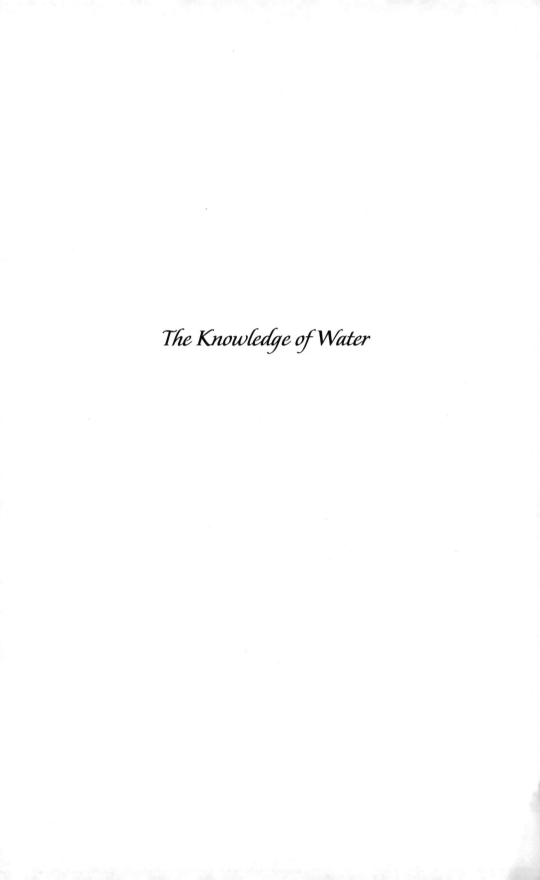

The Knowledge of Water

The

KNOWLEDGE
of WATER

SARAH SMITH

BALLANTINE BOOKS / NEW YORK

Grateful acknowledgment is made to X.J. Kennedy for permission to reprint a
somewhat altered form of the poem "The Cat Who Aspired to Higher
Things," which Reisden recited to Tiggy. Copyright © 1979 by X.J. Kennedy.

http://www.randomhouse.com

Library of Congress Cataloging-in-Publication Data
Smith, Sarah, 1947–
The knowledge of water / Sarah Smith.—1st ed.
p.   cm.
ISBN 0-345-39135-7
I. Title.
PS3569.M5379758K56 1996
813'.54—dc20   96-18438

Text design by Ann Gold

Manufactured in the United States of America

First Edition: August 1996

10   9   8   7   6   5   4   3   2   1

to Fred Perry
husband, partner, lover, friend

and in memory of
Rita Alice Contant Perry
1916–1994

and Owen Roger Smith
1923–1995

omnia mei dona Dei

Presentations of the past raise peculiarly intractable conundrums of authenticity. Every relic displayed in a museum is a fake in that it has been wrenched out of its original context. Riddled with the inconsistency of compelling yet conflicting preconceptions—the golden glow of nostalgia, the sordid squalor of savagery—all "olden times" are potentially fraudulent. "Is that object real?" is a query often heard at historic sites. "Are you really a weaver? Is this building real? Are you actually doing that work?". . . Object authenticity is equally problematic. It is a common delusion that works of art are generated by an exclusively creative urge. Like other artefacts, art is mainly fashioned to be appreciated and acquired by others.

—Mark Jones, *Fake: The Art of Deception*

Chapter 1

It takes a second to shoot a man. Thinking about it takes the rest of one's life.

At eight years old, Alexander von Reisden got away with murder. He was not called Reisden then; he ran, he changed his country, his name; as far as he could, he changed his memories. He was admirably thorough, for a child of that age. For years he did not know what he had done, or at least believed he didn't. He was careful not to notice that he didn't remember any of his childhood.

He didn't have an easy life. What one forgets does not go away.

He was caught, finally. The crime had been essentially self-defense and he had been very young; there was no question of prosecution. The three people who knew his story kept silent; no one else would ever find out, they all hoped. It was finished.

But Reisden had found himself out. He could no longer avoid thinking about murder, or wondering what sort of person would commit it.

He was wondering now.

The public viewing room of the Paris Morgue looked oddly like a theater. The walls were grimy plaster, furred with mineral deposits; the gaslit stage was marble, a white cheesy slab stained brown, separated from the audience by a glass pane running with moisture. Six corpses lay on it, dressed in the clothes in which they had been found, the bodies frozen and glistening. Seine water trickled under the slab, keeping them cold. Under the freezing chill and the smell of menthol and disinfectant, the air was unbreathable with the flowery whore's-talc of decay.

She was the colorful corpse, still drawing the eye: purple satin skirt spreading around her, red satin jacket, and several waterlogged postcards and parts of postcards, recognizable as Leonardo's painting, still pinned to her clothes. Over her heart her murderer's knife had ripped her jacket to pieces. Reisden remembered her on the steps by the Orsay, a wrecked beauty of a woman, standing with her eyes closed, singing in the ruin of a voice, *kiss me, kill me, oh how I suffer*, shuffling and swaying and holding out her hand for centimes. She had looked like trouble, and now, to someone, she was.

I wonder why he killed her, Reisden thought; I wonder how he came to it.

"How did you know her?" Inspector Langelais stood in the shadows at the side of the stage.

"She begged near the Gare d'Orsay, near where I work. She was the local colorful beggar. I gave her money."

"Jeanne Cavessi was her name," the inspector said. "A stage-performer once, back in the last Napoleon's time; in these last years, a woman of the streets. She had your card—?"

"I gave it to her once," Reisden said. "To put in the mirror of her grand salon. In her palace."

"Her palace?"

"Her imaginary palace." The Mona Lisa had described it to him: the tall wrought-iron fence around the park, the gardens; the rose salon, the *grande salle* with the mirrors, the withdrawing salon where no one but Victor Hugo had ever been, and the fourth salon: *which will be a surprise to me, it has been so long, I forget it.* "I collect hallucinations; I rather liked hers."

Langelais pursed his lips. "And this Artist, Her Artist, did you collect his hallucinations too? Is that why he wrote you?"

"I have no idea why he wrote me."

Limping, the inspector led the way out of the viewing room to one of the interrogation rooms, a bare cell painted the greenish ocher favored by French bureaucracy. Through the walls Reisden heard the rumble of the Seine. The two men sat on either side of a scarred deal table. Langelais leaned his cane against the table, took off his bowler hat. The ends of the inspector's white mustache were waxed and twisted, a style military men affected, and in his buttonhole he wore a service ribbon from the campaign of 1870, forty years ago. War hero, Reisden thought; entered the police force when the Préfecture had been virtually a branch of the army; now waiting to retire. The murder of "Mona Lisa," street beggar, was not being handled by the Préfecture's best.

Inspector Langelais took out a handkerchief and wiped his hands, then his nose.

"Do you remember when she disappeared, Monsieur le Baron?" he asked.

"About a week ago." The Mona Lisa had been singing Aida's farewell on the steps of the railroad station: *O terra addio*, wringing her hands and rolling her eyes in theatrical despair. He hadn't been in the mood and had gone round by the quai rather than spend five minutes listening.

And then she hadn't been there.

"Today you received this letter?"

"Yes, by the early post."

The inspector laid the photographic copy of the letter on the scarred table, then the original beside it, in a glassine envelope.

It was written on the cheap greenish notepaper that is sold by the sheet in any post office, in purple ink and an uneducated scrawl.

> Cher mseur le Baron de Reisden,
> You like me you have lovd a Womn of Knidness Greace & Beauty She us Not Recthd the End of the Rivr war She ws Mnt t Go It is not Rit tht Mona Lisa shd be in That Plasc like any Comun Folk Ples Help
>
> Hr Rtis

" 'The end of the river—' "

"Her palace was there," Reisden said. "At the end of the Seine."

"Her imaginary palace.—You knew her very well."

"Not at all."

"You knew this man, Her Artist? She had spoken of him to you?"

"No."

"Why should he write you?" Langelais asked.

Because I know what he's thinking, Reisden thought without wanting to; because I can know. "I have no idea." Painfully, with a sputtering unfamiliar pen, *son Rtis* had copied the engraved letters of Reisden's calling-card. "He had my card. He may have taken it when he killed her."

" 'You like me, you have loved . . . ,' " the inspector pointed out. "He believes you knew her well enough to 'help' her. That indicates he knows you."

Reisden shrugged.

"Perhaps someone you added to your collection. Like her."

"I don't collect people."

The inspector pulled at his mustache-points. "What does he expect you to do?"

"It sounds as though he expects me to bury her."

"Why?"

"I have no idea."

The inspector tented his fingertips doubtfully, rubbing the ends together.

"She had been in the Seine for several days," Reisden said, "but her body was discovered yesterday morning and the story was in the afternoon papers. The letter came from," he picked it up and looked at the cancellation, a slightly smeared RDU-LOUV over a red ten-centime stamp. "From the Hôtel des Postes on the rue du Louvre. From the time-stamp, he mailed it at ten last night. Louvre is the only all-night post office. Yesterday afternoon or evening he read that her body had been found and taken to the Morgue; he had my card, which he took from her body; he immediately wrote me. The Morgue disturbs him."

"But why did he write to you, Monsieur le Baron?"

"I really have no idea."

"Perhaps you had a—particular relationship with the lady?"

He was asking if Reisden had been her client. Reisden gave him two seconds of the look one gives to an absurd inquiry, if one is Monsieur le Baron and the inquirer is only a Préfecture policeman.

"Someone must have seen this man when he bought the notepaper," Reisden said.

"How do you know he bought the notepaper when he wrote to you, Monsieur le Baron?"

"A man who writes like this is unlikely to own any."

The inspector said nothing, a tactic designed to make the interrogatee say something. Rather to his surprise, Reisden said something. "Perhaps he simply needed to talk to anyone, and my name was the first to hand. He would want to talk."

He had wanted to talk.

Langelais blew his nose again, then folded his handkerchief elaborately. "Monsieur," he said, "I am afraid I must ask you one delicate question. In the investigation of a murder, one sometimes touches on—other events. Is it true that you," he hesitated, "killed your wife?"

Reisden said nothing for a long moment. "If you mean 'killed' but not 'murdered,' yes, it is true. My wife died in an automobile accident some years ago; I was driving the car."

"But you said at the time you had murdered her?"

"At the time I felt so."

The Inspector said nothing. Reisden said nothing. Everyone wants to know why; no one will ask. Just as well.

"You were in an asylum."

"Briefly."

The two men looked at each other. Shall I show him that it bothers me, Reisden thought; shall I pretend it does not; what would the normal man do? He tried to look neither defensive nor angry, the look of a man answering a question about his tailor or glovemaker; but that was not normal either, of course.

"You understand," the inspector said finally, "one must ask."

"I understand. But I don't know who killed this woman," Reisden said. "I don't know why he wrote to me."

"Perhaps he was an acquaintance in the asylum?"

Reisden smiled wintrily. "No."

"Or a patient at Jouvet?" The inspector examined Reisden's card. Dr. the Baron Alexander von Reisden, Jouvet Medical Analyses. The card did not say that Jouvet specialized in mental disturbances; it didn't have to. Jouvet was well known.

"I own Jouvet but I don't see patients. And as far as we can tell from our files, he isn't one of ours."

"Patients see you," the inspector pointed out.

"That may be; I don't know him."

"I think you do know him," the inspector said.

The inspector let the silence go on; Reisden looked back at him with the clear steady gaze of years of practice. You think I am guilty of something, Reisden thought; and I am. But don't look at me, look for this one.

"He's committed murder," Reisden said. "He wants never to do it again but he knows what he can do and he's afraid of it. He may write again: to you, me, the papers. He *will* write, he will try to explain himself," he said, "because he is a mystery to himself. He isn't ordinary, he isn't normal, he doesn't know what he is. —Catch him."

Chapter 2

"I wonder what makes people *commit* such crimes," Gilbert Knight said.

Mr. Gilbert Knight was a medium-sized, pale grey sort of a man: grey hair, grey suit, a sort of a fog come calling. He had the absentminded look of a not-too-successful bookseller, which he had been once. A small leather-bound volume poked out of his pocket. He had been at the Harvard library, he said, looking at an early North Italian binding, and it had been a forgery—"there are so *many* forgeries," he murmured regretfully, "so many people whose morals are *not what they should be.*" He had been in the neighborhood, Gilbert continued, and had simply . . . and . . .

"Uh-huh," Roy Daugherty said. They both knew Gilbert hadn't just simply wandered down into Cambridgeport casual-like; but Gilbert wasn't one to impose himself, even on his friends, he always apologized. He was unnerving that way.

"You want tea, Mr. Knight? Or beer?"

Gilbert Knight politely said he would take whatever Mr. Daugherty was having, but what he wanted was to worry a little; he usually did want that. He was worried about Europe, and about his protégée Perdita Halley, who was studying music there.

"The French do not wash their vegetables," Gilbert said earnestly, "or pay effective attention to their drains. Some of the French drains, Mr. Daugherty—some are *centuries* old."

Gilbert Knight had a nephew, who a few years ago had got himself engaged to Perdita. Perdita hadn't lasted with Harry, but she had with Gilbert, who was financing her piano studies. She was supposed to be a fine player, and was studying in Paris.

"How's she doin'?"

"She will have her debut concert at the American embassy in January. Not the Salle Pleyel, she writes, but a Paris debut all the same."

"Good for her," Daugherty said. "I remember when she was nothing but a little thing, and playing the pianny even then."

"I am on the horns of a dilemma about Perdita, Mr. Daugherty. I would like to give her something."

Gilbert fell silent, maybe wondering whether he should even mention it. Daugherty figured it was something Gilbert might consider indecently personal, like a new kind of toothbrush.

"Something," Gilbert Knight repeated apologetically, but with a small increase in firmness. "If she were to have a *certain amount*, to buy pianos and pins and—the things that women buy—my mind would be so much relieved. Not too large, but substantial, useful. The income of a nice little business."

Daugherty choked on his beer and turned it into a cough.

"But I really wonder whether I should."

"Won't break you." The Knight estate wouldn't notice one business more or less.

"Oh, the money does not concern me." Gilbert Knight leaned forward. "But if she were to have part of Father's estate, Mr. Daugherty, I wonder if it might really stand in the way of herself and—Mr. Reisden? I gather from his letters, they seem to be rather fond of each other," Gilbert said, "he and Perdita."

"Seemed to be," Daugherty said cautiously, "once."

"I do believe so still. He writes very little about her; if his feelings were simple toward her, he would be much more forthcoming."

This was dead right about Reisden.

"But if they were to think of—of course one cannot count on anything, one dares not—it would mean that Mr. Reisden might be put in the position of benefiting from one of Father's companies. And you know he would never do that."

Daugherty sighed and scratched at his short-cut hair. *All I wish to gain from having been Richard,* Reisden had said, *is not to be Richard any more.*

"Well," Daugherty said, "you might give it to her if she *don't* marry him."

"But that would imply some disapproval of—Mr. Reisden," Gilbert said, distressed, "and those are far from my feelings. I *do* wish," he said, and he said nothing at all for a moment, looking beyond the smoke-browned paint of Roy Daugherty's kitchen the way a man long alone looks toward the horizon, or like very old people do, waiting for they don't know what. *Mr. Reisden* Gilbert called Reisden now, as if he hadn't a right to first-name him. "He is not my heir; I know that; I have no connection with him, nor any responsibility toward him, that is the way we both wish it. But I do wish for his happiness."

"Is Reisden thinking of marryin' her?"

"Richard is not a man to marry easily," Gilbert forgot and said; and realizing what he had said, stopped, but didn't correct himself, only sat for a minute staring down at his hands before going on. "And, Mr. Daugherty, Perdita has done so very well with the piano: she will have her French debut in January, and come back to tour in America, and that will be the end of her time with Mr. Reisden in Paris."

"Then they ain't going to get married," Daugherty said. "So you can give her the money. My experience, people'd usually rather have money than get married anyway."

"Have you ever been to Paris, Mr. Daugherty?"

Daugherty's heart sank. "Can't say I have."

"If you were ever to think of going—I understand it can be quite splendid, especially during the winter season—this might be a good year; you might stay as long as Perdita's concert. If you were to go at Christmas, I should give you my Christmas presents for them, particularly for him. I should, of course, pay your expenses, and a fee."

Danger money. Daugherty took off his glasses and polished them. "You getting him something special, it needs me to go?"

"I had thought"—Gilbert Knight quavered—"of getting him a dog."

The air in the room congealed to ice, all but the butterflies in Daugherty's stomach, which felt like red-hot clothes moths. "You *ain't*."

Gilbert Knight's nephew Richard had been a fine boy, and a lonely one, eight years old; and he had lived alone with his grandfather, Gilbert's father, crazy old William Knight, who thought beating kids helped them, and the more beating the better. Once William had gone away from home for a week, and Richard had found a dog, a puppy named Washington, a stray. His grandfather had come back and discovered Washington. He had broken its back with his lead-weighted cane and then made Richard shoot it dead.

And on that same night, when old William had been about to hit Richard the way he had that dog . . . There'd been the gun, on the table between them, and the boy'd been eight years old.

Did you see who shot your grandfather? the police had asked Richard afterward, never thinking of the kid, who was practically out of his mind with shock; and a couple of days later he'd disappeared.

And they would have thought he was dead, but for finding, twenty years later, a man named Alexander von Reisden. Who had a face like a Knight, and couldn't remember anything before he was ten years old; but *I know who I am,* he'd said, *if I were your Richard, wouldn't I know?*

"He don't want no dog," said Daugherty, distressed; "what you think he wants a dog for?"

"We none of us wish to remember that trouble, but—" Gilbert Knight leaned forward and took Daugherty's arm, and the light on the table shone into his eyes so they weren't washy blue but suddenly, strangely, the pale steel of his father's, or of Reisden's. "He distrusts himself so— I think he might find a dog is simple— He wishes, I think, to take care of something," Gilbert said. "Someone. But he is afraid to speak. You do not need to bring him a dog, Mr. Daugherty," Gilbert said, "merely—*visit*— You have been a married man, you will be eloquent on the advantages of the state."

"Hmmph," Daugherty said, looking round his outdated dusty kitchen. Coal stove, a little dribbled with bacon grease from last week's Sunday breakfast; gas lamp with a tin shade. On the walls, the boys' school drawings were still tacked up, though Franky was in the Merchant Marine now and Bob had got married last summer. Pretty much unchanged since Pearl had run away with the Bible salesman twenty years before.

"*You* ought to have the dog," Daugherty said. " 'Twould be mighty simpler."

"I believe I have a sort of dog already," said Gilbert Knight. "You will consider it?"

"I ain't no such of a man to go to Paris."

Chapter 3

"The piano should be played like the body of a woman, messieurs—caressed, with adoration, with passion!" said Maître. "The audience," Maître said, "all those *chères femmes*, have not merely come to see you play the piano—but to *make love*."

In the echoing damp auditorium of the *grande salle du Conservatoire*, ten of the twelve students of Advanced Piano Class broke out into admiring laughter, baritone and bass snickers and one tenor giggle. To the right of Perdita, Anys Appolonsky sighed in despair. Perdita simply sat up straighter, scorning Maître and all his works.

"We demonstrate: Miss American, your Chopin étude."

Do we demonstrate, do we? Perdita Halley rose, gathering her skirt in her left hand. "Maître, my piece is—"

"I know, Miss American wants to play Busoni *forrrrrte* with the left hand; play your Chopin."

She used her cane to find her way among the shadows of chairs on the stage, found the piano bench, and placed her fingers. Maître had assigned her the Chopin a month ago; now, after long special pleading, she was being allowed to work on Busoni's transcription of a Bach chaconne. She wanted to rip into Busoni's heavy bass work, show off her upper-arm touch a little, and make the *salle* boom; instead she took two deep breaths, thought *I will not let him bother me,* and began the

Chopin. Lovely music, interesting music, but soft, pretty, *feminine* music—

"You see, messieurs," Maître said above her playing, "the pianism of women is like cut flowers, perfumed, decorative, but without strength, without emotion. One must have roots, messieurs, even in a bright little piece like this, one must be strong, like the trunk of a great tree, rising!"

Perdita pedaled the sound hard enough to crack a walnut and turned to face him.

"You would say, *cher Maître*," she said oh so very mildly, "that expressiveness at the piano should always come from sheer physical strength . . . ?"

"You confuse strength with pounding the keys, Miss American." The tenor giggled again.

Maître was known for teaching students how to play full out, expressively, the way a soloist has to do, and dear Arthur Norman at the New York Institute had told her she should study under him; but what Arthur hadn't told her was that Maître taught men and women differently. All that wonderful full-out passion, he taught to men; but what he wanted from women was a playing style as if one were really too too superior for any kind of emotion, attacking even forte passages with finger-touch and little genteel flexes of the wrists. That was bad for hands, dynamics, everything; he had ruined almost all his female students. In the concert hall he had made her cry from pleasure; he was a great pianist. He should have been that good a human being, that good a teacher.

The piano should be played like the body of a woman, indeed!

At four o'clock, after the last chord of lessons, Perdita and Anys took their poor selves outside and stood on the steps in the frosty November rain, silent under their umbrellas.

"At least this week he forgot to tell me to become a piano tuner," Perdita said.

"To you he's good." Anys sniffed. "Last week he say I play *like* pig, this week *worse than.*"

In counterpoint between the rumbling autos and wagons there rose the treble voices of two beggars, a match seller and a violet seller, competing for the passing crowds: "Buy my violets, I have three children!" "*Allumettes*, they always strike, my fine phosphorus matches!" The match seller had a grand bass, *fine phos-pho-o-rus matches*, like a Handel recitative, but Perdita held out her coins to the violet seller with children and got in return two bunches of violets, petals flaking from their blossoms, each soft, poor stem carefully pierced with wire.

"Lucy Anderson, Agathe Backer-Grøndahl, Amy Cheney Beach," Perdita recited, handing Anys one of the bouquets and sniffing the other. "Come on, Anys: Teresa Carreño. Ilona Eibenschütz."

Anys sniffed. "Essipova."

It was the litany that strengthened every female piano student: the women concert pianists. Lucy Anderson to Agnes Zimmermann, thirty-seven women. Maria Theresa Paradis had been born a hundred and fifty years ago, in 1759; Olga Samaroff was only seven years older than Perdita. Thirty-seven women in the lifetime of the piano; not very many; but they existed.

"And who is number thirty-eight?" Perdita asked Anys.

"Me," Anys said without conviction.

"Oh, Anys, you have to mean it: me, me, me!"

"For Maître we are not human," Anys sighed. "We are wooman. He doesn't care if I live or die."

"He just doesn't think." How could he think Perdita's reading of the Chopin was dynamically weak and not try to improve it, but simply use "female weakness" to make a teaching point? She couldn't break a bass string like Liszt, but she could reach the back of the house over an orchestra.

A couple of men students stood smoking beside them; Perdita listened to them throwing out judgments like old critics. "Fauré! His music's worn-out, administration has ruined him. Debussy, brilliant, there's nothing else to say!" In New York Perdita would have fallen into a lovely musical conversation, but fraternization was a sin at the Conservatoire.

"We must simply endure, like good professionals," she told Anys. "Let's get something to eat."

"A sandwich is too much. Maybe pastry."

"You should eat better." Anys was only fifteen.

"I go with you," Anys conceded.

Inside the warm bright bakeshop, sweet smoky ham vied with cheese, sugar-smooth *ananas au kirsch*, lemony chocolate-and-vanilla Paris-Brests, *tartes aux pommes.* . . . "We'd like two *sandwich au jambon,* a *Paris-Brest,* a *tarte aux pommes,* a big bottle of Evian, and some bottled lemonade—" The bread was just out of the baking oven; the smoky ham tasted faintly like Alexander's skin, a secret thought that made Perdita shiver.

"I have nearly to throw up when I hear Maître speak you," poor Anys said.

"Never mind him."

"But I don't learn. I am taking poison soon. I am returning to Moscow."

"Oh, don't leave me alone with him, Anys! That would be cruel."

"But I am stupid always." Anys was always sleepy, not stupid. She lived with a Russian family at Alfortville, got up every morning at five o'clock, took the train and the Métro to get to the Conservatoire, and stayed until ten in the evening; then she took the Métro and the train back out to Alfortville, and five hours later she started all over again. "It's better in Paris to be stupid, *nyet*? Stupid, pretty woman."

"What do you mean, Anys?" That was an awful thing to hear from a voice still half a child's.

"In Paris, you notice, is so many statues of naked woomen? Purity, Beauty, Awakening of Soul, Spirit of Science. Me it is feeling wrong I am dressed, I should be inspiration for someone, I should be *amante*, I should be mother, teach my children music is what Maître says."

Perdita felt for the girl's hands. "Anys, they're not used to taking us seriously, but *we are serious*. We are human beings like the men. We must be whole people, we must have our lives and our work."

"But sometimes it's me so sad, so sad."

Sometimes it was Perdita so sad too. She walked with Anys back to the Conservatoire and stood in line to get a rehearsal room; there were always more pianists than pianos. Down the echoing hall she heard a Conservatoire mama encouraging her sniffling daughter; "there, there, dear." She thought of how odd it was, how uncomfortable, to be a woman here.

Female weakness was part of Conservatoire myth. Women weren't supposed to be able to weight-lift, which everyone did in New York; women needed lunch. *Normalement* she and Anys would have brought their mothers to chaperone them and support their frail little stems; their mothers would have waited for them all day while they practiced, brought them a hot lunch from the café, tucked them in at night, and stayed up doing the washing. Perdita's imagination was harrowed by all those invisible mother-slaves; she heard them in the narrow Conservatoire corridors, their knitting needles ticking, waiting for years and years, making endless sweater-coats "to pass the time." But the mothers were women too.

Ideal women, the kind the students fell in love with; women the men students competed with; women who were mothers; women who sacrificed marriage and family for their art—

What kind of woman did she want to be?

There didn't seem to be a good answer but *the best parts of all of them*, which was impossible; trying to be too much, she would simply get in trouble.

She leaned against the wall and sighed, then stood up straight because Conservatoire students didn't slouch. She was still at the end of the line. With a faint sense of self-betrayal—she should be practicing, she should depend on herself—she retreated to the Conservatoire's phone closet, closed the door against being overheard, and called Alexander.

"Maître was *so dreadful*—" She let herself be comforted, wrapping herself in the warm velvet of his voice. *On January twenty-first,* he said, *you will play at the embassy. You will do very well; Henry de Xico will review you; and that will take care of Maître.*

Love seemed to be the answer to who she would be; she would love him and be strong from his strength. But that, which was what she wanted, made her frown; it was obscurely uncomfortable, like an inexpressive fingering or an interpretation only half worked out.

She couldn't be uncomfortable loving Alexander.

Chapter 4

"Darling, you realize Jouvet is far more trouble than it's worth."

In late November, Reisden had masons in to repair what appeared to be a minor problem with the foundations of Jouvet's building. The masons discovered trouble with the bearing beams; the carpenters discovered dry rot; and Reisden, who had never owned anything larger than a racing car, called in his cousin, the widowed Viscountess de Gresnière, who had recently rebuilt a wing of one of her country houses. On a rainy evening, Dotty toured Jouvet, holding up her narrow skirt fastidiously, wrinkling her nose at the must in the cellar, where the archives were stored, and frowning at the dry-wood smell in the examination rooms. At the end of the tour they went up to the fifth floor, to his apartment.

"You realize," she said on the stairs, "I have never been here before?"

"In three years?" he protested. "Surely you have."

"Never." The stairs were narrow, the stone steps dished with age; the plumes of Dotty's wide fashionable hat brushed paint from the plaster. "You come to my house; you take me to dinner and the theater; but you live like a hermit."

The door at the top of the stairs stuck; he put his shoulder against it. "This building has significant foundation damage and roof damage," Dotty said. "The slates have not been repaired since the fall of the Bastille." She touched the plaster with a finger gloved in glacé kid and broke away more flakes of paint. "That comes from damp. There are beetles, my darling. It will all be tremendous trouble to rebuild and will cost you millions."

"I hope not."

"Literally. I'm sure. You should sell."

"I don't want to." He got the door open and stepped back for her.

"Oh, my *dear*, how *awful*."

When he had bought Jouvet, three years ago, he had fallen heir to the apartment where five generations of Dr. Jouvets had lived. The last of them, who had died at ninety-four, had been a collector of antiquities, books, and scientific instruments. Marble heads still stared blankly from the upper shelves of the library. The large library table was piled with brown-paper bundles of books, which Dr. Jouvet had never opened. Through the rusty velvet curtains, in the music room, on the shelves by the piano, were displayed a gilded orrery, a pair of Sphinxes with the heads of women, and a collection of small blue Egyptian funerary figures. Reisden had never much considered where he lived, or thought of changing it; it was background, like the noise from the street. But Dotty stood in the middle of the room, slim and blond in her long gray chinchilla coat, and he felt an odd sense of being caught out, of failing to be like normal people.

"Forgeries," Dotty said, turning an ushabti in fastidious fingers. "Second Empire," she said in exactly the same tone, putting down the ushabti and narrowing her blue eyes at the faded plum velvet that shrouded the windows, as a soldier would regard the enemy. She marched into the unused dining room and through it into the kitchen, mowed down the tiny gas-cooker with one blue glance, and opened the cupboards. "*And* you have no plates."

"Jouvet's niece wanted the china," he said.

"Which you have not replaced in three years. You don't need it, you don't eat, you go out. Of course you don't have anyone in."

"Should I?" he said.

"Not until you have completely redecorated," Dotty said coolly. "I don't mean you, of course; I mean your wife. The woman you are going to marry, who will bring you the money you want, and tidy up and buy you plates and entertain for you."

He smiled and shook his head.

"You should marry again; you know you should."

She went back into the music room, pushed back the velvet covering from the piano, and opened the fallboard, examining it as if casually for signs of use. She struck a few keys. Out of tune: she smiled.

"Miss Halley doesn't come here," he said, understanding belatedly Dotty's desire to see where he lived.

"Miss Halley? Certainly she does not, what would you think of? She is a respectable girl." She played a few more chords, apparently unconscious of the dissonances. "I have met her. Yes. I took her to tea. A very respectable—girl. She is devoted to her music, and has an American 'agent,' and wants a career now, marriage and children sometime; *et patati, et patata.* She is fascinatingly self-centered, if that amuses you, and quite honest about it, but quite respectable—so far, my dear."

He raised an eyebrow at her.

"But she tells me, openly, that you and she correspond every day. And at the theater last night, André du Monde mentioned to me that you have rented his old banker's house 'for a blind young lady who plays the piano.' Really, Sacha."

One should never be surprised at the extent of Dotty's

knowledge. "André has got it quite wrong," he said. "*She* has rented the house. She needs a place to practice on Sundays."

"And you intend never to go there, I suppose," Dotty said.

"You suppose nothing of the sort," he said, "but you exaggerate; I shall probably go there once or twice, if she invites me."

"Oh, darling," Dotty said. "As if she won't. She's taken with you."

He felt himself reddening. "And she does *not* come here."

"As if there are no hotels."

"Dotty."

Dotty picked up one of the faience figurines. "I simply think, my darling, in any relationship, someone should be domestic. She believes she is but she isn't, and you—" She blew delicately at dust in the crevices of the figurine. "More than domesticity, someone must have money. She has no expectations; you make your money, and at the moment, my dear, you don't have enough. If you must rebuild this building, if you do not intend to sell—"

"I shall go to the banks," he said.

"You should marry a woman with resources; then you wouldn't need to borrow."

"I'm not going to marry."

She put the ushabti down and took his arm; she stood them both in front of Dr. Jouvet's dim gilded mirror. One blond society woman in a cloud of fur; one thin man, black-haired, pale-skinned, a face of bones and hollows, with inhumanly wary eyes. "Looks, family, a certain amount of money," Dotty said judiciously. "You could do very well in the marriage-market."

Family. He made a face in the mirror, leering like a stage madman. The face that grinned back at him was a Knight's.

"Me what killed me first wife?" he said lightly. "What woman wants to be the second Mrs. Bluebeard?"

What one chooses to forget comes back in disguise. He hadn't murdered Tasy, but for years he had thought he had— he'd been sure he'd murdered someone, who else could it have been? He had said he'd murdered her, to far too many people; he had tried suicide; he had been in an asylum; everything, everything. He had been memorable. What he had been set his teeth on edge.

"Oh, seriously, darling," Dotty said. "Bluebeard."

"Seriously. Suppose," he said, putting his arm around Dotty, "suppose that when our Tiggy grows up—" Tiggy was Dotty's son, Reisden's nephew, the six-year-old Viscount de Gresnière. "Suppose that Tiggy were to fall in love with a woman who, as a child—killed one of her family."

"What sordid things you come up with, darling," Dotty said, shivering.

"An excusable crime, let us say," he said. "But would you let Tiggy marry her?"

"Of course not. One doesn't want that sort of people, one doesn't want scandal."

"But I," he said, "a man who believed for no reason that he murdered his wife, will succeed in the marriage market."

"You want to marry," Dotty said, taking his hand, "and not only for the money, my dear; that counts for a great deal."

"I don't want to marry. I shall be an old eccentric bachelor, help raise Tiggy, and take Sunday dinner with you."

She smiled, half-pleased, half-annoyed. "Nothing would please me more, darling. But—" Dotty held his hand and counted off points on his knuckles. "You have your company, which is a splendid success and will make you money unless this building falls down. You have your Sorbonne research, so deliciously esoteric no one understands it. You have your suburban nest that I'm not supposed to know about, where you are playing appallingly at house with your American mistress. But she is going home; now you need a nice rich wife."

"Perdita is not my mistress." He looked away from Dotty. She took his head firmly between her hands and turned it back, tilting up her head to see into his eyes.

"Really," he said, "she is not anything to me."

"Darling," she said, "forget the past. Be agreeable to women. Talk about your preferences; say you enjoy the theater; mention your investments. You should meet Cécile de Valliès; she likes the theater. A widow, a darling person, with a great deal of property in Bourgogne, and two children. You like children, and with Cécile's money—"

"Dotty, my love—"

"I'll have you two to dinner; you can see. Meanwhile, what shall we do with your little Miss Halley? You can't make her pay the price of your self-consciousness, darling, it is too cruel. You must drop her and let her go home brokenhearted."

"No," he said, "I want her happy."

She gazed at him, assessing him with something almost like dismay. "Women are never happy," she said after a moment. "But I shall make her feel wanted—by the critics, my dear, not by you. Then she will go away. Then—?"

"Then," he said, "we shall all be relieved; but I won't marry anyone, not even your friend Cécile."

Chapter 5

"Sacha is asking me to take a great amount of trouble over you," said the Vicomtesse Dorothea de Gresnière.

Alexander's "cousin" had accompanied Perdita to Worth's, and now brought her back in the huge Gresnière coach to Dotty's house on the place Dauphine for tea. Cousin Dotty did not have a sweet tooth—Cousin Dotty did not have or do anything unbecoming—but she had heard Perdita did, Dotty said; and so tea at Dotty's included pastries from Rumpelmayer's. Perdita sat, hands folded for fear of knocking over one of Dotty's knickknacks, and ached with desire for chocolate. But when one has not very good sight, one learns to eat neatly by compromising with what one wants. Perdita, when she ate in restaurants, had her food cut in the kitchen and kept a little brush in her handbag to un-crumb her skirt afterward. But at Dotty's house—? "I'll just have tea, please."

There was the sort of silence that occurs when one woman thinks another is dieting for effect. "As you please," Dotty said. "Miss Halley, I wish to speak frankly about my cousin. You know Sacha is flirting with you."

"Oh, madame, we are good friends, that's all."

"I disapprove of women and men being friends; it is disingenuous."

"Between him and myself, it means only a mutual regard, madame."

It was more than three years ago now that Alexander had asked her to marry him. Three years, two months, eight days ago, on a September night on a train between Boston and New York. She had said yes; she had wanted him more than life; and so, the next morning, she and Alexander had gone together to the New York Institute of Music to say she would not be coming to study, because she was marrying and moving with her husband to Paris.

They had taken a cab to the Institute, in a brownstone near Greenwich Village. He had stayed in the cab; she had climbed the steps; she had stood at the open door and listened, and smelled— It had smelled like music, bow resin and dust and ink and sweat, and from inside she had heard a piano played beautifully. Go in and give it up, she thought, but the music went on, and on, and she had stood in the new city, in the sunlight, on the threshold of what, for all of her life, she had known she was.

And he had known too. He had taken her around the corner to a coffee shop and had let her cry against his shoulder for half an hour. Goodness knows what he had felt. *Don't we know who you are?* was all he had said. *Go, love, do it.*

Only a mutual regard? She loved him for who he was, for what he knew about her; but because he knew her so well, she could not marry him until she knew what she could do in music.

"Whom do you admire?" Cousin Dotty asked.

"I beg your pardon, madame?"

"Among the musicians. Whom do you prefer to play?"

"Oh: Brahms, Beethoven, Schumann; the moderns, Debussy—Ravel's *splendid*—have you heard 'Gaspard de la Nuit'?"

"One should never become too emphatic about living

artists; one runs the risk of being thought eccentric. You are actually engaged in music for hire, Sacha tells me. You have an agent," Dotty said as if she were lifting the word with silver tongs.

"I will if Harry Ellis takes me, ma'am."

"And this Mr. Ellis has asked you to get reviews from Paris," Cousin Dotty said, "good reviews, from which he can extract quotes, for posters." Dotty said the word *posters* exactly as if it were *roaches*. "So, in short, you have come to Paris for reviews."

It seemed a bald way of putting it, but Parisian reviews were a necessity for a musical career in America.

"Very well," Cousin Dotty said. "Sacha finds you attractive; he has a *tendre* for young musical women. But when he thinks of marriage again, he will be expected to do as everyone else does here, and marry according to his social position."

"I cannot speak of his plans."

"No, no, Miss Halley, I will have no missishness. I am speaking of your plans, and hoping that none of yours will interfere with his."

Perdita took a breath. "I like to play music. I like to solo with an orchestra, ma'am. I've been lucky enough to do some of it and I want to do more. As far as I know, my chances for that are in the United States. Your cousin understands that."

"Of course," Dotty murmured. "One wouldn't really hire American pianists for anything, would one? Not here in Paris."

Splendid pianists—splendid *men* pianists—were graduated every year from the Conservatoire. The French seldom hired any but their own; even German musicians were only for oom-pah bands and café orchestras. Women musicians were relegated to tea-dance orchestras in the suburbs, to salons, and principally to teaching.

Alexander knew that as well as she did.

"If you and he are simply good friends, then there is nothing to be said; I do not entirely approve, it is risqué for a young woman, but of course I apologize for any misunderstanding and I shall serve you to the best of my ability." She did not sound apologetic at all. "A proper wife will advance Sacha's interests. As his closest relative, I take an interest—that is all."

"What sort of woman would be a proper wife?" Perdita could not forbear asking.

"A Frenchwoman," Dotty said firmly, "a woman of resources and good family. I hope we understand each other, my dear. Let us move on to something more pleasant. Sacha and I are agreed that, while you will certainly play splendidly at the embassy, a second concert would not be amiss. Perhaps on— let us say the twenty-seventh of next month, you could play something professionally for me and a few of my friends? That will be the Thursday after your debut. I shall have a critic or so as well; perhaps we can get you extra reviews for your agent, your Mr. Ellis."

Chapter 6

Dotty was right. In every sense except reality, Perdita felt she was Alexander's mistress.

A respectable gentleman and young lady are never alone for more than ten minutes. She and Alexander had been together in a train compartment all night. They had stayed in the same resort town twice, for two weeks each time, though not at the same hotel. They had met each other on the beaches or at restaurants; they had talked about everything, the news, politics, his work, hers. She knew more about the chemistry of stimulus and response (his Sorbonne work) than if she'd gone to college, and he knew more about music. They had gone fishing in companionable silence. He had taught her to swim, at a pond in the country, alone. She had taught him cooking—men's cooking—bacon, lettuce, and tomato sandwiches, omelettes. He had taught her to make coffee. They wrote each other daily.

A respectable young woman does not exchange daily letters with a man; she never signs them *love*. And if she does, she means it; she never accepts a man, then tells him she won't marry him.

They had kissed, and more, too much for her peace of mind; sometimes only the touch of his hand would make her lose the thread of their good conversation. But they had done nothing truly wrong.

What did she like about touring? Heaven only knew. Touring was cold theaters and strange orchestras at eight A.M., going through a conductor's interpretation for the first time that day when you were playing it that night. Touring was a month, or two, or three, living on sandwiches from railroad dining cars, sleeping in Pullmans if you were lucky but mostly across two seats; bringing your own tuning forks and felting files because half the pianos on tour wouldn't have been felted in this century.

Touring was music: new orchestras, new interpretations, new colleagues and friends, constant challenge, and performance, performance, performance.

So she and Alexander had a friendship. An awkward friendship, that always made her worry it would slip down into that and nothing more.

She, like Dotty, distrusted friendships. Blind girls have friendships. Men tell blind girls they are good friends; men take blind girls out to lunch; but they don't take them to dinner, and never home to meet the family. Perdita was not blind, she was determined she was not; she was only very nearsighted. And Alexander said she was attractive, and never talked about other women (except Dotty), but—

Had what he felt for her simply dwindled to friendship? Had he told Dotty to tell her she was unsuitable?

She didn't want a friendship with him. She wanted Alexander to love her for her body.

She upbraided herself for caring nothing that he respected her.

Chapter 7

The Conservatoire was closed on Sundays. When Perdita had arrived in Paris, she had budgeted money for a place she could practice on Sundays, and Alexander had found an empty house with a piano, well within her budget, just across the river from Paris.

"Large, modern, and ugly," he said, "with an interesting garden."

"And what kind of piano?"

"An Érard concert grand; will it do?"

Courbevoie was only the other side of the Seine from Paris, a streetcar suburb, two and a half miles from the Arc de Triomphe; but it was country. According to Alexander, reading aloud from Baedeker's *Handbook for Paris,* it had a boulevard by the Seine, a main street with plane trees and shops, and the ruins of Louis XIV's stables. When they got to the Courbevoie tram station, they discovered the town also had a Sunday market tucked between the church and a street of little shops. They walked through the street market, where the women vendors of cheeses and pin-lace flirted, giggling with Alexander in soprano chorus—"Oh, *le bel homme,* you there, handsome!" They escaped the laces and the tinsmith, but Perdita fell victim to a trayful of fragrant, gritty lavender soap and bought three bars. Courbevoie felt hours away from Paris. She could hold hands with him on the street here, as she could not have done under the shadow of Cousin Dotty. She took his hand self-consciously, feeling whether her hand was welcome in his; he took it and she sighed happily.

Down from the main street, there was a neighborhood of houses on a sunny hillside sloping down toward the Seine. They turned right into a wide stone stairway descending between stone walls. "There is no street; carriages can't take the slope," he said. "This is the passage Mallais." She could hear the echo of horses' hooves from the boulevard below and the stuttering motor of a Seine barge or a car; but the arched bare branches of trees over the stairs gave the passage Mallais a romantic isolation. Eighteen steps; then her fingers, brushing against the wall, felt the bars of a door.

"I have the key," Alexander said. The big French lock screeched, the door hinge screaled, and they were inside the wall, in a silent garden.

This was the country itself. It was echolessly quiet and smelled, at first, only like freezing loam; then she took a step forward, through long, drenched, rustling vegetation, and it came alive with smells. Catmint, lavender, the sweet licorice of chamomile or fennel: someone had kept an herb garden here before it had gone wild onto the path.

"Who lived here?" Perdita found a modern iron rail. Long canes and thorns pricked her bare fingers; there would be roses here in spring.

"No one. The garden was leased to the painter Mallais, Claude Mallais, one of the grand old men of French Impressionism. I knew him a bit. Jove in a straw hat, with a beard down to his watch chain." Perdita had heard of Mallais; Dotty had one of his paintings. "He's dead now. The widow still lives next door. This house was built after his death by his old patron, a banker. It's very modern: central heating, electricity, a shower-bath, a telephone, and two indoor WCs." Unheard-of luxury. "But a gentleman's country villa is unsalable this side of the river, and the painter's widow feuded with the patron and has built a very ugly wall between this house and hers. The heirs are renting out the house for the cost of heating it, while they decide what to do."

He opened the door for her; her steps reverberated in an empty room. It was damp, like any house near water, and smelled of plaster dust and of never having been used. He began turning on lights, a brilliant blaze in the dimness. She saw something black in front of her, stepped forward onto a double thickness of rug, and touched the keys. It was the Érard; it had just been tuned.

"The heirs will rent it and the furniture with the house. You are tenant-at-will, one month's notice on either side. For a Sunday practice retreat, it's very reasonable; I'd recommend it."

She sat down, stripped off her gloves, and began playing. The room had echoes, but fabric on the walls would fix that. The Érard's action was stiff, in spite of the good name, but there were worse at the Conservatoire. "Can I play full out without bothering the neighbors?"

"Madame Mallais and her brother live the other side of her wall; she is supposed to be a recluse and won't bother you. The next nearest neighbor doesn't winter here."

"Oh, this is perfect." She stood and held out an arm for him. He took her hand and she drew him to her. They had not seen each other in a week; she stood tiptoe to touch her lips to his, and felt a reluctance in his response, but felt herself responded to; she smiled and put her arms around him, murmuring to him in whispers, hungry and content at once. The walls were high and the house quiet. "You are so clever to find this," she whispered, every word a little kiss against his lips; and for some time they were content, kissing, arms around each other, still with their coats on, clumsy as two bears. The house was so quiet behind its walls, Courbevoie so separate from Paris, that it seemed anything done here was in a world different from him being of an age to marry and her of an age to work. They kissed more warmly and less carefully, and it seemed natural and urgent and right to do it, and they were all alone.

He gave a sigh and broke away. "Come see the rest of the house, love."

It was half-furnished, barely that: in the large salon, beside the piano, no more than a chair; in the kitchen, two plates and a pot. The shower-bath had no curtains, the bathroom no towels or soap. She laid one of her bars of fragrant soap ceremonially in the zinc dish, taking possession.

He went out to buy a coffeepot and coffee (and, she reminded him, cups, sugar, spoons). When he was gone she explored the rest of the house. The door beyond the bathroom, the one he had not opened, led to the master bedroom; and the master bedroom contained a bed. Straw mattress, sprinkled with bay leaves to keep away mice; featherbed rolled up at the foot, smelling a little of damp; big French cylindrical cushion and pillows at the head. There were no bedlinens, no puffs or duvet.

She sat on the bed, and held one of the pillows clumsily to her; and lay down amid the acrid prickling spices, and buried her face in the pillow, clasping it to her, hugging it; and then got up hurriedly, brushed the bay leaves carefully off her back and skirts, gathered them from the floor, and spread them over the bed again, as if no one had been there.

Chapter 8

Perdita's ideal woman was Florence Fish de Pouzy, who lived at Versailles, near the old palace. Florrie had a big house with a garden; Florrie was married with two very young children; and Florrie had organized a Young Married Women's Musical Society, a quintet of married women players, and was keeping up her work. Perdita had a great curiosity about them.

"Won't you come out and play music with us and stay for dinner?"

Florrie was too rounded out to show herself politely in public; she was seven months along with a third child. She let Perdita hold sweet-smelling baby Martha, and Perdita stood haloed in baby-warmth, baby-weight, baby-smell.

"Those long fingers!" her mother crooned. "Feel!" Perdita gently felt the baby's tiny hand and little fat-circled wrist. "I'm going to start her on piano as soon as she's old enough to sit up, those fingers are so precious! Julie's hopeless, she doesn't have any musical interest at all, but Martha—"

"You are lucky," Perdita said: Florrie, who was married and a mother and a musician. Florrie was "suitable," of course; her family made half the ink in America. But what a life!

"Oh no," Florrie said, "*you're* lucky."

"What do you mean?"

The Société Musicale de Jeunes Mariées arrived one by one. All except Florrie were French with at least some Conservatoire training. The piece they were working on was Fauré's Quartet no. 1, which to Perdita had all the interest of a ball of yarn; but while the women tuned up she dreamed of being a Young Married Woman too.

From the first bars, Perdita was simply embarrassed to be there. The violinist was the only person who knew the music well; the rest barely had a notion. Florrie missed every single one of the glissandos; she played B when she should have played B-sharp; and she overpedaled her solo bit as if she were trying to catch rats with her feet. What had happened to Florrie, who had been so good at the Institute?

Afterward the cellist apologized and said her son had been ill with *un rhume féroce*, she didn't think she'd been able to do the piece justice; and the violist said everyone in her household had been prostrated, the children, the nursemaid, all the maids; her own ears were blocked. Florrie said her husband had been in England all week, she'd had to do everything. "And in your delicate state, too," the violist sympathized, coughing. The violinist, who had known her part, was silent; the other three asked Perdita for criticism. First learn the notes, Perdita thought, and managed to say a few things about interpretation, feeling like a person who has shown up properly dressed at a formal party to which everyone else has come completely naked.

"Won't you play for us?" Florrie asked. "She's so good, she's very good. Why, she can do the Paganini Variations—"

Perdita pleaded she could only do the second series, she was having trouble with the first; but she played the second series, and afterward there was a silence, and they told her how lovely it was, how truly lovely, what an inspiration she was to them; but that wasn't what they meant. And she said how lucky they were to have their families and their music, what a good life they led, but that wasn't quite what she meant either.

Over dinner the women talked with enthusiasm about their children. The violinist sat as silent as Perdita.

"Do you have children, Madame Clémence?" Perdita asked her.

"No," said the violinist brusquely. "I had one, she's dead."

Perdita sat silent, appalled.

When the others had left, Perdita stayed a while to visit with Florrie. "We weren't very good, were we?" Florrie said.

"Madame Clémence was," Perdita said soberly.

"What a price she paid, poor woman."

Florrie went over to a chair and let herself down; Perdita heard her heavy breath and the susurrus of her big dress whispering against itself. A slim silhouette was the fashion for women their age; Florrie sounded like an old lady.

"Three children in three years," Florrie said. "When I married Charles, I thought the housekeeper would take care of the house, the nursemaids and the governess would take care of the child—I'd only have one, can you imagine!—and I would take lessons from the best masters, and practice all day, and play in a quartet. I don't have time to practice. Two hours in the last two weeks, that's all, and as for keeping up with the literature—my dear!" Florrie said. "And Charles wants me to entertain his friends, and there are all the little errands, getting my watch fixed and having my clothes adjusted, planning who's coming to dinner and who can sit next to whom, talking with Cook and the gardeners and the housekeeper—we used thirty pounds of sugar in one week, thirty pounds for a family of four! I suppose I've arranged my life as I like it," Florrie said. "I only think sometimes, when I hear *you* play— How is your Alexander, are you still seeing him?"

"Yes," Perdita said.

"How do you—feel about him?" Florrie asked, but didn't give Perdita time to answer. "When I was at school I was crazy to marry Charles, I'd have done anything. And I'm happy," Florrie said. Her silk robe rustled as she shifted uncomfortably in her chair. "But . . . Be careful. Love isn't everything. You have such talent, you could be really good. Don't waste yourself on marriage."

"I don't think it would be a waste to have love and music both," Perdita said uncomfortably, "and Alexander has always encouraged me. I think it would be the best possible way of life."

"The best possible way of life—isn't possible," said Florrie.

Chapter 9

In early December, Reisden went to Rome for a neurochemistry conference and spent an extra day in Genoa sitting in the sunlight talking with old friends. He arrived back in Paris on Thursday afternoon, just in time to rescue Tiggy from Dotty's formal Thursday at-home.

"Where shall we go today, chéri?"

"To play with *your* toys," Tiggy said. "I want to play with the go-round-round and be a big animal. And then we'll go to the cinema."

"A well-chosen afternoon," agreed his uncle.

Reisden had space at the Med. School, part of the Physiological Psychology Lab: a bit of bench, a very good microscope, a centrifuge, and a neat litter of lab notes. Tiggy and he whirled the centrifuge, and then they went to Physiological Psychology's big central room, where the test equipment was set up. On the long table, someone had constructed a telestereoscope, a set of mirrors used to do vision experiments; Tiggy giggled in delight as he fitted his small jaw into the chin rest and looked into the confusion of reflections.

"How big an animal am I? Am I as big as a dog?"

"Bigger; you would see like this if you were a very large animal, chéri. A rhinoceros or a lion." Tiggy sat at the table, delighted, roaring *rrowl rrowl*, a small blond lion, while Reisden sorted his mail.

One of the letters was from a consortium of doctors who wanted to buy Jouvet. It was not the first time they'd made the offer, and Reisden reflected, not for the first time, that he should take it. The place made money, but he could make as much elsewhere; it took time away from his real work, which was here.

"Uncle Sacha," Tiggy hinted, "I know where there's a movie about a dog."

They both loved movies. They retreated to a storefront cinema off the boulevard Sébastopol, a dive smelling of hot film-stock, damp sawdust, and oranges, and watched (four times) the story of a heroic dog who rescued his young master. "That's enough," said Tiggy, replete with nougatine and heroism; his uncle admitted that he thought so too. They took the horse-omnibus back toward the Île de la Cité. Tiggy was allowed to ring the bell and twitch the reins over the three patient bus-horses. They got off the trolley at the place du Châtelet, where the buses wait for passengers before the long haul down the rue de Rivoli, and Tiggy begged coins to buy apples from the apple vendor by the theater. "Me, Uncle Sacha," his small nephew confided, "I'm going to be a tram driver when I grow up." From his small open palm the horses ate their apples delicately, long-toothed; he whispered into their steaming nostrils, patting their noses, a sturdy little blond Norman with an instinctive capability for animals. His father had liked horses. *How much he's like Esmé,* Dotty's friends said occasionally, and Dotty would look at her son narrow-eyed.

"Uncle Sacha, can I get a dog?"

"Chéri, you know your mama doesn't approve," Reisden said.

Esmé de Gresnière had betrayed everyone but his dogs and his horses. On his deathbed, he had called not for Dotty, but for his favorite hunter and the beagles. The dogs had disappeared afterward, to Tiggy's tearful consternation. Dotty did not intend her son to be at all like his father.

"Will you get a dog? Then I can come and live with you."

"Zoölater," said his uncle comfortably. "I don't want a dog. I don't like dogs. Come, let's get tea with your mother."

They crossed the Pont au Change and passed the Gothic bulk of the Préfecture, gloomy in the mist. They cut through the byways of the Palais de Justice down toward the place Dauphine, the wedge of ancient buildings at the pointed end of the island, where Dotty lived.

"Uncle Sacha, when you get married, can I be one of your witnesses?" Tiggy asked. "And hold the rings?"

"When I get married—?" Reisden said, startled.

"Mama says you're marrying Madame de Valliès."

"Does Mama," Reisden said. "She and I will have a word in private."

"Sacha, how could you bear to come back from Italy?" Dotty said as they stamped their feet dry in her black-and-white marble entryway. She waited for them halfway up the stairs, a cream silk shawl over her fashionable pastels. Her shawl and light hair reflected in the ancient mirrors on either side of the stairs: Dotty in a gray smear of ghosts. In Paris, Dotty said, it had hardly stopped raining since he left; it was *disastrous*. He made soothing noises appropriate to weather. Tiggy was sent off to have Miss Wallis change his wet clothes. "Bring us tea, please, Frérin, and please tell Miss Wallis that the vicomte must have his bath before he joins us."

"Oui, Madame la Vicomtesse," the parlormaid said.

Dotty's house had two drawing rooms, with a set of Louis XV glass doors between them, loot from the great auction at Versailles. In the women's drawing room, an under-parlormaid was clearing away the cakes and teacups from Dotty's at-home. He dropped into the straight-backed armchair that had replaced Esmé de Gresnière's; Dotty seated herself in a Louis XV armchair *à la reine*, her face shaded by a petit point fire screen.

"Would you like tea or whiskey? . . . Both," she decided.

"A hot grog." She leaned forward to set the poker in the fire. Frérin brought in a tea service and plates of English sandwiches, cheese, fruit, and plum cake. This was a new Frérin, Reisden noticed. All Gresnière parlormaids were Frérin, as the *maître d'hôtel* was Dumézy; who the original Frérin and Dumézy might have been, the Gresnières no longer knew.

"You're tired," she said.

"A long trip."

"You shouldn't take Tiggy out if you're tired, darling."

"I never mind him."

Dotty scraped sugar from a sugar-cone over a Limoges plate and dusted her hands off over the fire. The sugar, falling into the flames, made a momentary shower of sparks and a smell of caramel. He smiled, remembering her doing that over the schoolroom fire, one cold spring day at the Loewenstein schloss near Graz, how long ago? He had been twelve or so, raw from South Africa, prematurely tall, prematurely everything, suffering from nightmares he couldn't remember, knowing nothing but how to bluff; and she had seemed as finished and cool as porcelain, and then, after tea, had dusted her sugary fingers briskly over the fire and said, "Smell that, *na ja*! When I grow up I'll eat nothing but caramels."

She looked up and caught his eyes on her.

"I've forgot your caramels," he said. She laughed. He had not brought her caramels in years. They were bad for the teeth, she said. After Esmé had left her she had gone through the mercury cure and Salvarsan, and now she was fanatically careful of everything that might have been made fragile; she worried that her skin had aged, that her hair was thinning, that she would lose a tooth. She had a bad temper, a defensive bravado; she was young for a widow and extremely beautiful, but it was an open secret that Esmé had died of syphilis, and even if she were to wish to remarry, she was not likely to make a match.

Frérin came with a stein, and Dotty blended tea, rum, sugar, and lemon, drew the poker out of the fire, and plunged it hissing into the grog. "There!"

"Splendid, as always."

"As always, as always; that is the story of my life." She neatly wrapped the sugar in its blue paper and returned it to its box. "My gazette of the week: Frérin bent a spoon. Tiggy's friend Paul has chipped a front tooth, fortunately a baby one. Cécile de Valliès is thinking of having her hair dyed. I *may* go to Nice."

He shook his head and yawned behind the back of his hand.

"Oh, I forgot, and, you villain, you didn't notice: I have lent my Mallais to the retrospective."

Over Dotty's bow-front cabinet, Mallais's splendid *View of the Seine: Twilight* had been replaced with a school-of-Watteau scene of romping shepherdesses. "I shall miss it."

"I still don't know whether I should have lent it."

"Why?" he asked. Dotty was very proud of her collection.

"Oh, I don't know, I don't know . . . Betsy Ducret d'Hédricourt's not lending; she says she'd have to get a burglar alarm. . . . I wonder what Madame Mallais will put in the show. Perhaps you have met her," Dotty said, "since you have spent the last three Sundays 'talking' with Miss Halley next door to her?"

"I have not," he said curtly. "Met Madame Mallais. By the way, who has been telling Tiggy that I am to marry Madame de Valliès?"

"I have no idea," Dotty said coolly, "but I had Cécile to tea yesterday, and she is utterly taken with you. She thinks you are romantic."

"My G-d. Dotty, really, don't."

Tiggy came clattering down the stairs, followed by the long-suffering Miss Wallis, his nurse-governess, carrying a rather large model of the Eiffel Tower. "He would bring it, madame," Miss Wallis sighed.

"Miss Wallis, please wait with the vicomte for a few minutes in the dining room; the baron and I are talking. Tiggy, darling, get Cook to give you and Miss Wallis some tea." Dotty closed the glass door to the hallway. "This house is so inconvenient. Now then," she said, sitting down again. "Miss Halley. You're compromising her, darling, and you used to leave little girls alone. Truly, dear, shouldn't you be more circumspect?"

"There is no reason to be circumspect," he said. "We only talk."

"Especially if you like her a bit?" Dotty asked. "Do you? Like her a bit?"

"No."

She spread her hands in a gesture of regretful dismay, as if he had said yes, and he felt he had. "I'm sorry," she said, "I'm being terrible."

"You are."

"But really, darling, she is far too inexperienced to make a good mistress."

"She is not—" he said forcefully.

Tiggy was standing outside the door, forlornly, in his arms the Eiffel Tower in tin, trailing its electric flux wire and plug. It was officially Reisden's, given him by Tiggy for his last birthday. Tiggy had been appointed its caretaker until Uncle Sacha could find the right place to put it. This would take Reisden as long as possible, since Tiggy loved it. The two of them went into the hall to use the electric plug box and turned down the hall gaslight to get the full effect of the toy's Pharos lantern.

"*Il est si beau,*" Tiggy said. The tiny red lamp blinked solemnly over the sea-green-and-gilt panels of Dotty's hall, making red flashes in the mirrors.

"It's very good, *mon cher,*" Reisden said. "You're taking good care of it."

Tiggy sighed with embarrassed contentment.

"About what we were discussing," Dotty said. He looked at Tiggy, then, with raised eyebrows, back at her: in front of the child? She shook her head. "Since you must have—business—that takes you to Courbevoie," she said, "I wish you to do me a favor. Please find out something about this Madame Mallais. She still has so many of her husband's paintings."

"You don't mean to buy directly from her?"

"No, no, one must buy through Armand. Being a client of Armand is half the experience." The great dealer Armand Inslay-Hochstein had been Mallais's dealer from the beginning. Buying from him, Dotty said, was like having an audience with the pope. "I am only curious."

"Why? Are you up to something?" he asked. Dotty was seldom curious without a purpose.

"Oh, my darling, I am certainly up to less than you."

Dotty herself let Reisden out, going with him down the stairs to the quai-side door. There was a hallway between door and quai side; in the practical way of old Parisian residences, the street level of Dotty's elegant townhouse was taken up with a shop. Dotty's tenant was a jeweler; in the lighted window, gilded bouquet-holders jostled Florentine cameos, opera-glasses, and diadems glittering with paste jewels. From above the door arch, rain drifted steadily, and Dotty's door had developed a discolored streak to match the hollow worn in the pavement from centuries of rain.

"So," Dotty said, standing in the shelter of the hallway. "The twenty-seventh. Miss Halley is very pleased to get more reviews. I am inviting critics from *Figaro*, *La Grande Revue*, *The Musical Review*, *Musica*, *Parisian Weekly*—any more? And my very select friends, the ones who'll make the papers."

"Good," he said. Perdita was thinking only of reviews; very

well; he knew she was going back to America. Reisden shook out his soaked umbrella, brooding.

"Darling," Dotty said, watching his face. "How has this got so far?"

"It has got nowhere," he said.

"You should have enjoyed and forgot each other well before this. Why this particular one?" Dotty hesitated. "I know it's odd, my dear, but does she— She comes from America, where you were involved with that family with the murdered child three years ago. Didn't she know them?"

"Yes," he said in the correct tone of slightly puzzled inquiry, "but what has that to do—?"

"I do hate it you don't tell me anything about that, I know something happened, and I know it's *so* Arsène Lupin and Sherlock Holmes, darling, but if the reason for her is that she knows something important to you," Dotty said, "tell me?"

But, Dotty, he thought, I don't tell; you above all, especially not you, my dear. I don't tell anyone. Because you think as I do, as anyone does: that a child who murders, even for a good reason, is a warped thing.

And where does that leave me, except with a twenty-one-year-old who says she loves me and is passionate to work with American conductors? To just the extent that Perdita said she loved him, he did not trust her judgment. She was wrong about him and wrong about herself; he was Bluebeard; she would go home. She had better.

"I shall get you *The Return of Sherlock Holmes* for Christmas," he said, kissing Dotty's hand farewell, "and rat traps for the Giant Rat of Sumatra; but romance I cannot provide," and he turned down the quai toward the row of misty street lamps marking the Pont-Neuf.

"Villain!" she called after him, laughing.

Chapter 10

Leonard is ordinary.

Leonard is thirty years old. He lives in a world of unapproachable women, tormented by lusts that twist and petrify his body, that make him stammer. Those things he wants most to say, he cannot. The sight of a woman's booted ankle under her skirt in a café makes him rock back and forth, moaning inwardly behind his newspaper. Women ignore him, despise him, distrust him.

Leonard is extraordinary in only one thing, that he would do anything for love; and he has.

Leonard is a guard at the Louvre. At night the palace's twenty-two furnaces are banked; the cold of centuries comes out of the stone walls; Leonard and the guards like him wear capes and gloves, and warm their hands over their lanterns. It takes a strong man. Every half hour, guards are supposed to patrol every corridor, flashing their unblinking lanterns on Phoenician antiquities, cases of royal jewels, Veroneses, and fragments of Greek temples. Those men slouch off, they go down to the basement, to the guards' quarters where it's kept warm, and smoke their cigarettes and drink coffee.

But Leonard never leaves his post, he's reliable. He has to be. Every three days, he watches the Mona Lisa.

The Mona Lisa is worth any amount of trouble, any extreme of service. The more trouble a man has in loving her, the more worthy he is of her.

She told him so.

All through Paris he sees her. She appears on *baci*; she is a brand of milk and of cigarettes. The singer Mistinguett dresses as her; she appears in revues; little girls wear her on china lockets. There is a Mona Lisa laundry on the rue Quincampoix, the Mona Lisa café on the rue Léonard-de-Vinci, a Mona Lisa line of blouses, Mona Lisa matches, a Mona Lisa bath powder. In the Louvre itself, copyists paint her to sell to people who love her. She is everywhere: and wherever she is, Leonard looks at her in longing and pain. He knew her once and now he must remember.

Once she was alive and smiled at him. Once she would come to visit him. Leonard gave her a key to an old side door of the museum. She would pant her way up the Daru stairs, and then she would stand, her arms crossed over her bosom like a little girl praying, gazing at herself, and then she would smile at Leonard: so beautiful, her smile.

Who doesn't love a smile? Everybody does. Leonard is an ordinary man, he loves women, he loves to be smiled at and appreciated. "You are my gentleman," she said. "My artist, Leonardo."

A while ago—ah, Leonard can't think of it, some blackguard, some *vaurien* did it to her, she's dead, no, he can't think of it.

Leonard wants to give her a good funeral, but he doesn't have the money. She needs a funeral. At *that* place, where she is now, they keep the unfortunates two or three months, until the refrigeration doesn't work on them. Then—

When he is not on watch, Leonard sits cross-legged on his bunk in the guards' quarters in the Louvre basement. The long room smells of sweat, mildew, unwashed underwear. Around him other lonely men are sleeping. Above Leonard's bed, a copy of the Mona Lisa smiles from a cheap red frame. Leonard bought one from the copyist Jean-Jacques last August, when the tourists were away and the prices were low. He was meaning to give her to herself.

Leonard pinches himself to stay awake and writes, forming the letters painfully one by one, to the single name he knows. *Cher monsieur le baron de Reisden, it has been Three Weeks and she is still in the Morgue, why do you not give her a Funeral*

He writes them, then hides them in the single suitcase under his bed. He sends none of them. He doesn't want to offend the rich man, who has the money for a coffin.

Leonard stands night after night, in the cold and the dark, holding up his lantern in front of her, and he cries inside. It is pain for him to look at her, but pain is better than nothing at all. If he did not hurt for her, not hope for her, he would have nothing left of her.

Leonard loves the Mona Lisa.

Chapter 11

"I want to throw the Mona Lisa in the Seine," George Vittal proclaimed in self-adoration.

When I am dead, Milly Xico thought, when I am dead and go to H—l, I'll be riveted into an uncomfortable chair while my ex-husband and his girlfriend flirt in front of me, and for hundreds of years I will be forced to listen to George Vittal reading his own poetry.

"The only true art is the death of art," George intoned with unctuous slowness, turning over the fresh white pages with fascination. "I want to rape the corpses of the Académie, to sodomize Géricault, and cut the throat of Rosa Bonheur."

Oh, you're such a big strong man, Milly thought, scratching her pug Nicky's wrinkled forehead with one stockinged toe. George was a couple of years younger than Milly, just younger enough to be interesting, rather handsome, with a white-pie face like an aspirin tablet, flopping brown hair, and the lips of a venal pope; but how he talked; endless, endless. When one gives readings or makes love, the less one says, the better. Nick-Nack looked up at George, grinning and slobbering with approval. Milly poked his neck with a toe and frowned. With an oratorical gesture, George turned the page and went on.

> "All art before the twentieth century must go
> Except for Balzac Mallarmé and the Douanier Rousseau

Esther Cohen and Juan Gastedon
The rest ce ne sont que des cons—"

Bored, Milly looked round her, at the half-famous and near-famous gathered in a circle of Esther Cohen's uncomfortable chairs. There was Juan Gastedon, the soon-to-be-world-famous Spanish painter, with his big forehead and eyes like ripe olives; next to him the latest Juan's girl, whoever she was; they never stayed long enough to have names. Matisse; old Père Girault; Henry and his poopsie; and, as always, Esther sitting in her Venetian doge's throne.

Esther collected. Esther was American, Esther had money, of course she collected. Poets like George, journalists and publishers like Henry, writers like Milly, and artists. She crammed her apartment with big unfashionable Renaissance chairs, tables covered with carpets, chests carved into weathered tattoos like aboriginal faces; and on every wall were her friends' paintings: lush garish curves of red and bronze, disturbing red cubical cheeks, protruding salmon breasts, pale fruit, sensual flowers in yellow and pea-green and rose.

Esther wrote, too. She was short and weighed nearly two hundred pounds, or she would have danced. As it was she wore sandals, even in the winter. She had stubby toes.

Esther caught Milly looking at her and smiled lovingly. Milly sighed. Esther was kind, intelligent, much better to her than Henry had ever been; but Esther looked like a combination of your aunt and a truck driver, and Milly disliked even the look of men.

"I'll tell you how I would destroy the Mona Lisa." George gestured expansively, his arms over his head. "Twenty-eight copies! Twenty-eight artists! Twenty-eight bridges over the Seine in Paris! Noon! The bells strike! Men in black robes, like executioners, rush into the Louvre and snatch the painting! Immense numbers of confederates pass it from hand to hand, through windows, over rooftops, toward the Seine! Splash! Splash! Splash! Up and down the Seine, twenty-eight simpering pictures are hurled over twenty-eight bridges. The police rush in to arrest the perpetrators—but who can they arrest? It's a popular revolt! A revolution!"

"Oh, that's good," Henry said, clapping.

When the guests rose to look at the paintings and talk to George, Henry wound his way among the furniture, affable, smiling, well dressed, talking to the most important people. With his portly build and his beard, he looked like King Edward. He waved to Esther; he turned; his eyes lit up like the Pont Alexandre at twilight. "And here is my dearest, my dearest Milly! Milly, do you remember Julie de Charnaut?"

As if she didn't. Milly smiled at Julie. Clinging to Henry's arm, Julie-les-Fesses smiled back like a mannequin, as if she'd never cried when Henry had sent them both out of the house, Julie because of her jealousy, Milly to keep Julie out of the way while Henry slept with yet another woman. Julie had screamed and wept, walking up and down the paths in the Jardin du Luxembourg, dabbing at her eyes with a lacy handkerchief meant only for decorative crying, until the lace was soaked and dirty. "Milly, *we* know what a swine Henry is, don't we?" she had sobbed. "No one would believe what he's done to us—" *Us?* The last thing Milly had needed was Julie flirting with her. Julie had changed her hairstyle; her body looked pinched, not from conscience but from the new long corsets; her pointed little nose and chin stuck out from her hair like the muzzle of a Jack Russell terrier peeking from his mistress's muff. She had lost flesh, she was dieting to get the slender look, to please Henry, or what the magazines told her was the way to please a man like Henry, as if there were any way.

"Hello, Henry," Milly said, "hello, Julie," because it was beneath her to play who-says-hello-first with Julie.

"Hello, my darling. Hello, little Nick-Nack. Do you remember Papa?" Henry put out his large confident hand. Nick-Nack growled. Henry patted him anyway. "Ah-ah, puppy, has Mama been telling you bad things about me?"

Leave my dog alone, Milly thought, and smiled brightly at him. "Henry, look at you! You've grown so stout."

"Good living, my dear, good living. Julie, would you get us some refreshments? Milly, what will you have?"

"Oh, nothing, thank you."

He dragged one of Esther's chairs next to Milly and sat down, a little too close. "Julie, dear, bring me a whiskey. Tiresome girl," Henry added under his breath as Julie undulated off in her tight skirt.

"She won't find anything but spaghetti and bad wine."

"Then she'll cry," Henry said, "and not come back for five minutes." He looked unashamedly at Milly's breasts.

He had never really wanted any woman, Milly thought, only Woman; he had chased the will-o'-the-wisp Her through three thousand skirts, trying to find the right breasts, the right adoring eyes, the right amount of money. Milly was the only woman he'd married: she'd been the daughter of a friend of his mother's, as if he'd been a *pharmacien* from a country town, too shy of women to find one for himself.

"I had dinner with Michel," Henry began.

"And I had dinner with a man who's starting a new publishing house," Milly interrupted. "I'm thinking of doing another book." She wouldn't, but she smiled to see Henry worry. "It's time, don't you think? All those ones we did together, they're beginning to get old, no one reads them anymore."

"That's not what Michel thinks," Henry said complacently.

She saw the malign weariness in his lined eyelids. "Michel's bought them."

"Bought them?" Milly said.

"Rights to reprint. Outright. In perpetuity. All the *Midinette* books. I didn't want to tell you until it was a done thing."

My books? Milly thought. For a moment she didn't know what he was saying. Time stopped; even the fire stopped. For a moment no child turned in its mother's womb; no blade of grass sprouted in a park, no leaf fell; the clockwork of rain stopped ticking.

"You sold my books?" Milly repeated dumbly, quietly, and then at least hoping for something, "What did you get?"

"Yes, sold, sold, completely gone," said Henry, waving a hand as if she'd said nothing. "Believe me, I didn't get much. Michel thinks they have scandal value, that's all."

"And the money's spent, I imagine," Milly said.

"Of course, yes, gone immediately, I haven't seen money for years, I live on my debts."

You should have given me some, she could have said. But they hadn't been his to sell. It was she who had written them, it was she who had spent all those hours married to the desk, all those years. She smelled in her imagination the green odor of her mother's garden at Bresles, the rocky corner overgrown with feverfew where the cats had liked to roll, and saw the long pause of a dewdrop at the point of a tulip leaf, shining and quivering. What a story Henry had made of that leaf, with his thick blue editor's pencil: while the old schoolteacher declares his love, Midi looks at the downbent leaf, its tip drooping with a clotted and dirty raindrop.

Now Milly knew Henry's version of herself better than she remembered her own. La Midinette and her girlfriend Clémentine fishing for trout with their hands, Clémentine's pink skirts kirtled up to her knee, the trout stream brown and foaming between her pale freckled legs, while she held to the willow branch with plump white knuckles. "Middy! I'm going to drown and I don't see no fish!" Ursule. The old man with the hat. Madame Méry. All Milly'd have to do would be put pen to paper, they'd flood out of the inkwell. Little girls, school stories, comic old people, and the discovery in Paris that a man named Roland was the most wonderful lover in the world.

Henry had been Roland once, Roland whom she'd loved, whom she'd adored with her heart and her pen; and Henry had robbed her of her very memory, of her words.

"But there's money in it all the same," said Henry. "Michel wants to make us a little proposition."

"Us?" said Milly.

"You and me. He wants us to write another Midinette book. A little girl, a strong male character, something romantic, something a little—" Still seated, Henry shook his shoulders and hips, looking like King Edward doing the hootchykootchy. "That love of a young woman for an older man— That's what the audience likes. You could use my help."

"I could?" Milly said dangerously.

He leaned forward, his light eyes gleaming with the pleasure of a man who knows that, sooner or later, women never turn him down. "You're the best I've ever worked with, Milly. Wouldn't it be fun to be together again?" He rose from his chair, grasping his cane, puffing a bit. "And plenty of money. You're a splendid writer, you know. Much better than you think. I'll call you in a week."

He didn't give her time to say no. He would call in two weeks, or three; he would have broken up with Julie (again). He would wonder if Milly were free for dinner, and later in the evening, he'd say that, after all, divorce was just a word, and who would know? It would be a good dinner, he would be his most charming. And then she would let herself think the old phrases. *Eyes like a lion,* she had written about him.

Across the room, under Gastedon's big gray portrait of Esther, Henry was talking to George. Henry laid his hand on George's arm and said something; George grinned almost shyly. A pale young man, the type of herring-thin young man who freelances for weekly magazines, took out a minuscule pencil and notebook and began interviewing George.

"—the sensitive violence of lust—" George said.

"—is a very clever young man who publishes under my imprint—" said Henry, introducing George.

"—destruction, sadism, assassinations, anarchy—"

"—in my magazine every Thursday—"

"—floods, fire, young men raping the dead—"

"—*Modern Life.*"

Look at him seducing George, Milly thought. Me first, now George. And George was falling for it, of course.

"Oh, that's good," Henry said, laughing. "Go on, go on—"

What *I* need is a revolution, Milly thought. Against men, against all lovers who know who one is, against the very concept of love; against little girls who adore big strong men—against Henry—

Now that she was no longer a writer, Milly Xico was a theater artist, an attraction; and that evening she played the last night of her engagement at the Alhambra, *The Turk's Dream,* in which she sang and took a bath onstage. Afterward, depressed, she invited Nick-Nack and herself to have dinner at Le Départ. The Départ was a student café; inside, the students were singing, a boy was dancing on a table, a German band was playing; everyone was laughing and having fun, and they were all a decade younger than herself.

Outside the café, under the electric lamps, the Boul'Mich' was crowded. A horse-omnibus's iron wheels rattled against the street paving, and the people inside nodded in unison at each bounce of the bus. Across the river, on the Île de la Cité, the enormous flaming jewelry of Notre Dame's windows blazed frosty and glittering in the rain, and the bells rang, *bim dom boum*. Soup and then a steak, Milly decided, and *frites* three deep on the plate, soaking up the blood from the steak, and a demi of good cheap red wine. Nick-Nack struggled out of her arms and jumped up into his usual chair, looking out at the crowds like a dog Napoleon.

I have to do something about Henry, Milly thought. Has it really been three years since I divorced him? And he still treats me like this?

If you listen to bells you can hear your true love's voice. Boum bim dom boum, don't you love me? Dim boum dom bim, I love you, dear. Esther had been after her to give up touring and do another book. You should *write*, you should *use* your talent, I'll sup*port* you.

Henry said the same things. Bim boum bah.

Love made Milly nervous. Sex, that was easy; one says yes, one says no; but when the person was in love, who knows where it ended. Milly liked things clear and definite; love, like stories, should have a beginning, a middle, and especially an end. Love was depressing, a want beyond reason, a male want. I want the Mona Lisa to throw in the Seine. I want to own another person. I want you to write, dear. I want the moon.

Milly was through with writing, and love; all she wanted was to get rid of Henry.

Her demi-carafe of red had arrived, and she poured out a

glass and tasted, holding the prickly thin furriness in her mouth as a cat might hold a mouse.

Outside, on the rain-slick pavement by the almost-finished Métro station, four people and their umbrellas were making a little drama. From the old days when Milly had been Henry's society wife, she recognized one of them as blond, icy Dorothea de Gresnière, in a fantastic chinchilla coat, holding the hand of a blond little boy with hair like dandelion puffs. By her stood a dark-haired man: the black panther out of Rilke's poem, lean, dark, restless-eyed. On his other side stood a pretty young girl of perhaps twenty, the boy's nursemaid or the panther's prey. The vicomtesse was trying to get the man's attention. "Sacha? Darling?" But "Sacha darling" wasn't listening; he was talking with the pretty girl, the two of them framed by the new Métro entrance with its delicate mantis-head lights.

She was much younger than he, and she gave everything, looking up at him with the self-deluding ecstasy of a girl who puts all her pleasure in one man. Her umbrella slid under his, forming one roof that rippled sexually. Framed in thousands of francs of chinchilla fur, the vicomtesse saw the girl's expression and smiled tightly at "Sacha." He looked back at the vicomtesse, eyebrows a little raised. She lifted her eyes resignedly, to Heaven or to the bright electric sign of Le Départ. He smiled and shook his head slightly. She pouted, bored.

The viscountess would lose tonight's battle for Sacha, but in the end he'd go back to her. Milly looked at the girl who was so proud and smiling, and wondered what quarrels and betrayals and heartbreak lay in her future. "Someday she'll be an old woman like me," Milly whispered into Nick-Nack's warm hairy ear, "and live with her dog and eat at cafés alone. Will the dog be as nice as you, do you think?" For a moment a story flickered at the edge of Milly's attention. She shooed it away.

Love, who knows where it gets you? Into trouble, that's all.

"I'll get Henry," Milly whispered to Nick-Nack. "I'll make him suffer. He'll crawl back to me, with his stories and his dinners. And what will we do to him, Nicky-Nicky?"

Nick-Nack growled. Milly growled back affectionately. The steak had come, and Milly cut him a piece and tossed it to him.

"We'll feed you steak, Nicky, and let him starve."

Chapter 12

After she had left Henry, Milly had taken refuge on the rue de Bièvre. Her "apartment" was a single large room with an attached closet for her bed; it was furnished with plants that flourish in the dark, a rickety table from the *marché aux puces*, a chaise longue scavenged from an alley; today, in the rain, it reeked of sewage. Her pug Nick-Nack snorted lazily, napping in the warm cave underneath her knees; she reached down absently and scratched his forehead, then dipped her pen in ink and went back to her scarred table and her "science article" for the *Journal des Femmes*.

Paris floods, madame. Our City of Love, our city of milliners and theaters, designers and cafés, is at the mouth of five rivers. Into the Seine, above Paris, pour the Oise with its tributary the Aisne, the Marne with its Grand and Petit Morins, the Aube, and the Yonne. When it rains above the Galeries Lafayette, Milly expanded, *it's raining from here to Belgium, because all of northern France is subject to the same weather.*

Milly sighed, dipped her pen into her inkwell, and ran her fingers through her short hair. The inkwell was inscribed: *Prix des Femmes Écrivains—La Midinette à Paris, by Henry and Milly, Best Novel, 1902.* This prize inkwell had the shape of a twining woman in long hair and sinuous draperies, whose quill pen lay forgotten on her desk as she dreamed of a night of love. A woman full of ink. Her head hinged open. Milly shuddered and went on.

In a rainy fall like this one, all the rivers of northern France are flooding. If all that water came through Paris at once, it would flood our downtown to the arcades of the rue de Rivoli; the Eiffel Tower would have its feet in water. All our domestic arrangements would be—"Foutu," Milly murmured, tapping her pen against the side of the inkwell, and wrote with feminine discretion, *disarranged.*

Madame wanted to hear about disaster; Milly had to speak of soil composition. Milly glared at her interview notes and wrote on.

Fortunately Paris seldom floods. Our city is blessed even in her soil. Only a small part of northern France is rocky. Most is like your bath sponge— Always mention advertisers. *Most is like a Délicatesse bath sponge, able to soak up incredible amounts of water. In this benevolent soil, the most tempestuous floodwaters merely nourish the strawberries and pearl onions our cooks buy at Les Halles.*

Still, Paris has flooded, and terribly. Visitors to the Left Bank will notice, at the top of the picturesque rue de la Bièvre, an inscription recording that in 1740, water stood waist-high in the streets.

Outside her window, a broken gutter gargled; it had been raining for days. "Picturesque, isn't it, Nicky?" The dog snorted in his sleep.

More recently, our— Our oldest readers will recall? Our readers will recall their mothers speaking of? *Our readers with long memories will recall the Great Flood of 1876, when the Seine reached 7 meters 30, almost fifteen feet above its normal height.*

Fortunately, the engineers of Paris understand the problem. All through Paris, the Seine runs between high stone walls. At the bottom of the walls the Seine runs peaceably in its bed.

The *Journal des Femmes* was generous with photographs. Milly took a separate sheet of paper and detailed the pictures and captions she wanted. A historical photograph of the Great Flood of 1876, of course, showing the water high up in the walled bed of the Seine. To show how the Seine was measured, a picture of the hydrographic scales, the enormous iron rulers set into the stone walls of the quais. There would be, of course, a photograph of the walls themselves, rising above the Seine; below, on the broad quai promenades, lovers would be strolling by the river. *Journal* readers were married, poor goobs; there should be a sickeningly happy family among the strollers, a nanny with a pram.

Here at the side of the Seine we find our famous promenades, Milly wrote as a caption, *our broad stone walkways where visitors to Paris enjoy the splendors of our river. Above them soar our majestic quai walls, protecting us from flood.*

Soar, dreadful. Walls do not fly. Milly's pen hovered over *our majestic,* wanting to replace it with a simple *the;* but Madame loved adjectives as much as lace on an evening dress.

This year, throughout the fall and into this winter, it has been raining in the Seine basin. If it continues to rain, flooding will be as inevitable as the white sales. The river will rise, and our children will have the memory of one of Paris's most impressive sights.

But, thanks to the Métro constructions, all the quai walls are newly raised and strengthened. All ventilation windows are well above the height of the '76 flood.

Let it rain; Paris is protected.

Paris is safe.

Bah, thought Milly. She wanted disaster, any misery, as long as it hurt Henry. Henry still lived in their old apartment, with Julie to wait on him, George to write for him, her books to pay his debts. Milly had debts herself.

What right did he have to live so comfortably, first on Milly, now on George? La Midinette had captured the imagination for a while at least; she had made Henry money once, now it was George and *Ten Thousand New Perversions.*

What sort of disaster would truly hurt Henry?

Milly sat cross-legged on her sofa, absently scratching Nicky's head.

What if George stole the Mona Lisa and threw it in the Seine?

It was an interesting thought, but it wouldn't happen. George was lazy. Milly had known George since the time she'd been married to Henry, and she'd seen thousands of George's ideas fly by like colored snowflakes. One day it was a patented chair made of living women; the next, selling tickets to watch elephants defecate. But he was incurably lazy. George started magazines that never got to the third issue. George promised Henry translations of *Fanny Hill* but was too lazy to go to the library. Instead he wrote *Ten Thousand New Perversions* out of his head.

Throwing the Mona Lisa in the Seine was just one of George's ideas, no more likely to last than another.

Unless—

Milly threw herself at her desk and pen.

An Alarming Pronouncement by an Anarchist Poet— She dipped her pen in ink; the words flowed faster than the Seine in flood. *"Men in black will steal the Mona Lisa!" the poet and pornographer George Vittal has threatened. Together with a group of confederates, who are said to include the publisher Henry de Xico, Vittal has vowed to steal Leonardo's master-piece, the jewel of the Louvre, and throw it from the Pont-Neuf at noon*— she consulted her pocket calendar —*noon on Friday, January 28, less than two months from now.*

January 28 was Milly's birthday.

This year, Henry would remember it.

Chapter 13

To have a house of one's own is an intoxicating thing at twenty-one. Twice a week, instead of practicing at the Conservatoire, Perdita would take the Madeleine tram line to Courbevoie and spend the day. She would buy a bit of cheese, a *demi-bâtard*, an imported winter pear or apple; she would practice all day in the lovely country silence, with the rain making a frou-frou against the windows and the fire whispering in the hearth; and as often as he could, even with his schedule, Alexander was with her.

He worked at the kitchen table; she would hear mail being opened, pages turned, journals or Sorbonne lab reports or assessments of patients from Jouvet; sometimes there would be pencil scratches as he took notes, and occasionally a "Ha!" of triumph. He seemed, mostly, simply to be there, almost ignoring her, but sometimes, for a long time, she would hear nothing at all, she would feel that he was watching her through the doorway, and then her fingers would go clumsy and self-conscious; they would find an excuse for a walk, out into the rainy garden, to explore the fine old trees and the iris pond and to escape the house, which had suddenly become too intimate a space.

The most censorious watcher would have seen nothing to condemn. They were incautious, but respectable; it was a friendship.

Only a friendship? There was a part of him she did not know, and it was what he would do if she let him do what he wanted. Outside the clear comfortable boundaries of their relationship was the unknown territory of Alexander. And a part of her was outside it too, on the other side of a barrier whose existence they would be imprudent even to discuss.

She knew it had not been this way between him and other women; she didn't need Cousin Dotty to tell her that he had experience. When a man and a woman write each other every day, the woman will from time to time realize that the man is being discreet about something. It hurt her but she said nothing. She had had the chance of marriage; she did not own him; it was a friendship.

She thought about him constantly, his silences, his discretion, his presence.

Late one stormy afternoon in early December, a day when he was not at Courbevoie, Perdita went in search of dish towels at the Grand Bazar, a fusty, musty, cluttered store for buying everything; and while she was there she bought sheets and bedlinens. There was a bed, after all; it might sometime be convenient for her to stay the night; the Christmas and New Year's holidays were near, two long weekends one after the other. But she took a long time even by her standards, "looking" at everything by feel, and bought the best quality, stiff thick sheets smelling of lavender and trimmed with embroidery, luxurious French bedlinens and a thick puffed French comforter, as if she were preparing her bed for a guest.

Chapter 14

And then Mr. Daugherty wrote from Boston, saying he would come to her debut.

"We will not see each other while Roy Daugherty is in town," Alexander said, folding the letter. "Can you imagine what he would say to Gilbert if he knew that you and I were spending afternoons together, alone in a house?"

Perdita could hear the quotation marks around *alone in a house,* but he was serious.

"*You* are doing nothing wrong," he said. "But I shouldn't be here. I have had pointed out to me, quite correctly, that I am compromising you by being here. Roy Daugherty would think the same."

She would quarrel with him someday about Cousin Dotty.

"I do not want you to leave me," she said.

" 'Leave you' is dramatizing," he said.

They were sitting in the kitchen at Courbevoie, eating a late breakfast of tartines and coffee. It was a Sunday, and raining torrentially; when they had arrived the water had been running down the stairs of the passage Mallais. But they were warm and dry and above all they were with each other. "This is my house," she said gently, protecting it. She had never before had the privilege of someplace that belonged to her, someplace she could invite him without eyes overseeing them. "I invite you into it, as I might invite Mr. Daugherty or your cousin Dotty."

"Love, it isn't the same; you don't think it is," he said.

"Don't they think we can be respectable together?" she asked.

"No," he said frankly.

"You can't think you should stay away because of how it might look to others," she protested. "You would protect us out of knowing each other, Alexander."

Where else could they talk like this? Where else but behind these walls did they have this quiet space, this freedom?

She practiced that morning with automatic fingers, only half attending to the Chopin étude she was preparing for Maître. Everyone seemed to "know" what she and Alexander were doing, though they were not; everyone seemed to assume the nature of their relations, except themselves.

Why aren't we—? It was an unthinkable question.

When Alexander had taught her to swim, she had stood for what seemed like hours at the end of the dock. How long she had waited, before trusting him to keep her from drowning. She thought of his hands supporting her, against her ribs, through her thin wool swimming suit, and blushed unexpectedly all over her skin: the soles of her feet, the palms of her hands, on her neck, behind her ears, so that he must have seen something.

She practiced the Paganini Variations fiercely, polishing them for the embassy concert. The Paganini Variations take everything you have: they are intellectually so clear, like a mathematical proof, and emotionally and technically so varied; they wring everything out of both the piano and the body, fortissimo, prestissimo, octaves, sixths, cross-runs, singing runs like Paganini's violin. To play them at all, you must commit yourself completely to the need to play them, not only technically, but with your whole self. The technical challenges had taken her two months of daily coaching; years playing it would not exhaust the music.

Why could not her connection with Alexander be like that? How long was it honest and good to hold anything back? She could not marry him, she was not suitable, she was not French; but she wanted to make efforts for him, she wanted to take chances; she wanted to have as strong and honest a connection with him as she did with music.

"We are more than friends," she said, a little more loudly than she had meant. "I want to invite you into my house, more than the salon and the kitchen, all of it. I don't want to hold back parts of myself from you for respectability's sake, as if I were afraid of *anything* that could happen between us. I do not know what we are but I hope we are more than friends."

Not a word from him. She had said things that women don't say. She turned her head, trying to hear something from him, using her eyes as best she could, but he was only a shadow against the fire, silent, as if she had offended him or told him something he could not know. Why don't sighted people learn to talk?

"I only mean," she retreated, "you are like music to me. I mean that you are much more important to me than Cousin Dotty's or Mr. Daugherty's opinion. I will not chaperone my mind or my true feeling for you."

He thought she meant that she wanted to be unrespectable, she thought; and perhaps that was all she meant.

He said nothing for a moment, and then, "Thank you," as if they were only friends.

She ought to say she loved him. But she had said that, three years ago, and then told him she wouldn't marry him.

"Pay attention to your work," he said. "We will be reasonable, love, and respectable, and give Roy Daugherty no cause to interest himself in us."

They ate lunch at the restaurant on the main street, with its dubious "steack" and its murals of camels, peeling away from the mirrors; the rain ticked on the windows, the wind thumped the glass. "The weather's getting worse," he said.

"Yes, it is."

They didn't say much else. On the way back to the house, the rain became a downpour.

"I'm sorry," she said. "We *can* be just friends, that's all right. I want to be friends with you."

He hadn't brought an umbrella; the wind tugged her small red umbrella and thwacked it inside out; she had to lower it. By the time they got back, she was a drowned kitten. She peeled off her wet overcoat and set it on one of the two kitchen chairs. Her blouse was soaked, clinging to her shoulders, her skirt wrapping around her legs. She reached out and touched his coat, just as wet.

"I'm going back to Paris this afternoon," he said suddenly, "if you don't mind. After Italy, I'm behind on everything. If you would be able to get back without me—"

He had never done this before. They had so little time together, they had both always treasured it. She had spoken what she thought and felt, and he had found it ugly.

"I shall have no trouble getting back," she said. "Go, if you think you should."

When he was gone, she sat on the hearth-rug, her knees drawn up and her face buried in her arms. A respectable woman would have talked about her sentiments for him, perhaps asked him through friends if he wished to renew the offer he had made her three years ago, and intimated that it would not be treated so roughly this time as last; that would have been proper. But she hadn't said she loved him or would give up music. Instead she had urged herself on him as if she were a sandwich on a plate: here, take this, you want it; at least it wants so much to be eaten. She buried her nose deeper into her crossed arms.

Eventually, from the warmth of the fire, her wool skirt began to smell like a laundry. She made sure the door was locked and pulled the shutters closed; and then, quite alone, daring, she stepped out of the skirt and spread it on the hearth-rug to dry. Her shirtwaist was still sticking to her arms and bosom; she fumbled the buttons loose, having trouble with them because the buttonholes were damp and stuck. Her hair was falling down; she took out the pins and shook it loose, a lank weight reaching nearly to her waist. She sat by the fire and combed it with her fingers—she had no comb or brush here— and then rolled down her stockings and laid them on the floor to dry, wishing for hangers. She picked at her damp underclothes, her underskirt and corset-cover and combinations, peeling the cotton away from her skin. She should be practicing, but the piano bench was far away from the fire; the room was drafty and her underclothes damp, so that her skin rose in goose bumps immediately. She had no extra clothes out here; for all her fine words, this was not her house but the place where she practiced. So she sat by the fire, her underskirts carefully away from the flames, thinking of music but not playing, thinking of Alexander but—not.

Chapter 15

You are much more to me than Cousin Dotty's or Mr. Daugherty's opinion, he heard, and *You are like music to me.*

He sat in a café by the tram stop, drinking coffee laced with cognac, watching while one tram for Étoile and two for Madeleine sparked and sputtered past in the rain.

He did not want her. He could hurt her. He had his affairs with experienced women, who had little interest in him beyond the moment. Perdita one did not treat lightly. Her wet blouse had clung to her, so that he could see skin through the cotton and lace. He had seen the sheets on the bed. He did not want to be seduced; she was going back to America.

You would protect us out of knowing each other, Alexander.

He felt he was hurting her. She had offered herself, and would not believe she was too good a gift to take.

He wanted to go back.

What terrible thing would happen, if they were to be together between Perdita's embroidered sheets? He had at least experience to offer her. How to take pleasure, how to give it; how to set limits; how to prevent consequences; and how, finally, gracefully, to reach the end of an affair. He didn't make enemies of old lovers; he would not be a bad lover for her. He had seldom—never—been a woman's first, but he would not do it badly.

Oh, my dear, my dear, if I loved you less— He wondered at the verb, and rejected it. If I were only a bit less careful about you, I would be in bed with you now.

He could be a bit less careful. He doubted any physical intimacy could last much longer than Roy Daugherty's arrival; Perdita would not give herself to him when she would have to lie about it to someone from Boston.

That was part of the problem, he thought wryly.

He walked back along the high street, through the soaking rain, and stopped under the pharmacist's awning, as if he meant only to take shelter; and went inside. There were no other customers. He had with the pharmacist one of those conversations between gentlemen; "his wife" had been counseled not to have children, he said, and was sold a small red box labeled SALUBRIOUS PRECAUTIONS FOR MARRIED COUPLES.

Unlike Perdita, he knew what he was doing, but he felt surprisingly nervous.

He went down the stone steps of the passage Mallais, listening unconsciously for music over the wall, and stared at the garden door, still thinking this could end with smiles and a retreat to known ground. He used his keys to unlock the garden door, then the house door.

"Perdita?" he said.

She was sitting on the hearth rug, and she whirled, embarrassed. She had taken off her wet blouse, skirt, and stockings; apart from her corset, she was wearing only a thin underskirt and a combination, as naked as a well-brought-up woman would have been in the bath, more so than she might have been in bed. "Alexander?" She turned, hearing him, caught up her wet coat, and held it in front of her; but then she let the coat go and it fell in a pool at her feet. She simply stood, her hands at her sides, transfixed, and then—and he saw she was frightened— held out her arms to him.

He tried to speak; he could not. He could see her legs through the damp firelit cloth as if she were wearing nothing at all. Some strands of dark hair had fallen into the deep soft shadow between her breasts and lay against her skin.

He crossed the room and put his hand on her skin, very lightly, very carefully, a man wet and cold and unworthy of her. He was afraid of using any word to her, he could not use any of the ordinary euphemisms, make love, be intimate, take to bed; he wanted a word made for no one but her. His breath caught in his throat, painfully. She looked up at him, as if she were listening to him intently, and laid her hand over his.

She helped him take off his wet clothes. He was the one whose hands shook. They lay together in the bed. He got his voice back, somehow, explaining to her everything that would happen and might happen, in careful detail, as if he were giving a lesson, as if he were to be no more involved with her than the lecturer in her advanced class. It was all pretense. He was taking what he did not deserve; he was the womanizer Dotty thought him; he was the boy virgin he had not been since twelve.

"Will it hurt?" she asked. "I don't care. Let it hurt if it has to."

It was by no means well done; at the end she cried out in surprise and pain, pinned under him. She clung to him and bit her lips. There were drops of blood on the embroidered sheets. He stared at the blood, frightened by it, frightened by something it satisfied in him. Virgin-hunting is a perversion, but he understood it at that moment; the blood made her his. He had marked her, and she had let him, as if it were some sort of perverse ritual, as if she had asked him to tattoo her, to brand her. This affair would finish—that was what he wanted—but whatever else they were to each other after, it would contain this. He held her to him, possessive, afraid. *This is utterly wrong,* he thought, and *This is important.*

He had thought he had wanted her to go away happy, and in the long run that would have to be true; now, in this fragile and already passing instant, he only wanted her, this connection with her; what he had made him want more; he wanted to take her, have her, keep her, and never let her go.

Chapter 16

Between a gentleman and a lady there is a delicate connection. In her eyes he must be always strong, able to do everything, always right, always good, wanting only her good. He is a slave to her slightest wish, but she wants nothing he cannot give her.

It continues to rain. Against the windows of the Louvre, the rain makes a rustle of satin skirts; hail coughs against the glass. Down the echoing Grande Galerie, rain drips, and Leonard shivers.

The Mona Lisa asked him for two things. The first— happened, say no more than that, it happened; but once that was done the second ought to have been easy. To be buried in the Seine! To float down the river! It's not too much to ask, any man favored by such a lady would want to do it. Any man with heart would want to help.

But the Baron von Reisden won't.

Night after night Leonard stands, his lantern held high, gazing at an unchanging smile and wondering what to do next.

Chapter 17

"Let's go to the Louvre," Milly invited George.

Esther and Juan Gastedon, George and Milly went to the Louvre. Gastedon wanted to look at some sculpture; Esther wanted to be with Milly, who wanted to be with George; George wanted to hear himself talk. The Louvre was open from nine in the morning, one of the few warm places where homeless people and beggars could sleep. But art should shock the ordinary man out of his slumber, said George, walking through the echoing galleries of *le Lubre*, comparing art to sexual perversions in a voice too loud to be ignored.

"Onanism," George said cheerfully. He gestured with his cigarette at an Etruscan sarcophagus. "Necrophilia. Coprophilia. Love of one's secretions, or those of another."

"Marriage," said Milly. "There's a perversion. Have the police talked to you yet about stealing the Mona Lisa?"

"I'm not going to steal the Mona Lisa," George said. "Not to help you fight Henry." George was lazy but not stupid.

A girl still young was sitting on a bench, a silent girl with a big tender pale forehead. Milly watched her stretching her legs out in front of her, smiling tiredly, flexing her ankles, her skirt drawn up above her worn red boots. George sat down by the girl and laid his large hand in concern on her arm. "Do you not know that art is vo-yeur-ism? Viewing art is viewing sex, mademoiselle!"

The pale girl got to her feet carefully and moved away.

Juan was examining the *Deux Époux*, the *Spouses*, as if he wanted to steal that. Henry's bold eyes and gourmand smile stared out from the Etruscan male figure's wooden face. The white-faced wife leaned against him, mirroring his expression. Looking at pictures of herself and Henry taken during their marriage, Milly'd caught his look on her face, his self-indulgent heaviness, his sensual stare.

"If you and Henry threw the Mona Lisa in the Seine, it would be publicity for *Modern Life*—"

"Publicity?" George said. "It would be art. But I don't want to spend my life in jail."

"Henry is her art," Esther said acidly. "They have been divorcing for years, they are always divorcing, they are almost always almost divorced, but they are not divorced yet."

George gestured with his cigarette. "Henry is like all men; he wants to kill the woman he loves and he wants to adore her. Necrophilia's the only solution, but Milly won't lie down."

They headed upstairs, past an old soldier slumbering on a banquette and a rigid little seamstress huddled in her shawl, past gilt-framed saints, purgatories, and angels. Juan lagged behind, his possessive olive eyes sucking everything in. "Is there anything so fine as/Loving a dead man or woman?" George recited in front of a Crucifixion. They headed down the Galerie d'Apollon, past fauns, Laocoöns, and Ledas. George lectured on the appeal of bestiality.

Milly steered them into the Salon Carré.

The Mona Lisa gleamed in the center of the western wall, a greenish painting in a great gilt frame, which was in turn enclosed in a glass-fronted, white-painted, thiefproof box. Around her hung virgins and martyrs, Holy Families glowing with Italian light against the tobacco-colored walls; but the tourists only looked briefly at the others—check, check, check, now we've seen that—before gathering in a semicircle around the Mona Lisa. A mother held the hand of a little boy who shuffled his patent leather boots; a Scotswoman in a coalscuttle bonnet wrote in a notebook. Three adolescent boys, who looked as though they'd spent the night on the streets, poked each other in the ribs shamefacedly. Within her glass box the Mona Lisa hid, a moon behind clouds, a face remembered, a glimmering sacred heart behind a glass veil. From across the room, Milly could see the reflection of her own hat in the glass, and behind that, faintly, Leonardo's masterpiece.

"The glass reflect, and the brown varnish," Juan said. "So no one see."

"It could be replaced by a copy," George muttered. "*They* wouldn't care."

To one side, a boy at an easel was making a copy of the painting. He was a downy schoolkid, maybe seventeen, all ears and nose, the elbows of his jacket were patched and dusty; he had soft chapped lips and his straw-blond hair was a half hemisphere, as if someone had snipped it away under a bowl.

"You see Leonard?" Juan asked the boy. "He has terra-cotta for me, I want."

Juan had a friend at the Louvre, a guard who sometimes came to Esther's. Leonard sometimes stole primitive art from the Louvre basement for him. Now if *he* were to steal the Mona Lisa for George— January 28 was approaching and Milly did not want to be disappointed. She embroidered the story idly until she noticed the boy copyist looking at her.

"Hel*lo*," he said to Milly, and smiled, and blushed. He had beautiful eyes, the blue of a sky filled with Italian angels.

He was much too young for a copyist. Copying paintings was a job for mugs. In any warm museum, distressed gentle-women and ex–art teachers sat in shirtsleeves in front of their easels, dabbing away at a slightly too pink Rubens or dolly-face Madonna. They painted imi-Titians for provincial churches and rich men's mantelpieces. They had nerves, TB, an invalid mother. It was a job with dignity and nothing else. Copyists ate dinners of bread with a little smear of jam and called it high tea; copyists met at the flea market by the Porte de Clignancourt on Sundays and exclaimed over the delicious odd plates and threadbare overcoats they found, as if they could afford Limoges and *loutre*. Copyists were all about forty; so where had this little canary come from? Milly saw the control card tacked to his easel—MALLAIS, like the painter, the poor sweet little dupe. MALLAIS, JEAN-JACQUES. He was still trying to raise a mustache; over those soft lips it had a ridiculous lovable air like newly sprouted grass.

"I'm sorry," the boy said. "I mean—"

"That's all right," Milly said, smiling. She took a look at his Mona Lisa: not bad at all, only with rather large knuckles, just like his.

By the time Milly and George left the museum, the rain had momentarily stopped. In the sunshine, street vendors were selling Mona Lisa colored prints, Mona Lisa postcards, pink-and-green Mona Lisa lockets on necklaces. Nick-Nack, leashed and miserable outside the museum, jumped up to lick Milly's chin. George loped across the street, dodging an auto-taxi, and looked over the parapet of the quai at the wide promenade between the quai wall and the river. Nick-Nack sniffed the base of the parapet and lifted his leg against it.

Below them stretched the white stone pavements of the lower quai and the smooth gray-green Seine. Milly looked down on the promenade, saw a boy watering horses and a woman lavender seller wheeling a barrow upriver toward the Châtelet, where men were coming and going from the Samaritaine public baths. In the middle of the river a commuter boat was chugging past a barge; colored posters gleamed on the *bateau-mouche*'s square roof, SUNLIGHT SAVON, CHOCOLAT MENIER. The sun filled the quais with a flat, pale, tender light, which shone on the bared muscular arms of the lavender seller and on her red kerchief. For a moment Milly's revenge against Henry wavered and she felt the presence of something unpurposeful, unplanned, as iridescent and momentary as the green shine of a grackle's wing.

"Milly?" George said. "What's it about?"

Milly pressed one finger against the top of the parapet, over the hollow left in the sandstone by a prehistoric snail. "Oh, Henry?" she said casually. She looked at her fingertip; the shell had left a clear impression.

"He can't give back the copyrights," George said, "if that's what you want."

"I want you to throw the Mona Lisa in the Seine," Milly said.

"Why, to get me in trouble?"

Milly smiled at him from under her hat like a tiger from within a cage.

Chapter 18

"There is something I do not like about Mallais," Dotty said to Perdita icily on one of their endless trips to Worth's. "The endless paintings of Courbevoie. A single boring river suburb, when there is all of Paris to choose from! One becomes provincial, don't you think, Miss Halley?"

"I couldn't say, ma'am."

"I think you do not choose to say," said Alexander's cousin. "Courbevoie cannot possibly be good for one."

Good, no. Perdita was descending a moral slope, but at the bottom were parts of Alexander and herself she had never known before.

Sex had changed her very idea of herself. Her head and hands and torso, the sensitive ends of her fingers, her legs and feet, her heart and brain, her body with which she played the piano was also the instrument with which she made love. Much of what Maître said about the piano was suddenly comprehensible to her; she eavesdropped on the men's world with new knowledge. *Make love to the piano like the body of a woman*: she did to the piano what Alexander did to her, making it surrender its hollow spaces to her, making it reverberate and sigh and cry out in pleasure. With every note she played in class, she felt she was proclaiming what she knew, but she could not help it; the attraction of what she could do was like a drug; she felt she had suddenly been given immense power. Music changed for her.

And Alexander? If he was her piano, she was his. Had she ever doubted that she attracted him? "Kiss me on the eyelids," she commanded, his blind imperial lover; he did, long and lingeringly, and held her. "I was desperate for you," he said.

She scanted rehearsal time and concentration; she was spending all her time with him. The Young Ladies' Pension had eleven P.M. curfew, an hour after the Conservatoire rehearsal rooms closed; several times she arrived just as the clock was striking eleven, breathless, with her hair disarranged; how many times could she excuse it by saying the wind had tugged at her hat? She left for dinner and never returned to practice. He met her in dark restaurants; they kissed in doorways; he smuggled her into hotels. On Tuesday and Friday she took the tram or the railway to Courbevoie, where she should have been practicing intensely for her debut; but he came by another route, and whatever improvements had occurred in her playing didn't come from hours at the keyboard.

At the end of the long afternoons, when she finally put on her clothes, her body no longer seemed natural in them, as if her modest blouse and skirt had taken some stiffness from the damp. She was a naked woman, with all her heart; she could have showed her legs and breasts in public, Alexander had made her so proud of them; she could have dressed herself in only her tangled hair.

It was such great pleasure it seemed ominous: pleasure that didn't come from self-approval but from something darker, as if this pleasure were hunting them like dogs, day by day pleasure chased them and caught them and brought them down; and sometimes she thought they should try to escape, go back to the respectable friendship and the long conversations; but that was impossible now. Even when they simply walked on the quais and talked, even when they only held hands, they always knew each other physically, they were always partly in bed. They were like Mississippi raftsmen or canoeists skilled in navigating rapid waters, who even if they were rowing on a lake always had a tense necessary alertness between them, a shared sense of danger.

They could not live like this. Mr. Daugherty would come to Paris. They would be caught by someone. But they lived like this.

Chapter 19

On the second of January, at the street market in front of the church, Perdita first met Suzanne Mallais, the widow of the painter.

All Perdita knew about her at first was her voice, a comfortable unplaceable twang very like a Boston accent. Alexander was off buying hardware to mend a faucet; Perdita, string bag domestically over her wrist, was investigating cheeses. At the next stall, a fishmonger's, a twanging guitar string was bargaining for a couple of *morue* for her brother Yvaud and talking about her grandson and the weather. Wasn't it nice and warm, but such dreadful rain, *haing*? "Nayuh," Perdita imagined this Frenchwoman saying, "I been lookin' at the river; goin' to get us some floodin' in the ma'shes, I should imagine." Perdita listened unashamedly to this French version of a Boston backfence conversation while Madame the customer talked about Célesting's eel-soup recipe, Monsieur Yvaud's terrible "arthuritis," and the suspicious smell from the draings.

Like beauty, a handicap can be used or misused; Perdita used her bad eyesight to ask Madame the customer what fish she would recommend, and was soon in the middle of a satisfying conversation about drains, dripping faucets, and wandering cats. Madame the customer's black-and-white Léong was missing, and in this rain! The school grounds were all filled up with mud, Madame the customer said, *les p'tits enfangs* were crazy with the bad weather. Did Madame (meaning Perdita) have children yet?

No, Perdita said, not yet, and blushed, hoping Alexander wasn't close enough to overhear that *yet*.

The weather was awful for her business, Madame the fishmonger said despondently. Impossible to keep instruments in tune, Perdita contributed. Cut her grandson's business in half, Madame the customer said; tourists didn't come out to buy the Mona Lisa copies he painted. Only the dratted Parisiangs went out in such rain, those dainged Parisiangs who lived in the dainged house next door, Madame the customer said, and had *her* garden.

It was only then that Perdita realized who Madame the customer was; and her face must have shown it, because Madame the customer realized who Perdita was. A dreadful silence fell, a disappointed silence; they had been having fun.

Back at the house, she and Alexander discovered they had no pan to bake the flounder, no griddle or skillet. "Tell me more about the Mallaises," she said.

Fifty years ago, Alexander said, Mallais had been a market gardener. He had rented this steep bit of land, which then had been planted in fruit trees. He and his wife had transformed the garden and he had painted in it. They'd bought the corner lot and put up a small house. In the late 1870s, the banker Fernand Driesbach had bought the rest and had given it to Mallais to use for his lifetime.

"In 1900 Mallais died," Alexander said. "His patron decided to build his own house at the upper end of the garden. The day the builders started, the widow Mallais began to wall off her garden from his. It is a remarkably ugly wall."

Abandoning the fish, they picked their way down the steep

clay path, past the dormant flower beds. "Here is the wall," he said, guiding her hands to it. Perdita took off her gloves and felt rough gritty stone; on this side, where Madame Mallais hadn't been able to reach, the mortar lumped and drooled downward. The blocks rose as high as a small woman could reach with her hand above her head. Even to the touch it was ugly—Perdita could hardly imagine friendly, garrulous Madame the customer building this—but in one place the wall had been curved and stepped, unskillfully, around a gnarled old apple tree, as if Madame Mallais had been careful of the garden even while she ruined its beauty.

Last weekend Perdita had lost her gloves and Alexander had loaned her his; she'd hated to give them back because they smelled of him. If she were Madame Mallais, and the garden where her husband had painted was invaded by other people right after he'd died—?

"Now the family can't find a buyer, due in no small part to the wall. They blame her."

"I'm surprised no one *has* bought it," she said, "it would be such a good house for a family. And convenient, on the tramline . . ."

"And the Métro eventually, I suppose."

A few seconds of silence hung between them.

"I knew him a bit," Alexander said. "Mallais, I mean, when I was in Paris in '96. He held court at the New Athens café two or three nights a week. Dotty and I went to see him—even then she wanted to own one of his paintings—and he sketched her on the back of a menu and gave it to her. He was a big, laughing man with a splendid long beard and a big-brimmed hat. He would wipe his brushes on his vests and wear them, stiff with color, like canvases. Being a painter delighted him."

Alexander collected older solid men, stable, sensible ones, *pères de famille*. Know what people want to be by whom they admire. She smiled, wondering what Alexander would be like at fifty or sixty. Stable and solid, with a beard and a reputation for kindness? She would be forty or fifty then, becoming (she hoped) the sort of steady older woman she admired. Would she have got past touring; would she be giving concerts; would she be the sort of wife the man he wanted to be should have? She wasn't French, or rich, or of good family.

"What was his wife like then?"

"No one ever saw her. She was a laundress, or had been, and never came to Paris. She planted the garden; he painted it; that's all one knew. Look," he said, "this must have been *The Rose Hedge*."

"It needs cutting back," she said, feeling the long straggly canes.

"I think there's a pair of secateurs in the kitchen, among that stuff in the odd drawer."

He cut back the roses while she held the canes. They could plant a garden together, she wanted to tell him; they would; she felt for him something that wanted to make itself permanent. I will give up touring and stay with you, she almost said, but the words would not come out; she felt half-truthful, half meanly selfish.

He was pruning the roses the right way. She wondered who had taught him.

"You don't know Dotty's picture," he said.

"No." She could see pictures in very strong electric light, with a magnifying glass, but Dotty still had gas and candles.

"It was painted from where we're standing," he said, "looking down the slope and across the river. The time is late afternoon, almost sunset. At the bottom of the picture is a bit of the garden and the wall, quite dark. Above that, on the quai de Seine, a lamplighter is turning the gaslights on; and past him, taking up most of the picture, is the Seine at sunset, with the island of the Grande Jatte and the far side of the river turning red. One is drowning in the light, and there in the midst of it is the poor gaslighter, eyes on nothing but his lamps. . . . I think of that kind man in the café, laughing at the lamplighter and pitying him, and seeing and painting all that splendid light."

The sunset was reddening across the Seine. "Do you feel happy here?" she said, turning toward the fading center of it. "I do."

He came to her and held her close. But he did not say he was happy.

"I should—" she said, and stopped in frustration, and tried to go on.

"No," he said. "You shouldn't. The moral of Dotty's splendid Mallais is that the brightest things don't last. They don't need to. One simply pays attention while they're there."

She turned to him and held him convulsively. "You are my light," she said.

He said nothing.

They walked round the rest of the garden in the gathering dark; she felt smooth willow bark, the knobby roughness of apple twigs, buds in clusters. She waded through a patch of rustling iris leaves, marking the outlines of the pond that formed in spring. Alexander told her the names of Mallais paintings that had been made here, *Two Willows, The Old Apple Tree.* "One feels one's been here before," he said. That would mean a great deal to Alexander, she thought: a sort-of-memory that had no threat in it. Above her head, tree branches laced protectively. For three years she had lived in hotels; she was overcome by a hunger for domesticity; she thought about how this garden would be in spring, or warm in summer up on the hill, with the sunlight and a little breeze from the river. But by summer she would be gone.

Chapter 20

Perdita was due to be "visited" just after New Year's, and did not get her period, which showed her how much she was worried about her concerts. Many performing women are irregular before concerts; Alexander used precautions; she had no real reason to be concerned. Still, it was now possible for her to have a child. She felt a nervous anticipation, half the sense of her body's possibilities, half dread.

What if she did? They would marry; they would live here. She would take care of him. Alexander never ate enough, he simply forgot. He spent too much time at Jouvet, making sure the mad people were taken care of, and too much time dissecting frogs; he would spend the time with her instead. She would fix him delicious little meals. And she would play the piano—

When she was younger she had volunteered at the Children's Clinic, where there was a class for "girls in trouble" as young as thirteen and fourteen. Struggling through simple books and sums, at school recess they gossiped knowingly together with the air of grown women. *My boyfriend he's a marrying me next month,* and *when you due?* They were lazy as mud, especially when they had work to do: *oh, miss, I'm so sleepy, oh, miss, my stomach's feeling bad, I got to go out on the playground, I feel sick.* They had given up all their chances to better themselves; the settlement workers told them so. But their lives had seemed to Perdita secretly rich, secretly enviable.

Now I got somebody of my own, miss, a girl had told her, *now I got my own one to love.*

She had someone to love now, too. When she lay in Alexander's arms, when she should have been practicing, she surrendered delightedly to loving him. She wanted to love more still. She wanted to have his child. Someday, she said to herself, stroking his skin with the sensitive ends of her fingers, someday I'll have made a success of myself, I'll be the pianist I wanted, and then I'll give it all to you, to us. She thought of pouring herself like gold into his hands. And why should someday be later?

The rain whispered around them intimately, like bed-curtains shutting off the world; and she let him say cautiously that this would not last, and she knew it would, someday.

But she did not tell him, because she was not quite ready for someday to be now; she had something else besides him, and she had seen from Florrie what marriage did to the piano.

Chapter 21

On Tuesday, Perdita went to Courbevoie alone. She stopped at the Grand Bazar de Courbevoie to buy a skillet (what *was* the word for skillet in French?), then applied herself to Chopin and Liszt, but she was thinking of the couple who had lived here before herself and Alexander.

Cousin Dotty had told her something about them. Madame Mallais had been a housemaid and laundress working for a French painter's family. When Mallais had run away with the painter's daughter, she had gone too. The daughter had died and Mallais had married Madame. She had supported him by taking in laundry, but when he had become famous, he had left her in Courbevoie while he stayed in Paris among his friends.

"She was uneducated, poor—quite unsuitable—she would not have fit in Paris." Cousin Dotty had drawn the moral of their lives for Perdita. "He married her to legitimate their child. He was kind to leave her here alone; his friends would have laughed at her."

Perdita treated herself to a walk in the garden, thinking about that ill-assorted pair, the painter and his laundress, and ended at the bottom of it, opening the door in their high French garden wall. Madame Mallais's garden gate was only twenty steps to the left.

When you were young, she asked her invisible neighbor, did you think about him all the time and know you shouldn't?

Did you walk in the garden with him? Did you start with him and not be able to stop, not want to stop, but want to say something? Say *I'm not quite like what you want*? What was it like to begin to wonder if you should have his child and stay here? Were you glad when you did?

"Miaou!" Wet fur rubbed itself against her ankles. She jumped, startled, then knelt down, finding a chin to scratch, and gathered up a double armful of heavy wet cat.

"Minou, minou! Oh, you poor darling, did you get locked in here?" She squinted. "Are you a black-and-white cat? I think you are. Are you Madame's Léon?"

"Miah!" the cat agreed, purring. "Miauf?"

"No, kitty, I don't have any food for you, but if we take you to your mama—" She didn't know if she wanted to break in upon Madame Mallais, but now she could, before their awkwardness had had time to set hard. "Come on, Léon, and don't jump out of my arms on the street." Perdita let herself out of the garden gate onto the quai de Seine and pulled the bell at Madame Mallais's.

"I've found him—"

Léon purred enormously.

"*Is* he your cat—you know I don't see very well—"

Another moment of silence, but this time of another nature. "Oh?" said Madame, and then "Oh! Mais vous êtes *aveugle*!" You're *blind*, aren't you! Madame Mallais had *known* that, her tone implied, but hadn't seen the implications until just this moment.

"Come in," said Madame Mallais, opening the door. "You come right on in."

The Mallais garden was small, shadowy, and airless, like a city yard; as they went round the house, Perdita felt the ugly wall catch her skirt. They stepped over a patch of rustling dead iris leaves. Madame Mallais's backyard sloped upward steeply, like their own; it smelled of juniper and lavender, strong even in the January chill. But the air didn't stir as it did in the other garden; this one was small.

"We can sit in the tent, if you like," Madame Mallais said, "but my brother's asleep there. He has the arthuritis terrible—"

"Who's that?" a muffled bass voice complained just to the right of her. Perdita jumped. "Have you let someone in?" as if it were something Madame Mallais should never dream of doing.

Monsieur Yvaud had a much more educated voice than his sister—no twangs in his *n*'s.

"This is our neighbor," Madame Mallais said, "from next door, she can't *see*, Yvaud!"

"Oh?" Madame Mallais's brother said. "Oh," as if that explained everything. "*Bien!* Good to meet you, madame—mademoiselle—"

"Mademoiselle. Perdita Halley," Perdita said in some puzzlement. *Bien?* Nobody *likes* people who can't see.

"No one ever visits us," Madame Mallais said.

They ducked inside the tent and sat down, sheltered from the rain. The tent was small and smelled strongly of dead Monsieur Mallais's oils and turpentine, old pipe-tobacco smells, new pipe-tobacco smoke, and Monsieur's wintergreen liniment. "You're from that dreadful house, heh?" the old man wheezed indignantly.

"Our garden was special," Madame Mallais said, half apologizing. "It had a wonderful light, even in winter. You couldn't do a thing wrong there."

"You aren't the one who plays piano, mademoiselle?"

"Brother Yvaud loves to listen to you," Madame Mallais said. Monsieur Yvaud grunted in agreement.

They talked about her career for a bit—women's careers, if they're good for nothing else, at least make conversation—and Madame bustled about, showing Perdita her herbs, her little roses, her flower bed under the juniper, as if to reassure her that this garden was as good as the other. Perdita knelt down and touched the flower bed, lumpy in its winter sleep.

"I saw your garden today," Perdita ventured. "The buds are coming out on the branches."

"Never you mind for the garden," Madame Mallais said briskly. "Come, you have tea."

Madame gave Perdita tea and little toffeelike oatcakes that, Madame assured her, were exactly the recipe she had got from a Scotch governess she'd done laundry for when she was a girl, and a nicer lady you'd never want to meet. Brother Yvaud would take his tea later; he was "all strucken down," Madame said, and hadn't much use of his hands or legs. Madame's brother was clever: a stick strapped to his arm would let him turn pages of a book; a wire stand let him smoke his beloved pipe; he drank his tea through a metal straw. "He thinks of everything!" Madame said proudly.

The garden is my garden, Perdita thought, even if I've only rented it, and Madame is my acquaintance now; I have the right. "Madame, will you come visit and show us how the garden ought to be?"

"Us?" Madame Mallais said sharply. "Oh, I thought you were there by yourself—"

"A—friend comes to visit. *Un ami.*" The masculine word for *friend* was also the slang for something closer and less respectable. Perdita blushed. "I mean—he isn't my husband. Not yet. But we—" She had not thought of what Madame could think of her. "I'm just getting established as a pianist—I'm at the Conservatoire—they don't let married women study there, so . . ." She trailed off. "I'm sorry, madame, monsieur."

Monsieur Yvaud unexpectedly chuckled. "Oh, don't you mind not being married," Madame Mallais said. "Everybody starts there."

"You don't—mind, then?" she said, her voice quavering a little.

Madame Mallais patted her hand. "You take some cakes back for your young man. And I'll come to see you anytime."

"My—young man—could come to see Monsieur Yvaud, if you like. He must want company."

"Oh, Yvaud doesn't see people; he's dreadful sensitive about being crippled up; but you come back to see me again, and I'll come have tea with you."

Perdita climbed back up the garden slope. The evening was already dark and chill. They were a strange pair, Madame Mallais and her brother. It was morbid of Monsieur Yvaud not to want to be seen at all. (Perdita had actually got an impression of him in the strong light outside: a yellow-gray blob of a mustache, a black blob-beret, and to hold them together, a figure so stooped he looked tiny.) She was not at all sure brother Yvaud was really Madame's brother; why did they sound so different?

His arthritis bothers him so much he won't have visitors, she wrote to Alexander that evening. *She's lonely, but she wouldn't invite me in until she remembered I don't see well. They're nice but strange.*

And Dotty's acting oddly too, he wrote back the next day. *I wonder what is going on. Could you see any Mallais paintings? Madame is supposed to have all the unsold ones. Come have dinner with me this evening and tell me about it.*

She caressed the Braille typewriting as she would have smoothed his skin. *I can't,* she wrote; but she crossed it out and wrote *I will.*

Chapter 22

Reisden wanted her and did not want her.

He had not realized how wholly one could want to be with someone. In the lab he dreamed of her. Staff meetings at Jouvet drifted. On Monday he thought of being with her Tuesday; on Wednesday, of Thursday; on Friday, of Saturday and Sunday and the long precious night between. But he wanted more. He wanted to show her off; he wanted to introduce her at Jouvet; he wanted to say, *this one is mine.*

It was not, of course, a real relationship, either in life or in his head; it was far too intense. It was a reflection merely of his emotional needs. He wanted her so thoroughly because he could be unguarded with her; she knew everything; it saved him from having to explain again.

But he did not really want what he could not keep.

Perdita was not his, in spite of any mystical mark he had made on her; she gave herself to him, and neatly took herself back at the end of the afternoons; and he resented it a bit, which was unfair. He didn't want to take her work from her, and he didn't want to live with it, and he didn't want to resent her because she wasn't capable of married love yet. But he couldn't keep, he didn't want to keep, a woman who'd tour.

When he had married Tasy, she had been in the chorus of a traveling opera company and he a graduate student in biochemistry. His lab work could easily go seventy-two hours at a time; the opera traveled all over England—*Lakmé* in Glasgow, *Aïda* in Leeds; they had somehow had a life together, but he remembered as ruefully typical the time he had taken a freight train to Brighton in order to connect with her passenger train for York. They'd had three hours of blissful, frustrating second-class cuddling in a dark corner, after which he'd had to go back by the milk train to London. His life with Tasy had worked, barely; England is small. But from Le Havre to New York is five days by fast steamship, and New York is only the beginning of America, land of endless symphony orchestras.

And what did Perdita see in him, what did she want from him? Whom did she see instead of him? He had not been bothered by her eyesight before they had been lovers; now he was; it was a metaphor. Perdita eventually wanted children, and when he said he didn't, she smiled, looking past him with unfocused eyes. *Look at me,* he wanted to say.

The horrible truth, my dear, he thought, holding Perdita's warm body against his, is that I do know what I want. He didn't want a mistress; one leaves mistresses after one loves them, as he left Perdita at the end of their afternoons. The luxury of love was time, closeness, talking or reading together, body fitting against body, knees and arms, legs and hands, falling asleep together, domesticating the darkness with each other's presence.

Dotty was right; he wanted to be married.

When this was over, he would seriously look for a decent woman he could *have.* The wife for him would be about his age. She would have been widowed, or perhaps divorced; she had begun searching for a reasonable chance at a second happiness. She might have children, but they would be older, at school.

There would be no piano, none. No symphonies, no touring, no agents, no America. No leave-takings.

And the woman for him would have no curiosity. He

would not have to share everything with her, the whole ragged horrible story; she would simply assume that once he had been ill and now was well.

But he was out of his own control. When he wanted to chase after a reliable wife, he found himself instead with this lover: settling down by her, distrustful, doing the wrong thing; lying next to her, body against body, his arm cradling her. "Good night, my love," he said to her. "Good night, my own." Perdita was to him so much like Tasy, so much like having decided; of having found someone against whom everyone else was measured. What he felt for her was not an emotion to survive in a mirror but something for darkness, an emotion not even human, but animal, a relief, an exhaustion of all care, like that of a guardian dog falling asleep at his mistress's side because she is his. It did not have a name; certainly not love; it was not romantic; it was self-consciousness compounded; it was possession of what one cannot keep.

He should simply blurt out his horrible past to someone else, and sleep with someone else, and break the special relationship that held him to Perdita, and let her go.

Chapter 23

Murder is less terrible a thing than neglect. After New Year's, Leonard begins to realize that no one is going to bother with the Mona Lisa. The mirrors are soaped, BONNE ANNÉE *1910*, the *year* has changed, the *decade*, she is still *there*.

He is obsessed by the Morgue. Cold days make him think of the ice where they keep the bodies; the drip of rain, the drip of ice as it melts. The few sunny days create in him a nameless horror.

He reads, again and again, the few inches of paper in which the discovery of her body was reported. GRUESOME DISCOVERY, he reads. MONSTROUS CRIME. The grubby bits of newspaper almost comfort him. Such a monster must be obsessing the police of the Préfecture. Hundreds of policemen must be combing the streets. The Mona Lisa is not being forgotten. The police are after the killer.

A monster. A *vaurien*, a blackguard with his long knife, a good-for-nothing, a—

But even the police must know he cared for her, that "monster" who "perforated her body with his knife." She was sick. The monster had pity. The monster was a gentleman.

The rain drifts across the quai du Louvre like black funeral crepe.

Baron de Reisden why do you Ignore your Duty Why do you take no Trouble for her

Leonard pins a postcard secretly inside his tunic, where it rustles like a disappointed and angry heart.

Chapter 24

Surly you doant No Wat Yoar supos to Do—

S	The letter lay on the table at the Préfecture, all seven pages of it. The police photographers had already been at it and had got several prints, most of them unfortunately Reisden's. Down the linoleumed halls, the wind howled like a faraway madman.

"He kills her violently, Monsieur le Baron, and then he writes to you that you should put roses into her hands when you throw her into the river." Inspector Langelais looked at the letter with the combination of professional interest and personal unease that a bomb squad shows for a bomb. "Roses!" repeated Langelais.

"He wants to be caught," Reisden said.

"If he did, he would try to bury her himself!"

"He's not to that point. But he wants to talk." Her Artist had written about the first time he had seen the Mona Lisa, dancing in front of the Gare d'Orsay. He had written minute details of the funeral he wanted for her, which involved Notre-Dame, the peerage of France, and the pope. He had even included instructions for her reception at her palace, at the end of the Seine. "He's obsessed with her, he can't let her go. This is a way of continuing the relationship."

Langelais grimaced.

"Have you never arrested a man crying by his wife's body?" Reisden asked. "Why is he crying? Because she's left him."

"Ah, yes, all the violent ones are sentimental," Langelais said, "but this was a vicious crime. He used two knives. He cut both her wrists, stabbed her repeatedly, finally slashed an artery." The inspector twisted his mustache, fuming. *"Roses?"*

"He cut her wrists?" Reisden said. This detail had not made the papers. "That's usually part of an attempt to make it look like suicide."

"He stabbed her thirty-seven times!" said the inspector. "It wasn't suicide."

Reisden left Langelais at the Préfecture with the letter. He was supposed to be attending a neurology lecture, but he'd heard the speaker before and would catch up on any news at the reception afterward.

He strolled aimlessly along the Right Bank. By the Mégisserie bird market, the roosters ruffled their feathers despondently and the pigeons cooed in the rain. Reisden stood in the rain watching the lights, the carriages trundling past, the birds, in that nerve-ridden mood where every ordinary thing seems fragile.

He had a theory about the crime, and didn't like it.

Past the rue St.-Honoré, the somnolent cabbage-smelling greenhouses of Les Halles glistened, reflected in broken chunks on the pavement. He walked up the rue Montmartre toward the Hôtel des Postes on the rue du Louvre.

Under the awning of a café, half-protected from the rain, a child was selling boutonnieres from a heavy shoulder tray. Reisden bought the contents of the tray, ten francs' worth of small white roses, petals adhering to each other from the damp. He made the child give them away while he watched, gave her two francs more for dinner, and left before some do-gooder, or the child herself, began to think he was buying her. She would be back on the street tomorrow with another load of roses, and eventually she would be on the street without roses. Someday no doubt she'd be singing on the street like the Mona Lisa.

Dotty was right. He should marry. One needs someone to love without making a fool of oneself.

Inside the Hôtel des Postes, winged women in marble brooded over the ranks of telephone kiosks; at the long counter, expressionless uniformed men took coins and passed out stamps and stationery. A fat woman was complaining bitterly over ten centimes. Reisden took his gloves off, smeared his hands with ink from the bottle on the counter, did his best to look unbalanced, and stood in line to buy a sheet of cheap notepaper, an envelope, and a ten-centime stamp. An unusual purchase by a gentleman, but the postal agent barely raised his eyes.

No one had seen Her Artist buying stationery. He had left no fingerprints. He was simply not likely to be caught.

He walked back toward the river, past the dark bulk of the Louvre; at the Pont-Royal he crossed the Seine and stood at the end of the bridge, in the lights from the Gare d'Orsay, looking upriver toward the Vert-Galant.

On the upper quais, by the big railroad station and the hotel, there were crowds at every hour. From the side of the hotel hung enormous electrical fixtures, lighting everything below like foggy moons. A train was chugging along the railway cut from the Gare des Invalides. On the lower quai was a mooring for barges. Two were there now; porters were unloading wood and barrels of flour, and a small mountain of gravel blocked part of the downstream side of the bridge. *Bateaux-mouches* with their red and yellow lights dotted the river. The whole of the Seine in central Paris was busy, lighted, filled with boats. Anywhere on the Seine was an impossible place to kill someone, unless the man had wanted to be caught.

G-d, how he'd wanted to be caught himself, in his time, and hadn't had the sense to know it.

Foggy rain was drifting across the river. The lights glinted on the hydrographic scale, a vertical strip of rain-darkened iron running up the nearest bridge piling. Trees leaned out from the downstream wall, their leafless crowns above the quai, making deltas of shadow in the electric lights. He looked upstream and saw, with almost a shock, the only dark place in the river, the park of the Vert-Galant with its dim spike-crowned lamps, a notorious place for lovers.

There. It had been there. She had taken him to the Vert-Galant, acting perhaps like a lover, and then—

"Monsieur de Reisden?"

He jumped like a guilty man.

"Inspector," he said.

The inspector's face was a blank in the dusk. He has been following me, Reisden thought. Monsieur de Reisden was an ex-madman, who lived near the river and had known the Mona Lisa. Monsieur de Reisden had been to the post office; there he was staring at the scene of the crime. Reisden would have arrested himself.

"I know what happened between him and the Mona Lisa," Reisden said.

Chapter 25

By this time the Mona Lisa had been in the Morgue six weeks. They examined her in the back autopsy room, under the harsh electric light. Reisden attended autopsies in his work; he didn't like them; but he had the strength of stomach to turn over the corpse's hands (club-fingered, surprisingly small) and to examine the palms and wrists with the autopsy room's pocket-glass. The Mona Lisa's skin slid liquidly; on the back of her hand, it tore. He went out the back door of the Morgue and stood in the northern wind off the river, breathing hard, wiping his fingers against the cold granite exterior of the building.

"This was not a murder," he said to Langelais. "Not initially."

"What do you mean?"

Reisden took out his silver Swiss pencil. "Hold out your wrists. This is a knife and I am cutting them." He drew the tip of the pencil across both wrists, very gently; the pencil glimmered blue in the dusk. "I am right-handed, you are facing me; I cut both your wrists from my left to my right. The wound starts at the thumb side of your right wrist; its trailing edge is at the thumb side of your left. I don't see that on her wrists." He drew the pencil from outside to inside of the left wrist, switched it, and with the left hand drew from outside to inside of the right. "Now I am cutting my own wrists. Opposite directions, slanting slightly downward, leading edge of the wound at the thumb side of both wrists. That's what I see. He did the rest, one presumes, but she cut her own wrists."

Langelais pulled at his beard. "That's very clever," he said.

"She cut her own wrists, and then— She was leaving him, or she asked him to kill her." *I gave hr Evrything she Wantd bcas She Ws Good to Me:* Her Artist had said it three times in seven pages. Poor Her Artist, writing obsessively in his painful scrawl, explaining how good the Mona Lisa had been.

"Of course," the inspector said, clearing his throat. "This letter, for instance, gives you a complete alibi, if you can account for the time when it was mailed. Yesterday evening, Monsieur, six P.M., at the rue du Louvre; you were certainly elsewhere."

"Yesterday evening, six o'clock." He had been with Perdita. "I was alone, I'm afraid," he said.

"Ah, that's unfortunate."

"If I were this man, I should have made sure to provide myself an alibi."

The inspector looked away. They both knew Langelais would not arrest Reisden unless he were so gauche as to confess; Reisden was a baron and the owner of a company, and one does not get far by prosecuting the *classes dirigeantes*. But they both knew as well that Reisden was acting oddly.

"I think she asked him to kill her," Reisden persisted. "It's not a good theory but it's the best I have. There were no cut marks on her palms; when one is being knifed, one puts up one's hands in defense and is slashed across the palm, but she had no cuts. She didn't resist him. And now he is a murderer." *I ms hr so mutch*, the man had written. "You know quite a bit about him from the body. He's right-handed and a few inches taller than she. He has perhaps been rejected for military service; at least he has no military training. He should be easy to find among her clients."

"You say you didn't kill her," the inspector said, "or I *would* think you did." He smiled, but for effect, baring his teeth politely in his beard. "Military service?"

"One learns to consider how well armed one is, and to stab upward. He simply pummeled her with the knife. He had no idea how to kill her."

"Ah."

"He needs to be found," Reisden said.

The inspector fumbled with his mustache. Langelais wanted a simple case.

I am going to get in trouble over this, Reisden thought; I should leave it alone.

"You will never find him," Reisden said, "but I think I can."

Chapter 26

Saturday, January 8, it rained ferociously; water poured over the pointed roofs of Jouvet and gurgled down the drains into the courtyard. Apprehensive patients arrived huddled under black and brown umbrellas; ambulance drivers took refuge in the waiting room, smoking and complaining, while their horses waited outside under oilcloths and blankets, heads bowed, manes streaming, stamping their feet in impatience to be home. Reisden's sour-faced secretary, Madame Herschner, stalked the laboratory, sniffing disapprovingly as she constructed a supplies list; and Reisden sat with the accountants, who took two hours telling him that Jouvet was prosperous enough to float a bank loan.

For the last three days an advertisement had appeared in the agony columns of the least literate newspapers of Paris. *MONA LISA ARTIST—Must speak with you. Leave message, Hôtel des Postes, rue du Louvre.* The plan was to persuade Her Artist to agree to a meeting, at which the police would capture him. Having committed even to this little, Reisden wished he had known better.

About noon, after the accountants had left, he closed the door to his office and took from a cabinet under the bookshelves an old Edison dictating phonograph and a wax cylinder in its box. He lowered the playing arm very carefully onto the wax-covered cardboard and listened through it once. Through the jingle of wear and needle noise, he heard a red-haired girl of eighteen making a recording. Tasy stood in front of the recording horn, singing, until again she fluffed the last high note, again broke off, and used the last half inch of wax to record a message to him. *"Ya lyublyu tebya, Aleksandr!* I love you, Alexander," she said and the needle ran off the wax. She had made it ten years ago today, on the morning of the day they had married.

Every play of a wax cylinder destroys it a little more. Nothing was left of Tasy's voice but a high soft burr and a memory. With efficient speed he put away the machine and its single recording, as if taking time over it would expose the moment as outworn too.

He would not use Tasy as an occasion of self-pity. He called up Dotty. "Lunch?"

"Oh, darling, I'm having lunch with Cécile. You could join us. She is really a lovely woman, dear," Dotty said. "And such a lot of property in Bourgogne."

He laughed. "Is Tiggy there? I shall take him out and buy him a dog."

"I would never speak to you again. No, he's at Paul's for the day. . . . Darling, if you are feeling infinitely obliging, there is one thing you could do for me."

He caught the note of brittleness in her voice. In that tone she had asked him, three years ago, if he could possibly find out where her husband had gone.

"Your Mr. Barry Bullard, a most unpleasant man. Yesterday, darling, he came to see me. He told me—" Dotty took a rather shaky breath. "He told me he's looked at my Mallais, and, darling, he says there's a detail of it that's rather off. I don't believe anything is wrong, but of course it is terribly disturbing. The retrospective opens next week. Could you speak with him?"

"Is that why you've been asking about Madame Mallais?" he asked.

"No, no, not at *all*—nothing can be wrong, I bought my painting from Armand—"

"Are you really not free for lunch?" he asked.

"I can't," she said.

"Then you are giving me tea and you will tell me all about it. Five o'clock."

Chapter 27

I t was also on Saturday, the eighth, that Milly Xico unexpectedly made the acquaintance of Perdita Halley.

La Parisienne had called; one of their regular contributors
was sick in bed; a photographer was at the Conservatoire with
twelve girl students, ready to be interviewed. Could she do
"Girls of the Conservatoire," eight hundred words, by this
evening?

Of course she could.

She was bored with the revue she was rehearsing. It was in
an old dump of a theater near the Boulevard Poissonnière, the
sort of place that books a woman who is almost thirty-three
and used to have a name. At the back of the theater, drops
clinked monotonously into a tin pail. The house manager
coughed; the director sucked throat pastilles; the girls of the
chorus shivered in their short skirts and tight knit vests. In the
wings, the young girl comic singer, who was looking suspiciously thick about the waist, conferred with a knowing-eyed
Englishwoman who sang opera to "clear the seats." A continu-
ously playing revue was only a step above having no work at
all. If only I had money, Milly thought. Onstage, Nick sat on a
bentwood chair, head down, shoulders up, and Milly bent her
body forward with the saccharine suppleness of an English
singer and cooed hoarsely:

"Said the kitty-cat
To the dog who sat
On the hearth-rug, 'My dear . . .' "

"Wait, wait!" the director said. "The dog doesn't look as if he's enjoying himself."

"It's not the dog they come to see, after all." Milly put her foot on the chair seat and snapped her fingers above Nick's wrinkled little muzzle. "Meat, Nicky! Smile!"

Nick rolled his eyes up, sighing a cloud of steam.

"Miau-Ouah-Ouah!
What a funny pair we'd make
Life would be a piece of cake
If you loved meee . . ."

Milly faced downstage, Nick faced upstage, rump to the audience. Milly sang "It's No Sin." Milly sang "A Woman's Heart Alone." Milly picked up Nick-Nack and sang:

"What can a man do that a dog can't do?
I'd rather have a dog than you. . . ."

She kissed Nick-Nack on the mouth, touching warm furry rubbery lips and smelling meaty breath, and one of Zosmé's 16 Count Them 16 Dancing Girls laughed nervously.

"Fine for Xico, Dancing Girls up please!"

"I think she *French*-kisses the dog!" she heard one of the girls whisper.

"Not in rehearsal, idiot!"

Now the Conservatoire. Passing hurriedly through the streets of the quarter, Milly had an impression of shop windows—play publishers, music publishers, makers and repairers of instruments; one shop sold only bows and tiny copies of violins and cellos. A café, the Viola, gave off a smell of fried potatoes; Nick whined and looked at her with sad bulbous eyes. "Not yet, Nicky, we have to pay the rent."

The girls of the Conservatoire were lined up in a row, all in white blouses and dark skirts. Most were debutantes, polishing their musical talents before they married. Two girls at the end of the row caught Milly's eye, one very young, soft and sad and heavy-faced, the other dark-haired, slim, passionately gesturing with big musician's hands. The second girl seemed familiar, the way fresh young faces often are. Milly tried to place her and failed.

"Smile! Say *yes*!" the photographer said. "Now line up for Madame Milly."

Where *had* Milly seen that girl before? Each of the girls sat down at the piano and played a few bars; each sat next to Milly and answered questions. Agnieszka Appolonsky, the sad little pillow, twisted her fingers nervously. Miss Perdita Halley, American, gave a charming and very self-possessed interview for them both. Miss Halley was appearing professionally twice in Paris within the next couple of weeks: on January 21, under the sponsorship of Mrs. Bacon, the American ambassador's wife, and the week after, the twenty-seventh, at a reception given by the Vicomtesse de Gresnière.

That was who she was, the little companion of the black panther and the vicomtesse: the girl with the umbrella.

Oho, classy; a Conservatoire student! A Conservatoire student who was the lover of a man who had a great understanding with the Vicomtesse de Gresnière. That frigid blonde, dark "darling Sacha" with his ironic and protective glance at her, and the girl between them—

Milly was nothing if not decisive. She had a use for darling Sacha.

"How do you know the vicomtesse?"

"Oh, her cousin, the Baron von Reisden, is—a friend of my family. An acquaintance."

So, thought Milly, the relationship with "Sacha" was a secret, though not to Dotty.

"My magazine likes fashion interiors," Milly said, "and I am supposed to write about one girl in particular. Is it possible to photograph you at the vicomtesse's?"

Chapter 28

Making Miss Halley's acquaintance was no harder than to pet a stray kitten. Milly had planned on taking her to tea and making common womanly cause over something. What it turned out to be was hats. As they left the Conservatoire, Miss Halley's hat broke its brim in the door.

"Oh, what a shame," Milly commiserated. "I know a hat shop—"

Milly had a favorite cheap atelier, where millinery was made in the back room and sold in the front. In a tiny electric-lit room, at a long table jumbled with ribbons, flowers, and feathers, three women in aprons created a hat for Miss Halley: a dark brim of enormous extent, a splash of marigold-orange trim, a this, a that, not too much, not too little. The milliner suggested a boa-length scarf to match, deep eggplant with marigold tassels. "Does it really look suitable for Paris?" the girl asked shyly. "I do like to be fashionable enough."

Poor baby, dressing for a man.

Madame la Vicomtesse's house was a stony pale building on the narrow place Dauphine. The vicomtesse's entrance hall was hard black-and-white marble, its walls twined with lifeless painted roses; the stairs and her formal reception rooms were lined with mirrors, dimmed as if by the smoke of some long-ago conflagration too solemn to wipe away. Madame de Gresnière herself sat upright in a chair from the ancien régime, a

Wili in pale pastels, her hair so blond it was almost white; she looked at Milly haughtily, without interest, from sad blue eyes, the eyes of a woman deeply wronged.

Sacha arrived halfway through the photography, black and feral, bringing into the overheated and wax-perfumed air a chill smell of the rainy streets outside, of subways and formalin. Not for him the vicomtesse's pale, elegant, and fragile chairs; as if it belonged to him he took the clubman's leather chair by the fire, next to hers, stretching out his long legs. He and the vicomtesse exchanged murmurs, leaning toward each other. He had raptor's eyes, light irises ringed with dark: carnivorous, watchful, uncontent by nature. He devoured the girl Perdita with his eyes, turning away, then back, as if taking time over his meal, and the vicomtesse watched jealously.

Should there be flowers in the photograph? The photographer wanted an interesting composition. Madame la Vicomtesse vetoed flowers on the shoulder of Miss Halley's dress (a Worth!), but monsieur thought flowers were a necessary cliché for a young woman pianist. Madame, smiling with mixed jealousy and patience, sacrificed some of her hothouse blooms, but frowned as monsieur added to the bouquet the flower from his own boutonniere. The girl stood between them, glowing as the flowers were pinned on by the baron, submissive as the vicomtesse repinned and rearranged them: perhaps insulated from all this by her eyesight, perhaps simply wise.

In the vicomtesse's dressing room, Miss Halley changed back into street clothes. The private rooms of this formal house were exactly like the public ones: corroded mirrors framed with olivewood and gilded *boiserie*, silk wall coverings, gilded chairs, but here Madame de Gresnière had installed electric light, a secret sin, to see how she would look in someone else's house. Miss Halley had a magnificent figure and that warm tint of skin that looks rosy under electric light. She wore completely plain underwear, flannelette like a schoolgirl, tight across the breasts, an attractive awkwardness; Milly got a piquant sense of this girl and the baron in the bedroom.

They all had tea and little sandwiches on Limoges china. The sprays of flowers on the Limoges matched those embroidered on the chairs. The vicomtesse's son joined them, the Vicomte de Gresnière, every little blond hair combed straight for tea with his dragon mother. Pouring tea from a silver pot, Madame talked about fashions. Pastels and pearls were all the rage this year; nothing overdone; nothing too *colorful*. Miss Halley lowered her eyes. The baron looked at the vicomtesse intently; Miss Halley's hand brushed as if accidentally against the baron's, and rested there; the vicomtesse regarded them with a prussic-acid smile. Miss Halley excused herself with a quick twining of her fingers around the baron's, asking, "Would Madame mind if I played the piano?" No, please do, said the vicomtesse, clearly glad to get rid of her. The little viscount nestled up against his uncle's elbow; the two of them read a book on animals; and Madame de Gresnière, making polite conversation with Milly, turned on them a look as tender and proprietary as a mother and wife.

From the mirrored hall an ordinary telephone buzzer buzzed like sleepy bees. A very proper butler knocked at the door, announcing the telephone as if it were a visitor: Mr. Barry Bullard, for Monsieur de Reisden. Madame jumped, and a tense look passed between her and Sacha. He went to answer the phone.

"Are you a student of pictures?" the vicomtesse asked Milly. Milly admired her pictures, which did not require admiration: who can quarrel with names, and Madame de Gresnière was a collector of names. "The Turner is in the yellow drawing room, the Renoirs in the dining room. My Mallais—" She broke off. "My late husband collected English hunting scenes," she said dismissively, "they are upstairs."

"Ah, English hunting scenes," Milly said dismissively, too, like a woman who throws such things away every Tuesday. She smoothed her silk skirt, which was on loan from a designer who hoped to be mentioned in *Femina*.

"Oh, that is unfortunate," the baron said from the hall. "Bullard, are you sure?"

"Do you collect?" the viscountess said, but half-turned toward the baron's voice.

"I don't doubt you," he was saying, "but this is really difficult. Yes, I'll speak with Dotty—"

There was a silence; the baron re-entered the room. The baron looked meaningfully at the vicomtesse, the vicomtesse apprehensively at him; they both glanced at Milly.

"I must go," Milly said.

"It has been such a pleasure," the vicomtesse said perfunctorily. The baron nodded; he had said almost nothing, and said nothing now.

Outside, Milly rescued Nick-Nack and gave way to curiosity. *Difficult, unfortunate?* "They're too rich, Nick my sweetie," Milly said, gathering him into her arms. "They have nothing to do. So the vicomtesse loves the baron, the baron flirts with his mistress while he reads aloud to the vicomtesse's son, and as if that isn't enough, he looks at the vicomtesse to see the effect on her. Them and their custom-painted china. I'll bet she smashed a piece once, Nicky, and didn't rest until she had it repainted. I wonder what they think their problems are?"

Suddenly, down through the bare branches of the quai des Orfèvres, in the circumspect street, with its jewelry shops and its view of the Seine, there fell a cascade of music and light. Someone had opened a window; a pianist was playing. Milly stepped into the street in time to see a parlormaid throw crumbs from the window of the salon above, adjust a curtain, and close the window again; the street darkened. But a momentary lightning had struck, leaving an imprint, a shock inscribed on the air, so that even the raindrops paused.

Miss Halley? That little girl with the flannel underwear and the adoring looks? Milly remembered her air of competence, of having given interviews before.

So Miss Halley had something, this little convent novice with the generous breasts and flannel underwear. She was a Turner or a piece of custom china, bought to furnish the house. But she was not fitting in, and soon the vicomtesse would get rid of her.

Miss Halley's future, Milly understood, depended on the reviews from her two performances this month; and the more important from the social point of view would be in the salon of this very Madame Chinchilla-and-Limoges, the Vicomtesse de Gresnière.

Yes, definitely, Milly thought, she could bring Sacha into her plot against Henry.

And on Saturday, the eighth, Roy Daugherty arrived in Paris.

Chapter 29

Arc de Triomphe, Champs-Élysées, the Eiffel Tower; Paris was full of famous things, but Daugherty wasn't over-impressed. It was a handsome city, but Gilbert Knight was right for once, it was dirty. Flowers all over, even in winter, electric lights on every street, cafés with tidy green awnings, but every pretty woman on the street was standing next to a little yapping French dog, squatting to do its business. The Latin Quarter: if it'd been in Boston they'd have had it for a slum. A block away from the postcards and the Seine skulked winding narrow streets, scabby with centuries of soot; buildings leaned against each other, shored up with pilings, and the sewers ran open down the middle of the street. The Panthéon. The Paris Métro. Every café had a flower vase on every table, and in every flower vase floated a dead fly.

Paris had street gals, just like Daugherty'd heard. They stood in front of all the subway stations. A girl with a neckline down to here passed him near his hotel and gave him the eye. But they all spoke French, which made them next to useless.

Saturday afternoon, Daugherty scouted out Jouvet, on a quiet street near the Gare d'Orsay. An office-block sort of building; one corner was much older, a picturesque, blackened old tower looking like a church, with a peaked roof and punky stone carvings rotted through. Reisden's English-speaking secretary, a dragon of an old lady with fourteen chins and

120

brooches stuck all over her frontage, looked at him like he was a lemon she had to eat and said Reisden was out. "I will give 'im a mess*aizh*," but Reisden didn't call back.

He stopped at Perdita's hotel. She'd gone away for the weekend.

His first Saturday evening in Paris, Daugherty sat in a café, drinking a thimbleful of expensive coffee, and drew in his worn detective's notebook caricatures of the girls with striped stockings that sat at the tables around him. He bought the *American Register* and read that he'd arrived.

On Sunday morning he visited the Viscountess de Gresnière. Reisden's "cousin" lived on the island in the center of the city, in a museum sort of house fine enough to make your palms sweat: mirrors reflecting in mirrors, curvy-legged chairs with cushions embroidered as fine as if they'd been painted, and not a one of them you'd dare sit down on. She spoke perfect English with an accent that reminded Daugherty of Reisden.

"Ah yes, Mr. Daugherty, the detective; I know of you. You are at the Hôtel d'Orsay? I don't know where Sacha has taken himself, but you do know Miss Halley? You have known Miss Halley since she was a child? How nice." She smiled in a way Daugherty didn't quite understand. "I have the address where she is staying."

At her direction, Daugherty took the Western Railroad out toward Colombes and Asnières. Under the Levallois bridge, where he got off, slow barges nodded gently in the water. Upriver he could see the steep Courbevoie bank, with its big enclosed yards and large houses. He squinted upriver through his glasses, and found the right house in the thin winter sunshine, modern brick and glass at the top of a long garden. A corner of the garden was cut off by a wall, making a triangular plot with a poky little pink cottage jammed into it. A stout old lady came out the cottage door, threw her washwater on the ground, sniffed the air, and went in again. A Sunday horse-drawn bus, half-empty, jingled down the street by the bottom of the garden. A woman in a wide hat and a scarf with orange tassels came out of the house, looking very French—

French she looked, but Roy Daugherty had no trouble recognizing Perdita, or the man in shirtsleeves who held her back a moment to kiss her.

It was Reisden.

Chapter 30

The morning started badly. After church, Perdita and Madame Mallais were going to do their marketing together; and Alexander had asked Perdita to get into Madame Mallais's house.

"Don't speak to her about the forgery," Alexander cautioned. "There are only three places from which the forgery could have come: Inslay-Hochstein, Dotty's household, or Madame Mallais. It's not Dotty. Dotty says it's not Inslay-Hochstein."

"But Madame Mallais?" Perdita said, carefully putting out of her mind Madame's odd attitude toward blindness; she liked Madame.

"Brother Yvaud?" Alexander said.

"He can't use his hands."

"Can't he, or is that what she told you? If she brings him outside, I can look at him over the wall. If she doesn't, Dotty would appreciate your having tea again with them and trying to find out."

After church, she and Madame Mallais wandered through the street market, avoiding the bright-colored rugs that were spread on the edges of the sidewalk. Madame Mallais chattered happily about the best laundries in town and how good the sunshine was for brother Yvaud's arthritis. I will not spy on them, Perdita thought, but asked after brother Yvaud's health.

"He's still all wrought up with the arthuritis, mademoiselle, hands and feet and knees and even his neck. It's this rain."

"How did it start with him? What does he do for it?"

Madame Mallais listed all brother Yvaud's medicines: honey mixed with vinegar, salts of this and copper of that. It sounded a great deal like what Great-Aunt Louisa had taken for her arthritis. Madame is a good ordinary woman, Perdita thought, who was deserted by her husband most of her life; and I bet when he came home she did his laundry all the same. Dotty, go find your forger elsewhere; it didn't happen in Madame's house.

"I liked you from the beginning," Perdita said impulsively. "Because you curved your wall around the apple tree."

"Not a very pretty wall," Madame Mallais said, half apologizing.

"Well, I don't mind it, and you have a right to build on your land. . . . My Alexander's cousin has got one of your husband's paintings," she said, following the impulse. "A *View of the Seine*."

"Oh, that one. That gaslighter never looked up at the sky. We wished he would."

"Alexander likes the pink shadow." Something about a pink shadow was supposed to prove it was a forgery.

"Mallais thought that shadow was clever as anything, it wrought the painting together so."

"Did he?" That was information she would pass on to Dotty.

Perdita had forgot her shopping list; all she could remember were homely items for Boston cooking, a beanpot, a good black-iron cornbread pan. Alexander came up with European things that seemed to her exotic and even useless: a pepper mill, sugar in a cone. Differences in upbringing are never stronger than in the kitchen.

Suddenly, as she was standing by the tall iron fence by the church, pricing green beans, without warning she panicked, as though she had begun to cross the street and had heard hooves pounding toward her, but didn't know from which direction they came. She backed up against the fence, breathing heavily; she was safe on the sidewalk, there were no horses, but she had heard something. She held on to the fence, taking shaky breaths, and listened, chill in the sunlight because of the sweat that had come out on her, staring at the grey blurs of people passing, and listened again, and heard footsteps she knew.

Her ears sang and she could taste her breakfast at the back of her throat. The familiar creaking boots came closer.

"Perdita, honey?"

"Oh, Mr. Daugherty, how are you here?" All she could think of was Alexander, still at the house. Mr. Daugherty is here because he got our address, she answered herself.

And he got it from Dotty.

"Are you just off the train?" she said brightly, and his silence answered her.

"Oh, honey," he said, "I was coming out to see you, just friendly like, and I seen *him*." Mr. Daugherty waited for her to deny it. "He's just visiting you early," he said. "Like a—friend, ain't he?"

She and Alexander had been caught, and by someone from Boston. Someone from home.

Chapter 31

"He got to marry you, honey," Mr. Daugherty said. She got rid of Madame Mallais somehow and took Mr. Daugherty to the house. She had to take his arm as they went down the stairs. Instead of letting herself in with her key, she rang the bell, hoping that would give Alexander some warning. But it didn't; he answered the door, and then there was a silence that it seemed nothing would ever break.

The worst of being blind is a silence like that, when no one is telling you what's going on.

"Reisden. I got to talk to you about this."

"Go inside, Perdita," Alexander said.

She sat inside, in the single chair in the salon, trapped in the silence between the walls. She heard them talking, and once Roy Daugherty shouted. "Ain't you ashamed?" he said. I will not be ashamed, she thought, but she was, not for Alexander nor what she'd done, but what Mr. Daugherty's voice made her feel, what she would feel about herself if she were judging herself in Boston, a woman with her lover in a half-furnished house. She closed her eyes, horrified, sick, feeling ice in her stomach.

"You got to marry her," she heard Roy Daugherty saying from outside, as if she were his to dispose of. It stirred up in her the same instinctive anger that Maître did, and panic, shame, fear. She stood up, swayed, and had to sit down again.

It was silent outside. Alexander came in alone.

"He's gone," he said.

She let out a breath she hadn't known she'd been holding. "What does he—think?"

He made an impatient sound in his throat. "What one would expect. He is willing to do nothing until tomorrow morning; then I must tell him what I mean to do."

"We aren't his business," she said, very slightly emphasizing the *we*. What *we* mean to do.

"Of course we are," Alexander said. "He's come from Gilbert. He doesn't say so but of course he has." He had been speaking in the same harsh tone he must have used to Mr. Daugherty. His voice softened and quieted now. "I cannot have Gilbert think I've ruined you. I owe him that."

Ruined, she thought dispassionately. "Nothing you do to me will hurt me," she said, raising her head. "And I owe Uncle Gilbert too; but what he thinks does not change that."

"Daugherty wants us to marry."

"Oh," she said, hating the way she said it, long and drawn-out and with a rise at the end, impatient.

"Now. This week."

She didn't say anything for a moment. "It's not his *business*," she said. "I love you. But not this way, Alexander, I want it my choice and yours, and coming from who we are, not what people think." He said nothing; she stumbled. "I know it's respectable, and we should talk about what Uncle Gilbert thinks. But—" She didn't know what she was saying.

He got up and fed the fire; the log thumped and made a hiss. "The point is that you want the music," he said.

What did he want her to say, *oh, yes, we'll marry now,* like that, as if they had only been waiting to be caught? That would make despicable everything they had thought and done.

"I want to get reviews here, Alexander; then I want to tour;

and then I do want to marry you. I won't be touring forever. I'll come back here and try to get a place—" She said it rashly, badly. "It's only that I want to see how well I can play. You understand that, don't you?"

"Yes," he said. "I do. Is that your plan? To work your way up from America to Europe?"

It was as good a plan as she had, apart from splitting in two or somehow persuading him not to notice when she was gone for months at a time.

He brought a chair out of the kitchen, set it by her, sat down. He took her hand. She put his hand between her warmer ones; his own was cold, half-frozen, he had been outside without a coat all this time talking to Mr. Daugherty. He needs a good wife, she thought. He drew his hand gently away, only clasped hers, like someone who is giving bad news, but wants you to remember that he's a friend.

"Just go to America," he said.

She held his hand harder. "I could be good in America," she said, "but I couldn't have you."

"No," he said. "You can't have both."

The fire ticked. The sun came through the windows onto their joined hands. Perdita remembered Madame Mallais talking about the sunlight in their garden. *There was always so much, even in the winter; you couldn't do anything wrong there.*

"I love you," she said, which she should have said before.

He didn't say anything.

She did love him. It committed her to too much, but she did.

"I could give up the piano," she said. "Women get tired of the circuit. Everybody does. I could get tired before I started."

He made an impatient sound.

"All right, I could do it for a year, and then give up. I'd have done something, I'd have reviews. . . . Could you wait a year?"

"I could," he said, "but you're a musician. The music won't stop in a year. How long did your thirty-seven women play the piano?" he asked. "Did any of them stop at twenty-two?"

"No," she said after too long. They played all their lives, of course, if they could; who wouldn't? "I'll go amateur, like Florrie."

"No, you won't," he said. "You've told me about Florrie."

He had always believed in her; now it made her frightened.

"I will—" she said, and stopped, not knowing what promise she could give him.

"No," he said in a harsh voice. "Go back to America; have your touring career. I want you to be happy."

He sounded angry. She was angry too. " 'I want you to be happy,' as if it's your gift! Are you trying to *make* me give you up? You can't *make* me give you up, Alexander, no more than Mr. Daugherty can make us marry."

"No," he said. "I'm sorry, Perdita. This doesn't work. I'm giving up you."

Chapter 32

She stood up; her knees gave way and she sat down on the floor. He helped her into their bedroom. She lay down on their bed and sat up, gasping. It was too cruel to be lying on the bed alone. What she wanted was his love; but what he brought her was tea, English-style with milk and too much sugar, and crackers out of a tin. She was hungry, suddenly, almost sick for food, for whatever he would give her.

"It's shock," he said.

She drank the tea down scalding and began to cry.

"Don't," he said.

"How can you say *don't*? You can't decide this by yourself." Her heart beat so fast she could barely talk. "There are two of us, Alexander."

"You are twenty-one," he said. "I remember being twenty-one; I was married to Tasy. One is capable of anything; one wants to be married because that is what adults do; one will win the Nobel Prize; one will do anything. Perhaps you will; you are really very good. I won't get in the way of that," he said, "but I want someone."

It was the cruelest thing he had ever said to her.

"Aren't I good enough?" she flared. It was that or hear that she had been cruel to him. "Is it because Cousin Dotty doesn't like me? *I want you and music*, Alexander, I'll do everything I have to, and I can, I'm not a fragile little thing. But if you care for her opinion that much, you had better say so."

They had dropped hands; she depended on touching him during the silences in their conversation, to understand through her fingers what he was saying and feeling; and now, though she stretched her hand out, he did not take it, and the silence went on and on. "I want someone who's here," he said.

She didn't know what to say. She had said it already. It was a matter of not just love but time, and he had told her they'd run out of it.

"Alexander," she said, and said the unthinkable. "Richard."

He didn't say anything.

"What will I do without you?" she said, suddenly helpless.

"What will you do?" he said as if it were obvious. "You have such a passion for music; follow it."

She stared at the shadow that was the man she thought she knew; she was too stung for tears. "That is cruel," she told him. "That's cruel."

He sent her back to the Young Ladies' Pension in a cab, in the middle of Sunday. She made it up the stairs, tearless and straight and careful under her fashionable new hat, and then sat on her neat narrow single bed, with the knobs on the iron bedstead pressing into her back, cross-legged, with the pillow over her knees, and pounded her fists into it, crying, until the interwoven springs under the mattress creaked and sang like their bed at Courbevoie. This morning they had lain together there, they had walked together in their garden. She had thought *this is where we start, not being married*, as proud as if she'd already had the ring on her finger.

He had said he loved her.

Oh, now she longed to show him she was domestic, now

she longed to be caught, like any poor wretched girl who had to marry; now she wanted him and nothing but him; now she valued marriage.

But what had she given him? Even when they had been together, she had been always the piano student, always practicing, playing scales against his ribs, but not feeding him. He wanted a wife. Cousin Dotty said he did, but it was true.

In the narrow bed in the narrow room, with her arms around the pillow, she cried because she could not give what he wanted, or because he wanted the wrong thing, or she did; because she could not fill that central place in his life; because she was furious at him; she cried most of all because she saw how shallow she must be for him, how self-centered, how unworthy of marriage, because she loved the piano; but didn't he understand how she desperately wanted to marry him? She cried silently, so as not to disturb all the girls in the rooms around her; she thought again and again, I'll give it up, I want him.

But he knew her too well.

She stayed up all night, trying to pretend that she had changed her nature; but the next morning, after the café au lait and bread and jam she felt too sick to eat, she telephoned Mr. Daugherty at the Hôtel d'Orsay.

"What Alexander said is right. There is nothing between him and me."

She hung up the phone and leaned against the wall of the phone cabinet, dizzy with the shame she'd hoped never to feel; and called Alexander, told him what she had said, and hung up on his long silence; and then got her hat and her music and went off to practice at the Conservatoire, because that was who she was.

Chapter 33

In the morning Daugherty went to see Reisden at Jouvet.

It looked prosperous. The brass plate by the entrance read ANALYSES MEDICALES JOUVET and was polished so Daugherty could count his teeth in it. Inside the green carriage gate was a neat courtyard, shadowed by the square tower Daugherty had seen from outside. It looked even more like a castle; from the peak of its stone roof, a little wooden flag swung and creaked. On the first floor of the tower was the office for the doorkeeper. Down at the bottom of the courtyard, three vehicles were standing: a motor ambulance, a horse-drawn carriage, and a fast-looking black-green motorcar that had to be Reisden's. Up a couple of stairs and through glass doors, in the modern part of the building, was the clinic.

A female nurse behind a counter pointed him to a yellow-lit waiting room. A couple of patients were sitting nervously on the benches, an idiotic-looking girl with her mother and a twitching man trying to read a newspaper. "Jer ver vwahr Reisden," Daugherty told the nurse at the desk, and sat to wait too. There were testimonials on the walls; Daugherty tried to read them, but they were mostly in French. Patients came to wait and were shown toward the back. One man read the testimonials and nodded slowly, like he figured he'd come to the right place but didn't give much for his chances.

The clock hands crawled round. Finally the old lady with

the fourteen chins led him down a corridor, up a flight of stairs, and through a laboratory, vinegary smelling and busy with people in white coats. On the other side of the laboratory was an oak door with cracked, old-looking panels. The secretary opened the door, sniffing with disapproval, brooches and chains jingling on her bosom like warning bells.

It was an office, dim and smelling of old fires. Reisden was sitting in a leather chair behind a big desk, head back, eyes closed, talking into a phone transmitter. He looked worn-out, with remorse, Daugherty hoped.

"Yes, Bullard, I have it here. Dotty's pulling it from the show," he was saying, "rather than exhibit what might be a forgery. No, we didn't look at Yvaud; something intervened. I need a private detective who knows art. I thought you might— Good." He opened his eyes and saw Daugherty; his face went blank. "Tonight's the earliest. You'll show me what you see wrong with it; bring me names. Thanks." He set the telephone down on the desk and hooked the receiver to it, then stood up behind the desk as if their conversation was going to last thirty seconds.

"I want to know what you're going to do for Perdita," Daugherty said.

"I will leave her alone," Reisden said. "Nothing more will happen that you would disapprove."

Daugherty planted himself in one of the two big leather chairs in front of Reisden's desk. "That's what she said, so I guess you two think that quitting is going to make everything right."

"I don't," said Reisden. "But it's the only thing I will do."

"Then I got a long conversation to have with you, son."

Reisden closed the door and sat behind his big carved desk and leaned his elbows on it, looking directly at Daugherty. He was too thin, and he still didn't care much about what he wore, and he had chemical stains on his hands. But Reisden took the carving and the gilt and leather top for granted, it was just someplace to sit at while he stared you down. Daugherty had forgot how much of William Knight's arrogance Richard had.

"You have really only two choices," Reisden said, in the tone of a man saying *surrender or die, I don't care which.* "One is to tell Gilbert Knight what you have seen, which would greatly hurt everyone. The other is to say nothing."

Daugherty had forgot, too, how Reisden started a couple of steps ahead of you.

"You got to marry her. She don't know what she done, and maybe you don't, but she ain't respectable unless she gets married. I known Perdita since she was this high, and I ain't letting that happen to her. I can't go along with her being ruined."

"Whether she is no longer respectable is your decision."

"You wouldn't say that to Gilbert," Daugherty said.

Reisden looked down, to his credit.

"You seduced her, son, there ain't another word for it. You probably never meant to marry her if you ain't insisting on it now. But I thought you had some care for her. Don't you know what happens to a woman when a man does this to her? No one will cross the street to talk to her."

"She won't marry me," Reisden said. "She knows who she is. She wants her music."

"You won't take responsibility for what you done, is what you mean. Son, if you was at home and she was mine, and you tried to hide behind that kind of excuse, I would need to horse-whip you."

He'd gone too far, saying that; you didn't ever talk about beating up Reisden. The man's eyes blazed and he stood up. Daugherty took hold of the chair arms; he wasn't moving. They looked at each other for a long moment, two dogs deciding whether to fight.

"I don't want trouble with you," Reisden said.

"That's a shame," Daugherty said, "because you got it,

son," but quiet, not setting Reisden off. "I ain't fighting with you but I ain't giving in."

"Did Gilbert send you?" Reisden said. "Why?"

"Why do you think, son? But if he saw this, he'd wish he'd never heard of you."

"We will have coffee," Reisden said. He went to the door and talked to the secretary.

Out the windows, Daugherty saw other windows in another office building across the street. On the shelves back of Reisden's desk were scientific books, titles with *Neuro-*, *Physio-*, and *Patho-*; a skull sat on one shelf and on the paneled uneven wall hung the etching of a flayed man gesturing like an actor. The bookcases and desk and telephone were modern, but the room had an ancient air; the fireplace was big enough to stable a pony and the mantelpiece was held up on either side by two almost life-size stone figures of men in capes and short britches.

Above the mantelpiece, casually leaning against the paneling next to a square French clock, was a painting.

It was Reisden and Perdita's garden, where Daugherty had been yesterday. A steep slope, half grass, half trees and bushes; a house at the bottom; the street beyond the garden wall; and taking up the top half of the picture, the river, an island, and the far shore. The river ran between stone walls pink with the last light. On the street a lamplighter was turning on the gaslights while a horse and carriage trotted by. Daugherty sat with his mouth open, looking up at the lamplighter, who was busy doing his work and not noticing the glory all around him.

If a man looked up and saw that terrible surprising beauty—Daugherty felt diminished and grand at once, like in a parade when the flags go by. It made him want to be better than he was.

"I never seen anything so handsome," he said reluctantly, not wanting to change the subject.

Reisden came back and sat down at his desk. "Spectacular, isn't it. It belongs to my cousin Dotty and it's apparently a forgery. It should be a Mallais." His eyes flicked up to the painting and back to Daugherty. "By the way, was it Dotty who told you where to find us?"

"Don't matter where."

"No," Reisden said after a moment. "I suppose it doesn't. Something was going to happen sooner or later; it happened now."

The secretary brought coffee, looking at Daugherty suspicious-like. She left the tray and closed the door behind her. Reisden offered Daugherty a coffee cup, then poured himself coffee. He sat down behind his desk.

"May I explain about Perdita?" Reisden asked.

"You go straight ahead."

Reisden gestured toward the painting with his cup. "That," he said. "The painting. I used to look at it for half an hour at a time. I don't see why it's wrong yet, I'm still too close to it, but I will; so I know enough not to believe in it." He looked at the painting silently, his coffee cup clasped between his hands, not drinking. He was wearing a signet ring, an old one with a stone; still holding the coffee cup, he rubbed the ring with the fingers of one hand as if it hurt him. "Perdita has tried to tell me that she can get along without the piano; she said she loves me enough for that. I don't believe it. I tried to believe it, it was a thing I think I wanted, a forgery, like that, very handsome; but a forgery."

"Then you oughtn't've done what you done."

"I knew that before I started," Reisden said.

Daugherty picked up his hat. "I don't want your coffee. You know what you got to do. I'm going to stay in the city till you do it."

"Take her home," Reisden said. "Let her have her reviews, then take her home."

Daugherty opened the door. The secretary was at her desk, leaning a little toward the door the way potted flowers in a parlor lean toward windows. She had been typing a letter, officially, but unofficially she'd been listening; and now she turned away and began pushing the keys of her machine, paying proud attention to the letter and none to him, the way lonely folks ignore people.

He saw again the blond woman, Reisden's cousin, in her lonely quiet house, smiling rigidly as she gave him directions; he heard Perdita saying *nothing between us* on the phone as if her heart would break. *I knew I shouldn't have done this*, Reisden had said. Daugherty had a sudden miserable sense of himself blundering through something as frail as a spiderweb.

"Excuse me," he said, "I got some more to say to Reisden," and opened the door again. Reisden was still at his desk, staring at nothing.

"What?" he said, proud and sharp and not giving anything away.

"*I'm* a detective," Daugherty announced loudly, as if Reisden didn't know it. "You said on the phone you was looking for a detective about a job," like he'd been calling about a job.

"You don't know French," Reisden said, "or art."

"No," Daugherty said, and pulled out his address book. He opened to a page at random (it was a sketch of a French girl). "But I got the names of French detective agencies here, from— because I have 'em. And I might as well be useful, Reisden, because I ain't a-goin' to leave."

The French clock on the mantelpiece ticked on. The rain glistened and ticked in tiny reflections on the glass.

"I know I shouldn't do this either," Reisden said. "All right. Stay."

Chapter 34

"First of all, now," Barry Bullard said, "I can give you a bit of a background to the question of forgery, if you'd care to 'ear."

Beyond the small windows of Reisden's office, the street was darkness with a blurred line of lights. Daugherty, seated in one of the leather chairs, opened his battered leather notebook to a fresh page and headed it *Painting*. Reisden was by the window drinking black coffee and Barry Bullard was at Reisden's big desk. To Daugherty's surprise Bullard had turned out to be a black-skinned man. He was lean and balding, with dark prominent eyes; he talked English-style with a thick accent and wore a suit as good as Reisden's.

"Right, then. Technically, a forger is a man who creates a painting in the style of another man and signs that man's name to it. And you would think 'e'd do it for the money alone. But at a certain level of skill a forger is an artist. Giovanni Bastianini's *Lucrezia Donati*? Renaissance portrait bust, 1865. Wonderful piece, break your 'eart. The Vicky and Albert 'as it."

Daugherty carefully wrote "Forger=artist."

Bullard propped the painting up on the other leather chair, leaning against the back. "This is a great painting," he said, "done by a remarkable artist. But this little bit of work right 'ere." Bullard tilted the electric desk lamp to shine at the center of the painting and pointed with a long dark finger. "You see that bit of pinkish purple? Looks like a shadow, underneath that tree on the Grande Jatte?"

"The island," Reisden said to Daugherty.

"On the island, right. That's a fishing shack. 'Orrible color of paint. Only, you see, it was painted green until 1903, Mallais died in 1900, and 'e's supposed to 'ave painted this in '95."

Reisden knelt to look at it.

"When I saw this," Bullard said, "I said this could be a Mallais colored shadder, 'e did 'is shadders very colorful at the end, so I looked at the painting closer and I saw this treatment of the edge of the quai wall. 'E'd only begun to try this very thin overpainting with contrasting color before 'e died." Daugherty squinted at the line of paint. "Stylistically 'e might 'ave done this in 1903, '04," Bullard said almost fondly, "apart from being dead, I mean. It's flaming brilliant. But 'e wouldn't 'ave done it in '95."

"Are these your only proofs of forgery?" Reisden said.

"Enough so I 'ad to mention it, Mr. de Reisden," Bullard said.

"Yes, I know, I'm just thinking as Dotty will. She'd be relieved to have no problem." Reisden stood. "If it is a forgery, and let's assume that it is, who might have done it?"

"Normally, for this grade of work, I'd say Italians."

"Italians?" Daugherty said, thinking of the North End or the Black Hand.

"Exporting art is illegal in Italy—*unless* it's a *reproduzione*. In Italy, your artists 'o want to make money paint reproductions. You get your villains there, trying to smuggle real paintings, and your usual chappies selling muck to tourists. But most of your Italian reproducers take apprentices, they grind their own pigments, it's a craft. Beautiful stuff, there's this bloke in Padua does great Rubens *bozzetti*."

Reisden nodded.

"But this one, 'e's French. Look at the quality of that light

on the Seine, that water, it's dead right. 'E's local. 'E works at
Puteaux, Levallois, the Grande Jatte, Courbevoie."

"What else do you know about him from this painting?"
Reisden asked.

Bullard shook his head. "Frenchman wot paints. All French-
men paint, it's a disease with 'em. You get your disaster, your
'orse foundered in the street or your Métro excavations, you've
got your Frenchman painting it." Bullard came round the desk
and looked at the canvas himself. "It's so flaming good the
forger might be a known painter, like Trouillebert with Corot."

"Don't recollect them," Daugherty said.

"Trouillebert got 'is start doing Corot forgeries. 'Appens all
the time, one painter imitates another. Macurdy did a series of
Pasquier forgeries. Marian Blakelock forged 'er father's paintings. George Inness, Jr. did George Inness, Sr. Corot forged 'is
own stuff."

Reisden lifted an eyebrow.

"Corot? Great teacher, 'e was. 'Ordes of students. They'd
go out to the country and paint with 'im, same locations, same
subjects, same days. And Corot'd go round to these blokes with
their little easels all set up in the 'ayfield, and 'e'd take 'is brush
and 'e'd dab 'ere and dab there, just fixing things up. And when
the light got bad and they knocked off for tea, 'e'd 'ike round
again and say, 'That's good enough to be a Corot,' and 'e'd sign
it. Never took a penny. Don't you never trust a painter."

"Do you know French painters who could forge this?"

"I could give you a list. Someone young. Someone not suc-
cessful yet, or not enough. Painted with Mallais when 'e was
alive, or 'as some of 'is stock— Now that's an idea," Bullard said.
"I think I 'eard Madame Mallais never sold off Mallais's stock."

Daugherty looked at Reisden blankly.

"Stock is whatever a painter 'asn't sold yet. When 'e dies, 'e
leaves stuff, canvases 'e never finished or didn't like, drawings

or preliminary sketches. Some of it's good pieces the artist kept. On some the paint's flaking or whatever; the dealer gets a bloke like me to restore it, then sells it. Some paintings aren't finished and you can't do anything with them. Madame Mallais never sold off 'is stock, she's been consigning it piece by piece."

Daugherty scribbled *stock* in his notebook. Reisden got himself a second cup of coffee and offered the pot around.

"Why can't one finish unfinished paintings?" he asked.

"A painting finished by another artist doesn't represent the intentions of the first one. Ruins the value. I'm a good enough faker," Bullard said, "but when I restore a canvas, it ain't what it was and I know it."

"Repainting is a form of forgery," Reisden summarized, "because it compromises the artist's intention?"

"That's right."

"Is the customer informed when a painting is finished by another artist?" Reisden asked.

"Supposed to be."

"How?" Reisden asked.

"In the accession book. When a dealer gets a painting, 'e describes it in a book, like an inventory book. The description includes at least artist, provenance, size, and price paid. If the painting's restored, that goes in the description. Or if it were finished by another artist. But you'd never see that in an ack-book; the painting wouldn't 'ave any value."

Bullard passed the painting over to Daugherty, who looked curiously at a blue number stenciled on the wooden frame of the canvas.

"That's the accession number, the painting's number in the ack-book. It 'elps to establish provenance, if it ever comes in question. You know what provenance is, am I right?"

Reisden nodded; Daugherty shook his head.

"Right. The goal of provenance is to trace your painting

that you 'ave in your 'and back through every sale or gift to the painting it's supposed to be. With a modern painting, your provenance can be very simple. If the dealer 'as the work from the artist himself, then under 'Provenance,' 'is ack-book would say 'From the Artist.' That is the direct provenance, it's the most valuable."

"And if the artist is dead?" Reisden asked.

"If the artist's dead, and the dealer 'ad it from the family, the ack-book would say 'From the Artist's Family.' That is the next best provenance. In France provenance from the artist's family 'as the same legal force as if it were from the artist."

"Surely the family occasionally tries to pass something off," Reisden said. "Such as a painting finished by another hand."

"Flaming right they do, but most of the time the families aren't so much crooks as pure bleeding idjits. Maurice Guzot's own son brought in a painting once, swore his father had painted it, it was a Renoir. Signed. I ask you." Bullard held up his hands in a very French shrug.

"So. Who else can establish provenance?"

"In France, again this ain't true for other countries, you can take the artist's dealer as a provenance: 'From Armand Inslay-'Ochstein.' But for preference there, and always otherwise, you 'ave to 'ave documents, such as your bill of sale or letters relating to the gift or sale. For a modern painting, if you can't establish provenance, it don't look right and you won't get your price."

"And accession-book records are kept how long?"

"Forever. Inslay-'Ochstein's got 'is from the bleeding Revolution."

"This painting has provenance," Reisden said, "courtesy of the Mallais family. From Madame Mallais, who used to be a laundress and has lived in the country all her life."

"That's right, Monsieur de Reisden. Its description would be 'From the Artist's Family.' "

"And if it hadn't, Inslay-Hochstein could provide provenance."

"That's right."

"And now Madame Mallais is living with a man named Yvaud. She did have a brother Yvaud," Reisden said, "in a manner of speaking, the son of the family she worked for before her marriage. That family were painters. Yvaud would have been a painter. He is supposed to be arthritic in the hands; Madame Mallais did her best to persuade—someone who visited them—that he has no use of his hands."

Reisden stood in front of the painting, scrutinizing the purple spot at the edge of the quai. "Once the artist is dead," he mused, "under French law a painting can be authenticated by the same people who have the most to gain financially from the estate. They have the power to control the size, composition, and value of the estate. They own unfinished works. They are not necessarily honest. They do not necessarily have expert knowledge or even ordinary knowledge of art. But they may be able to paint." Bullard nodded once, gravely. "Madame Mallais has said this is a Mallais," Reisden said. "And so it is a Mallais, legally, isn't it?"

"Makes you wonder about the law, dunnit."

"It's a rather elegant solution," Reisden said.

"French is what it is. Inslay-'Ochstein's got other Mallais canvases," said Bullard. "They're goin' to the Winter Salon on account of the retrospective. I wonder if I ought to 'ave a look at 'em."

"Yes," said Reisden, "I wish you would."

Chapter 35

During the week of the tenth, one of Milly's articles was "The Métro: Is It Safe for Women?"

In early 1910 the "Necropolitan" was still under construction. The huge St.-Michel station had opened the previous weekend (*Femme-Paris* had run a picture of two duchesses and a minister's wife, all in full-length fur coats and fur hats). But the station was only partially constructed; the part serving the North-South Railway Line was still being finished.

The new electrical lines of Paris ran in sheathed cables attached to the roofs of the Métro tunnels. The Métro suffered an average of fifty short circuits a day. Most of them were minor, a momentary loss of power, a flickering of lights.

But on Sunday, the ninth, the first full day of operations at St.-Michel, three short circuits caused significant damages in the Métro, one blowing up a transformer with such force that a part of the sidewalk exploded. On Monday, the tenth, another explosion shot a manhole cover through a crowd of women inspecting white-sale items in front of the Galeries Lafayette; by great good fortune no one was injured.

Milly's article concluded that French ingenuity would shortly cure the problem, but for the moment one might take the horsecars.

Milly blotted that article and took a clean piece of blue paper for another. *This year one must go to Nice! While rain constantly patters on the umbrellas of Paris, white beaches and comfortable hotels beckon on the Côte d'Azur. . . .*

No one—certainly not Milly—connected the explosions with the rain. But it had been raining for weeks now, for months. Milly had written that the land around Paris was like a bath sponge, capable of soaking up immense amounts of water.

She had not thought that eventually the land, like a sponge, might grow full.

Chapter 36

Milly waylaid the Mallais grandson at dusk as he was trudging from the Louvre to the Palais-Royal Métro stop. She swung up beside him and put her arm in his.

"Don't tell me you don't remember me. George Vittal introduced us. I'm Milly."

"Uh—" He was as delicious as a pastry, his nose bigger than his chin, his eyes as blue as aquamarines. "Um— You're Milly Xico!" He blushed red, then looked stricken.

"You can walk me to the subway," Milly said. "Don't mind him—" Nick-Nack was sniffing at the boy's pants leg.

They walked toward the dangerous subway, then stopped to chat. Jean-Jacques said he'd seen her sing at the Ba-Ta-Clan and retreated into embarrassed silence. "Do you like macaroons?" He bought her a bag from a street vendor. Milly crunched cookies and kept hold of his arm.

"Where do you live?" she asked him.

"In the fifth arrondissement."

"So do I. You could bring me back to my flat."

He goggled at her.

It was perfectly innocent, like giving a toy to a baby. She showed him her apartment, a little garden flat tucked into an old building in the Maubert, near the river. She showed him her kitchen, her sofa. She showed him her bedroom, and so on, and so on.

She loaned him a robe and put on her favorite silk pajamas. They sat on the hearth rug and she wriggled her bare toes in front of the fire, watching him blush while he looked at her. "You're—" he said. "I mean—I never knew— I mean," he looked at her, "I'm not very experienced, you know."

Milly knew exactly how experienced he was.

"You're so beautiful," he said. She let him go on for a little while, then asked him to tell her all about himself. He was an engineering student at the Sorbonne.

"But you're so clever, so young!" Milly cooed. "And a copyist, too! That takes so much skill!"

Oh, that, he said with the nonchalance of Mallais's grandson. Anyone could paint. "I always do the Mona Lisa. It's efficient. I do two hours a day, more on the weekend, and I think about my class assignments. The tourists pay the most for it, too."

He would have talked about his methods for an hour. He always did the Mona Lisa as accurately as possible, on old wood, he said; one could get wood at any junk dealer.

"My copies are supposed to be good," the innocent said.

You sweet boy, Milly thought. They sounded as good as forgeries. He didn't paint badly, either. Good enough to fool Henry. Maybe even George.

"I—I'd give you one," Jean-Jacques offered.

That was exactly what she wanted, of course. "Oh, that's so nice of you!"

"It's a great mistake taking men home," she told Nick-Nack when she'd finally got rid of the boy. "Oh, yes, it's true," Milly said, scratching him on the belly. "It's true, it's true. Now we will have supper all alone, won't we, lovey? And I think we'll start with dessert, because we're such complete savages." She tossed Nick his butcher's bone. In the kitchen was her stash of chocolate bars. She unpeeled silver paper carefully, got out her silver toasting rack from England, and poked up the fire. She sat on her haunches, barefoot, her knees hot, turning the chocolate carefully inside the toasting rack. Done just right, it would be burnt bitter and stiff on the outside and warm and almost liquid on the inside. She could smell the hot silk of her pajamas, and a burnt-feathers smell came from the hairs on her arm.

"When I am rich," she told Nick-Nack, "I'll have the perfect long-handled chocolate-toasting rack, I'll have one made . . . it'll be silver with an ebony handle, and I'll have a little friend with aquamarine eyes who will paint me pictures, I'll have a little mistress, but nobody will own me, I won't live with anyone except you." She unbuttoned the top of her pajamas, slipped it off entirely, and crouched naked to the waist like a Sphinx, toasting her chocolate.

This was the right sort of love affair, the essence of love: sex in the afternoon and dinner afterward with the dog.

"Now all we have to do," Milly said, "is get 'darling Sacha' to do his part. And Leonard, of course."

Chapter 37

"Armand Inslay-Hochstein, a dealer whom Dotty idolizes, may have sold her a bad painting," Reisden said to Daugherty. "But she doesn't want to believe it. The widow of Mallais, one of his best painters, may have done the same to him, and fooled him with it. Dotty of course cannot be the one to discover this; she would not take it well. Your job is to manage a very private investigation, to find out what happened, and to report back to me."

Daugherty would work with a French investigative firm, Lebonnet & Duroc, who probably could have handled it themselves. He knew why he was involved. First, from Reisden's point of view, it got him out of the way; and second, because in every investigation that might come out differently than you hoped, you keep one stupid guy around. If things go wrong, it's the stupid guy's fault.

Bonnet and Doc would handle investigating Hochstein's finances and questioning the viscountess's servants. Roy Daugherty would just bumble around scratching his head and asking dumb questions and wait to get blamed.

Well, he'd done it before, and the person who knew the viscountess best was Reisden, and the expert on the painter's widow was Perdita, and the stupid guy got to spend most of his time around Reisden and Perdita, asking them whatever came into his head.

"Do be comfortable, Mr. Daugherty."

Reisden's "cousin" received Daugherty in the apple-green salon. On the piano, in the dimness, a single candle shone. Cousin Dotty was a beautiful woman, fashionable, but with features like an old painting, long-nosed, heavy-lidded, a face oddly like Reisden's. She had his look, too, like she owned where she was. "Please sit down," she said, more or less an order. "That chair might suit you."

Daugherty lowered himself carefully into one of the comb-thin chairs. It didn't break.

"Sacha tells me that you are—assisting—the agency he has chosen to investigate my painting. I confess I am at a loss to understand what assistance they require."

"I'm managing the investigation," Daugherty said, which is what the stupid guy says.

"I believed Sacha would do that."

"You ain't paying me, if that's what you mean."

"That is not what I mean. When Sacha 'assisted' you in finding that dead boy in America, he was very unhappy and disturbed for months afterward. If my painting is a forgery, Armand must take it back; if it is not I shall be glad to keep it; but I do not like your being here at all."

Daugherty had not heard about *unhappy and disturbed.* "Reisden asked me to help, is all, because you got you a problem here."

"I am grateful; please do believe I am," she said dismissively, "but I feel I must speak with Sacha about the way I wish to have this handled. It is a delicate matter, Mr. Daugherty."

"Well, you do that. Meantime he says I got to investigate whether someone mighta switched your painting when it was in your house. You know of a servant, someone you maybe fired, would do such a thing?"

"I often let servants go, Mr. Daugherty. I have high

standards." Cousin Dotty rose gracefully and drifted over to a cabinet with a curved glass front. "Mr. Daugherty, you mislead yourself with servants. A painting is so difficult both to forge and to transport. My mother-in-law collected snuffboxes." Daugherty peered at the dim palm-sized boxes crowding the shelves. "The light is bad," Cousin Dotty said, and brought the candle. The shelf came alive with tiny enameled paintings, glittering jewels, and red reflections off gold.

"Have mercy," he muttered.

"Mr. Bullard looked at them, and at the Turners and the Renoirs; they are all quite in order still. Even our Corot is genuine, which is, I understand, a rarity. Why should a servant forge a Mallais?"

Good question. "Who'd you think did it, then, missus? Ma'am?"

"Certainly not Armand." Mallaises were hard to get, she said, because the family sold only one or two a year. Three years ago, in April 1907, Armand Inslay-Hochstein had offered her one. She had arrived barely after Madame Mallais had brought it, had taken the painting home immediately on approval, and had bought it without ever returning it to the dealer. "I knew instantly that it was of the highest order, and I am seldom wrong."

"So this Inslay-Hochstein wouldn't'a had time to switch it?"

"One cannot possibly suspect Armand. He cares so for his gallery; when his son was born he gave the infant a Renaissance silver rattle 'to train his eye.' One knows from Sherlock Holmes that it is always the least likely suspect, but really, *Armand*—"

"Uh-huh," Daugherty said. "Glad to know he ain't a suspect. Then who is?"

"Moreover," Dotty said, "Armand allows unconditional return."

This went entirely over Daugherty's head. "Ayuh?"

"Unconditional return, Mr. Daugherty, means that if I should ever be dissatisfied with my Mallais, for any reason, I may return it to Armand for the original purchase price. He guarantees to take it under any conditions, at any time, even if it should have been proved to be a forgery." The viscountess smiled. "He is far safer than the stock market."

"Then who'd it be? Mrs. Mallais?" Daugherty said.

"One has heard of the family forging when they have run through their originals. But surely, since she has sold very little—?"

"Well, then that don't leave no one," the stupid guy said.

"It leaves, Mr. Daugherty, that Mr. Bullard is mistaken."

What it left was Dotty acting peculiar, first saying the painting was bad and now backtracking, but he wasn't going to tell her so, not yet anyway. Instead he gave her an out. Bullard had put together a list of painters who he thought could do quality forgery. Daugherty asked her if she knew any of them.

"Paul Vécherier?" No. "Herbert Weiss?" Never; absolutely not. "Jean-Jacques Mallais?" Was he a relative of the painter? In any case she didn't know him. "Juan Gastedon?" The name was familiar, she thought, but no. She had heard he was quite talented.

She hadn't heard of any of them.

Chapter 38

Daugherty went to see Reisden, hoping for a little talk, but Reisden gave him a list of Mallaises in private hands. "Go look at them." Which meant, Get lost.

Under a gray sky, Daugherty set off with his city map. The first painting was at a theater owner's office, a peculiar place decorated with bones and skulls. "This Mallais reminds me of going on rounds with my father," André du Monde said. "He was a doctor. He would take me to deathbeds at night. We were very close." Daugherty looked at the painting, the daybreak shadow of a tree on snow, ominous and clean as a picked bone.

Another painting was a flower meadow in a pretty apartment on a boulevard. "It reminds me of being in love," said Mrs. de Valliès.

Daugherty took his list round to cream-white French apartments with gray views of the Eiffel Tower, the river, and the Tuileries Gardens. Quite a few of the owners had lent to this big Mallais show that was going to open in a week. When the pictures all began to whirl in his head, he stopped for lunch at the Café Américain, and then walked down through the wintry streets to Galignani's English bookstore by the Palais Royal, where a clerk hunted out a book about Mallais that would have something more educated to say than *art reminds me of love*. He took it to a café and read about sensitivity and

Impressionism, genius and passion and the cult of the artist and suchlike stuff.

He decided to visit "Armand."

The Inslay-Hochstein Gallery was a sort of combined museum and funeral parlor; every room was swathed in dark velvet, and in each room a single light shone on a single painting. An old gent and his wife were gathered round one of the dear departed, murmuring in exactly the tone you'd have said *Don't he look natural, you'd a thought he was asleep.* Daugherty was afraid to cough for fear he'd accidentally spend money.

He gave up pictures for the day and went to see Reisden at the Sorbonne.

"Did you see Armand Inslay-Hochstein?" Reisden asked.

"If he were there, I wa'n't quality enough to see him."

The lab where Reisden worked was a much less fancy setup than Jouvet; the whole lab was two big dim rooms and a warren of little offices. Reisden didn't even have an office, just a part of a lab bench, where he was frowning through the eyepiece of an oversized microscope.

"There's a lot of hooharaw around art, Reisden, seems to me, when all folks are really looking at is what their dad was like and whether anybody loves 'em."

"Usually that's what people look at." Reisden straightened up and closed his eyes, pressing his eyelids. "One of the dangers of scientific research. Seeing what one wants."

"What you looking at?"

"Go ahead." Daugherty squinted through the eyepiece; the lens of his glasses clicked against the lens of the microscope. All he could see was a yellow-gray blur.

"Frog muscle," Reisden said. "Stimulated to exhaustion, minced, run through a centrifuge, stained, and smeared on a slide. Maurice O'Brien sees, and I quote, 'unidentified hexagonal crystalline structures at the limit of visibility.' John Lamb sees them. I don't. I've been trying for a week."

"This is still frogs?" Daugherty said.

"Still muscle contraction; stimulus and response." He massaged the back of his neck tiredly. "This is my hand; why does it move?" The stone in his ring glinted like a lion's eye.

"You thought of getting some sleep?"

"No." Reisden led the way into the corridor and opened one of the doors; inside was a sitting room, shelves piled messily with books, a couple of chairs, a table, and a sink and counter with unwashed, unmatched cups. On the counter, above a turned-off Bunsen burner, was a flask partway full of some dark liquid. Reisden took one of the cups, rinsed it under the sink, poured some sludge from the flask, tasted it, shrugged, poured it back in, and turned on the Bunsen burner.

"Stimulus and response, huh," Daugherty said, looking at the unfamiliar machines in the big room. In one corner was what looked like organ pipes; in another, a one-handed grandfather clock with a bell. On the table was a thing made of mirrors, like a bird landing with outstretched wings.

"Stimulus, response, and perception," Reisden said. "Berthet, who's the lab head, believes that the process has three stages. Stimulus, the electrical impulse acting on the muscle. Perception, the physically measurable response, the contraction of muscle, the twitch. And consciousness, the intelligent being's perception that it has been stimulated and has responded. The perception of the perception." He flexed his hand. "This is my hand; how do I know it is moving?"

"You know unless you're stupid," Daugherty said.

"Not so simple. We never actually see or touch or experience anything; we experience electric impulses in the brain. Some of them come from light striking the retina and producing neurochemical reactions in the optic nerve. Some have other sources, like hallucinations."

It sounded like magician's patter to Daugherty.

"Let me show you." Reisden started up the pendulum on the grandfather clock, then made an adjustment to something, a knob or lever on the side of the case. "Tell me whether the bell rings before the pointer reaches the red mark on the dial. Look at the bell first, it's trickier." Daugherty looked at the bell; *tock, tock*, went the pendulum; the bell rang, and Daugherty looked quickly at the pointer, seeing it just reaching the mark.

"Bell first or pointer?"

"Bell."

Reisden adjusted the knob again. "Now try. Look at the pointer this time." That was easier; the pointer reached the red mark, then an instant later the bell rang.

"Reisden, you do something to the machine and things come out differently. I know that."

Reisden took his hand away from the frame; there was nothing, no knob, no lever, just the plain oak case. "The two take place at the same time," he said. "Always."

"You fiddled them, I saw you."

"I didn't adjust the machine, I adjusted you," he said. "What the consciousness is fixed on appears to happen first. I changed what you noticed."

Daugherty poked at the side of the machine, looking for clues. "That ain't fair."

"Berthet and I try to measure experimentally the relations between perception and consciousness. I come from the perceptual end, measuring quantifiable phenomena; the muscle hasn't contracted unless I can measure lactic acids, that sort of thing. He's the psychologist. He comes from dreams of men running. Does dreaming of running build up lactic acids, or dreaming of light make the iris open?"

"Does it?" asked Daugherty.

"We think it can, sometimes, which is rather exciting."

"Sounds like measurin' fairies to me."

Back in the room with the coffee, Reisden took a cup and sat down in one of the chairs, leaning tiredly against the back. "Consciousness has a language. Dotty told you I had a bad time when I got back from America. What happened is that, for about three months, I would occasionally look in the mirror and—" He looked for words. "I would not be there. I think I could see myself, but what I perceived was no one."

"Musta been fun," Daugherty said, trying to joke it away and thinking of what Cousin Dotty had said.

"Oh, it was terrifying. Things happen in the mind. I had spent twenty years not seeing what I had done, willfully not seeing it or its effects." He broke off. "And the mind learns. Certain ways of seeing, certain ideas, come more easily. I began to wonder what I had learned to think after four years of being booted about by William and almost twenty years of lies. I wondered how much the machinery of my consciousness had been damaged."

Daugherty cleared his throat uneasily.

Reisden tasted the coffee and dumped it out in the sink. He stood there, looking at the coffee drain. "This is an apology," he said. "I ought to be saying it to Perdita, but I'm not going to talk to Perdita, so you have it instead." He twisted off the ring he was wearing and handed it to Daugherty, who took it curiously. An old signet ring, gold and carnelian.

"That's the Reisden family ring," Reisden said. "Leo von Loewenstein gave me it. I never wore it until these past three years. I had lost touch with everyone in my supposed family. Now I have Dotty and Tiggy. I chose them to be mine," he said, "and I want to make it at least a good, solid forgery, a compelling forgery, like the Mallais; one that no one will ever spot. I want Dotty to see her cousin when she looks at me."

"She don't know who you are? You never told her?"

"No."

"Hmph."

"I'm not good at being Reisden. I know well enough what he would do, and I don't do it. I bought Jouvet when he would have stayed in stocks. I spend too much time on Jouvet. Above all there was Perdita. I'm faked," he said. "Reisden would look at the pointer, Richard would hear the bell; I hear the bell. Dotty always sees the pointer."

Daugherty felt this whole thing was being complicated to death.

"I don't know truly what made William," Reisden said. "I know of people like him. Sometimes it's disease and one can actually medicate them. Sometimes they do what they do because it was done to them— It was done to me. I learned how William thought. I am his grandson.—Perdita and Gilbert think Richard was the victim, in spite of his having murdered William," Reisden said, "but I think that's very naive."

He poured himself another cup of coffee out of the same beaker, began to drink it, stared at it, and poured it in the sink. This time he poured the rest of the beaker out as well. "I am trouble," he said. "Daugherty, be good to her; I can't be."

Chapter 39

Daugherty took Perdita to dinner. "How'd a girl like you do such a thing?" It was like Pearl running away with the Bible salesman.

"I'm not ashamed," which told him she was.

Daugherty explained to her that he had taken on investigating the forged painting. She knew about it. "Do you have any clues?" she asked. He told her about provenance and the French law that let families establish it.

"You don't think Madame Mallais would involve herself in forgery? She's a nice woman."

So were you, honey, he thought; a nice girl. "Who do you think did it?"

"One of Dotty's servants," she said, "or her picture dealer. She doesn't want it to be her dealer but she thinks it is."

"Wouldn't be her?" Daugherty suggested.

"Not even Dotty would do something like that and then ask Alexander to fix it."

"Honey," Daugherty said, "why won't you marry him?"

She shook her head. "He doesn't want to marry *me*."

"You think so?"

"He doesn't want to marry someone who'd tour. He wants a wife. It isn't because of me specifically, or anything but music and what he wants. If I loved him enough I'd give up music. I just—don't."

"Ain't nothing to do with love, honey." It was cruel but Daugherty ought to say it. "You chose him instead of music, doing what you did. And he chose you instead of—whatever he wants, if he don't want you."

She went so pale she looked plain. "I didn't *choose* not to have him," she said. "I don't choose to give him up, I don't want to choose. You tell him that." She reached into her handbag and handed him a square of pasteboard. It was an invitation to a recital at the American embassy, sponsored by the ambassadress, Mrs. William Bacon, on the twenty-first. Miss Perdita Halley, winner of such-and-so and this-and-that prize, would play. *A stunning new talent*, said *The New York Times*. Refreshments to follow.

"I don't want this, it ain't worth your good name." Daugherty pushed it away, and then saw he had hurt her.

"You come," she said. "If you think I ought to give up music, you hear me play first."

"I'll come," Daugherty said reluctantly, "but I'm bringing him."

"He'd come anyway," she said. "He won't marry me but he'll come to my concert."

She looked like she could go right from dinner to the funeral of all her best friends. She was just off a lesson, she said, so excuse her if she wasn't cheerful. She listened to all the news from home, and took a bite of dinner, and then put her fork down while she chewed dutifully and swallowed hard.

"How do you like Paris?"

Well, he said, 'twasn't the same without knowing the language.

They made a list of places to go and things to do, and phrases he might want to use there. *Ung biyay, due franks.* Her list was long on concerts. "Ain't there anything but pictures and concerts and art?" Daugherty asked.

"You can go up the Eiffel Tower, and there's the subway. The Métro. It's lots grander than the one in Boston, and they've just opened the part under the river. There's an enormous station, it echoes like a cave." She sounded like a little girl again. "Do you remember riding round the loop in Boston?"

"You come show me this big new station. What's it called?"

"St.-Michel."

Chapter 40

It is a relief to have made a difficult decision; Reisden told himself so. He talked with Dotty on Monday; she apologized for giving Daugherty the address. "I shouldn't have done it, darling," she said, "and you have every right to be angry."

"I do." She had forced what he should have done. "At least something is settled," he said.

"Cécile de Valliès is coming to dinner with a few people tomorrow night. I have a box to Bordet's new play. Are you free?" she asked. "Do you wish to be free?"

He dined at Dotty's on Tuesday night and went to the theater with her party. Cécile de Valliès was among the guests; he exerted himself to please her, and she clearly wished to please him.

He drank far too much and then escorted her home in a taxi. She lived in the sixteenth arrondissement, in a residential hotel very much like his own. During the drive she talked about her children, who were away at school. He said he liked children. Hers, she said, were very well-behaved, polite and intelligent; their names were Eugénie and Frédéric. She discreetly mentioned a château and other properties, left to her outright. She liked the musical theater, but of course the classics too; she had never thought about neuropathology, but she was sure it was fascinating. She had a soft, agreeable profile, a pleasant and frequent laugh; she dressed well; he was sure her cook would be good and her housekeeping impeccable. With her he would never need to sleep alone. She would not be overly curious about him. He would never be afraid of what he might do to her, never hurt her or be hurt.

He was comparing her with Perdita, which he should not.

He had taken Madame de Valliès back to her house with the deliberate intention of being unfaithful to Perdita, if the occasion offered. She owned a Mallais, which was upstairs; she offered to show him. "I never do this," she said, "but—the charm of this conversation—" He watched himself, an automaton, accept the offer she had not quite made; he watched the two of them sip their drinks and admire her Mallais. He wondered if the painting were a forgery, and wondered how much of the whole evening had been a forgery; he watched the smile on her face, constructed for him, and felt the same smirk on his, constructed for her; and was tired of what he ought to have wanted. "It has been far too pleasant an evening to prolong," he told her, and took his leave, and spent the rest of the night walking the streets through an intermittent downpour, in a black vicious anger at himself and Perdita and Dotty and even the innocent dull Madame de Valliès, whom he would not marry and for preference would not even fuck.

Wednesday morning, at his office at Jouvet, he threw out Perdita's letters, all of them, three years' worth; she had written to him even in Paris, on days when they hadn't seen each other or been able to telephone. Every one was signed *Love, Perdita*; there was even one, a scrap of music paper, with the closing and signature alone. Nothing to write, nothing to say, only love. He forced himself to notice that her handwriting was that of a very young woman.

He took the wastepaper basket up the private stairs to Dr. Jouvet's apartment; he dumped its contents, envelopes from the early mail, the wrapping of a newspaper, and the letters, into the empty bottom drawer of his bureau. He did not lock the drawer; that would have been to give them some value, even to hurt.

On Wednesday evening Reisden took a couple of visiting German colleagues to the Folies Bergère, where one goes only with visitors. All that female flesh, all those charms, nine hundred costumes, thirty-one changes of scene; the curvaceous Miss Campton, the amusing Jane Marnac; Léonette Roberty and her exotic dancers; tableaux of live women mannequins, "At Great Catherine's Court," "The Studio of the Masters." All the women were beautiful, all the costumes revealing. At the entr'acte they paid to go into the promenade, where the two Germans eyed the whores. "Ach, G-tt, women aren't only better than men, they have better bodies."

He thought of Perdita's body, soft specific places; he put her out of mind.

He thought of the women onstage; but he could not enjoy them comfortably as bodies, he insisted on seeing them as performers. Approximately eighty chorus girls. The average chorus member spent three to five minutes onstage, then had ten to twelve to change costume and be in place for her next appearance. The languid beauties onstage, dressed as peacocks, were in the middle of a two-and-a-half-hour sprint of changing and performance; which made him think of Perdita's stories about the horrors of touring. He had hoped the stories had meant she didn't like it.

This, students, is how obsession works, circling back forever to the same unavailable object. He should simply go backstage or to the promenade and buy himself a woman.

"Dr. de Reisden?" One of the ushers approached him. "You have a telephone call."

At first he could hear nothing on the line but shouts and confusion. "Monsieur, I'm calling from the Café du Départ. We regret there has been an accident on the Métro. . . ."

When he arrived, the police were setting up barriers around a hole in the sidewalk in front of the Café du Départ. It had begun to snow; around the site of the explosion and at the entrance of the Métro station, the slush was blackened as if by smoke or dirt. The wounded had been taken to the Départ.

He saw Daugherty first, sitting at a café table, bleeding profusely from a nick in his ear and pressing a towel to it; and then he saw her. She was covered with dirt and plaster, spotted with Daugherty's blood, holding his hand with both of hers and talking to him. "Are you all right?" she was saying or something like it, but she leaned forward, straining for the answer, and she held on to Daugherty's hand tightly as if to keep track of him, as she would never have had to do if she could hear.

For a moment he didn't do any more than look at her. He saw her vulnerability, understood what that straining for words might mean, and for a moment of horrified triumph he believed she had gone deaf, enough so that she had to give up music— He wanted to take her in his arms, wash her face clean, bathe her skinned knuckles, cover her with kisses; he wanted not to be left or to leave, he wanted someone, he wanted to love; he wanted her, her, *her*.

And how did he propose to do it? By depriving her of her hearing. He felt dirtier than either of them. The desire to hurt in order to possess is wrong.

"You'll be all right in a few minutes," he told her, formally, *vous* not *tu*.

"I'm already beginning to hear things again," she said,

"and you see I found Mr. Daugherty, and he's all right. So I didn't need to have you called—I'm sorry—"

"Oh, that's all right," he said quickly. Everything was all right, wasn't it. "I was bored." *Stupid fool.* Better than to say he had been thinking of her.

"Oh, well, then."

"Would you like a towel to wipe your face?"

"Yes, please."

He watched her as she cleaned her face with the hot damp towel, wanting nothing more in the world than to touch her; but he only jammed his hands in his pockets and turned away from her to watch the other victims of the explosion being dusted off and given coffee and brandy. There was Daugherty at the coffee line, holding the towel to his ear, the other hand gesturing to Reisden: go on, you talk to her, go on. Reisden shook his head. "I'm leaving now," he said to her, "I'm glad you're all right, goodbye."

"Goodbye, Alexander. Thank you for coming," like a hostess.

"Goodbye."

Idiot. Fool.

He left.

Chapter 41

Cher misieur le Baron,
I wnt 2 the Hottel des Posts the Polis hv got it
Wached I think they Now abt wear Yu cld Rit to me I
hope it wasnt Yuo wo told them to Wacth Loking for yu
to Do Rit by Her Soon

Hr Rtis

I will Come to Yu

"You set up a police trap for a man with a knife in the Hôtel
des Postes," Reisden said, "where there are bystanders
every hour of the day and night. The trap was to be at the meeting place, not there. And he saw you before you saw him."

The inspector looked wrathfully at his sergeant, who
looked at the floor.

"What do you intend to do now?"

The police had recovered a clear palm print and set of
fingerprints from the letter. "We'll send these through the
Bertillon files, Monsieur de Reisden," Langelais said. "We'll
find something."

"Not soon enough." The Préfecture identified prints by
characteristics but filed them by name, having no better system.
A search often took weeks. "He might try to come here; that I
can't have. I'll suggest a meeting to him."

Reisden's secretary gave him a horrified look.

"He's suspicious already, monsieur," said Langelais.

"I believe I can get him to come."

Langelais looked at him with uneasy speculation. "How?"

"By writing as he would write." Her Artist now had his own folder in the Jouvet archives; Reisden leafed through their typewritten copies of the first two letters. "Madame Herschner, take this down. 'I miss her so. Without her I do not know who I am. Help me. I must speak with you, I must talk about *her*. . . .' "

A police trap requires a space that is apparently open but can be cleared of bystanders, not an easy thing to find in Paris. The various public gardens were out; so were private spaces such as the zoo, the Arènes de Lutèce and the Cluny gardens, which would be full of tourists if the weather turned passable. Père Lachaise and the other cemeteries were out; relatives would be visiting the tombs. The inspector suggested Jouvet; Reisden vetoed it. "Jouvet is not a place where the mentally disturbed are captured."

"Yes, that's true," said Madame Herschner.

Versailles was too far, though the leaf-strewn and deserted rooms of the old palace would have made a properly haunted meeting place. Reisden called André du Monde, who knew every odd place in Paris. Du Monde offered the garden of his house; Reisden declined with thanks, since André refused to remove his principal garden ornament, the small traveling guillotine that had beheaded his great-grandfather.

Reisden thought of the large garden at Courbevoie. On Sunday Perdita might be there. He thought of going to see her Sunday, talking with her, explaining—something, somehow— and told himself to stop.

"The Dogs' Cemetery at Asnières," Madame Herschner suggested. "Barry's Tomb."

Barry, no connection to Barry Bullard, had been a Saint

Bernard dog who had saved forty travelers on the old Simplon Pass before the railway tunnel had been opened. The forty-first had thought he was a wolf and had killed him. The proprietors of the Dogs' Cemetery had given him a tomb worthy of a Rothschild, with the epitaph THE MORE I SEE OF MEN, THE MORE I LOVE MY DOG.

Langelais thought Barry's Tomb was perfect; and so the rendezvous between Reisden and the murderer was set for three-thirty P.M., Sunday afternoon, at Barry's Tomb, symbol of fidelity, at the Cimetière des Chiens at Asnières.

Chapter 42

"Leonard, I need a frame," Milly says. "Like that one. It's a present for George, but I want him to think it comes from you."

She shields her eyes and squints through the glass at the Mona Lisa's enormous gilded frame, carved with egg shapes, knots, and acanthus.

"You can get me one. . . . Of course you can, you get terra-cottas for Juan."

"That's d-different."

"I'll give you as much for a frame as he does for one of those masks. And I want you to write George a letter to go with it. 'I am giving you this to help you.' The frame has to be the same size as the Mona Lisa," Milly adds. "Measure one of Jean-Jacques's pictures."

That feminine look, that smile: Leonard trembles, thinks of Milly's ankles, feels angry, feels guilty.

Leonard steals things from the Louvre, of course. The Louvre has things it doesn't know what to do with, little terra-cottas from archaeological expeditions, granite busts, masks, statues, one isn't well paid. . . . After his shift, Leonard goes down to the basement of the Louvre and opens one of the storeroom doors.

The beam of Leonard's lamp shows shelves of hacked savage work. Faces red as blood and white as the corpses in the Morgue; half-open eyes, staring hollows; mouths open in horror. Leonard closes his eyes, snatches one, rolls it in a sheet of yesterday's *Petit Parisien*, and stuffs it inside his tunic; against his undershirt it's scratchy and heavy, concealed guilt. He closes the door, glad to be a civilized man.

But a frame? The Louvre has a roomful of seventeenth-century gilded frames, left over when the big Rubens canvases were restored and restretched in the last century. Leonard opens the door and gazes respectfully on the royal glitter of gold. It's wrong to steal them. So much gold on those frames, it's like stealing gold louis, and they're all hand-carved. No picture has been in these frames in a hundred years, but the Louvre keeps them out of respect.

He won't do it, Leonard decides. It's not the act of a gentleman, stealing things people want.

He needs to feel gentle and good. Or bad, evil, unrepentant. When he thinks of her he feels worse and worse, he wants to feel bad. *Fearsome wounds,* the newspapers said. *Fearful strength* and *madman.* Easier to be that sort of man, and not care.

Leonard's ordinary. He does care. He sits in a cheap café eating his dinner, struggling with words on green paper, writing with a worn-out pen he stole from the post office. *Pls get Hr from the Morg*

He looks in the mirror and sees his own face, untidily mustached, a man a little too old to be young; an ordinary man.

Chapter 43

On Thursday, with his ear bandaged up, Daugherty went to the Louvre to see the Mallais canvases.

The old palace was guarded by a vicious spiked wrought-iron fence. Daugherty crunched across a gravel courtyard the size of a football field, found his way inside and up a dark flight of stairs—at the top was a statue of a woman with wings but no head or arms—and came out into a long corridor, chock-a-block with pictures and furniture and statues and every sort of gaud, half a museum, half a warehouse.

Daugherty ran his finger over the guidebook map. Left here.

Modern Art: A long, overheated, wine-red room, crowded as Leviathan's stomach, the walls jammed with double and triple rows of gilt-framed paintings. Landscape. Naked woman on a couch with a fan in her lap and not a thing on but shoes. Same woman in a dress. Another naked woman. Man and woman harvesting, looked like they knew what they were do-ing; late in the day for it, though. Landscape. Three men wear-ing theater getup and crossing swords. Another naked woman. Woman in a veil. Two marble statues of Virtue and Purity with come-on smiles.

412, Huet, Floods at St. Cloud; 216, P. Delaroche, Death of Queen Elizabeth of England— Here they were— Mallais, *813, Fields at Sunset (early work, 1863), 324, Bath-house of the Samaritaine.*

Fields at Sunset Daugherty didn't like much. The other one was a stunner. It wasn't anything but a picture of a French bath boat, one of those big white barges you saw moored at the promenades. There were people by the boat, little daubed figures, a man rolling a barrel, a woman porter carrying a basket on her head, two men talking. Above the boat was the quai wall, trees just beginning to leaf out, a set of steps up to the street, and some buildings. But you knew to the day when it had been done, that first real spring day when you start thinking about baseball. Underneath the boat, the mud pluming off the bow, that was spring runoff, and all those little daubs looked happy.

Daugherty sat down on a bench and read his book about Mallais, looking up every once in a while at the painting.

In the photographic frontispiece, there was the man himself, a big smiling barrel with a beard, leaning forward in a chair, smoking a cigarette. Claude Mallais had grown up in Alfortville, just upriver from Paris; his father had been a ship's chandler. He had studied at the School of Fine Arts and with Corot (there was that Corot again) but hadn't had any particular success. He'd gone to study in Normandy with an obscure painter named Duféray, whose daughter he'd—married, the book said. The book had a pencil sketch of a poorly-looking girl in Civil War clothes; she was sitting in a rattan chair, talking to a big muscular woman with a laundry basket on her hip. Daugherty turned the page. There the tired girl was again, thinner, on a couch, and there, in a colorchrome plate, she lay with a white veil over her face, flowers strewn over her. The family must have been poorly off, because the flowers were plain day lilies out of the garden, cropped with all their buds. It took Daugherty back to his mother's funeral.

Mallais had vowed he would never paint again after his wife's death. (Daugherty wondered when he'd done the one of her funeral.) He'd destroyed most of his old paintings. Then, a year or so later, he'd married the big girl with the laundry basket, his dead wife's foster sister, Suzanne.

First important paintings: *La Veille*, 1870—that painting with the veil over the dead wife; *Les Bains de la Samaritaine*, 1871. Daugherty flipped the pages over and saw the color plate of *Bath-house of the Samaritaine*; it didn't give half a notion of the painting. He leafed forward and saw later pictures, landscapes mostly—some of Reisden's garden—and sketches and paintings of Mallais's only child, a daughter. Mallais had developed distinctive style and subjects, the book said, painting the edge between city and country, the landscape of the suburbs. There were family photographs: Mallais with the long-legged daughter, his arm around her shoulder; Mallais painting in a hay field, wearing a broad-brimmed hat, his back turned to the camera; Mallais painting in the rain, sheltered under a canvas thing like half a tent. *Although the most congenial of men*, the caption said, *when he painted Mallais insisted on complete privacy even from his closest friends.*

At the end of the book were sketches of landscapes and of a blond little boy, the daughter's son, pulling a wheeled toy horse. Here was a photograph of Mallais at the daughter's funeral, and after it were the last photographs of Mallais, an old man, getting thin, leaning on a cane. He was standing on the grass underneath a spruce-gum pine, and Mrs. Mallais, the washerwoman, was sitting on a checkered tablecloth breaking one of those long French breadloaves. Big arms, wide hips, graying hair, crooked front teeth, and a comfortable smile.

The last photograph was of some lonely rocks on a coast somewhere. Just when a storm was coming on he'd gone out to paint the Bergac rocks, and a big wave had got him. . . . Wasn't that just the way it happened. Summer folk standing on rocks, looking at the waves with their mouths hanging open, a big one comes along, "warn't that wave enormous, Mabel!—Mabel, where are ya?" Family had never got the body back.

Funny to think that artists got drowned like ordinary folks.

Daugherty stood up and stretched and looked around the room, and an odd thought struck him: all these pictures had actually been painted by real folks like the Mallaises, mostly ordinary except for being painters. He wondered what had got them into it. He understood forgery; it was money. But painting wasn't any kind of stable or respectable life. You had to wonder why they hadn't gone into something solid.

He looked again at the pictures of naked women, and grinned. There was that.

Daugherty walked into the Grand Gallery with its big frosted-up windows; he breathed a hole in the frost and looked over the river to his hotel. Here the paintings were Crucifixions and Virgin Marys and long dark saints with their eyes rolled up. He poked into some of the other rooms, meaning to go back to see the Mallais again. Off the Grand Gallery, halfway down, was a room with more religious pictures and a white-painted, glass-fronted box with a guard standing by it. Daugherty took a polite glance around, trying not to disturb a kid who was working away at his easel in the corner of the room, and then peered inside the box for curiosity's sake.

Well, here was a shock.

It was the Mona Lisa. It was the actual Mona Lisa. She looked like you'd think, smiling that closed-lip mysterious smile. She had narrow sliding eyes and narrow hands with wrists crossed like someone had told her her hands were pretty. Daugherty grinned and stepped back, sort of shy, not knowing what to do, and stood for a moment making sure he'd seen her. Well, he thought, now I seen the Mona Lisa.

The copyist was still scritching away at his canvas, and Daugherty wandered over to look at it. It wasn't a canvas at all, but slick white paint over a board, and the copyist was painting over the white in clear thin layers. He was painting another Mona Lisa. It was astonishingly like.

It was sort of comfortable seeing a painting being made, like tinkering or a construction site, not like art at all.

Daugherty had watched for a good few minutes before he saw the name on the copyist's easel.

He took a second look at the copyist, then brought out his Mallais book and turned to the drawings. There was the blond little boy, the grandson, years before, with his toy horse, and here he was, same big ears, painting away at a Mona Lisa.

And there he was, too, on Barry Bullard's list that marked Daugherty's place in the book.

Daugherty hadn't counted on "Jean-Jacques Mallais" looking like his boys had in high school, hair and sleeves a little the wrong length, top lip trying to grow some hairs. His jacket elbows were mends on top of mends.

"Vous—êtes—le—Mallais, le grandson?" Daugherty said.

The kid looked suspicious and sullen, the way kids do when you mention their families.

"Jer aime Mallais," Daugherty said encouragingly, and then had recourse to his *Traveller's Manual of Conversation*. He hated to play the stupid guy with this kid, to be the dumb American who just wanted a Mallais copy— "In the Shop" didn't have a sentence for what he wanted to say. He liked that bath-house painting and he'd give a fair amount for a copy of it. He wanted something closer to the art than the book was.

"Les tableaus—de Mallais—vous—copiez?"

The boy got all grim and white-faced and shook his head no.

Daugherty wondered if he'd said something wrong. He tried again. "Vous copiez me a tableau?"

The kid shook his head even more violently, his eyes wide.

Daugherty had seen that look before. That look got hauled

into every police station in every city, every weekend, and it always broke your heart, the look of a kid who'd got himself in real trouble for the first time.

"Vous copiez me a Mona Lisa?" he said mechanically. The kid smiled.

Outside, rain blew gloomily into Daugherty's face. He stopped at one of the street traders, where an old lady was selling jewelry under an umbrella: little china lockets of the Mona Lisa, pink and green. He bought a few of them for souvenirs. What would he do with a Mona Lisa from Jean-Jacques Mallais? The dripping gate of the Louvre looked like a prison gate, and Daugherty thought about the cheap long muffler the boy had been wearing, the muffler of someone with no overcoat. He looked up the boy's address in his pocket guide to Paris; it was in the fifth arrondissement, a poor neighborhood.

Jean-Jacques Mallais was on Bullard's list because of how many of his grandfather's paintings he'd seen, and because he copied paintings. The little boy in the book, with the pull-toy and the wagon, would have had paintings all around the house, more Mallaises than were in the Louvre, than even a man like Reisden had seen.

And he had that look on his face like a boy caught stealing.

Chapter 44

Daugherty found Reisden at Cousin Dotty's, just about to collect his nephew Tiggy. "Reisden," said Daugherty, "I got to talk to you about a painter I found."

"A forger?" But for the moment he was with the little boy. "Where shall we go, chéri?" he asked, kneeling down to talk to him.

"*Visiter les animaux,*" the little boy said, looking up at Daugherty shyly, "*am Zoo.*"

"Come with us, Daugherty."

They all went along to the zoo, which had a giraffe and a bear pit, snakes and lions, and a black panther, which Reisden said had had a poem written about it. That was Paris all over. They walked into the big birdcage for some protection from the drizzle. Tiggy fed the birds from an end of bread in his pocket, standing on the path in his sailor suit and coat, breaking off and tossing bits of bread in short little-boy throws. It began to rain harder, and they went inside the Museum of Natural History, where the great bones of the dinosaurs stood still in the watery light, and Tiggy stood with one hand on the railing, looking up, awed.

"Right fine boy," Daugherty said.

"I think so."

"How old is he?"

"Almost seven. His father died last year, but was gone in

all senses well before that; I don't think Tiggy remembers him."

When folks lost their minds and died, it was likely to be one thing. The wife would have had it too, and all too often the kids. "Boy's well?" Daugherty asked diplomatically.

"Yes; that was the one thing Esmé did right. He begat the next Gresnière generation, and then—" Reisden shrugged.

Daugherty thought about catty Cousin Dotty, beautiful and sharp as a knife, and didn't dare ask.

"Tell me about this painter," Reisden said.

"I met Mallais's grandson today," Daugherty said. "Boy's a painter, a copyist. I asked him to copy a Mallais for me," and Daugherty explained how the boy had looked, all white-eyed, the sweat coming out on him.

"No, he's too young. He would have been fourteen in 1907."

"He's real young, but I called up Bonnet and Doc, and they got their eye on him already. Just about the time your cousin got her painting, he had a big fight with his grandma. He stayed with friends a couple of months. What does that sound like to you?"

Reisden shook his head. "One doesn't commit forgery so young."

"Son, boys do any kind of mischief at fourteen; I raised two of 'em."

Tiggy, done with the dinosaurs, climbed up onto the bench. Reisden dropped the conversation to show him the animals in the tiles on the wall. *"Tu vois le rhino, Tiggy? Tu te souviens du poème du rhino?* 'All four of thy uncle Erics/Gnash their teeth and have hysterics—'?"

The little boy giggled and chorused, " 'Mamma smashes glasses, cusses: /At least we've no rhinoceroses!' *C'est* nonsense, *c'est ce que dit Miss Wallis.*"

"Ah, but child, *c'est de l'*English nonsense. *Ça te fait du bien. Apprends bien ton anglais, je te lis Edward Lear.*"

"You're talking to him in different languages," Daugherty pointed out.

Reisden looked surprised. "He knows them all. Dotty and I talk English, French, and German with him more or less interchangeably."

"So he knows 'em. And you don't think a kid brought up around paintings would know how to paint, twice the age Tiggy is?"

"Not well enough to have done Dotty's painting."

"Maybe that painting come out of stock and he finished it."

"I'd much rather Yvaud."

They took little Tiggy home and had cocoa and bread and butter in the basement kitchen—you didn't think of people with titles eating in the kitchen. An English lady brought down Tiggy's model of the Eiffel Tower so he could show it to Daugherty. From upstairs Daugherty heard a hen party going on. Tiggy sat for a while on Reisden's lap, both of them reading a book about a faithful dog, and then Tiggy went off for his bath.

Reisden took up the conversation again. "One doesn't commit premeditated crime at fourteen."

They looked at each other.

"And where would be his motive?" Reisden amended.

"Didn't do it, then," Daugherty said. "Least he didn't mean to."

"Possibly he's nervous because he knows who did."

The kitchenmaids were busy in the kitchen, scrubbing up the pots, getting ready for whatever next meal Cousin Dotty was serving; a girl came downstairs with a load of china cups and saucers on a tray. "It's time for us to get out of the way." Reisden let them out the street door; they headed back toward the Pont-Neuf and the Left Bank, into the icy rain.

Reisden stopped to look at books in a box on the parapet of the quai and bought two for Tiggy, a French picture book of sinuous cats and a flip-book with a clown and jumping dog. Reisden riffled its pages as if things like this were still new to him. If Richard Knight had ever had toys, Reisden wouldn't remember it.

"You like Dotty's kid fine," Daugherty said.

"I like both of them," Reisden said.

"You ever going to have kids of your own?"

"No," Reisden said, "Tiggy is it."

"You could marry Dotty," Daugherty said, "if 'tweren't for Perdita." It wasn't quite a question.

"*Dotty?*" Reisden shook his head. "She's my cousin."

There were things Reisden didn't see about Dotty, Daugherty thought. They walked back to Jouvet in silence.

Even this time of the evening Jouvet's waiting room had people in it, and on the second floor of the building, lights were blazing in the lab. "Busy," Daugherty commented. "Any place we can go and talk quiet?"

"I'll show you the archives."

The archives were down some back stairs into a basement. Reisden led the way; Daugherty followed. The darkness was full of the sweet mildewy smell of old paper. Reisden turned on dim electric lights and Daugherty saw rows of oak filing cabinets against stone walls. The wires for the lights ran along huge punky beams, low enough to make both men duck their heads, and, with the rain, the basement was damp enough to make Daugherty's shirt wilt.

"The Jouvet archives," Reisden said, "the reason I bought Jouvet. The Physio. Psych. lab was trying to save them as the company was being closed down; I asked why someone didn't buy the company, since it seemed a working proposition, and everyone looked at me. Just as well, given what the market did in '07.—This is the best multi-generational data on insanity in France, here in this room," he continued. "It's difficult to get data on heritable mental disease. One can't run advertisements. 'If you are mad and many of your family have been, call Orsay 6523; small stipend.' The families are terrified; they lie. But the Jouvets loved the mad and they loved records, and generation after generation of families went to them; and the Jouvet heir was going to throw everything away."

Daugherty sniffed the mildew. "Wonder you keep 'em down here."

"I haven't a choice; the building needs repairs." Reisden leaned his back against one of the cabinets, his hands in his pockets. All this with Perdita had hit him hard; he looked tired. "I've applied for an enormous bank loan and this spring we fix all the floors, and the foundations, and the roof, and then these go up to the third floor."

Daugherty opened a drawer himself and peered at the records. Old thick paper with old-fashioned writing; newer, browner paper; printed forms, all in neatly labeled folders. One of them was very thick and seemed to cover a long time. Reisden looked over his shoulder. "Those are the Guérarts. Antoine, Dénis, Edmond, Émile, Hortense-Émilie, Marie twice, Paul, Paul-Antoine, Paul-Émile, Paul-Joseph . . . Classic hereditary schizophrenia. One wonders what they think at christenings." He closed the file drawer and stood looking at it. "Can you imagine telling a child, 'I have chosen to pass on a mental illness to you'?"

Daugherty thought he'd say something, then he'd better not, then he did. "Far as I know, wasn't any Knight crazy but William."

Reisden looked up sharply.

"I know that for sure," Daugherty said. "I spent years hunting Knights. You remember they wasn't just looking for you, they needed any heir at all. The Knights weren't a crazy family, not like them Gerrarts."

There was one of those silences that you don't want to break, the other person has to speak first. Reisden jammed his hands in his pockets and stared down at the floor. "Clement Knight killed himself," he said finally. "Isabella probably. Gilbert is relatively sane but has phobias. Richard—"

"William raised all of 'em, son."

"He raised me," Reisden said, "until I killed him."

Daugherty nodded, but not because he agreed with Reisden. William Knight had warped everyone he'd touched, like a frame around wet wood, bending it to one shape or snapping it. Teaching 'em to jump when William rang the bell. If William had a dog he'd kill it, if he had a boy he'd beat him; that was William; that was what Reisden had to think was his heritage.

"You ain't William," Daugherty said.

"I am very like William," Reisden said. "I like control. I like—" He hesitated. "Owning people. I'm delighted to have all these." He gestured at the files. "Bless you, my children, Papa Reisden has you now, and you will not be thrown out for trash, but live forever in a research study at the École de Medicine."

"That ain't wrong."

"No, but I do want to win." His lips tightened. "When I wanted Perdita, I wanted to be more important than the piano. I wanted to be absolutely sure of her."

"Uh-uh. William beat kids and you take Tiggy to the zoo."

"And then I congratulate myself that I am not William, which makes me wonder whether I'm doing it for Tiggy or merely want to approve of myself."

"Could do both," Daugherty said.

"You are a sensible man," Reisden said.

They climbed the stairs from the basement and the records.

Outside, in the dark, a man and a woman were toiling up the steps of Jouvet, him helping her, and Reisden looked across at them, part clinical, to see what was wrong with the woman, part—Daugherty knew the look—just longing, brooding, a man without a woman looking at a man with one. And then he shook his head and looked away.

Chapter 45

Saturday Reisden spent at the Sorbonne, drafting a plan for a series of experiments. When one really wants to work it doesn't rain. By four, Reisden was staring at words that had made sense an hour ago, while through the window of his Spartan university office, the sun was setting on what had been a warm and perfect day. Perdita would just be getting out of class; on a day like today, with such weather, he would have been waiting for her.

He could call Perdita at the Conservatoire and, one, make it clear she could go to Courbevoie to practice on Sunday, because he would be at Barry's Tomb; two, suggest that they should both go to Courbevoie and talk; three, invite her to someplace private, not Courbevoie, where they could talk, but not near a bed, not in the house they had shared; four . . . *I want to be more important than the piano*, he had said to Daugherty. Five, let her tour; give up having her; not give up wanting her. Six.

"I will not tell Gilbert Knight I debauched you," he said aloud. What else had he been doing? Utter *fool*, self-righteous *idiot*, what had he been doing? "Debauching," flaming h—l.

Barry Bullard called. "I got more information. Come 'ave tea?"

Reisden joined him at a Chinese chophouse in the medieval warrens of the Quartier Maubert, at the disreputable eastern edge of the Latin Quarter. The soot-black medieval walls were covered with fans and torn bits of brocade; from the beams hung red-paper lanterns inside which candles jittered. The air caught at the back of the throat, foul with smoke from the kitchen and the tobacco haze of *mégots,* cigarettes made from the tobacco of cigarette ends found on the street. Reisden had smoked one out of curiosity; they tasted like horse dung and were amazingly strong. Most of the Maison Choi clientele were Chinese or porters from the Halle aux Vins; two men discussing art were to be pitied and ignored.

Bullard ordered Chinese high tea for them, with no reference to the menu, in Limehouse-accented Chinese.

"I went to see Armand-'isself and mentioned I 'ad me doubts about the painting. 'E practically took me 'ead off, marchin' up and down that bloody Aubusson carpet of 'is. 'E could swear to that painting 'isself, see, there was the ack-number, which 'e'd done in blue ink because 'e was out of the usual black. And the 'eliotrope pink was a bloody Mallais shadder like I'd ought to 'ave seen fifteen times before; 'e'd got another like it in for the show."

"He has another?" Reisden coughed and drank harsh green tea.

"Eugène de Cressous's, painted in '97. Inslay-'Ochstein says it's typical of Mallais's late work, and I say I ain't seen anything like it before, and 'e says that's not 'is fault, and 'e smiles nasty-like."

"And the overpainting?"

"Typical, 'e says."

"So no one has forged anything. What do you think?"

Bullard shook his head. "Dunno. I really dunno. The Cressous canvas is fabulous. You're coming to the Winter Salon opening Monday night? Take a look." He masticated a bit of chicken, thinking. "Wish I'd never said nothing, t' tell you the truth."

"Are we making trouble for you?"

"Nah. Armand'll cool down right enough. But—" Bullard put down his chopsticks and tapped with a long finger on the plank table. "'E believes in those paintings, 'e don't want to give up on 'em. If 'e worries your cousin's ain't right, 'e'll get someone to write on Mallais for the *Art Journal*, praise the late-period shadders, and use *View of the Seine* as an example. But it ain't because 'e thinks it's bad. 'E really loves the paintings." Bullard's mobile mouth turned down at the corners. "Makes me wonder if I'm seein' things. They're flamin' good pictures."

"I know. I was very happy with *View of the Seine*."

"Everybody wants to be 'appy. That's why forgers get away with it," Bullard said.

Chapter 46

Anys Appolonsky left the Conservatoire.

It happened during Advanced Class. As Anys was sitting down at the piano, Maître said something, not much worse than the things he usually said, but Anys gave a thin little scream, banged the fallboard down, and ran out. Perdita could hear her crying in the hall.

"Mademoiselle l'Américaine," Maître said. "You play instead."

She rose and sat down at the piano and had actually played a few bars before she knew for certain how angry she was. "*I can't sit here and hear her out there—*" She went outside and held Anys, poor shrieking and sobbing fifteen-year-old Anys, who was crying out in Russian all down the echoing corridor. The knitting mothers moved to give them a place, but apart from that left them alone. Anys cried so hard she had to be helped to the ladies' toilet to throw up, and then needed to be sat with in the lobby while the concierge called someone from the Russian Hospital. Don't take her to the hospital, Perdita thought; just someone take her out for dinner and tell her she plays Tchaikovsky like a dream, and then send her home early and let her get a good night's sleep; but nobody did, and finally someone came and gave Anys a shot that reduced her to mumbling, and took her away in a cab through the rain.

And that left Perdita alone.

Using her cane to grope her way, she went to the ladies' room in the basement and cried in one of the cubicles. (There were so few women instrumentalists, she had the *salle des dames* all to herself. This seemed so sad she cried harder.) Who would she take out to lunch now, who would she fuss over and care about? Who would she love?

When I am famous and rich, she thought, I will start a fund to provide mothers and cats for poor Conservatoire students; and that made her almost laugh in the middle of her tears. It was comforting to think of helping someone, even in fantasy.

Madame Xico invited her to lunch.

"How's your 'Sacha'?" said the journalist. "Oh, there, there," patting her hand as Perdita, mortified, burst into a whoop of tears. "Take my handkerchief."

She refused it, and took it, and buried her hot face in the square of perfumed green silk. Madame Xico's handkerchief smelled of chypre, cigarette smoke, lip-tint, and dog, a very modern smell.

"Believe me, your Alexander, you're better off without him. Isn't she, Nicky? Here, Nicky, give Miss Halley a kiss." Perdita hugged Nicky and cried into his muscular little neck while he snuffled at her ear.

"Men are a mug's game," Madame Xico said. "I only like dogs."

Madame Xico had been married "very young" (a year older than Perdita) to a much older man who was important in Paris publishing. Before she was married she had not been a writer at all, she said; her husband had encouraged her. And then he had got tired of her. He wanted someone younger, more pliable.

"He wanted a wife," Perdita said bitterly. "Someone suitable, who wouldn't ever leave him."

"Him? He wanted a girl. . . . Why don't we go shopping again? Saturday, after your lesson. Then I'll take you out and show you some of Paris. We'll go to a salon," Milly said. "Esther Cohen's."

"I'd like that." She would like anything that kept her from thinking of Alexander.

The music had lost all its life. Perdita banged away at the Paganini Variations and another of Chopin's endless dratted glittery nocturnes, but she felt as if she were a piano roll, a set of mechanical fingers. Oh, the blasted piano: it made her back ache to play it. She put her head down on her arms, right at the keyboard, taking up a practice room and not practicing, a sin.

Her whole body ached, her stomach, her arms, her breasts where he had laid his head. She cried silently at night into her pillow; she woke up tired, her head bursting, her nostrils stuffed with tears.

She would forget Alexander, but she wouldn't go back to America. She would live in Italy. She would learn to smoke, like Madame Xico. She would take long walks on a beach; people would talk about her in hushed voices. She would never marry, though men much better than Alexander would ask her, and she would always wear black. Some Italian conductor would hear her play, solitary in her palazzo, and ask her to play for him . . . it would be the beginning of her European career.

She never fantasized about finding love, of being domestic with her husband; it was always music; she was shallow. Alexander had known that, and forgiven it for a time, but wanted more. She felt as if, trying to love, she had been just

like Florrie and the Young Married Women, not even conscious of how bad she was.

She wiped her tears against her sleeve, and sniffled, and
went back to practice.

She went round the corner to the pastry shop. The patisserie
was overheated, greasy, and full of garlicky-smelling people;
the sweat came out on her. She bought a cheese sandwich and
a bottle of Evian, and took them back with her, waiting in line
for the next piano; but she couldn't eat any of the cheese, only
picked tiny bits of bread out of the sandwich and held them in
her mouth. Instead she practiced, her fingers against her arms,
thinking of intonation, cradling her aching heart.

She was suffering; she was enraged at him for how much
she hurt; it was nothing like romantic disappointed love, it was
like robbery, an obscure disease, a parasitic infection, leaving
her with no dignity, nothing but need.

She had no one to share with, even in her triumphs. One
afternoon that week, for the first time, she played all through,
almost to her satisfaction, the first series of the Paganini Variations. What a delight! What a day! Before she remembered, she
wanted to call Alexander and share it with him.

Chapter 47

"I still got that problem about Madame Mallais and her brother," Mr. Daugherty told Perdita. "And it's her grandson now too."

He had invited her out for tea, but Perdita hadn't been able to face a café, with all the noise and smells and people; she asked if they could just walk. It was dark gray out, wet, cold to the bone. They sat on a bench, on a boulevard, as if they were waiting for a tram. Her hands were freezing. She wanted to go back to the Conservatoire, find a practice room, and cry. "You look right peaked," Mr. Daugherty said. "The both of you are miserable, seems to me."

The both of us deserve it, she thought. "Tell me about your detecting."

"Well," Mr. Daugherty said. "Dotty's servants check out, near as we can tell. And this Inslay-Hockstein man? When Mrs. Mallais come in with Dotty's painting, there was a man in the gallery. A judge buying a flower-picture for his sister's birthday. He fell right in love with that Mallais painting, and he didn't take his eyes off it from the time it was unwrapped, all the time 'Armand' was stenciling the identification number on it and writing it in his book, until Dotty come and took it away. Practically had his nose to it. The painting Mrs. Mallais brought was the one Cousin Dotty took."

"So," she said defensively.

"So, Mrs. Mallais. Keeps herself to herself inside that wall. Lives with a man you say don't seem much like her brother. Had a big fight with her grandson over selling that picture to Dotty. The grandson paints copies."

She hadn't heard about that.

"Could be Dotty, though," Mr. Daugherty said. "Maybe."

"Don't you get me started on Dotty; I've a mind to accuse her of anything."

There was a little pause in the conversation; Mr. Daugherty took up another subject. "I went to the Louver, Perdita, and I was wondering why some folks decide to be artists. Thought I'd ask you, since you are one."

"I don't have any idea," she said snappishly. "I thought it was something I could do to get boys. If I'd known then what I do now, Mr. Daugherty, I'd have taken another line."

"You going to give up, then?" he asked hopefully.

On the boulevard a horse omnibus went past them: shaman's rattle, snare drum, bass drum, bells, cymbals. Two women behind them were discussing their health, *poumons, misère, chérie, tsk!:* violins bowed and plucked. Her hands were freezing; she tucked them in her sleeves. When she got back she would go to the ladies' room in the basement and run hot water over them to get them warm for practice, and perhaps cry a little. "No," she said. "I'm not."

"It's no sort of a steady living, and girls don't get the"— Mr. Daugherty cleared his throat. "Advantages."

"What advantages?" Only the moment this afternoon when a little glissando had turned into something utterly different, something to be run through the hands like silk. Only moments like that.

"Never mind. You been going at it forever," he said.

"Since I was five."

"Every day?"

"Even Sundays. After church," she added hurriedly.

"Have mercy, honey, you don't know anything else."

"Maybe I don't," she said. "But when you know you love one thing, or one person, what else do you have to know?"

Oh, Alexander, Alexander; tell Alexander that, she wanted to say.

"Seems to me," he said, "you still got to know a lot."

"Madame Mallais isn't the kind to make anybody do anything wrong," she said. She decided to be extra fair to Dotty. "And I don't really think Dotty did anything either. She's too proud to lie," she said.

"Honey, pride's what blackmailing's about."

"Do you think someone would blackmail Dotty? What about?"

"You know her," Mr. Daugherty said. "What happened in 1907, when she bought that painting? Reisden ever tell you anything about that?"

"Nineteen oh-seven? To Dotty?" Perdita had been working on a Liszt piece then; she played it against her sleeve, bringing things back. "At the end of 1906, her husband left her and went to Cairo."

"Huh."

"Alexander went after him but couldn't bring him back. In April, Alexander came to visit me in New York."

"You didn't ask him why he come?"

No, that was the last thing she would have done. "I only cared that he was there," she said.

"Uh-huh," he said, "uh-huh"; she was embarrassing him.

"He talked about Dotty. He said she'd been in a lot of difficulties."

"Oughta ask him what. Or you could ask her, maybe, be sympathetic, like women do."

She snorted. "I don't believe I'm talking to her."

"Talk to him, then."

"I'm *not* talking to him." Would he come to Mrs. Bacon's? To Dotty's on the twenty-seventh? Would there be a Dotty's on the twenty-seventh?

"You doing anything tomorrow night?"

"I'm going out," she said haughtily, not thinking it necessary to mention it was only with Madame Xico.

"We're going to see a painter named Juan Gastedon. Fine painter, he mighta done Dotty's painting. . . . You could come with us, you wanted."

"If he's a fine painter, he's not a forger. He wouldn't want to waste the time."

But, she thought, why did she waste the time on Alexander, why did she waste the time on believing she wanted him, when even she knew that she had given him up for music?

Chapter 48

Saturday the fifteenth was a lovely day; even at dawn you could tell it was going to be nice; but while she was standing in line outside the Conservatoire, waiting for the rush to get the best pianos, Perdita felt very dizzy, as if she were going to fall down.

Of course she would feel sick, she told herself; she'd been overpracticing, she hadn't been eating well, and she wouldn't be with Alexander at Courbevoie tonight. Hadn't he told her that mental states caused physical effects? But, holding on to the iron railing, shaky and half gagging, she felt panic gathering in her stomach. It didn't matter what caused it; her sight was bad, losing her balance frightened her, it made her feel as though she had to hold on to someone, and there was no one.

She was just feeling sorry for herself, but at noon she went to see a doctor.

She had a keeping-ring of her grandmother's, a plain gold ring that could have been mistaken for a wedding band. Since what had happened a month ago at Courbevoie, she had kept it on a chain on her neck, underneath her blouse and chemise. She still had it on the chain, with a Mona Lisa locket Mr. Daugherty had brought her from "the Louver." On the way, in the cab, she put on the ring. The doctor might wish to examine her, and she was not a virgin. The stratagem shamed her.

"And what is the difficulty, *jeune madame*?"

Dr. Magnin was an Englishman who had been on the bar-
ricades at the time of the Commune; she had got his name
from the Canadian embassy (not asking herself, either, why
she had phoned the Canadian embassy rather than the American). He spent more time telling her about the Commune than
examining her, while she turned the unfamiliar ring around on
her finger.

Her stomach was upset, she said, and she had felt dizzy.
She was really feeling better now. It must have been nothing.

Anything else?

She felt sleepy—depressed—

Any lateness of the monthly flow—tenderness in the
breasts . . . ?

She swallowed, suddenly frightened. "Yes."

"Ah, then, madame, perhaps we have some splendid news
for your husband!"

"But that can't be. My husband uses—" She was not sure
she was even supposed to know the word.

Dr. Magnin questioned her. Did her husband take precautions reliably? "Yes," she said sharply, "very reliably." Carefully? Every time? Of course; he was a scientist. Ah, a scientist,
said Dr. Magnin. Then her sensations must be only the natural
timidity and eagerness of the young wife. She sighed, feeling a
lowering of emotional level that was only partly relief.

She was very lately married?

Yes, she said, crossing her fingers in the folds of her skirt.

And depressed? At such a beautiful time of her life? Was
she educated, perhaps?

She was—had been—at the Conservatoire.

"Ah!" Dr. Magnin said. "That's it." She was dangerously
overeducated. Any sort of study greatly increased female irreg-
ularities. Had she suffered from lateness before? Ah, you see.
Too long daily practice at the piano harmed the delicate

anatomy of reproduction; nature became unable to throw off the impurities of city life. Her husband should require her to take daily strolls, to gather flowers in season, to prepare herself mentally and physically for the sublime lot of woman. And, of course, her husband should not be timid; this was not the time for precautions.

"Madame, in my experience the educated young woman is always apprehensive before she is blessed with a family. But the state itself is quite different. Many of my female patients, upon learning their condition, have described a bliss, an ecstasy, even a sense of *forgiveness of sins*. The young mother is fulfilling her allotted role in life. She thinks of nothing but the infant; she dreams of nurseries."

He gave her some stomach tablets and a pamphlet, "Some Interesting Facts of Great Value to Women," took ten francs, counseled her to drink only bottled water, and sent her away.

Class was Chopin Preludes no. 11 and 13, lovely to play but cut flowers. She went into the *salle* with the men, and performed badly, and was justifiably hauled over the coals, another Saturday afternoon at the Conservatoire; and then she sat listening to Paul Favre and all the other men caressing the piano like the body of a woman. She sat, her hand over her mouth, her eyes cast down, as if she were thinking; but she was only feeling her blouse tight and painful over her bosom.

Chapter 49

"Interesting facts. 'One of the most frequent causes of congestion of the pelvis,' " Madame Xico read, " 'is the "décolleté" evening dress and the bell-shaped nether garments.' Nether garments! Where'd you get this?"

"A doctor," Perdita said.

"Why do they suppose women wear corsets?" she continued, leafing through the pamphlet. "To attract men; to be the right sort of woman, not 'loose'; I'll bet you wear one for the baron. Henry used to have me tight-lace to nineteen inches round the waist; me! The doctors tell women not to wear them, but they say it's 'unnatural' for a woman not to want to attract her husband. . . . 'Children a Woman's Highest Duty, Nature's Most Wonderful Miracle, First Indications of the Blessing of Motherhood, Evils of Abortion . . .' Look here: 'Everything that causes an increase of blood to the womb and ovaries should be avoided. In this category belong sexual excitement . . .' " Milly turned the pamphlet over. "*Bien sûr,* a British doctor.—Men write these pamphlets for men, to reassure themselves that women don't exist. Eh, it's like a melodrama, these women! The bad women wear the 'bell-shaped nether garments' and smoke and play the piano all day long, and the good women dream of Nature's Most Wonderful Miracle.—Are you pregnant?" Madame Xico asked.

"*Madame,*" Perdita pleaded in a low voice. They were in a public café.

"It's all right, there's no one here who cares. If you are, call me Milly," Madame Xico said. "I'm calling you Perdita. Is that why he left, because he thought—?"

"No. Of course not."

"What a time for him to desert you, when his cousin's supposed to introduce you in Paris! Believe me, he thinks you're giving him a little responsibility."

"I just wanted information," Perdita said, "that's the only reason why I went to the doctor."

"As if you can't get it for six francs. Semiramis," she said to the barkeeper, "sell us a copy of— Yes, that." Madame Xico— Milly—handed over what felt to Perdita like quite a thick pamphlet. "If this is any use to you."

It was a delicate way of putting what was probably a question about her sight. They were sitting near a good light; Perdita took her magnifying glass out of her handbag, peered through it at a page, and nodded. "Let me see your magnifier," Milly Xico said.

"It's extra strong; Alexander found it for me. He's good at finding things like that."

"Look at my finger, the cuticle is like chick feathers. You don't read much, eh?"

"Alexander reads to me at night. Did read." What a voice he had, it was like lying bare-skinned, being caressed. She would not think of that; but who would ever find her a scientific magnifier again?

"I'll bet he never read you any of *my* books. You're really not going to get back together with him?" Milly seemed very interested in this.

"No. I had a—" She lowered her voice. "An *affair,*

Madame—Milly, that's the only word for it, and it's done. I'm
not right for marriage; I'm too devoted to music."

"He thinks so, because you're not devoted to him!"

They continued their conversation, discreetly, as they
walked toward the Grands Magasins de la Samaritaine, the
Samaritaine department store. Even though the sun had set,
something of its warmth remained; the streets were crowded
and animated. Milly Xico's hair smelled strongly of tea; she'd
just hennaed it. She took Perdita's arm. Perdita was reassured
by the contact, to have an arm to hold when one had spent the
morning being dizzy.

"Men are a mug's game," Milly said. "Look at what men
do to us. They idealize us when we're young, they marry us, tie
us down to motherhood or their social lives or just to their idea
of us, and if we aren't what they think we are, they blame us!"

"He wanted to see how it would work out," Perdita said,
"but when it didn't, then—" He had said it all, *I want to marry
someone.* "Milly, I feel like a freak, he is a good man and he
wants to marry and I want him but I don't want to marry
him."

"He doesn't want you. Men don't want women, they want
mamas and girls. How did you start having your affair?"

"Milly," Perdita protested.

"We'll walk on the promenades if you're shy," Milly said.
They descended the stairs, slippery even after this day without
rain; Perdita held hard to the handrail. They threaded their
way through stacks of boxes, coils of rope from barges, quai-
side debris. Perdita sat on a coil of rope, feeling a little tired.

"Tell me," she said, stalling. "How did you meet Henry?"

"Oh, Henry, he was a friend of my parents, he came to my
house, he courted me, we got married, all that. You?"

"I was engaged," she said, "a long time ago, to someone else. Alexander—showed up. All summer, he and I kept

meeting each other, everywhere it seemed, he was new in town, everyone noticed him of course, I thought I was just noticing him too. But he seemed to me to be so always *there,* in the barn, in the summer kitchen, at a dance." It was useless to talk about this truthfully without saying how she had felt. "Oh, from the beginning, I wanted just to touch him—I wanted to put my fingers on his face, to feel him, it was more than just wanting to know what he looked like. I could feel him wherever he was in the room. He was like sun on my skin."

"Ah, *oui,*" Milly said, a little impatiently.

"There wasn't any place for us; there wasn't anywhere; I couldn't do anything because I was engaged and I was a respectable girl. I gave up being engaged, I had to, but I was still respectable. And finally he was going away, forever, and we said goodbye—" That last evening, she had sat with him in Gilbert Knight's kitchen, stiff in her new gray suit, remembering to call him by a new name, not so much as touching his hand. "We went to the station together. He got on the train, and it was about to leave, and I got on too."

Simply by being on the train with him, overnight, she was as good as ruined. "Get out, go back," he had said. No. "I'm going to marry you," she had said. She knew how young she had been, and what he had seen in her. She thought of what he had said once about Tasy: *We were sure of each other.* He had been sure of her.

And then she had shown him she didn't love him.

"I couldn't be enough of a *woman,* Milly. I wanted him completely, and I didn't want him enough. His first wife always wanted to be with him; that's what he wants from love. I want to be with him too, but . . ."

"Women are never enough for men," Milly said. "My Henry. I was never enough for him. I could never give enough, nothing I did was enough, I never touched his center. I was his light, his moon, his stars; but I wasn't his newspapers, his clubs, I wasn't his friends. He asked me to write for him; I wrote my life. He edited it. He showed his friends how young and pretty I was, but I got older, I had bronchitis all the time— he never spent anything on our house, it was always cold. I cut off my hair; he kept me around because I said clever things, and I brought women to the house, clever pretty women, my friends. My particular friends," Milly said, "you understand?"

"Yes," Perdita said. "I understand, Milly."

It was getting darker and the evening was getting colder, but neither of them moved from their seats on the rope coil.

"And he liked that, for a while, but then he got tired of it. He cheated on me with one of them, then he cheated on her with me; then we all got tired of it and I moved out and went on the stage and he divorced me. He had a good sense of publicity, Henry did; he used to dress Polaire and me up alike and take us out on leashes; plenty of people want to look at me still, so I'm all right, I make my way. But relationships between women can never be so unequal," Milly said. "I like women better."

Perdita wasn't naive; in music, some women live with other women. People like that were occasionally troublesome, usually quite ordinary, sometimes good friends; more or less like other people; really more like other people than she was, who wanted a man she wouldn't marry. "Friendships with other women are important," she said. "To talk with someone who's like oneself, who's an equal; whom the law doesn't give more power, or less; who isn't too much older or too much younger, or if she is, doesn't try to take advantage of it— That's like friendship with another musician." That sounded bloodless unless you were a musician.

"Friendships like that end up in bed, if they're important."

"Well, they do or they don't, Milly." They hadn't with

Perdita, and she supposed they never would; but what did women do, when they weren't capable of loving a man even when they loved him? "It matters more that they exist than where they end up."

"Where doesn't matter?" Milly laughed.

"I mean that—bed—is only a part of the piece. It's like practicing; every time I work at a piece, there's the chance that the music I find under my fingers will be something different than it has been before; that because I know it better and I'm improving my skills toward it, I'll find something new, profound, an idea, something that is so true it'll frighten and exalt and change me. Love and friendship ought to be true like that, Milly, and bed should be only a part of it, like an instrument in the orchestra."

"The ideas you get at the Conservatoire. And Esther thinks I'm a romantic!"

Perdita was glad to hear there was an Esther in the background. "What happens in bed, I mean, ought to be love, and love ought to be real, not done for show, or pay, or anything but truth."

"And what was your truth with him?"

She thought, and her exaltation burst like a bubble. What she had felt in the doctor's office, apart from panic, had been excitement; she had wanted to be happy at whatever cost, snatching and stealing what she wanted, breaking all the rules, grabbing everything, a music career, Alexander, Alexander's child. "I wanted to have him." She hesitated to tell this part to Milly; it was not something Milly wanted to hear, nor she to tell. She crossed her arms, feeling the ache in her breasts and the duller ache in her stomach. "I—got him into bed. It felt dangerous that he could give me a child, but I loved that danger. It was part of my being a woman toward him."

Her stomach felt queasy, disturbed. She sucked a peppermint

lozenge and offered one to Milly. "I wanted him to see things were simple," she said around the peppermint, "and to prove I loved him. You should see him with his nephew. He's— sweet."

"What about marriage?"

"I don't know. Married women have trouble keeping music."

"You wanted Nature's Most Wonderful Miracle and you didn't want to be married?"

"Oh, someday, but— I really *care* about music." Saying it sounded like a brag, like Florrie's friends saying, *We love our children so, we really don't have time to practice.*

"Maybe you don't want a man," Milly said.

"Milly, is it that different?" she asked, daring.

"Yes." No word from Milly for a while. "Yes, but— Lovers are always trouble. Husbands and kids are worse. Anyone who ties you down is bad. What would you do with a kid?"

How could she go on tour with a baby? She couldn't; touring would be too hard on a baby; it would be cruel, as if she could push the baby around because it was small. "I was fooling myself," she said. "I wanted to think I could do everything."

"You ought to do everything, at your age. It's sensible."

"Nobody can, though. I can't." Florrie had been right: the best way of life isn't possible.

"Flirting with getting pregnant," Milly said, "for me, that's like going round with a man who threatens to shoot you. That's Russian roulette, that's not romantic. 'He throws me through the fourth-floor window, oh! What joy it is when someone loves me so!' You're an idiot."

"I just wanted things to happen, somehow, without my having to choose. If I got in trouble, it would be obvious I hadn't meant to do it. But I did; I chose everything I did."

For her and Milly, at least, the worst of an awkward moment had come, and passed. Whoof, Milly said, it was cold! Perdita agreed it was. The sun had set. They brushed off their skirts and strolled down the promenade toward the Samaritaine bath-house and the stairs to the upper quai, Milly still holding Perdita's arm, but in a different way, more like a friend.

"Did you ever try to get pregnant with him?" Milly said.

Perdita flushed. "I didn't think of it. I wish I had."

"What an idiot!" Milly said again. "Look, here's the Samaritaine. We'll do our shopping here, and then we'll do another errand. I worry about you."

Milly led her through the perfumed confusion of the department store: whiffs of scent, sparkles of glass from countertops, whirls of bright and pale colors, the smell of garlic and furs, and saleswomen inquiring, *"Mesdames, vous désirez?"*

"No one wears flannel underwear in Paris, not at your age." Milly handed her a fistful of softness. "And you should try a *soutien-gorge* because your bust is big." Perdita retreated into a fitting room alone. The underwear was black, and made her Conservatoire outfit of white blouse and dark skirt secretly much more daring; but the *soutien-gorge* made her blouse really too tight under the armpits.

"Then we'll get you a blouse." Milly found a wonderful French blouse, very thin dark wool, soft as flower petals, but with a neckline Perdita wanted to pin. "No, no, leave it open, that's the look this year. Very sophisticated, and with your skirt it's a dress. That locket's a little . . ." Milly's voice trailed off dubiously. "The Mona Lisa, after all!"

"It felt 'a little,' but a friend gave it to me."

"Oh, friends."

They went to the perfume counter and, with a saleswoman hovering, used the testers shamelessly. "The luxury of poor women," Milly said, "to douse themselves from every tester on the perfume counter." The Perfume of the Lady in Black was Milly's favorite, she said, because it was overdone; sex should make you laugh, *hein*? Majestic was Dotty's perfume; ugh. Ylang-Ylang was sandalwood, a favorite smell of Perdita's. Milly said she'd known a *horizontale* who'd drunk it. Perdita dabbed a drop of the perfume onto her finger and just touched her tongue to it. "Ptew! Milly, what happened to that woman?"

"Dead. But she died celebrated, my dear! That's the suicide to aim for, not stab yourself on a man's—"

"*Milly,*" Perdita said.

Milly priced an evening dress for the premiere of *Chantecler*—too expensive—and bought a *fantaisie*, a tuft of red feathers to trim her hat.

"Now," Milly said, businesslike, "that other errand. Before you get into trouble, I'm going to teach you what every young girl should know." They walked up the rue Auber toward the huge bright and noisy St.-Lazare railroad station. "Do you see that group of women by the café near the entrance? No, of course you don't, but trust me, the brightest café sign near any railroad station draws them. You ask them"—Milly raised her voice—"*s'il vous plaît*, ladies, do you know the location of a glove shop in the neighborhood?"

Several raucous women's voices answered. What do you want with gloves, you and your little friend? Ask a policeman! Ask your pimp! Perdita concluded that gloves were not gloves and that these women thought she and Milly were, as Uncle Charlie'd used to say, cops or worse, reformers.

"Say something, Perdita," Milly said.

"*Nous ne sommes pas des gardiens de la paix,*" she said in careful French.

"*Américaine, la petite?*" She and Milly were surrounded and jostled: elbows, perfume smells, liquor breath, tobacco and garlic and sweat. The women exchanged raucous murmurs.

"Hey," one of the women said, "you're Milly Xico!"

The woman got Milly's autograph and led them away from her friends toward the steps of a nameless hotel in a side street. "Madame Bézou, here, see her."

Inside the hotel it smelled like a train station in a bad neighborhood, or a hospital, too many people together in a place none of them wants to stay long. Madame Bézou smelled like soaps: hand soap and floor-scouring powder, carbolic and oil tar, heavy-perfumed, faintly greasy smells thick in the air. She had hair the color of fresh rust and the slow careful steps of a fat woman. She talked in half sentences, always interrupted, while a harried undermanager and his assistant bustled in and out, getting supplies for "hotel guests." From out in the corridor, Perdita heard a woman laughing or crying, low stretched-out sobs like Anys's. She crumpled her skirt in her fist.

"It's a crusade—with me, good product—I'm educated—convent school," Madame Bézou said. "Out on the streets at fourteen; daughter in Abbeville—eighteen." She puffed, short of breath, mincing back and forth on painful feet, reaching down a box of something from her supplies. "Men only had to look at me—I was always in trouble—dining-room tables, instruments dirty as the Bièvre—" Perdita's stomach turned over. "My daughter—only been in trouble once!" She sat down again with a wheeze and tapped her fingers against the table. "My triumph, mesdames—*c'est du progrès*—whatever you want—I supply—clean!"

"Gloves," said Milly. She opened the box, straightened Perdita's index and middle finger, and rolled a "glove" efficiently over them.

"This is where you get them," Milly said. "This is what they're for. Roll them, don't pull them, and you don't have to care what men want."

Perdita took the proffered small box, paid, and left silently, walking quickly, breathing heavily, away from the darkness of the rue de Madrid toward the bright place St.-Lazare. Milly steered her into Hodgson's Bar and they sat, conspicuous, two women among men's bass voices. "You look pale," Milly said.

"I didn't want to be there."

"If you're going to live your life, chérie, getting a big belly won't make you a queen. Be responsible for yourself. Men won't protect you."

What Alexander used, what *he and she* used—had used—came from a place like that: that was all she could think. Underneath, like a bright thread of panic, was the thought that Milly had just shown her where girls in trouble could go.

"I'm going to have a vermouth," Milly said.

"I am too," said Perdita. She wanted to get her period and not to think of this.

When their order arrived, the smell of the alcohol reminded her of the medicinal stink of Madame Bézou's room. Rubber and vinegar, disinfecting alcohol, dried herbs, soap upon soap, and below it, like a ground, the dark musty odor of Madame Bézou's abused body. The paper parcel from La Samaritaine was on Perdita's lap, with her old underwear in it, and the black silk and the low-necked blouse were on her body; she could smell the Perfume of the Lady in Black on her fingers and the bitter aftertaste of Ylang-Ylang made a harshness at the back of her throat. Sex was not simple, it frightened her. Everything frightened her suddenly, the unclean Madame Bézou's "clean product," the box, the end of her affair with Alexander, the bruised heaviness in her breasts and hips, the sensual underwear she was wearing.

It would have been so much easier to pretend to be delighted with marriage, to have got married to Harry or to Alexander, to anyone.

Instead of respectability she felt a swooping, vertiginous kinship to all those women there, to the Mona Lisa, to Milly, as much as to the moral virgin she had been. It was all the same, Perdita thought, none of them really knew what to do about sex. Some women covered sex up with romance or with medicinal briskness, made it a business, or a religion, or a romance, some called it illegal or immoral, some wanted children, but everyone was driven to it. Sex was like, when you were a child, feeling a loose tooth wiggle and knowing it was going to fall out, no matter what you thought or did about it. Sex was like standing bare-legged and barefoot on the beach when the tide was heavy, standing still but feeling yourself moving quickly, drawn out to sea, sinking as the sand built up around your ankles, standing still but moving in every direction at once until you were whirled about and ill; and then when you were caught, some big wave came and soaked your skirts, slapped and soaked your legs and belly, so that you struggled out just in time and shrieked and ran for the shore; until one time you stayed, while the water rose and you got wetter and colder and you'd get in trouble and you knew it, but you stayed.

"I'm going to have another," Milly said.

Perdita shook her head.

"This woman I read about last week," Milly said, "at Avron, Madame Pimoule? The man raped her, then he strangled her, then he stabbed her, then he stuffed a handkerchief down her throat and threw her in a ditch. When a policeman's killed, like this Deray last week, the government gets involved, they arm the police. But a woman's murdered *three* different ways and it's an inch in the police blotter, that's it, goodbye, do you think they arm women?"

Perdita took deep breaths, trying to think of anything but sex. The vermouth was making her giddy.

"The same day, rue Orchampi in Montmartre, a concierge, Madame Toujan, raped and strangled. At Batignolles, a twenty-year-old apache girl, your age, chérie, shot by her boyfriend. On the rue Richer, a hairdresser, Madame Muller, assaulted by *two* men. George says it's all part of the sex act. I say"—Milly raised her glass—"revenge on all men, and long live dogs."

"Where *is* Nicky?" Perdita asked.

Milly laughed. "He has a girlfriend today. It's a living, after all! He has papers."

Chapter 50

On Bullard's list of forgers, Daugherty figured the likeliest was a Spanish kid named Gastedon. On Saturday nights Gastedon was always at the open house of an American woman named Cohen. Bullard introduced Daugherty to an acquaintance of Miss Cohen's, a Boston engineer named Peter Lawrence, who'd take Daugherty there tonight. Reisden would be late; he was seeing a banker about a loan.

Esther Cohen's place was at the bottom end of a dark courtyard. "Who sent you?" a woman asked Daugherty at the door. It reminded him of being sixteen and going to Mrs. Adams's joy house in Montpelier.

"He's with me, Esther."

Esther Cohen ignored them after she let them in; she strode across the room and sat cross-legged on a big dark throne. She was a sight, dressed like a monk in robe and rosary beads, her hair shaved short as a man's.

The whole setup was like Mrs. Adams's, only with costumes. A man with woman-length hair, wearing a sheet and leather sandals, flip-flopped up to the Cohen woman and began talking. Another man, thirty or a couple years younger, with a big round head like a white jack-o'-lantern, was standing talking to a woman in blue, ordinary enough, but his hands were on her rump, feeling around lazy-like. She swatted him away, not meaning it. Daugherty wondered was there an upstairs.

"That's Gastedon."

You noticed his eyes, like a shark's, round and black. Papers littered the floor beside him, and he was pulling more papers out of a child's school satchel and drawing on them. He drew fast as if he were trying to win a bet, and he looked some ways like a gambler, concentrating on that pencil like dice, seven-come-eleven, covering the paper front and back with scribbles. Daugherty saw Gastedon draw the long-haired man's sheep profile, the folds of the sheet, a portrait of a man with horns, a naked man with erect penis, crowded and overlapping. Daugherty had the same feeling that he'd had in the Louvre, looking at Jean-Jacques paint the Mona Lisa. Art was like building. But Daugherty had never seen an artist draw a penis before.

"The example of the Greeks, Esther—" the man with the sheet was saying. He was American, sounded Midwestern, Minneapolis.

Gastedon mumbled something in French, not looking up from his dice game with the pencil.

Esther, the doorkeeper woman, nodded. "That is it," she said. "The first man who makes a thing must make it ugly." She lifted her shaved head; she had the frog face of a schoolmarm but squinting, vivid, irregularly set eyes. "They cannot afford grace or beauty because it must be new, art is inevitably new but beauty is never new."

"That is," said the long-haired man, gesturing like a Greek orator, "that is *exactly* what is wrong with your theory."

"Raymond," said the man with the pie face. "Any theory is wrong. Sex is never theoretical—"

"Radium paintings," a moon-faced woman proclaimed anxiously, her glasses glittering. "Radium increases sexual potency—"

"What do you think of the paintings, Mr. Daugherty?" Peter Lawrence asked.

He nodded over at the group, Cohen, her friends, and Gastedon. "Been lookin' at the folks."

"There's Raymond Duncan in the chiton, Isadora Duncan's brother; the one who paints with radium is Laure Cheneau; Marie Laurencin in blue; the tall one is George Vittal, the poet. But look at Gastedon's paintings."

"Any of these his?"

"Most of them."

Daugherty stared at the walls, embarrassed. There were a lot of them and they were like what kids might do. Dirty-minded kids Franky's age. Angular pink bosoms, stark red roses in a fleshy pot, yellow walls, faces that were nothing but black lines on salmon. "Well," he said politely.

"Gastedon is trying to see in a new way," Peter Lawrence explained. The vocabulary of art had expanded; old polite forms were no longer enough. Gastedon's art took in the language of engineering, which was an innately beautiful way to show the mechanical aspects of human beings; it included animal references, primitive art, the art of children, deliberate crudeness—

Daugherty examined the paintings. There was a big painting of Esther Cohen looking like a squashed toad; flowers with sharp thorns, colored like flesh; a nude with a conical demure torso and legs and, turned backward on her body, a face that looked like it'd died violent.

It was this last one that caught him. The face was like that little young whore he'd seen once at Mrs. Adams's, drunk so bad she was staggering, and spilling out words you never wanted to hear from a woman's mouth. Once he saw that one, he began to see more of them. Flesh like thorns, like maps, like rocks and toads; roses like women's parts— He didn't want to know about this. There was a reason for all the secrecy, Daugherty thought, the passwords, the disguises; there was something ugly happening here.

He felt, suddenly, as if he'd come to someplace farther away than Paris.

"Radium is the male force of science," the moon-faced woman was saying in the background. "When I'm painting, I'm a man."

As if being a man made things easier.

"What do you think of them?" It was Reisden, standing next to him, looking like a man who'd spent all day not thinking of a woman, and resenting it, angry-eyed and tired of being dragged around: like one of those paintings.

"Dunno. Pretty troublin' stuff, Reisden."

In the entryway, floor to ceiling, hung pencil sketches, some well framed, some in cheap frames without mats. A sketch of George Vittal hung at eye level, inscribed *To Esther* and signed *Gastedon*, emphatically underlined. On the same sheet there was a color drawing of the blue woman, much more Louvre art than the painting.

"Gastedon?" Daugherty said. "That one too?"

Reisden nodded, studying it.

"I'd take him for the forger," Daugherty said.

"He's a better man as Mallais."

"No," Daugherty said, surprising himself. "I mean—at least these ain't forgeries." He remembered what Perdita had said, that a good painter wouldn't spend his time on forgeries. "Don't mean I like them."

Jean-Jacques Mallais, Madame Mallais's grandson, came sideways through the door, almost bumping into Daugherty, recognizing him, and nodding awkwardly. Behind him came a man of perhaps thirty-five, brown-haired, muscular, simpleton-faced, with a big French walrus mustache—Daugherty'd seen him, too, somewhere, but couldn't place him. Jean-Jacques was carrying a rain-speckled brown paper bundle. A copy of the Mona Lisa, probably. The mustached porter stood gazing at the wrapping, sucking in his lips. Behind the three of them came a man who looked like King Edward. He began to move around the circle, kissing hands and smiling.

"It's my ex-husband," Milly said, pulling Perdita back with her into Esther's vestibule. "Let's stay here for a moment. I want to see what he's doing."

The King Edward man—Henry de Xico—was making some sort of speech. He stood in front of the fireplace; he brought George Vittal to stand with him on one side, and on the other, Gastedon. He hand-waved at each of them in turn, like a magician. Gastedon bent down and brought up something, picture-sized and picture-shaped, with a cloth over it. Like a magician, Xico whipped the cover off.

It was another Mona Lisa.

It was bright. It was the same Mona Lisa, but bright, as if it had been new-painted. Pearly, creamy skin; rose and smoky shadows in the famous smile; satin sleeves colored as bright as a goldfinch. It wasn't the same as the one in the museum. But it looked real.

"G-d," Reisden murmured, "*that* makes Gastedon a suspect, doesn't it?"

"The swine!" Milly whispered. "That pig Henry! He wants George to throw a *copy* into the Seine!"

De Xico was talking. "Two weeks from now," Reisden translated for Daugherty, "January twenty-eighth, at noon, Xico, Gastedon, and Vittal will arrive on the Pont-Neuf. They will display the old Mona Lisa together with the new. They will throw the old Mona Lisa off the Pont-Neuf and crown the new.... I must tell Dotty, it'll be almost outside her windows."

Jean-Jacques Mallais unwrapped his painting. The mustached man barely spared a glance for Gastedon's Mona Lisa, but he picked up Jean-Jacques's and set it on a chair.

The speech was over; the guests drifted away. Gastedon asked the mustached man something. The man dug in the big pockets of his coat and brought out, wrapped in shabby newspaper, a clay head, a cruel slab-nosed mask with bulging eyes, like you might buy in some Mexican market. Gastedon set it on the table and ran his hands over it as if it were the most beautiful thing he'd ever seen. Gastedon and the man spoke, then the man picked it up and rewrapped it, holding out his hand: Give me money. Gastedon turned out his pockets. He had no money.

"Gastedon's poor," Daugherty said to Reisden.

"And he improves masterpieces, and he and Jean-Jacques know each other—"

He broke off as though someone had cut his throat.

Perdita'd come after all. She was talking to Esther Cohen and a short-haired Frenchwoman in a suit. The Frenchwoman was pretty enough, but Perdita looked prettier than Daugherty had ever seen her, casual and elegant and just a little daring. Why, Daugherty thought, she had makeup on.

"You knew she was coming," Reisden said.

"Didn't, son, but you're old enough to take care of yourself."

Reisden gave him one look and faded back against the wall, thin as ice and twice as cold, watching her.

Daugherty went over and told her hello; he didn't mention Reisden and she didn't ask where he was. Gastedon was sketching Perdita, all straight lines, a Mona Lisa pose, unfocused eyes. By the time he was done, Reisden was there too, looking at the sketch, looking at her, eyes to make the paper burn, but didn't say anything. She didn't know he was there, or if she did, she wasn't telling. They stared past each other. She took Daugherty's arm, reaching almost past Reisden, and introduced him to her French friend. "This is Milly Xico, Mr. Daugherty; Milly, *je vous présente Monsieur Roy Daugherty, un ami qui vient de Boston.*"

The Frenchwoman smiled up at him flirtatiously and mockingly.

The three of them went around the pictures, where Daugherty said nothing because he didn't want to tell Perdita what these pictures were about; instead he watched Reisden ostentatiously looking at the mask and the sketch and the pictures, and not coming up to say hello. In the far room there was a little upright piano. Perdita gravitated to it; she couldn't see it, must've smelled it. She played while the Frenchwoman sang music-hall songs.

Milly, the French gal's name was; she leaned forward so, Daugherty could see straight down the low neck of her blouse. He thought her hair was dyed, and he was certain she was wearing makeup, and he knew more or less what kind of a woman she was; but what was Perdita doing with her?

They broke off a moment while Perdita spoke to the Frenchwoman. "She ought to sing in a lower key, don't you think, Mr. Daugherty? Like this." She imitated a singer's growl.

Above her head the Frenchwoman's eyes met Daugherty's. They were blue, like sapphires. He felt a little jolt around his stomach.

"Milly, connaissez-vous cette chanson—?"

Perdita began to sing in a soft voice, low-toned, a song in English that Daugherty had heard once in a Negro bar. (Where'd *Perdita* heard it?) After a minute Milly joined in, *la la la* in her big rough voice, and all the time she looked at Daugherty. It had begun to rain again, and the pattering of the rain on the roof of the studio mixed with their voices. People quieted around them; Daugherty forgot about Reisden, watching Perdita and the French gal.

The stars are a-shining, hear the turtle dove,
I say the stars are a-shining, can't you hear the turtle dove,
Don't you want somebody,
Somebody to love. . . .

Something went past Daugherty like a ghost: like the memory of times at Mrs. Adams's, so that he was hot under his suit and his collar was tight. From the wall the flesh flowers watched him. The Frenchwoman's bosoms were lightly freckled, the freckles were hardly visible, like sand, as if she had been swimming at an ocean beach. He wanted to brush them off.

The evening was coming to a close. Jean-Jacques went off, casting Milly a last hopeful glance. Milly had other plans.

She drifted past the chair where Jean-Jacques' painting rested. She looked at the Mona Lisa; she looked at the fire.

The elephantine American, the one with the glasses, should be good for at least a late dinner. (She wondered if he wore flannel underwear, too.) And there was Sacha-the-panther, who had made his little girl cry, who'd deserted her at the first hint of trouble—but who'd bought Gastedon's sketch of her tonight, after all. Why, to put on his wall with his other trophies? To show the vicomtesse?

Tonight he was not only a hunter, he was hungry; those light eyes never left Perdita.

If Milly were to go off with the American, Perdita would be left with the panther. Milly's imagination furnished quarrels, surprises, silk underwear instead of flannel, jealousies, desires—

"Have 'Sacha' take you home," Milly said into Perdita's ear.

"No!" Perdita whispered back, but Milly was gone. In the fireplace, dry wood was snapping out sparks and something fat was hissing. Perdita moved away. People were getting their coats. She didn't know where Milly had put hers.

"I'll walk you as far as the taxi rank," Alexander said, "if you're leaving." He got her coat without waiting for her yes or no.

They walked toward the cab stand, he guiding her arm. Not speaking, she felt her other senses all the more keenly: the pressure of his hand on her elbow, his smell of chemicals, the wet wool of his coat, the warmth of his body. They stood in a doorway waiting for taxis. There were none; the stand was deserted.

"I've lost my magic," he said. "I used to be able to call up taxis at will."

They stood in the narrow door together. She was cold and tired and shaky-legged; she thought of leaning against him. If she touched him she could tell what he was thinking, what expression was on his face. If she touched him—

She stood carefully apart, listening to his breathing.

"Milly Xico is in search of prey," Alexander said.

"Mr. Daugherty? She doesn't like men, Alexander."

"Then she'll spit him out before completely consuming him. It will do him no lasting harm."

If Mr. Daugherty were a woman, Perdita thought, it might. Her breasts ached fiercely; her hips felt full. *Congestion of the pelvis,* Dr. Magnin's pamphlet called it. Due to sexual excitement. She was—like a person who has given up a drug, and now wanted it. "I wonder, will he do what he doesn't approve of?"

"Sometimes one does, love," he said.

It took that little, it was that simple; a slip of the tongue, a word, *love.* She turned and put her hands on his face, and felt his breath ragged on her palms. At that moment they heard a taxi behind them; he helped her in and got in after her.

They went to Courbevoie; and in the taxi they kissed and held each other frantically, not speaking. He unbuttoned the neck of her blouse down to her waist; he unhooked the tabs of her corset. She felt triumphant, panicked, sad. It had been clearer when she loved him, clearer when she knew she would leave him; even Milly's ambiguous friendship was clearer than this, even while she wanted shamelessly to have him. What shall I do, she thought, and even, What shall I think? But they arrived at Courbevoie and she had no answer. Panting, disheveled, she wrapped her coat around her disarranged clothes; they left the taxi by the quai de Seine, and went into the garden of the house that was no longer quite theirs.

In the garden it was still almost warm, a night to watch the winter moon and feel your breath fog around your face. They weren't ready to go inside, to find whatever they would find in the house. He put his arm around her (his hand brushed against her sore breasts and she breathed hard, half a gasp, half a sigh). The chill from the river rose around her knees, under her skirts, around her waist. He closed the garden door; she shivered, feeling the fog crawl on her skin. He opened her coat and began to rub her body with the flat of his hand, as if he were seeing every inch of her naked with his palms. She shuddered with pleasure and the cold.

There was some paving by the rosebushes, some flat stones; he put his coat on it as a pillow and laid her down on it, and lay on top of her, pressing her down; she was almost crushed, and struggled, but the struggle was part of what they were doing; she pressed herself against him. She was not in control of this because of something she had in her handbag, she was not in control at all, because she wasn't going to do anything about what she had in her handbag; she was in danger, in trouble, exalted, worse, she was helping him. She opened up her buttons, she slid her narrow skirt up and her petticoats aside. She would do anything to keep him, she thought, anything at all, give up her music, her future, her good name, anything; she could not stop herself giving them away.

It was cold, freezing cold, raining; her hair fell down around them; they were entangled, entangled, in her wet hair, in each other's arms, with each other again.

Chapter 51

He is listening to her play the piano. It is a concert somewhere, in a theater; she is onstage, back to him, and he is in the wings. He smells a theater: dust, cobwebs, the persistent stink of gaslights and rosin. Since he has known her, he dreams smells, as she does. There is applause; he holds up the green-glassed flashlight that is her mark for getting offstage. She walked toward him, trusting.

He is driving her in a car across some flat endless road in America, land of symphony orchestras. They crash against the tree in an explosion of glass; he flings his arm up and is thrown out of the car. Her scream breaks off.

Now I will be happy, he thinks. The worst part is always that one is happy to have survived.

But he feels tremendous hurt, an agony of loss. She is lying on a marble-white bed under a thin veil, a yellow wax woman with bruised blue lips, half-open eyes. He holds her hand between his own. Her hands and fingers were sensitive, a piano player's; now for a moment they seem to stir in his. He takes her in his arms, rubbing her skin, blowing breath into her, trying to give her his body warmth.

He woke himself trying to wake her, and woke her in the bed beside him.

"I'm sorry, I'm going for a walk, I can't sleep."

He walked in the rain through the shuttered main street

and the market of Courbevoie, trying to will away panic and despair. He wanted to escape the connection between them; it would only hurt them. He wanted to be with her every moment of the night.

After what was probably hours he went back to the house. He listened at the bedroom door for her breathing; he furtively shone their flashlight in on her. She was curled in the bedclothes, asleep, her arms around his pillow. He watched the rise and fall of her breath and thought of the green-glassed flashlight in his dream. He did not know how she actually got offstage; the flashlight was a dream invention; but he saw her again, coming toward him, toward hurt and capture, down a path of light.

In the morning, Perdita's stomach felt queasy again; she ate a stomach-mint from her purse and got on her dressing-gown and slippers. Alexander was asleep in the living room, not even his coat over him, with a scientific journal fallen on the floor by him, and the fire and the furnace had both gone almost out.

She would be a good housekeeper. With her white cane she groped around the basement until she found the furnace in the center and the coal bin off in a corner. She lugged a hod of coal from the bin to the furnace, raked up the banked coals from last night, and spread the new coal over them. She toiled upstairs and stood shivering, waiting for the heat to rise, thinking of the cold air on her legs last night.

She practiced, using the edge of the kitchen table as a silent keyboard, then left off. She hadn't the heart for music, and her fingers thumping the table would wake him. She wanted to let him sleep; until he woke, he was her lover.

When the room began to be warm, she went into the kitchen, drew water for coffee, and put the kettle on the stove's gas ring, one of Alexander's efficiencies; he had installed it over New Year's so they didn't need to build up the stove fire before having coffee. If Alexander were neither rich, handsome, nor clever, he would still be the man who made it easy to heat water in the morning.

As she stood by the counter measuring coffee, it suddenly smelled so nauseating that she felt weak-kneed and a rush of saliva came up into her mouth. She let the measuring spoon fall and leaned over the sink, away from the gritty, burned smell. She gagged and swallowed, and finally, when she was sure she was not going to be sick, she sat down on the floor, breathing heavily, and put her hands over her face, shutting out the world, almost cowering.

"Perdita?" He was standing by the door. He did not kneel down and take her in his arms, as he would have before they had broken up; then he did, but she felt the distance even while he held her. Today they should have learned how to be sensible again, they should have taken themselves back to Paris and said goodbye, or at very most they should have agreed that Mr. Daugherty would not separate them. Sickness was a distraction from that important business; instead, here she was, trying not to throw up on his shirt. He's disappointed in me, she thought, and thinking of all the people who would be disappointed in her, she closed her eyes and moaned.

"Oh, my dear." He carried her back into the bedroom (it was like a parody of a marriage) and helped her out of her dressing gown. Underneath it she was wearing nothing. Last night they had not thought of clothes. "Do you want your nightgown?"

"Yes," she said faintly.

He helped her on with it and began to button it for her. His fingers moved across her breasts very gently, perhaps by accident, but she felt painfully seen and wondered if her bosom felt as big to him as to her. There was a silence. Perhaps he was looking at her. His hand stayed on her breast, fingertips only, as if it helped him to think, as if he were considering what to say.

"Have you been sick like this before?" he said.

"A little bit," she said, "for a while."

Neither of them said anything for a moment; she wondered if he thought she didn't know what this sickness meant, and whether he was unsure himself; and then he said "Have you not seen a doctor?" just as she said, "I saw a doctor yesterday."

"And he said—?"

He said I am not pregnant, she had only to say, and everything would be put back as it should be; they would have their chance to be sensible about each other, to give each other up or at least to choose better; they would have all the chances that they did not really have. "I asked him," she said, "if precautions, of the kind we take, could ever fail. He said no—" She didn't say any more but she didn't finish the sentence, leaving it starkly a question.

Alexander took one indrawn breath. "He is wrong," he said.

"I thought he might be," she said. Now she had said it and she couldn't take it back.

"But he examined you—"

She shook her head, apologetically, no, and didn't know whether she was apologizing for the doctor's incompetence or for having accepted the doctor's answer.

"You had better be examined," he said.

A doctor came, a Frenchman indignant at being called out on Sunday. The doctor poked and prodded her stomach efficiently, distantly, he didn't approve of her, turning her this way and that, moving her knee aside impatiently, as though he could have conducted her life much better than she had herself, down to every motion of her body. She was wearing her keeping-ring, but their half-furnished house would fool no one; he called her mademoiselle. He told her nothing; he went out in the salon, where Alexander was waiting, and told Alexander. She lay in the bed and listened to the doctor say, in a sarcastic jovial way, that Mademoiselle wasn't dying, ha-ha, far from it; *mais non, elle est bien florissante.* She was flourishing. She got up; she swallowed hard, buttoned her dressing gown to the neck, and began to brush her hair. The door closed behind the doctor and there was a long silence, while she waited for Alexander and counted brushstrokes, seventy-eight, seventy-nine. . . .

He came into the room and sat down beside her; after a moment he took the brush out of her hands and held her hands in his. His were freezing and, just a little, shaking. He sat beside her and put his arm around her.

"Will you marry me?" he said.

It took courage to say that, but it seemed so incongruous a thing to say, she bit her lip so as not to laugh. She would marry him now, she had to. She had wanted to prove she loved him.

"You don't have to. There are alternatives."

She did have to; she was in trouble. Some girls went "on a long visit to a relative," then came back alone and pretended that nothing had happened. But can you imagine dropping out of the Paris Conservatory because you were going on a long visit to a relative? It was funny. And besides, she wanted to marry him. She covered her face and laughed in a painful series of hiccups, and he held her tightly and almost shook her. "Don't," he said, "don't. Perdita, don't." Finally he slapped her, quickly and apologetically, across the face. It made her stare; I must have been having hysterics, she thought; but still she fell back across the bed, her hand to her cheek. She sounded so like Anys, so like the woman crying in the corridor at Madame Bézou's, so like every woman in the world.

"You don't want to marry *me*," she explained.

"We can be married only long enough to legitimate the child, if you wish to have the child," he said. "And you do not need to have it."

She thought of Madame Bézou's. That was the alternative he meant.

When they had first made love, he had told her that *concepti* (that was the Latin word he'd used) were only seedlings. Weeding was not immoral, he'd said.

"Weeding" was the right thing to do, she knew that. They oughtn't to marry each other; they had made that so clear.

Seedlings. Volunteers pulled up from the garden in spring, nothing but two leaves and a stem, softening and drying out on the brick path. When she had been a little girl, she had rescued them all and planted them again in a corner of the garden.

She couldn't be a little girl now.

She sat in a fragile silence in the kitchen with him, drinking hot milk flavored with coffee. It still tasted black and gritty. *I want that danger,* she'd said to Milly only yesterday. *It will frighten and exalt and change me. It is profound and necessary.* She smelled on her hand the remains of the Perfume of the Lady in Black, sweet-bad and spoiled, reminding her of the rubber-and-vinegar atmosphere of Madame Bézou's. She laid her palm on her stomach, feeling nausea like a tangle of string tensing and knotting.

She went into the salon and stood by the Érard, not playing, but with the fingers of one hand touching the keys. She couldn't touch a key, couldn't press one down, the sound would have been too loud, too lovely.

Two choices: her career, their child. Alexander had already told her she couldn't have both.

"Would you like to take a walk?" he said.

They went to the Grande Jatte, where they had never been, a little island with only two streets, thick with fog. They walked past boatbuilding shops—she could smell tar, pine, and paint, and the sharp smells made the saliva come up in her mouth again. They went down some steps between a boat-builder's and a villa, and turned onto a slippery clay path where she had to take his arm and hold up her skirt out of the dirt and leaves, clumsy and awkward and womanly.

This was a waste place, the path barely a track between saplings, the whole island closed up tight, a summer place seized by winter. He led her right to the edge of the water, where the Seine chewed at the bank. He stood with his back against a tree and held her against him, his hands on her arms. She thought, one push, one stumble, would have sent her into the Seine, and she almost wanted it. "Are you dizzy again?" he asked. No; she thought of women: wives, mothers, girlfriends, prostitutes; inches in the daily paper; voices near a railroad station; the click of mothers' knitting needles in the corridors of the Conservatoire. A river of women, who were people individually but together were invisible and silent, so that no one thought of them.

He held her, it was all he could do; he walked with her in the bit of woods behind the boatwrights' and villas at the Grande Jatte, where Seurat and Monet and Mallais had painted. He looked blindly at the low arches of willows, dim in the fog. When he stopped, she stood in his arms, subtly rigid. He didn't know what to do: with her, to her, for her.

She had stood by the piano and not played, simply touched the keys. He hadn't said *I'm sorry* again, it was beyond being sorry for. He stood at a great lonely distance from his life and hers.

He had nothing to offer her, nothing to give her, not even love. He had thought he had experience. His precautions had never failed before.

He wanted to keep her.

Walking through the fog, they found themselves on a path, at the end of which was a patch of purple. Not only the door of the fishing shack was purple; the whole tiny one-room construction was a bright red-purple that reminded Reisden of Esther Cohen's paintings. From the boatbuilders' yard above came the smells of glue and paint and the urine smell of fresh-sawed oak. By the fishing shack, someone had built a small smoky fire in a circle of stones among the damp leaves, and a girl about thirteen years old was crouched by the fire, cooking a spitted fish, while her younger brother stood by the fire and kicked bits of grass into the sizzling flames. Their father was on the bank below, fishing.

He looked for a moment at the children, silent, transfixed by the children.

The girl stood up, brushing damp leaves off her wool stockings. The children's father, seeing a stranger watching his children, climbed the slope.

" '*Sieur, 'dame, vous cherchez—?*"

Mechanically, Reisden asked why the shack was purple, and when it had been painted.

The girl rolled her eyes and knelt down by the fire again, dismissing them. "It's because of Nathalie," her father explained. The boy nodded in a superior way. "It was her favorite color," her father said. "When she was six years old—"

"When I was six years old," Nathalie grumbled. "Oh, when I was six years old! It's a *stupid* color, Papa. All my friends laugh at me."

"Stupid," the little boy agreed.

And he could not stop looking at them. *Monsieur, your mistress is going to have a child:* that was what the doctor had told him. He thought of the children's stories he read Tiggy. Stories for children are always about threats: the child cut up and buried under the juniper tree, the child turned into a slave, the child sent into the woods, to the hungry monster. Reisden looked down the slope at Nathalie and her brother, and saw the father looking up at him, guarded and uncomprehending, with the eyes of the good woodsman or the rescuing shepherd. "Take care of your children," Reisden said abruptly.

These innocents had never heard of Mallais. Reisden confirmed that the shack had been painted in 1903, and left them bickering when the fish would be done—"Papa, don't you think I'm old enough to know *anything*?" Behind them, as he and Perdita climbed the slope, he heard them on the edge of a quarrel, their voices sharp with relief.

Take care of your children, she heard Alexander say, and neither of them said anything else until they had walked back to Courbevoie. In the market square, they stopped by the church. Services were over; they went in.

Inside the dimness of St.-Denis, a flare of candles marked the statue of the Virgin Mary. *My soul doth magnify the Lord. . . . May it be with Thy handmaiden according to Thy word.* Perdita sank into a chair and listened to the silence, the immense stone silence of a French church, hollow and reverberant, an urn for music.

To try to make a decision about children and motherhood inside a French church—

It would be so easy to think there was no decision, and to take neither credit nor blame. But that would feel like Florrie and her friends, saying *We have to do this* and *We have to do that.*

From the nave she heard a priest saying something, and then a baby crying; and what reminded her of her duty made a noise among the pillars and the arches and reminded her of music.

If she loved Alexander most, in the way he thought he wanted to be loved, she would do what he thought was right, and what was really right for them, which was not to have a child, at least not now; but the road to that led through Madame Bézou's. If she were the good woman she thought she was, she would accept marriage and motherhood and say goodbye to whatever else she might have been.

She might have the child and give it up to someone else. To whom, Uncle Gilbert? (No; of course he would want it, but he had an heir; it would be very cruel to the child.) She could give it to Alexander, who did not know the first thing about a child and would probably leave it in a taxi, the way he did his umbrellas. She could have the child and keep it, but not marry, and that would gain her nothing, because she would lose her good name and not be able to tour. Audiences don't care for women without husbands.

What would happen if she "weeded" it? For her it would be like what had happened to Richard. A feeling of relief, of gratitude at first, and then a sense of something terrible.

For Alexander it would be terrible, and he didn't dare know it. Look at him with Tiggy; and he was telling her she could take his child away from him, but what had he told the

man on the Grande Jatte? The same thing he should have said
to her.

"Weeding" would solve some things; it was *a* responsible
thing to do. But they would know what they had done. And it
would get into his sense of himself, and their caring at all for
each other, and her music—

Mean little shallow soul, poor freak, that was all she cared
about: Aborting a child would hurt the music.

St.-Denis had been built in the eighteenth century, a light-
filled cube with a rotunda and a Louis XVI altar, where no
doubt, in the Revolution, the French had worshipped Reason.
From inside the door Reisden watched Perdita, sitting in a little
rush chair in the attenuated light of the nave, the orange feathers
drooping from her hat, her cheeks pale, her gloved hands
clasped.

He doubted very much that her God would advise abortion, and so she would marry him, one way or another; and a
marriage in form was too European for her Boston soul. She
would pretend that she wanted marriage in the full sense of the
word. She would try to make it work.

My wife, some malicious element of himself whispered. My
child.

He thought of ingenious schemes to save her. They involved
feeding her substances that were after all systemic poisons, arranging a "miscarriage" before she committed herself. . . . Oh
G-d. Shameful and typical. He was a liar and a murderer, he
was trained to do it.

A group was coming down the aisle from the sacristy: a man
whom Reisden recognized as the butcher from the high street,
a big mustached man of thirty, perpendicular in a tight-fitting
suit; an old woman and a middle-aged one; a priest; two or three

children; and, last, a young woman carrying a baby. It was a christening. The group gathered around the font, Vermeer-distinct in the chalky light. No, he thought, no, no, no. The baby began to cry. He saw Perdita turn suddenly in her chair, listening intently, as if the cry were her own voice.

Without any warning, and as physically as if the sight were water thrown into his face, he saw an explosion of candles, night, something in a white veil. A wedding. No. A child's cap floating in a copper christening font, and the water around it all red, a child's christening clothes clotted with red, and he tried to turn his eyes away; and incongruously, saw the girl, Nathalie, sitting at the edge of the Seine, threading her hook with bread. The hook glittered; she raised her eyes and looked at him.

He went outside and stood shaking on the steps, in the rain, intently watching the puddles, which for him were still running with clotted red. He abhorred the moralism that be-lieved, if choices had to be made, an unborn human life was al-ways better than an adult woman's. His irrational mind saw hooks and instruments, a basin full of blood, and a child.

Never kill a child; never hurt a child; there was Richard.

Perdita came out and stood beside him. Her face was half an hour of anguish. He was glad she couldn't see his.

"I can't do it. I'm sorry," she said, "Alexander, I'm sorry, I can't make it come out any other way, for me it would be murder."

He had expected moral sentiments from her, but not from himself, not that wrenching hallucination, nor this relief.

"Murder lasts," he said. "Don't do it." He did not know whether he was telling her truth or an enormous lie. At a chris-tening, he thought, the Guérarts say, *This time it will be differ-ent,* and when they talk to their children, they say: *I wanted you.* I want you. Give me yourself. Hurt for me.

"I am going to marry you," she said. "I mean I want to, if you'll have me. Not in form, Alexander. I haven't had a moment's happiness since you left. I'm not going to have music now; Mr. Ellis wouldn't put me in front of audiences with a baby and no husband, and I won't tour with a baby even if I could do it, it would be cruel. I love you," she repeated, almost to herself; "I have loved you ever since I first knew you, and now, Alexander, I want to live in a better way, I want to put everything else aside and give my *whole* heart to you."

She held her hands out, hoping for his. He clasped them in one hand and put his arm around her. Every word of it would have been laughed off a stage. She had never wanted marriage since the moment on the Institute steps, three years ago. She did not want it now. If she had been honest, she would have asked for a marriage in form.

He was asking emotional clarity of a confused girl, ten years his junior, who wanted to do the right thing. She was trying for more than she could do. One always does.

"I want you," he said. "I want it to work out for us."

The word stopped him for a moment, *us,* as he had not used it in ten years, meaning my wife and me. And for one moment he was shatteringly happy, happy without believing it, wanting to believe.

Everyone wants to be happy, even the forger; even the forger wants to pretend his work is true.

Chapter 52

Leonard sees it now: the Baron de Reisden does nothing for the Mona Lisa because he has a woman of his own. She's a pretty girl, delicate, but vague-eyed, smelling of perfume. Around her neck she wears a cheap necklace with a portrait of the Mona Lisa. It is a strange little detail, tasteless, mocking. They leave together. She takes his arm, and sex stirs between them like a miasma.

Leonard follows them.

In the mist, he sees them stop together at a cabstand. They talk; they move together, then apart; they turn to each other, they kiss. They sway back and forth in the doorway, a four-legged, two-backed monster. A cab stops for them, has to wait for them while they untangle.

I miss her so. I must speak with you, I must talk about her. I am not worthy of her. Liar. Liar.

Leonard stands deserted on the street, shaking.

Sunday. Leonard takes the tram to Asnières. He waits across the street from the cemetery, watching Barry's Tomb, symbol of fidelity. On the little island the fog is soft and warm as squirrel fur, but with sudden shudders as cold gusts blow across the grass. Two black pigeons peck at the gravel; the lights are haloed in the fog. Below the walls, the Seine murmurs, and from the fog around them toll the little bells of the barges, the bells of ghost churches at the end of the river.

In the cemetery, suspicious loiterers wait. An old woman has been tending a little grave for an hour. A man in top hat and black overcoat waits by Barry's Tomb, but it is not the baron. A man detaches himself from the yellow-lighted gatehouse, a man in a uniform, with a badge of authority gleaming on his cap.

A woman walks down the street under a red umbrella leaking blood.

Here are the river, and the bells, and a barge moored, fogbound by Sunday; there's only the single policeman, but a bargeman loiters on the shed of his barge, neither doing anything nor inside in the warmth, and on the street outside the gatehouse a *tondeur de chiens*, with his painted scissors and his comb, is clipping the same white poodle for the third time.

And there's the baron now, at the far edge of the cemetery, a tall dark-haired man, elegant in a rumpled black overcoat, standing not where he is supposed to be but half-hidden under some trees. He is speaking with a white-bearded man, who looks at his pocket watch as though the two of them are impatient for a wife or mother to finish her duties among the tombs.

They are standing close to the iron railing around the cemetery. Leonard opens his umbrella, a man on his way to buy a bottle of wine, the newspaper, a loaf of bread; he pulls his scarf up around his face. By the iron railing is a tram stop; beyond the railing are the baron and his companion. He waits by the tram stop, facing away from them, jingling sweaty centimes in his pocket, listening.

"I spoke about these letters with Aristide Berthet at Physio. Psych. Berthet thinks the spelling's so bad that the man is likely to have other verbal difficulties, and in consequence psychological ones, possibly quite severe. They are likely to have been noticed when he was vetted for the army. He may be a vagrant; he's unlikely to hold more than a menial job. A typical background for a murder on impulse."

Leonard feels his lips draw back in an incredulous snarl. Ah, that's not him. He has a good job, he can *read*, after all. Impulse? No! Love, love, love!

He almost goes over to the fence to tell them so, but isn't that what they want? They'd have trapped him then.

"Berthet says Our Artist is likely to turn suddenly violent." That's what they want, yes, they want to trap a monster they've created, the man who kills on impulse, that's what they put in the paper; that's the one they want. They don't care about Leonard at all.

Leonard stubs out his cigarette and walks away, raging.

Chapter 53

Alexander and she would be married on Monday, the twenty-fourth, eight days from now. It would be simply an official ceremony, he told her, like the signing of a contract. Did she want a church wedding, which would be more difficult? No.

There were formalities to be gone through, he said, French officialdom being what it was, papers to be collected and signed. He would take care of all of those; she was simply to practice for Mrs. Bacon's.

What did Mrs. Bacon's mean now? She was a professional with an engagement; she would keep it; but it couldn't mean anything.

He would tell Dotty on Friday evening, he said, after the debut, which would give Dotty the weekend to get used to the idea. "I hope she'll make no difficulty about the twenty-seventh. It's all the more important for you to get reviews now," he said.

Why? It didn't matter, she said.

"It will be better for us if you have music," he said.

She would devote herself to Alexander and the child, she said; she would be Dotty's sister-in-law as best she could; she would learn how to be a European housewife, how to do Alexander credit.

But there would be time and leisure for her music, he said, and he wanted her to keep it up.

He had an errand in midafternoon, which he was willing to give up, but she sent him off to Asnières. "Go," she said, "please go, I want to be by myself in our house for a bit. I'm perfectly all right." *Our house,* she said, like a wife. But when he had gone, she sat at the piano, and then nerved herself and got her hands down on the keys and practiced.

She gave it a good three hours, and then, when she was tired, she thought out what she had to do.

After Dotty's, she would not simply give up touring, and being managed by Mr. Ellis, and all the opportunities for music in America: she would not so much as practice. She had spent too much of herself on music. If she were not vigilant with herself, if she let music preoccupy her, she would be in marriage what Florrie was in music now, half-trained and full of excuses. She would love Alexander and the child.

She was badly sighted, which meant things took time. Counting the laundry took twenty-five minutes for Perdita, ten for a normally sighted woman. A normal woman who wanted to go shopping went shopping; for Perdita it took any number of days, first rounding up a sighted friend to help her, then doing it when they were both free. Love shows itself in the use of time, in details and choices: practicing scales against checking the household laundry; keeping the garden neat, taking classes; eating sandwiches at midnight on the train, making sure dinner is on the table when he comes home, cuddling the baby, checking the notes in another edition because the first edition might have got something wrong, dressing so Dotty might approve, being there for him, being there; doing what makes you the person you choose to be. Love is inexhaustible, but details go on forever, and the test of love was which she chose, laundry or scales.

It all came down on her at once, and she sat silent, her hands helpless, unable to play.

She cried (it was only shock; she'd get over it), and practiced a little, and wiped her eyes on her sleeve, and touched the keys one by one, *feeling* them while she still had the right to feel them in the way she wanted, as the crown of an orchestra, a voice in the chorus of music, the wonderful thing she had been given in order to give it up.

Alexander's household would have servants, she supposed. She would have to think of servants, a housekeeper, a nurse. Would she and Alexander live here? If not, where? What would she wear to be married in? Who would help her shop for it? Would Milly? Did it matter? Dotty was the one who cared about that, and Dotty would be furious.

Could Dotty tell to look at her? She held her hand against her flat stomach. It didn't matter; Dotty could count to nine; if she were angry without reason now, later she'd have cause.

Dotty would have to be persuaded, somehow, that she was good enough for Alexander. She would have to be a good housewife. She thought of furniture, of plates for dinner parties, of silverware, of damask dinner napkins; of where napkins came from, who folded them, who ironed them, who set them out on the table and cleared them away and sent them out to be washed yet again. Dotty fussed over a bent teaspoon because it was one of twenty-four; because it had to be fixed or replaced or matched. She would have to fuss over teaspoons too. She would have to play by Dotty's elaborate rules, which Dotty had spent her whole life devising.

If she had to, she would.

Eventually she got up and put on lights; it was quite dark by now. The house was cold and damp; neither of them had thought of the furnace all day. She put on a sweater, then her coat.

She was getting hungry. She felt around the counter and in the cold-store; there was nothing to eat. The canned goods were featureless cylinders; she got her magnifying glass out of her purse and held cans nearly pressed against her nose to see the labels, but the light was too bad.

The market would be closed by now; she'd have to go out to a café.

She decided she would open just any can, but she could not find a can opener among the sharp and unfamiliar shapes in the half-empty drawers; she felt so worn-out and hollow, she sat down at the kitchen table. On the table she found the opener (it must be Alexander who hadn't put it back, she thought, and almost cried from sudden frustration at him). She chose what turned out to be canned peas. She stood at the sink eating peas out of the cold broth with her fingers, then suddenly felt, not so much sick as horribly frightened.

There was a tapping at the door. "Mademoiselle? Mademoiselle Perdita? I thought I'd just come up to see you," Madame Mallais said.

Of course—she pulled herself together—after she'd been sitting here for what could have been hours, with a coat on and the shades probably not down. She would have come to visit too, if she'd been in her neighbor's place and seen something wrong, and felt as shy for breaking into someone's privacy. "It's all right," she said. "Come in."

"You haven't set up your kitchen yet?" They had thought they had, but— "I brought some soup," said Madame Mallais. Not soup but *soupe*, French stew. "And a *demi-bâtard* loaf, and some of my gingerbread." There was a mingled-hot-food smell like a basket being uncovered, as if someone's mother had come to visit, comforting and not asking too many questions. One of the invisible river of women.

They heated the stew on the burner, and sat in the kitchen and ate bread and butter and drank hot milk mixed with coffee and sprinkled with cinnamon. For a wonder, Alexander and she had bought cinnamon.

"I'm going to be married in a week," Perdita said finally. "I'm happy about it; I've wanted to marry him for a long, long time." The words made her throat dry, they were so true and so incomplete.

The two women sat in the kitchen silence. Madame Mallais had found and started up the kitchen clock, which kept up a hollow French *toc, tac, toc.* We have a kitchen clock, Perdita thought, but still no pepper mill, which Alexander thinks is a necessity.

"It's different, to be married," Madame said.

"Oh, yes." Perdita pressed the backs of her wrists against her eyes.

"For me, it didn't feel right at all. I had always been the servant," Madame Mallais said, "and now I was Madame. I had to wear a hat and leather shoes, and gloves to make my hands white like a woman who sat in the parlor all day."

The clock ticked unmercifully in the silence.

"Yes," Perdita said. "It's—being someone else, doing other things, all of a sudden. Being someone I don't know. Doing things I'm not good at. That's difficult. I'll make do."

"Oh, but you'll do your *piano*!" Madame Mallais leaned forward and grasped her hand strongly. "You won't change that. And that will give you strength."

"I'm going to have a baby, Madame Suzanne, and—my sight isn't very good—I'll have all I can do."

"Ah," Madame said practically. "That's why you're getting married so quick?"

She nodded wordlessly.

"Are you happy?" Madame said.

"I wanted to marry him," Perdita said again.

"And the baby, that's all right?"

"That's *good*," she said, surprising herself a little. It was, too. She loved Alexander so inadequately that he thought she did not love him at all; but a baby she knew how to love. Now she had made her decision, she dared to think of the changes in her body as someone else, the beginnings of a person: oh, she thought, I do not want to hurt *you*.

"The music won't let you go," Madame Suzanne said solemnly.

She thought of Florrie trying to do her glissandos. "No, it'll let me go just fine," she said.

"The—laundry didn't let me go," Madame Mallais said. She called it *laungdry*. "You smile, but I liked laundry. And I was a gardener. Not much for talents, but—! When I was round out to here, the laundry was never done right, no one scrubbed out the grime from Mallais's shirts, and there weren't enough roses, only weeds, but I couldn't give it up, here." Perdita heard a hollow thump; Madame Mallais had struck her bosom with her hand. "My mind said to me, do the laundry, do the garden, and you'll be—"

"You'll be distracted," Perdita said. "You'll spend time on it rather than other things. I would be distracted, Madame."

"Busy with nothing finished." Madame Suzanne sighed. "Selfish, slatternly—calm . . ."

Perdita shook her head. "I want to do better than that for Alexander."

"I couldn't keep my gloves on," Madame Suzanne said. "I needed my river and my dirt. I had to take myself back a little," she said, "to love anyone at all."

Take yourself back? You can't take yourself back from a baby, you don't want to. From an exigent cousin-in-law, who was everything Alexander had for family? From Alexander?

He was the only one who urged her to keep up music, but he didn't mean it. Music would only get in the way of love.

"Please," Madame Suzanne said, taking both Perdita's hands in hers. "Please play your piano, Mademoiselle Perdita. I listen to you going on hour after hour, all by yourself, and I lay wages it won't let you go no more nor my work did me, and you'll end up in trouble and grief."

"What do you mean, madame?"

One of those long silences, that might have meant something to a seeing person but was only frustration to Perdita. "It wouldn't be right to tell you," Madame Suzanne said. "It was something that happened to me, but it couldn't happen to you."

"I can't," Perdita said. "He thinks he wants me to, but he wants someone else, and I have to be the someone he wants now. I do love him, and I will be happy to have his child." Her voice began to quaver. And I will not cry, she said to herself firmly, I will not cry; but thinking of the baby broke her; she thought of the music she would not be able to share with the baby or give to the baby, because she would have given it up, and she put her hands over her face and was gathered into Madame Mallais's motherly arms and cried, sobbing uncontrollably, mourning the piano.

Chapter 54

Leonard is oddly pleased with being angry at the baron. It goes with the weather, which is strangely warm, strangely—loose and lax, almost breathless, deceiving, like a woman. Monday the Louvre is closed; anonymous in a bowler hat and brown checked suit, he makes his way through crowds of shoppers. Under multicolored umbrellas, women pack the white-sale tables outside the Samaritaine, the Grands Magasins du Louvre, the Cour Batave; women busily pick over pillow shams and tables of lace blouses; he bumps up against them, saying "Ex*cuse* me, m-ma'am" in a surly voice as if that blonde he has elbowed, that brunette sparrow, that gangly woman is to blame. "Watch where you're going, m-madame! Who do you think you are?" He is looking for a smile, an apology, but he cannot ask for it, that would make him ridiculous, with his stutter; his anger makes things easy; angry, he can move at will among this crowd of women, boorish among the silk and lace, in the rain.

Every one of them, he thinks, every one of them is no better than she should be; every one of them has been in a fiacre, been like an animal in some doorway, every woman is half a monster, spreading her legs for a man. But not for him, ordinary Leonard, gentleman Leonard, Leonard gets nothing; worse than nothing. "I'll do it if you love me," some woman says in the crowd. And a wagon clatters past; water spurts from under its wheels.

"He knows you by sight. He knows where you work. We must try again," Inspector Langelais told Reisden.

The murderer hadn't shown up at Asnières; or he had probably shown up as Reisden himself would have done, coming early and seeing policemen taking their places. Instead he had sent another letter.

Yu wrnt at Barris Toom I was (presumably "saw") *u at the Fens with anothr man there but u Lie I AM NO MRDURER / Yu sd youd HELP but a Lie yu don't Love hr Help hr Imedatle or Yu Wont Lik it.* It was a postcard of the Mona Lisa, and had arrived with this morning's earliest mail.

Threatening, pleading: *I am no murderer,* Reisden read. *Help.* "He's breaking down."

"Can you stay away from Jouvet?"

"I live here."

"Stay inside, then, as much as you can. The police will keep a watch. Take guard. Keep out of crowds, monsieur."

Once a month Reisden sat in on patient assessments, and on Monday morning the seventeenth, one of the patients was a child, an anemic frightened boy who saw weather demons. When the sun shone he was more or less normal, but when it rained, "the exhalations of the atmosphere permit me, monsieur, to see the demons rising from the furrows. What concerns me, monsieur, *ce qui me concerne bien* is that *they are always there,* and it is only the weather that lets me see them from time to time." The morning was heavy and greasy with rain, which engorged into slow drops and zigzagged down the windows of Jouvet; the child spoke in a pale painful voice, while his eyes rolled from corner to corner of the room, following something furtive and invisible. I should get rid of Jouvet, Reisden thought, this is unbearable; he looked at his steepled fingertips, which were white, then watched the boy's stats being entered. *Fabre, Étienne, 10 years old, persistent hallucinations,* blood pressure such-and-so . . . Étienne Fabre, ten years old, would go in the records and someday into a research study; and there might be a cure for demons.

A technician tapped the barometer outside the assessment room; some mental cases vary with barometric pressure. "Broken, *merde!*"

"I'll leave it at Auzoux," Reisden said.

"You're not to go on the street," his secretary fussed at him.

"I'll take the car."

Dr. Auzoux's Establishment was an ancient slumped curiosity shop on the rue de l'École de Médicine. It had a respectable selection of medical and laboratory supplies—glass cover slips for slides, blades for cutting and slicing, formaldehyde by the liter, stains, articulated skeletons from cat to man—but its distinction was its shopwindow full of elegant ominous curiosities, blanched two-headed kittens floating in cloudy bottles, ants in amber. Inside the shop, gaslight shone green in the gloom, and a mummified clerk and three customers turned simultaneously to look at him.

"Broken barometer? I win my bet, you're the seventh today!" The clerk mummy turned the gaslight up to shine on shadowy hanging barometers. Every glass tube was as if cracked, the mercury balled at the bottom. "It's not broken, it's the air pressure, monsieur!" he cackled. "The barometers can't measure it!"

There was a great depression throughout Europe, the clerk

said; it was bringing rain from the sea. "Ah, that's what one wants, rain," said one of the customers sarcastically. Outside, the air was as heavy as if one were breathing through wet wool; the rain fell almost reluctantly, hanging in the atmosphere, making a stifling fog. "They say it's flooding in Switzerland and all through the mountains."

Reisden visited his notary and changed his will in Perdita's favor. He did not believe in Her Artist's power or desire to threaten him, but he attached to the will a sealed codicil, to be opened in the event of his death before marriage, stating that he had been betrothed to Perdita, acknowledging her child as his, and making provision for it. He suspected he was doing this simply because of the poetic name for such sealed documents (they are called mystic wills; one wants one as one wants a vast black cloak and a familiar spirit). But writing for the first time *my child*, for a moment he could not go on, overcome by a wash of shame and longing.

Demons in the air.

He went round to a framer with Gastedon's sketch: Perdita as the Mona Lisa, enigmatic smile, unfocused eyes, but the hands Reisden had seen a thousand times when she was practicing, the right hand crossing over the left as the fingers of the left hand curled in a chord. He went back to the office and filled sheets of paper with ideas, obsessing again. Who were the married women pianists in Paris? She should know them. Who would give her private lessons? When could she have some form of a career again: when the child was three, four?

He wrote a *petit bleu* to her: *I love you. Practice, practice, practice.* He would give her as much of music as he could, having taken it all.

Chapter 55

"Tell me what you've discovered about my painting, darling."
Late Monday afternoon, before the opening of the Salon d'Hiver, Reisden went to see Dotty with financial reports on the suspects. In the grey stifling rainlight all the mirrors seemed fogged and the gilt chairs were steel. In the other half of the salon a maid was dusting and puffing up the pillows on the chair seats. Dotty closed the door between them and sat down gracefully in a little chair, motioning him to his armchair.

He showed Dotty the figures. Madame Mallais lived simply, paid her bills on time, and had a bank account. Jean-Jacques Mallais lived from the copies he made. The painter Gastedon scrounged from his friends; his rent, on a falling-down Montmartre studio, was paid by Esther Cohen.

"So they are all poor except the widow, which one would expect."

Dotty stirred the coals of the firewood with the poker, and used the tip to spear a clinker.

"My darling," she said, "has Mr. Daugherty spoken to you about another suspect? Are you being discreet with me?"

"No." He had not seen Daugherty since the detective had left with Milly Saturday night. A thousand years ago. "Who?"

"Your charming Mr. Daugherty came to see me this

morning," Dotty said, an edge in her voice. "He asked me about *my* finances, and found them rather suspicious."

"Suspicious?" Reisden said. "Why?"

"He seemed to think I pretended to own all this." She gestured at Gresnière family heirlooms. "He was offensive, really, and I'm afraid I am offended. He insinuated, darling, that *I* might have had my Mallais copied and sold," Dotty said, "because I needed the money."

"Why? You would come to me or Ferval—" Dotty's other trustee. "There's no reason for you to want for money."

She looked down at her hands, touched the skin of the left hand with the long fingers of the right, ran her fingers up and down the index finger of her left hand, touching the small swellings at the joints. "To quote Mr. Daugherty, I am being blackmailed by some 'dunkhead who thinks I got money because I live in a museum.' The blackmailer, who is as ignorant as Mr. Daugherty, is asking for more than I can pay, and for some reason I cannot come to you."

"Are you being blackmailed?" he said casually. It was an ingenious theory, but not likely. He had known Dotty since he was twelve; she had no secrets left, at least from him.

"I, darling?" Dotty leaned forward as if he had said something fascinating. "No. I am only a bird in a gilded cage. I have nothing to conceal. I wished to be separate from Esmé, my desires are exceeded, he is dead. I have no lovers," she counted off on her ringed fingers, "no secret drug dependencies, no illegitimate child of my youth who requires establishment as a hairdresser; I have nothing. I only wonder why he should think of blackmail."

"To be comprehensive, I should expect," he said.

She gazed at him, an unreadable expression in her blue eyes; it was almost concern, but her lips were compressed.

"He does not know me," she said; "he does know you."

"Have I stolen your painting?" he said. "I do hope not."

"No, my dear, but you do have something you don't wish me to know: you have taken up again with Miss Halley. Carmencita Gomez de Castro was at Miss Cohen's. Miss Halley arrived with a woman of no repute, but left with you, and Miss Halley did not arrive at her hotel; I had a question for her on Sunday morning and found she was spending the weekend 'at her American friend's in Versailles.' My dear, I was not aware you were American."

"It is not obvious," he said, smiling to cover a ridiculous panic.

"Don't joke. You told me she was over."

"She was. No longer." Now I am going to marry her, he did not say. "What has this to do with your painting?"

"I am not being blackmailed, but I wonder if you are, dear." She stood, gracefully, to rearrange a vase of flowers on a table near the windows. She moved a couple of the hothouse stems, considered the effect.

"I? Of course not."

"Miss Halley is no one, my dear. She has no family, no background, no resources. You agreed with me hardly ten days ago and now you are back with her. What has happened since?"

Everything, Dotty.

"I think I must lead you," she said. "What has happened is that Mr. Daugherty has arrived. Mr. Daugherty, who is the friend of Miss Halley; Mr. Daugherty, whom you knew mysteriously in America; Mr. Daugherty, who believes you must marry her to preserve her reputation. Mr. Daugherty, 'investigating' at your suggestion, has been making clumsy insinuations about me and my poor little painting. I find that low. I have nothing to be concerned for. My dear, let me inquire again: do you?"

"No," he said forcefully. "Dotty, that's nonsense."

"Does he have a hold over you?"

"No."

In the other room, the parlormaid was showing an inordinate interest in dusting one small ornament. Dotty knocked on the glass. "Frérin, I think you are needed downstairs." She watched broodingly as the parlormaid left. "Now they will try to listen through the hot-air vents. I don't accuse Miss Halley of any bad intentions. Tasy was young, talented, and musical. Miss Halley is young, talented, and musical. One excuses that. But, darling," she said, "what—odd thing—happened in America, when Mr. Daugherty knew you there three years ago?"

"Nothing."

"You must not lie to me. . . . Armand Inslay-Hochstein spoke with me this morning," she said. "He said that, while supervising the hanging of the Mallais exhibition, he has had occasion to reexamine my Mallais. He congratulated me on a remarkable painting and asked my permission to write an article about it. So Mr. Bullard has simply made my purchase more valuable." She leaned back in her chair, touching her joined hands to her mouth as if she were praying. "I am completely reassured. I believe we have no further cause to investigate anything. Mr. Daugherty may be sent away. My dear, can you do it?"

He stood. "This is exactly what Inslay-Hochstein would do if the painting were a forgery."

"But Armand is quite clear it is not."

He looked down at her. "Dotty. Bullard told me this is what he would do."

"I am very tired of your Mr. Bullard." She stood too. "I don't care about the painting. Mr. Bullard has gone quite beyond himself; the value of the painting is safe, that is all I care about. I worry about *you*, my dear. Can you send Mr. Daugherty away?"

"Yes, but I don't choose to."

"You are committing yourself more and more extremely to a girl who does not love you." She crossed the space between them and put her hands lightly on his shoulders, looking up into his face. "Sacha, do you know what you were like after Tasy died? Do you remember I came to see you?"

"Of course I remember."

"We had tea in a café on Bedford Street." She put her face against his shoulder and one arm around him, the other hand still on his shoulder, fisted, as if pushing him away. Her voice was light and fast, as if discussing what she would wear to the Winter Salon. "You said you could see Tasy on the floor, dead. You said you could not bear your own thoughts. I was terrified," she said, muffled, "I told you, make yourself safe, get help, promise me you won't do anything; it was all I could do, because you had always been honest with me; and you promised. Well, my dear," she said, raising her head and looking at him with eyes half-resentful and half-frightened, "you left me a note, apologizing, which was not what I had in mind; and I will not have it happen again."

"It will not happen again. I treated you badly," he said. "I was ill at the time. That was nine years ago."

She was keeping her voice low because of the servants. "I do not want you to be lonely, but you cannot fall in love with someone you will lose. She wants her work and a nice gentleman who won't get in the way. If she were more honest, or loved you more, she would realize that she couldn't be fair to you."

"You are misunderstanding her."

"You know you will lose her. Send them away, or I am going to find out what hold Mr. Daugherty thinks he has over you."

"One doesn't do that, love," he said.

"I will," she said. "If I have to, darling, I will, because I will not lose you." She pushed herself away from him and sat down in her chair, not quite so gracefully as usual; she looked at him with bright eyes in a bleak face. "Must I? Can't this nonsense go quietly away?" She put out her hand to ring for tea.

He put his hand over the silver tea bell.

"It is nothing like what you think," he said. "I shall tell you everything either late on Friday or early Saturday; until then I can't. It is not the sorrows of young Werther. But meanwhile you must let it be."

She looked back at him, head high.

"Promise me," she said.

"What?"

"What you did last time. But this time don't lie to me."

"I can promise that," he said. "But I want you to promise something in return."

"Certainly, darling; what?"

Promise to stay by me, he thought. Ask me why I am back with Perdita. Let me tell you we're getting married, and then, my dear, help us make it work.

"Promise me when I need help, you'll give it," he said.

She stared at him. He did not ask for help. It was not that kind of relationship that he and Dotty had.

Chapter 56

Somehow, after that drama, they managed to accompany each other to the opening of the Salon d'Hiver as if nothing had happened. It is an advantage to be raised in a diplomatic family; one learns to keep one's emotions in separate drawers.

The Salon d'Hiver is the big winter show of fashionable, accepted artists. The Grand Palais had been open for about an hour and was already the human equivalent of a quayside traffic jam. A scarlet shoulder bumped against them, studded with buttons and looped with gold braid; electric light sparked on a river of diamonds. The maroon-draped walls were hung with post-Corot groves and school-of-Monet flowered fields, elegant and reassuring. Crushed against Reisden's chest, Dotty smiled and waved at a friend, making conversation with moues and gestures over the din. Her kid gloves waved in the air; the citron-and-black feathers in her hair tickled his nose. Her mouth was curved into the half smile of a Frenchwoman being seen at a party. Beyond her Reisden caught glimpses of Tout-Paris: low-cut gowns, white ties, tight tall collars; a woman's bejeweled fingers; a critical top hat inclining to left and right; the discreet red wink of a Legion of Honor ribbon in the buttonhole of an evening coat, and the fat red bankerly face of the Russian attaché Agafonov.

"Sacha, there's the Infanta Eulalia!" The Spanish royal, as Germanic and blond as Dotty, inclined her head. Dotty made the proper deep inclination of the head, almost a courtesy, a miracle to carry off in this crowd. Reisden bowed as an enormous Zieten Hussar officer blocked the infanta from view. "Darling!" Dotty waved past his shoulder, already on the next encounter.

Behind them, a well-known society painter was receiving congratulations for his latest, a group portrait of the musical daughters of a duchess practicing their scales at home; he was murmuring "thank you, thank you *so* much," over and over. Dotty turned and nodded encouragingly at the painting.

"You have caught the quality of the interior beautifully."

"Thank you *so* much, Madame la Vicomtesse."

Behind them, crushed against a palm tree, two Japanese women gestured to each other, silk flowers in their enormous wigs, the ends of their trailing sleeves rain-spattered above their pattens. "Okura," one chirped to the other; *au courant*, Reisden realized she was saying.

"There's Armand," said Dotty.

In the noisy crowd, Armand Inslay-Hochstein had gathered the ultimate compliment, a circle of empty space; he was ignoring his onlookers, examining instead a very small canvas hung in a corner. He was about fifty-five, a massive handsome man, graying hair cut brush-style, beard long and square; an Assyrian king. He nodded, said a few words to the painter, gave him his calling card, and moved on, leaving the painter leaning against the wall, open-mouthed, holding the card in both hands, carefully, like a live and beating heart. An eddy of the curious gathered to look at the card. A powerful man, Inslay-Hochstein.

"Introduce me," Reisden said. Dotty did, and they walked round for a few minutes with the dealer, greeting his artists, stopping twice to look at a canvas by someone new. "How do you spot what you like, in this crowd?" Reisden asked him.

"Oh, darling, he's one of the show judges," Dotty said. "He's spent weeks seeing everything."

Inslay-Hochstein gave a deep quiet laugh, not at all concerned to be caught out. "One must be a bit of a showman, Monsieur de Reisden. What I see here, madame, are the artists. Will *they* do? Then I may give out my little cards."

"And do you always examine a painting carefully?" Reisden asked.

"Always."

"But not Dotty's Mallais?" Reisden said mildly. "She told me she took it away barely an hour after you first saw it."

"After it came to my gallery, monsieur; I had visited it for years!"

"Putting Armand on the spot was quite unnecessary," said Dotty.

It took them an hour to make their way through small talk and elbows to the rooms devoted to Mallais. Here the crowds were relatively quiet, a few well-dressed people looking at the exhibition labels to see who had loaned what, a group of umbrella-wielding cultural tourists following a lecturer like ducklings.

"I was merely exploring an inconsistency," he said. "*View of the Seine* is here after all."

"Of course," Dotty said.

Dotty paused casually near *View of the Seine,* examining her fan, which had broken in the crowd, and was rewarded by the almost immediate appearance of Count Robert de Montesquiou, hound-thin, painted, and venomously drawling, trailing several young men. "Have you *seen* the *foul* Lara canvas, four little girls playing music as if they were plunging their fat fingers into a box of petits fours—but this—this, dear vicomtesse—you should hear what our incomparable Inslay-Hochstein is saying about it—the promised *land*scape, my dear!" Montesquiou raised one circumflex eyebrow and aimed his monocle at the canvas. Dotty smiled graciously; her Mallais was earning its keep.

The tourists eddied around Dotty and the dandy, inspecting the painting, Count Robert's monocle, Dotty's citron-and-smoke silk, and the young men's flowing ties. The lecturer urged his gaggle into the next room. *"Veuillez m'accompagner s'il vous plaît, 'sieurs, 'dames!"*

At the rear of the group of tourists, clearly enjoying herself, was Madame Mallais.

"Excuse me," Reisden said to Dotty and the Comte de Montesquiou, and followed her.

"Here we see, 'sieurs, 'dames, souvenirs of the great painter." The retrospective was as much a homage to Mallais as to the splendid canvases. In glass cases around the room Reisden saw brushes and a palette, photographs, Mallais's Pan flute, his big straw hat, and one of the famous painted vests. Framed above it was a *Spy* color caricature of Mallais in evening dress, straw hat, and paint-splattered Impressionist vest: Painter, with Vest and Beard.

The lecturer took a stance in front of a large canvas. A blue spruce dominated the picture, and spreading out below it was an extraordinary shadow, glowing with color against the grass. "Like the *View of the Seine*," he began, "the *Spruce and Shadow* (1898) is a masterpiece of the late period. It is the property of the noted collector Count Eugène de Cressous. . . ."

So that was the Cressous canvas, the other colored shadow: a stunner. The shadow was a combination of deep blues, light greens, and yellows, flecked upward as if it were springing out of grass. The tree stood blocky, massive, rocklike, an immobile silvery blue, almost the color of the sky, its stillness as impressive as the shadow's vigor. Reisden had seen the top of this spruce above the wall, a tree like any other. It made him feel as sometimes Perdita must, utterly blind.

Madame Mallais was standing in front of the painting, a small stout woman with gray hair, one hand fisted on her hip, like a woman at the bird market looking at a rooster she might buy. Her hair was piled up in a washerwoman's bun, firm as a brioche, and on it perched a hat, unfashionably small and slightly dusty. That long black veil straggling down her back must surely be the crepe from Mallais's funeral. She was carrying a tiny steel-mesh purse with a hinged top, a kind Reisden remembered Dotty having had in the 1890s; with it she wore a voluminous carpet-like green jacket and wool gloves, neatly mended.

She saw she was being looked at and blushed, suddenly self-conscious. Broad red face, gray hair, wrinkles; the air of a servant on her evening out; enjoying the paintings when she wasn't being watched, shy when she was. Mallais's laundress would never have been at ease at Mallais's opening parties.

"I'm from Courbevoie," he said. "I'm Alexander von Reisden, Perdita's fiancé."

It was the right thing to say. She beamed at him; the wrinkles were from a lifelong smile.

"Oh, you're her young man!" She pronounced it *maing*; the accent alone would have got her laughed out of Paris. "I've seen you up the market, buying one of those patent potato parers. I said to myself, here's a serious one, he spends twenty minutes buying a knife. I'm the widow Mallais, Suzanne Mallais."

They looked at each other as two people do, just introduced, who both care for the same person. She was uneducated and pronounced her own name Suzaing. But not a pure bleeding idiot: Madame Mallais stood looking at him for long seconds, holding his hand and smiling warmly; but he felt seen, as if he were a hunting dog and all his breed marks were being added up. Madame Mallais was not entirely sure he would do for Perdita and meant to find out.

"*Je vous félicite,*" she said: "Mademoiselle Perdita and I

had a bite together last night. Poor little girl, she thinks she won't make a good wife. But she's just young, and that cures itself." She looked at the cut of his evening coat. "Get a good housekeeper, m'nsieur, and a good baby nurse; *help her keep her music,* and she'll be fine."

She cocked her head like an owl and looked at him: well?

"I hope she will have her music," he said a little stiffly. He was unused to other people knowing his business, or making it so personally theirs. But he had said he was her neighbor; that made them her business, at Courbevoie.

"You're going to help her?" Madame Mallais persisted.

"As far as I possibly can. Her career should have been in America."

"Art for a woman, m'nsieur, it's *bieng* difficult," Madame Mallais said. She held her mended gloves out in a gesture half-tentative and half-blessing. "She wants to do it so hard, but she thinks she can't."

"I hope you'll be a friend to her."

She said nothing, head still on one side. She was not letting him off, she was not insisting, but she had not yet heard the answer to her question. And you? What about you? Are you on her side, are you her friend? Can you help? He saw suddenly the young painter's wife, wheedling credit out of the greengrocer, the butcher, and the dealer in art supplies. Mallais had not married her by accident.

"I want her," he said. "And I want the child, and she says she wants to marry me. I hope so. But marrying me means she must stay here, she must give up the course of her life." He was apologizing too much, in the way of a guilty man. "I wish I knew what to do. I wish I had the answers."

"You should be careful of having answers," she said. He thought she was laughing at him; then he realized that he had somehow passed inspection. "It's not my business, after all!"

she said. "But I like your wife. Don't you have answers too quick, either of you; they don't keep."

My wife. "Thank you," he said.

She nodded. They said nothing for a few moments. "I'll come visit till she's sick of me," Madame Mallais said. "Do you like the paintings?" she added a little shyly.

"Very much. It's odd living where they were painted." He looked at the label of the *Spruce and Shadow.* So did she. "One feels one sees very little."

"Ah, that's what it is, painting. There'd be my little spruce, and then'd come the painting and it'd look like that." He thought of what it would have been for her, living with Mallais. Utterly blind.

"Still, *Spruce and Shadow*! Think of it!" she snorted.

"What was your title?"

"Oh, we didn't call it anything. The picture over the sideboard."

"Who makes up the catalog titles?"

"Monsieur Armand, he's very smart about it."

Inslay-Hochstein again. "Eighteen ninety-seven, at least?"

"It's late spring," she replied. "Forget-me-nots, the first of the mustard—yes, it's May or early June. But which year, who knows?"

She had lost him. "Forget-me-nots?"

"That's what's wrong with the title!" she said. "It's not shadow, it's my garden." She leaned forward over the velvet rope and ran her thumb just above a light streak in the blue, earning a scowl from a guard. "That's my lavender, that silver-green, and those touches of yellow, that's wild mustard. Some people rip it out; me, it's just a flower that grows too well," she said.

No colorful shadow?

"Now this one." She pointed at the painting next to it. "This

I know was done in—what year did Claudie get married?—
1892," she said triumphantly. In the picture a young russet-
haired woman in lilac smiled in front of a great bank of roses.
"The material had stripes, it was the hardest-made dress I ever
sewed, and we ate our hearts out about whether the color'd go
with her hair—so when it came out right, of course she had to be
painted! Oh, there's my grandson," Madame Mallais said.

Reisden looked for a picture and saw the boy.

"Jeang-Jacques, *viengs un peu*, it's our neighbor—"

Jean-Jacques Mallais, Roy Daugherty, and Milly Xico had
entered the room together. Milly was flirting with Madame
Mallais's grandson and Daugherty indiscriminately. George
Vittal, behind them, was declaiming. "The attempt to repro-
duce visible reality pretends to substitute for the act of sex, but
it's a *tribade*, no penetration—" Daugherty's neck was red,
from Milly's fractured but utterly frank translation of Vittal's
remarks, and perhaps from Milly's neckline.

"*Oh, là, là,*" Madame Mallais muttered; the boy was staring at Milly with baffled adoration.

"I wouldn't take Milly seriously," Reisden said.

"Ah, m'ngsieur, you'll see, when you have children!"

Madame Mallais neatly severed her grandson's conversation
with Milly by getting him to meet Reisden. Jean-Jacques was
sullen, his eyes drifting over Reisden's shoulder in the direction
of Milly's brassy voice. He wanted to be an engineer, the boy
said in a mumble; he didn't like painting. He grew enthusiastic
over cities of the future, tropical climates, Africa. He talked
about the virtues of native materials, palm thatching, mud brick,
and pilings over lakes. "Construction, monsieur, is culture made
visible, expressed in its most technically advanced, most suitable,
and simplest form!" A quote from some text, surely, but one he
had taken to heart; the boy's blue eyes glowed.

"If you're going to be an engineer," Madame Mallais said

protectively, "you should go home and study, it's too late for you to be out." She gave a meaningful look at Milly Xico.

Jean-Jacques sighed and said, "Oh, *Grand*ma."

"My grandson is taking me to the tram station," Madame Mallais announced firmly. "Good night. Good night, M'ngsieu' de Reisden. If I came across a housekeeper, or a—?"

"Yes, certainly. Good night, madame; a great pleasure."

"Oh, *Grand*ma, really, I'm not a kid, after all."

Milly, unmoved by the departure of her admirer, stood looking at a landscape of the garden, her chin down. Dotty was still talking with Robert de Montesquiou; George Vittal was lecturing a couple of student types, towering over them, gesturing with a vast earnestness. On the silk lapel of his evening jacket, Reisden noticed a tiny construction, fastened where his boutonnière would have been: a salmon-skinned, bug-eyed head on springs, nodding and wagging its jaw as Vittal talked.

Esther Cohen and Gastedon had entered the room; Gastedon was standing in front of *Spruce and Shadow,* studying it intently. Vittal drifted over to him; Gastedon pointed; Vittal gestured. Gastedon indicated the line of the garden, which echoed the line of the branches. Armand Inslay-Hochstein had arrived and joined them. Inslay-Hochstein made the same gesture; yes, that's it, he said; the painter and the dealer continued talking, with Vittal interjecting occasional remarks, and then Inslay-Hochstein simply began to listen to Gastedon, the same intrigued look in his eyes as when he'd seen a good canvas.

"What'd you and Mrs. Mallais say?" Daugherty asked.

"Shh," Reisden said quietly. "Look at those two. Do they know each other?"

Daugherty squinted at the dealer and the painter. "Nope."

Inslay-Hochstein reached toward his waistcoat, hesitated, then brought out a card and handed it to Gastedon. Without premeditation? Gastedon took a look at it, took another look, and openly stared at the card. If he were an aspiring painter who had not known he was talking to one of the most power-ful dealers in Paris, he might look as stunned as he did now.

"So what'd she say?" Daugherty asked.

Inslay-Hochstein was treating Dotty's Mallais as if it were a forgery, needing to be shored up; but here was the man who could have painted it and they did not know each other.

"We talked about *Spruce and Shadow*," Reisden said qui-etly. "The 'shadow,' by the way, is a garden; and Dotty tells me that Inslay-Hochstein—"

"Garden?" Daugherty said.

"What?" Reisden said, his eyes still on the dealer and the painter. "Keep your voice down."

"Did I ever show you that photo of Mallais and his wife, just before he died? In my book I got? You ever see it?"

"No, I don't think so."

"Well," said Daugherty, "there ain't no garden."

There they were, Madame Mallais and her husband, in the photograph, 1899, the year before he'd drowned, sitting under the spruce tree. One or two years later than the supposed date of the Cressous canvas. And underneath the spruce tree, no flower bed; nothing to paint; nothing but grass.

"Madame Mallais has a flower bed there now," he said. "She might have been planning it when the picture was painted."

"Might have," said Daugherty.

She had spoken as if she had seen it painted. *There'd be my little spruce, and then'd come the painting and it'd look like that. . . . We called it the painting over the sideboard.*

"Who's this Cressous guy?"

"An art collector. Very well known and very knowledgeable."

"Wouldn't he a known it if he'd bought a forgery?"

Chapter 57

General Count Eugène de Cressous lived in a château about seventy miles from Paris. He was a big, red-faced man whom one expected to see charging about his domain on a hunter, or in a staff job in Paris; but Cressous was in a wheelchair, having lost both legs at Sedan forty years before, and instead of colonizing West Africa he had directed his energies toward Impressionists.

He lived in his picture gallery, which was the ballroom of his château. From floor to ceiling the walls blazed: Renoir, Monet, Cassatt, Sisley; roads, trees, fields, women in rowboats, women in gardens.

"Best painting Mallais ever did!" Cressous boomed. "I know that photograph of them. She put a garden in that spot afterward, did she? Very handsome of her. Life imitating art. Homage to my painting."

"Do you know her?"

"Never had the pleasure. Retiring sort of woman." Cressous showed Reisden his other Mallaises. He had eight, four of which had gone to the show. He talked until the shadows lengthened about the difference between a Mallais pink and a Renoir pink, Mallais's use of impasto, and dating a canvas by brush technique.

"Do you ever have trouble with thieves?" Reisden asked.

There were four servants in the room, all male. "What

about thieves? Trouble with thieves, boys?" said General de Cressous, and they chorused:

"Not—much—sir!"

"So, without any doubt, this is the painting you bought."

"Of course."

Cressous, an expert, had bought a forgery. Inslay-Hochstein, a clever man and an honest one, had sold one.

Unless—

Reisden drove to Bergac, where Mallais had drowned. The rocks of Bergac were like Gastedon's paintings, heavy, rough, and crude. The water chewed around them, sucking at them, and waves exploded against them, drenching the path. From above, the waves swirled hypnotically, an invitation to jump. Reisden stood on the cliff looking down at them, examining the rain-flattened grass and the clay on either side of the path. The rain blew horizontally in his face and stung like nails.

In the café by the train station, he had a conversation with the barmaid and the town fiacre driver. Mallais had never painted at Bergac before. He had arrived in the late afternoon, on a January day, alone. He had said he had heard of the Bergac rocks and wanted to paint the waves. It had been storming, although not so badly as today. They had recognized him by his painted vest and straw hat, which he had had trouble keeping on his head. The fiacre driver had taken him to the bottom of the path. Mallais had left the straw hat in the cab and walked up the path, leaning on his cane.

"You shouldn't have taken him, Jules," the woman at the *comptoir* fretted. "A famous painter and all."

"Thought he just wanted to paint the waves," the fiacre driver muttered, red-faced.

"People have jumped from the Bergac rocks since there

were rocks, monsieur," the barmaid told Reisden, "but still this one didn't concern himself."

Reisden called Daugherty from the post office at the next large town. "I want Mallais's medical records, and I want financial records on Madame and Inslay-Hochstein; and when I get back I want to try out a hypothesis on you."

He had *petit déjeuner* with Daugherty in the Deux Magots on Wednesday morning. It was raining tempestuously here too, wind rattling the awnings over the café. Reisden watched the carriages and automobiles pass on the Boulevard St.-Germain: bays turning black in the rain, the liveried coats of the coachmen covered with black rain capes, and the autos with their curtains closed, chuffing past mechanically at the regulation ten kilometers per hour, so as not to frighten the horses.

"I have two theories," Reisden said. "In both of them Inslay-Hochstein is involved. In one of them, Madame Mallais is helping him. Tell me what you know about their finances."

"Got 'em here." Reisden borrowed his notebook and looked at the figures.

From 1900 until 1907 Madame Mallais had sold very little. But during 1907, in a very short time, she had disposed of three canvases of much higher quality: *View of the Seine* to Dotty, *Spruce and Shadow* to Cressous later in the spring, and in early November, to Betsy Ducret d'Hédricourt, *The Old Apple Tree*, which hadn't been in the show; the venerable Betsy refused to loan out her paintings.

Since 1907, the two paintings Madame had sold appeared to be genuine Mallaises: midlevel, not mediocre, but not up to the level of the three 1907 stunners.

"She didn't need money." Daugherty had decorated the

financial figures with sketches of apple trees and spruces, and not a bad copy of the lamplighter in *View of the Seine*. "But Bullard says Inslay-Hochstein almost went bust in 1907."

"Because he has unconditional return," Reisden guessed.

Around 1900, Inslay-Hochstein had discovered American collectors. Because of unconditional return, he had become a favorite among Americans wary of forgeries; the Americans had spent money freely; Inslay-Hochstein had forgot his natural caution. But in March 1907 the American stock exchange had panicked. Some collectors, needing cash, had taken advantage of unconditional return and simply turned in their very expensive paintings.

Inslay-Hochstein had been desperate, until Madame Mallais had decided to sell three important works—works of such quality that they had to be bought.

"And," Reisden said, "in return she took paintings, not cash."

"Why'd she want more paintings?"

"She didn't," Reisden said. "Left to her own devices, Madame Mallais would have bought property or turned the money into gold coins and hidden them in the garden. Inslay-Hochstein persuaded her," he said, "because he had paintings and needed money."

"Is that legal?"

"Legal and profitable, as it turned out. He cashed her out for a better price once the market recovered."

Reisden tapped the figures with the end of his pencil, then brooded, looking across the boulevard. A bicycle messenger went by, spraying a flat disturbance of water from his wheels.

"Suppose Inslay-Hochstein looked through the Mallais stock," Reisden speculated. "He found three canvases that could be outstanding, but weren't finished. He had someone— who? Gastedon, whom he didn't know?—someone finish them. Three unsalable canvases became three splendid Mallaises. Madame Mallais provided provenance for them, and in return he gave her genuine paintings. Over the course of ten months, Inslay-Hochstein sold the Mallaises. Then the market corrected itself. He sold no more postmortem Mallaises; he didn't need to and he is reportedly an honest man; but he sold the paintings she had bought and made a better profit for her. To quote Bullard, it's a flymin' good deal and everyone's happy. Even the people who bought the canvases."

"Maybe she thinks selling 'em was legal," Daugherty said. "I know that kind of old gal, Reisden. She ain't going to do anything illegal, but if they was from her stock, if her man painted parts of 'em, she might have an *opinion* they were all right, and she wouldn't test it any too hard. It ain't as though she's selling dead dogs. Bullard don't even know for sure *View of the Seine*'s bad, and Cressous don't mind his *Spruce and Shadow*."

Reisden himself had thought they were splendid. And Cressous not only had bought his painting, he was letting it be exhibited. "They're terribly good." He drank his coffee, which was bitter cold. "I hope it's not Madame involved in this. I've met the woman; I don't think she'd fight with her fourteen-year-old grandson and send him out of the house in order to sell forgeries."

"Who is it, then? Brother Yvaud?"

"I have a theory about Yvaud." He was shy of it; it was what he wanted to be true; but it was as unlikely as Cressous buying a forgery.

An enormous procession, apparently a funeral, came slowly down the avenue, the rain soaking the black plumes on the corners of the coach and the plumes springing from the horses' bridles, until the irritated horses shook the wet sprays out of their eyes. Behind the hearse walked a vast train of mutes, black-clad, black-umbrellaed, black crepe and black plumes in their top hats. Behind them, men in slouch hats carried placards lettered in gold and red. SUPPORT THE STRIKING NURSES OF LILLE, VETERINARIANS SUPPORT THE HORSESHOERS OF THE TRAMWAY LINES, WE DEMAND AN 8-HOUR DAY, and the inevitable LONG LIVE THE WORKERS, DEATH TO THE RULING CLASSES. A chauffeur in a dark green Mercedes leaned on his horn and sped past, his mudguards flinging water on the strikers.

"Maybe she painted 'em herself," Daugherty said.

"Madame Mallais, of all people?"

"Well, I been thinking, Reisden." Daugherty looked down the road after the horseshoers. "Ever since you and I went to Miss Cohen's. About painting—" Daugherty slurped his coffee. "It don't take no sort of education to paint like Gastedon and Mallais, all you got to do is use your eyes. It seems like to me," he stabbed a finger after the procession, "any sort of person, one'a them horse-copers, who he took pains over it, and kept thinking about it, he could do a sort of painting."

In front of them, on the café table, lay Daugherty's open notebook, full of sketches. All clever, all amateur.

"She'd been lookin' at her husband painting; she'd know all his tricks."

Henri Rousseau had been a postal inspector, Gauguin a sailor and a stockbroker, Corot apprenticed to a cloth merchant. Mallais had worked as a paint supplier and a market gardener. Reisden thought of all the market gardeners who had not become Mallais. "A laundress could paint, I suppose," Reisden said. "Anyone could paint. A lawyer could."

Daugherty looked at him, defensively shy behind his glasses.

"But I don't think she would," Reisden said. "She wouldn't think of it. It would be her husband's job."

Daugherty didn't deny it. "Mighta helped him with his canvases," he said.

"That would be possible," Reisden said.

"She mighta wanted to just try her hand." Daugherty's stubby pen made circles over the open page of his notebook; catching Reisden's eye, he scribbled *Mme M? Why?*

"Then why only three paintings?" Reisden said. "Why did she stop?" He knew that much from Perdita. One didn't stop.

The rain was becoming heavier; a waiter went out with a broom and poked at the sagging awning, which emptied in a Niagara, splashing the steaming glass. He thought of Madame Mallais telling him anxiously to let Perdita keep her music.

"Once she started, if she painted that well, she wouldn't stop," Reisden said.

"So who is it?"

"Second proposition," Reisden said, "which solves almost everything, if one doesn't laugh at it. It explains why Madame Mallais and Inslay-Hochstein felt free to sell the paintings and why Cressous bought his. Let us consider brother Yvaud. Was Mallais arthritic?"

"Dunno. His doctor's dead."

"In 1900 Mallais went to Bergac, which is a suicides' leap, and he disappeared. No body. No inquiries, since people are terribly polite after there's been a suicide. But instead of killing himself, he took the cliff path to the next village, shaved his beard, and in due time appeared as brother Yvaud. Mallais is still alive," Reisden said, "and still painting."

"Huh."

"Consider it."

"Don't make sense. Why'd he pretend to be dead?"

"That is the difficulty," Reisden said.

Chapter 58

He thinks you don't so much as recognize him, he thinks you're stupid, he thinks you're a *murderer*, my G-d!

The baron has advertised again in the personals. He doesn't apologize. He doesn't say he misses the Mona Lisa, he doesn't talk about the police. He asks for another meeting. Leonard can pick the place, as if it'll make a difference.

If he tells the baron beforehand, the police will be there.

Leonard has been patient. But good doesn't get anything, does it, good goes hungry, good doesn't bring the Mona Lisa to Heaven, does it?

He should be this monster, this man the police have made up. That would be a different story. He *would* have two knives. One a penknife, the other an apache blade, a *surin*, eight inches long and rubbed to a razor edge. A monster like that would be respected.

Smoking on the balcony, he sees a great black hearse rolling down the quai du Louvre. Behind it is an army of mincing gentlemen in black gloves, black morning coats with black trousers, black top hats with black plumes, black wide umbrellas: the Undertakers-Mutes' Workingmen's Society, prim and trim and lifeless. From above, on the balcony, they are a river of black plumed with the grey rain. Among them float signs with large red letters.

DEATH, Leonard sees.

Milly comes to see Leonard; she's still looking for that frame.

"Your friend, that g-girl on Saturday, with the Baron de Reisden. Who is she?"

"Perdita Halley? Can you imagine, a Conservatoire student, talented too, and she wants to give it up for a man. He only wants her for love in bed, and she wants to be loved, so she believes him. Come on, Leonard, I need that frame."

You told me how to find her, Leonard thinks. Perdita Halley. At the Conservatoire.

Chapter 59

Monday it rained. It was too warm, almost breathless. This is the last Monday I'll have at the Conservatoire, Perdita thought, smelling Monday morning in the practice room, the faintly stomach-turning odor of perspiration. Next Monday she would be married, a loving wife.

But for this last week she had the concert on Friday: she had the pleasant horror of last practices, polishing the rough bits, eating lunch worrying about the dynamics of a transition in the Chopin, walking back to the Conservatoire and suddenly realizing a fingering that would make it work. The hours flexed through her hands without her noticing.

Alexander sent her a *petit bleu* on Monday. As she fell asleep that night, she realized she had not written him back.

On Tuesday, Perdita spent the day at Courbevoie alone; Alexander was out of town. At teatime she had an unexpected visitor: Madame Suzanne, bringing crackers and peppermint tea. They went walking in the garden in spite of the rain, which fell like peppercorns on their umbrellas. Perdita slid down the garden path, slipping in the clay and holding on to the rope Alexander had rigged beside it until they should get a better banister. She and Madame took shelter underneath a tree. Outside their garden wall, on the quai de Seine, a man with an accordion was playing "Le Temps des cerises." How did he do it in this rain?

Madame Suzanne told her again to keep up her playing.

"What you love gives you strength for the rest," Madame Suzanne said. "Women aren't meant to be clear. They're meant to be overbusy and muddled. Play your piano! A half an hour a day, if it's no more; you don't know where it will lead. It's important."

"No," said Perdita, getting a good idea, "you come here and dig in your garden." You shall have your piano, she thought. "We'll take the wall down, if you like."

"Ah," Madame said sadly. "You're a kind girl."

At the house, having tea, they talked about upset stomach and what to do about it: dried mint leaves for tisane, peppermints from the *pharmacien*, and dry salty English crackers. Drink nothing but Evian or Perrier water, Madame Suzanne counseled; no big meals, lots of small ones; keep rested; keep your feet warm and dry (they both laughed at this, it was raining so hard); wear flannel underwear. And then suddenly Madame said something about herself.

"When I was a girl," she said, "before I had Claudie, I painted too."

Perdita's breath caught; she swallowed. "You did, madame?"

"I'm from out in the country, you know, and I never could have borne to write 'Suzanne Mallais' as if I were an artist; but I painted, me."

"You gave it up when you married," Perdita guessed.

"I gave it up, the way you mean to. But that's why I say *do your piano*. Years later," Madame Suzanne said, "when Mary Cassatt had a show here in Paris, I went. And there was the name on the paintings," she said. "Mary Cassatt. Not Philippe or Jules but Mary, Mary! A woman! As if 'Suzanne' had been possible!" She turned toward Perdita; Perdita saw the rough pink blur of her face. "Oh, you educated women, you women with opportunities, like Mademoiselle Cassatt and you, mademoiselle, you would have been a light to me, when I was young."

I won't be guilty, Perdita thought. I chose what I had to.

"Did you want to keep on with your painting, after you got married?" she asked.

Outside, the wind threw rain against the windows; from down at the end of the garden, a barge moaned on the Seine.

"Ah, mademoiselle, it never let me go."

"Did you—" Perdita took a deep breath. "Did you ever take yourself back about *that?*"

Madame Suzanne hesitated. "No," she said brusquely, as if the question was something that had to be brushed off and treated as unimportant.

"You did—laundry," Perdita said. "And that made you happy."

"Yes, I went to the river and did my laundry, and I *thought* like a painter—I *saw* like a painter," said Madame Suzanne. "And the gardening. It gave me pleasure to make things."

Oh dear, oh dear. "It *is* possible for you to paint now, madame, you know it is. You can go to the Grand Bazar to-morrow—today!—and buy an easel and paints and canvas, and you can paint, even for just a half an hour. You don't even have to sign your name," she said, "but you can. It's all possible." Rehearsal time or no, "I'll go with you today, right now, even in this rain."

Silence from Madame, so Perdita hoped that she was considering it; but then, "Ah, I wasn't thinking right, was I? Every kind of work's the same. If it's important to you, you can't spend only a half hour on it; it's a life."

Perdita reached out and took her hand: Madame Suzanne's hand, Madame who had wished, and had wished, and had not known that what she wished was possible; but who knew it was a life. "Please," she said, "*please,* madame, do your painting now."

Chapter 60

Wednesday morning she felt sick to her stomach and had to keep opening the window for the fresh air. The rain and wind drummed against the window and it was freezing. Sitting at the piano in coat, scarf, hat, but no gloves, sucking a peppermint, she worked on "passion—lightness of touch—expressivity."

Wednesday afternoon, class with Maître: the last Wednesday class, the last class but one of all. The selection he gave her for Saturday was bright and light and sparkling: cut Chopin flowers in a crystal vase. Two of his other students, including Paul Favre, were giving concerts in the next week; he mentioned theirs, and, after a reluctant pause, hers.

After class he asked her to stay.

"Your program, what are you doing?" She had shown him the program weeks ago. She told him again.

"You must change it."

This was persecution. "No," she said, reasonably but definitely, as if she were negotiating with an impresario. "It suits my strengths and the acoustics there."

"Mademoiselle American, you're not playing for Americans, but for our critics." This had some validity; she hesitated. "You should play something American. Perhaps Stephen Foster. 'Old Folks at Home.' "

She had had enough of this man. She stripped off her gloves, stuffed them in her jacket pockets, sat down at the piano, and began to play. "Concord House": modern, big-toned, tough to do but good real music, to challenge good real pianists; Foster wrote for singers. Women pianists are like cut flowers, my Heaven! Oh, let us have Chopin, of course Chopin, and Liszt, and Schubert, but the big stuff too, the strong, the big music—

Utter silence when she finished. She listened for sighs, shuffling feet, anything.

"No woman can play music like that," Maître said. "If you call that music. The upper-body strength is lacking."

"We use Érards in the Conservatoire, Maître, but it's hard to get a big Germanic sound from an Érard. This composer uses a Steinway, and"—trump card—"he thought I was strong enough for the piece when I worked with him."

No need to mention that the composer was an insurance salesman in New Jersey, whom she had met on the subway. He was another Madame Suzanne; he did write real music, though.

"When you play for your husband in America, certainly, he'll get you whatever instrument you please," Maître said; "talented wives are indulged far more than real artists, I assure you."

"Talented wives can be real artists," she said. She had unconsciously folded her hands over the top of her stomach; she had begun to catch herself doing it. She clasped them in her lap.

"Mademoiselle American, when I was a young man and idealistic, I believed the aspirations of women. 'Women want to be artists, just like men! Look at Clara Schumann!' So much time I wasted. Talent in a woman is like a fine setting for a jewel; it draws the male eye, and so the woman becomes the Marquise of This or the Countess of That, and then she has succeeded in life. But for a man, mademoiselle, talent itself is the jewel!"

She understood him, but she didn't sympathize. "But don't you see, sir, that when you assume all women want only marriage, you create what you see? You are difficult with all of us equally, but you are training the men to be professionals. You were training Anys to be a professional's mother. You have told the men that they should play the piano like a woman's body; you haven't told us that we should play ours like a man's. You don't treat us as if the piano were sensual or necessary to women."

"Crudity is not an argument, Mademoiselle Halley; speaking like a man is not playing like one. Men create music; women have children. Once I recommended a married woman to a post, and then, when the arrangements were made, Madame could not fulfill them, Madame was having a family. I was a laughingstock."

She pressed down both hands in her lap; her stomach turned over. "Women do want to be artists, like men, sir! *Je m'excuse.*"

She took refuge in the women's room in the basement. She had said things that shamed her, because she was giving up, had let him think she disagreed with him when she really did not; the place of a mother was by her child, a wife by her husband. But to assume that, rather than have the woman herself decide it, that was where Maître was wrong.

One day there would be a woman with a deep enough soul to be wife and mother and artist, and the luck to be able to do everything; and what would happen to a woman like that, when Maître had already decided her fate for her? If she were already married, she could not enter the Conservatory doors as a student. If she could, she would be trained to be a mother of talented men. If she somehow was good, Maître would not recommend her to an agent or booker. She would stifle in the desert of her abilities; no matter what she did, she would be less than she dreamed.

All Perdita had done was make it harder for that woman.

Chapter 61

On Wednesday night, when Perdita got her umbrella at the desk, the concierge said a man had left a rose for her.

"That's not allowed, mademoiselle," the concierge warned her.

Alexander knew it, of course; even phone calls were discouraged; she usually called him from the café. It was good of him all the same; she loved flowers. She felt guilty because she had not written him. It was not that she had nothing to say, but when she tried to write, her pencil circled in the air above the writing board while she considered how she should behave toward him, how the good wife she wanted to be would behave and write and feel. He had not written since the note Monday; perhaps he had the same difficulty writing; perhaps the flower was an apology. She sniffed it; it had lost almost all its scent. "Who left it? A tall man, a cello sort of voice?"

"As if I had time to worry about students' love affairs! There's a note."

Outside, the wind buffeted her umbrella like a sail, the rain pocked the cloth. She hurried round the corner to the Café de la Vielle. A little queasy from the smell of chicken stew and cigarettes, she got out her glass to read the note; but she must have dropped it, it was gone. What had he said? She bought a telephone call to Alexander. "Thank you for the rose."

"Rose?" He hadn't sent one. "You have an admirer."

"A hopeless admirer." Oh, it was fun to flirt with him again. She was forgetting how much she liked him.

"I am threatened; I'll come with a cab."

He did, and brought her a handful of elegant smooth-stemmed blooms smelling of Chinese spice. She showed him the anonymous noteless rose, which was small and rather flustered, dropping petals, as if it had been stepped on. They laughed at it. She told him what a pleasure he was, what a good man to be with; the sort of thing that a wife would say to her husband, the sort of love notes she should have written.

But she did not tell him about Madame Suzanne, and she did not write him on Thursday, either, though she tried.

Chapter 62

Baron Reisden Se I now ho yr girl is   Help th Mona Lisa or I wl take car of Yrs   I wl se you b4 yu se Me

Leonard tries not to think about having sent the note, it isn't like him. Of course it isn't, he has written it as though it were from the monster, he has given it a monster's touch, winding it around the thorns of a rose, and he has sent it by messenger boy. Writing the letter eases his restlessness only briefly. He sucks his thorn-pricked thumb, feeling angry and romantic at once, as if he is asking her to go out with him. From this he will get some response.

The note lies on the cobblestones, curled from the flower's stem. The ink blurs in the rain, and the thin green paper softens into pulp. The remains of the note slide across the cobbles, down the stone *bouche d'égout,* and into the sewers of Paris.

Water washes the note through the clay pipes of the sewers into one of its great arched tunnels, the Central Collectors of the sewer system. Following the course of an old branch of the Seine, the water carries it all the way down the boulevard Haussmann. It eddies under the Opera (the famous lake of *The Phantom of the Opera* is part of the sewer system) and passes near the new Métro works under the Gare St.-Lazare. Near Lazare the note, now pulp in water, mingles with water from the other two great tunnels, the Rivoli Collector and the Louvre Collector, and heads northward toward Asnières and the mouth of the Seine.

The rain has fallen so long and so hard that all these sewers are full.

And Leonard feels full too, crammed and restless, because now the idea has come to him it is so easy to think of doing more than a note, a note is useless if the baron doesn't reply, and *you know he won't* says a voice in his head.

The Seine has begun to rise. It's disturbing. In the grey dusk, the water has taken on an odd metallic color, like rust, and a smell; it crawls up the stairs toward the Vert-Galant. There are floods coming from the mountains; the paper says that in Switzerland there are avalanches.

Leonard holds his lantern up close to the glass of the Mona Lisa. In the background he sees great rocks ready to tumble, and brimming water ready to engulf the stream below. He sees a river in the foreground; a tiny tower that looks like the Eiffel Tower; on the right, the unmistakable shape of the Pont-Neuf. From the mountains, cataracts of water plume down toward the valley outside the Mona Lisa's window.

Chapter 63

"All right," Reisden said, "why *would* Mallais pretend he was dead?"

They were sitting outside the Sorbonne reading room, where Reisden was supposed to be doing research. It was too early for the usual crowd of student smokers; they had the bench to themselves.

"Suppose Mallais were painting from photographs," Reisden said. "Impressionists paint from the immediate impression—of course—from momentary effects of light. But if Mallais is brother Yvaud and is actually arthritic, he's also become slow. He would want to paint as comfortably as possible, in a warm room, with photographs to remind him of the shapes of the shadows, and use his imagination for the colors."

"That don't seem wicked."

Reisden gestured toward the mural opposite them, a Puvis de Chavannes labeled *The Muses' Song Awakes the Human Soul*. The Human Soul, a rather chunky girl in draperies, was holding both hands to her ears in the attitude of Munch's *The Scream*.

"Look at how this man paints, all lines, all abstractions. He'd photograph models for expressions and poses. But Impressionists are meant to catch the passing moment as it happens, not"—he mimed taking a photograph—"get it taxidermied."

"There's different ways to paint?" Daugherty said. "Ayuh. There are, ain't they."

Reisden tactfully said nothing. He watched Daugherty looking from his notebook to the mural, the mural to his notebook.

"I could go to Courbevoie," Daugherty said. "Take my bird glasses and look at this Yvaud. 'Twould be mighty exciting if he was alive."

"Maybe he'll come out today." For the moment it was not actually raining.

"What're you doing today, Reisden?"

"This morning," Reisden said firmly, "I work. This afternoon I go to see bankers and sign loan papers."

He owed a report draft and was checking article references, a necessary job he loathed. He sat in the reading room, waiting for his bound journals to be delivered to his seat, stared at the white-green shade of the student lamp, and thought about Jean-Jacques, the Mallaises' weak link. An academic has access to information about students. Reisden thought of what he might find in the Sorbonne registry office; he was already in the right building, and his volumes had not been delivered yet; he walked downstairs.

Jean-Jacques did excellently in engineering courses, was chronically late in paying school fees, lived on the rue Maître Albert, and (one of those random facts that universities accumulate about students) had worked as an artist's model in an atelier off the place de la Sorbonne.

Which was two blocks away. He asked the reading room to reserve his journals.

At the atelier he was in luck. The model, a vast young southerner named Philipon Soubise, had got the job from Jean-Jacques and knew him. Soubise was an engineering student as well—he had the muscles of a man who assembles buildings with his unaided hands—and sometimes stood Jean-Jacques a beer. "Poor as half a pair of shoes, that boy, and proud! His grandmother'd like to help him, but he won't have it. I don't know why. Works like a tram horse. He's had only one treat since I've known him, but that was something! It's the little men have all the luck with the women, you know, us big ones go begging." Soubise leaned forward. "Milly Xico. Would you believe?"

The ancient rue de Bièvre, where Milly Xico lived, had been a canal in the year 1300, when Dante had written parts of the *Divine Comedy* there. It was now covered over, but the street still pooled constantly. Raddled frontages leaned forward, trying to see their faces in the water. A pipe jutted from a window on the second floor; as Reisden watched, unidentifiable substances splashed from the pipe into a puddle, spreading slow, eroded rings.

"Madame Xico?" the concierge said. "Third door on the left, second courtyard."

Reisden crossed a courtyard almost turned into a hall; the sky was only a gray damp slit above him. An abrupt open space between plastered beams held a scummed fountain and a lead gargoyle from which water dribbled. He ducked under an eighteenth-century brick bridge the width of a window, made a right turn past Renaissance beams set into scabrous plaster—it reminded him of Jouvet—and came out into a courtyard in which a spindly linden tree shared space with two potted dracaena. He knocked at the only door.

"J'arrive!"

Her apartment smelled of mold and cigarettes. She had been working; behind her, he saw a manuscript on blue paper spread on a wooden folding table. Her pug lay snorting by the fireplace. The apartment was small, a central room furnished with a threadbare rug, a sagging tapestry-upholstered sofa, a Buddha from which the gilt was peeling, a single straight chair drawn up to the table, and many plants: durable rubber plants, snakeplant, damp-loving ferns. Through a half-open door he could see her bed. She pulled the door closed and offered him coffee.

"Have I ever—gone out with him? Well, yes. Once. To get a copy of the Mona Lisa, of course!"

"Do you like the Mona Lisa?"

"Absolutely adore her." She looked at him over the rim of her cup. "But where is she now? He hasn't given her to me yet."

"Did Jean-Jacques ever talk about his grandfather's paintings?"

He had not.

"Has he ever, to your knowledge, painted a copy of a Mallais?"

"He never paints anything but the Mona Lisa. He told me. He only wants to copy one thing, and tourists buy the most copies of the Mona Lisa."

"Has he ever spoken about his grandfather?"

No.

They talked briefly about Perdita, and then fell silent. She gave him a short direct look, half teasing, half challenging, half in search of information—which halves added up to more than one, and so did the look. There was an oddly attractive reserve about her, the air of a chorister in a medieval manuscript; her big eyes were surrounded by kohl as if they had been painted for a psalter, and crowning everything was the famous frizz of hennaed hair. She was past thirty; her nose was too large for her face, her chin too pointed, her mouth too thin and thoughtful; she had the bruised fullness under the eyes that is the beginning of bags, and the dints at the corner of the nose and mouth that show where the lines will be. She was intensely attractive, and knew it.

"More coffee, Monsieur de Reisden?" She fixed him with stunning sapphire eyes. They looked at each other with momentary speculation. There was the slightest pause, invisible to any onlooker but each other; on the part of each, the slightest shake of the head.

"When Jean-Jacques delivers your Mona Lisa, would you tell him I'd like to see him?"

Jean-Jacques' address was a student hotel, the cheapest kind of housing, and Jean-Jacques rented a room under the eaves, the cheapest kind of room. He did not bother locking it. His garret contained two Mona Lisas in process of being painted, his books, and his badly washed underwear and socks set out to dry; no Mallaises, no seventeen-year-old engineer, no clue.

Reisden left a note for him: *I would like to speak with you about your grandfather's paintings,* and gave his address.

"A man who was fond of the Mona Lisa?"

Inspector Langelais had told Reisden that the Mona Lisa had lived somewhere near the Maubert market. It was close by; he went there. The police had been there before him, but the sellers of violets and tooth-powder, bundled up and miserable in the cold, were eager to talk. By the statue of Dolet, the cigarette seller La Brûlante brushed gray hair out of her eyes. Yes, there had been a man, she said, lighting one of her own *mégots* with a nicotine-stained hand. He was a postman or a watchman. No, interjected trembling-voiced Michie who sold cheeses, he was a gentleman; he gave her jewelry. He was Italian, added the one-legged mender of pots; she called him Leonardo.

Her Artist.

"That's the man. What else do you know? He killed her and he's still loose."

Hein! But no one had seen him; no one knew his age or where he lived. "She said he lived in a palace," said Michie unhelpfully. Eh, the pot mender said, after all, Mona Lisa was *un tout petit peu*, and he rocked his spread hand in the gesture that indicates everything from senility to the more acceptable manias. Hadn't she said President Fallières and the Count of Paris were her clients, and last New Year's, Victor Hugo had brought her roses?

"All the same," Michie said, blowing on her cold fingers, "there must have been something to it, that palace. Perhaps he had his own house."

Chapter 64

Preparing to marry, in France, meant filing endless forms: their birth certificates, Tasy's death certificate, further depositions and certificates because they both were foreign, Reisden had been married, his wife had died abroad, he was Catholic but atheist, and Perdita was Protestant, all of which were *anormale*. Since the separation of church and state, most people married twice: at the mayor's office, for legal reasons, and at the church to please the curé and the relatives. They were having only a civil marriage, which meant an unexpected visit by a priest from St.-Sulpice, anxious to reclaim Reisden's lost soul and to convert his wife.

The ceremony would take place at the *mairie* of the first arrondissement: tastefully decorated, respectable, the choice of fashionable agnosticism. Lunch afterward would be at Voisin's on the rue St.-Honoré, in a private room. They would honeymoon in Nice, since everyone honeymoons in Nice. And they would come back, he hoped, to the sound of sawing and hammers as Jouvet was repaired.

He had not yet managed to sign the papers; the one bank official who was absolutely necessary to the mortgage had been in Switzerland during the recent floods, and was still not back.

Thursday noontime, after her practice, Perdita came in a cab to see Dr. Jouvet's apartment. One day before her first

Paris concert, she was nervous and subdued, but she made a good impression. The staff did not even pretend to be working; he had to "show" her the patient assessment rooms and the labs in order to let them get a sufficient look at her. He and she went up the narrow stairs to *chez Jouvet* and she took in everything gravely, without reaction. He showed her Dr. Jouvet's piano. "I had it tuned for you," he said. She touched the keys politely. Bait to keep her here, he thought, and she knows it.

They hired a cab and crossed the Seine. It was officially in flood from the same storm that was delaying his bank man, but there was nothing much to describe to her; it was a foot or so higher than usual. They went to a goldsmith's on the rue de la Paix, where he picked out the favors for the witnesses—gloves, gold-and-pearl *pensée* pin for Dotty, silver cigar cutter for Daugherty, and similar for the other two witnesses, who were his lawyer and André du Monde. He bought his and Perdita's rings and left them to be engraved. Perdita would wear her Worth dress; the men would be in morning suits (Daugherty must hire one). Dotty would be perfectly outfitted, as always, and annoyed that there had been no time to get new clothes. Ten years ago Reisden had simply eloped with Tasy; the formality of this marriage suited him, as if he were emphasizing the difference between then and now.

They had lunch at the Ritz (after buying wedding rings with one's fiancée, one should lunch at the Ritz). She was very quiet. "Are you all right?"

"Oh, yes. Are you?"

"Nervous for tomorrow?"

"Ready as I'm going to be." She smiled. "More nervous for Monday, Alexander."

"Jouvet," he said. "What do you think? I live there, but we won't have to."

"Whatever you want, Alexander."

"Would you rather live at Courbevoie?" Have an opinion, love, he thought. Perdita without opinions made him nervous.

"At Jouvet you'll be closer to your work."

"I want," he said, "to be close to you."

"Then Jouvet."

"We can have both, if you like. Courbevoie is a better house for a family."

She smiled wanly. "Two houses. I'll have plenty to do."

"What sort of piano is it at Jouvet?"

"It's a Bösendorfer Concert Imperial," she said, smiling unconsciously, shaking her head. "How *could* his niece not have taken it, Alexander? It's like leaving a Stradivarius in the attic."

"She left it for you," he said, only half joking.

"I'll lock it and throw away the key," she said.

"I'll exert my husbandly authority," he said. "Don't think of depriving yourself of the piano. I want us to be happily married, love."

She sat silent.

Chapter 65

By Thursday afternoon, when he went out with the smallest member of the wedding, the expected flooding had visibly arrived; the Seine had risen by inches since noon. From the hired cab, he and Tiggy stopped to see the Vert-Galant; the steps leading to the river had disappeared, and water was running over the pavement by the base of the old willow. "Look, you'll see, your park trees will have their feet in water," he told Tiggy.

"Will it hurt them?"

"No, chéri. It happens to them often in winter." A man was hopping across the half-submerged pavement, looking as though he were skipping on water. Tiggy laughed.

At Au Paradis des Enfants, the big toy store, Tiggy was informed that it was absolutely necessary to buy a party favor for a child his age. "Who is it?" asked Tiggy. "Is it me?"

"Perhaps."

"It *is* me," said Tiggy with great satisfaction. They looked over tin trains, tin trams, real boats that one could sail in the Luxembourg basin; blocks for building a château; board games, Goose, Snakes and Ladders. "That's brilliant," Tiggy decided. "It's a formidable game, I play it at Paul's house."

"Shall we have that one, then?"

"Oh, we have to *consider*." While Tiggy internally debated the merits of every possible toy, his uncle looked at those in the

296 THE KNOWLEDGE OF WATER

next section, toys for *bébé:* silver rattles and bells, ivory teething rings, balls, blocks, and infinite numbers of books to read to a very small child. He paid for Tiggy's choice (it was Snakes and Ladders after all) and added to it a ball with a bell inside.

"That's for a baby," Tiggy said. "Not for me."

He turned the little red rubber ball in his fingers, squeezing it nervously, examining its blank surface while the bell chimed.

After the wedding, everything would be easier for them, it must be, when they could name all their relationships, husband, wife, father, mother. He could be in love with his wife, his son, even a bit with his wife's husband and his son's father, more so than with the tangled connections he had now.

He had not written Perdita this week, and had noticed she had not written either. They had too many inner reservations. But a child— He saw this ball rolling across the floor toward a baby, who reached out to catch it, and he was overcome: hopeless, desperate, concerned, confused, wanting the future to be so much better than he thought it would be.

Chapter 66

Perdita didn't practice the last twenty-four hours before a concert. After she left Alexander, she went for a walk with Milly. They would have gone down to the promenades, but the Seine was splashing almost over them, and so it was on the quai du Louvre, leaning on the wall with her elbows while Milly looked out at the Seine and Nick-Nack barked at it, that Perdita told her older friend she was going to marry.

Milly's silence was shrewd. "Why don't you see Madame Bézou?"

"I'm not going to."

"Because of the grand mystical duty of women? Nature's Most Wonderful Miracle? You're ready to do this?" Milly said. "Get married, give up everything for him?"

Perdita raised her chin. "It's the right thing."

"Oh my G-d! The ideal woman does the right thing! Is *he* happy, at least?"

"Yes. I hope so."

"And you?"

She didn't want to think too much about what either of them felt. "I am happy," she said firmly. "I will have this child."

They walked in silence down the quai. The sky was dark gray and it was cold enough to make Perdita hunch her shoulders and clasp her hands together in her muff. The Seine smelled sour, like clay. Something scraped against the pavement.

"That was half a tree. You should see the water, it's yellow as goose shit. Yellow water and gray sky, and branches sliding down the river like skiers. I think you're very stupid, you know. It's only a cup of tea, and some cramps, and then you get your time of the month."

"Milly, please don't."

"You're just scared. Go someplace nicer than Madame Bézou's. There's nothing to it."

"I'm afraid what I'd think of myself."

Milly didn't say anything, then: "What do you think of yourself now?"

They crossed the street and walked through the Tuileries Gardens toward the café; Milly was taking her to tea with some friends. Milly's pug snuffled in the grass. Perdita sat on a bench. The gravel was wet; her shoes were squelching. Expectant mothers should keep their feet dry. Behind her, the branches of a tree dripped moisture. She shoved her muff up on one arm, took off her glove, and pulled a branch through her fingers, feeling the knobbed swellings of its buds. She had felt buds on Madame Mallais's apple tree, in Madame Mallais's garden full of light, how long ago? Not even two weeks.

Buds to leaves and flowers; flowers to apples, to seeds, to make more apple trees, to make more apples. She had a sense of herself as a woman, the way men thought of her: a place to grow children, an orchard. Her breasts were heavy and their tips chafed under her corset. Amy Beach, she thought. Katherine Ruth Heyman. Julie Rivé-King. Olga Samaroff . . . The rumor at the Conservatoire was that Samaroff was definitely marrying Stokowski and giving up her career. More evidence that Advanced Piano was wasted on women; Samaroff had performed only a few years beyond her Conservatoire training. A man with her talent would have been onstage all his life.

"What are you really afraid of?" Milly asked, sitting by her.

She was afraid this child would be a daughter and learn music; and then the daughter would grow up and have a daughter, while men played the piano. She was afraid of the apartment at Jouvet. It was so full of things, piles of books she could not read or deal with, furniture that Alexander said Dotty didn't like, little unfamiliar gritty shapes she had held and prodded with her fingers. (Dr. Jouvet's ushabtis: what were ushabtis?) She was afraid of Dr. Jouvet's silverware, heavy in the hand and smelling of silver polish and devotion. How would she know when they needed cleaning?

She was afraid of the piano.

She remembered, shivering, how she had reached to the bottom of the keyboard, her fingers trembling, had found extra keys in the invisible black, had sounded the lowest note, C below bottom C, a growl. It was out of tune, of course. How she had wanted to run and get her tuning kit, to *hear* it, the whole sound of the piano, the wonderful middle range, the deepened bloom of the extra strings, the female voice of the treble. She wanted to play it, to lose herself in it, for hours and hours, for days, forever.

"I'm afraid of doing what I want instead of what I ought."

"*Merde,*" said Milly, "that's easy, do what you want."

"I can't." She *was* doing what she wanted, she was marrying, she had chosen that.

"I heard you play once," Milly said. "You were good."

I *am* good, she protested inwardly. "Come hear me tomorrow," she said. "You can hear me again, once. Maybe twice, if Dotty doesn't have a fit and cancel her salon."

"Say 'This is a disaster and I wish I didn't think I had to get married.' Then I'll come."

Chapter 67

It was Milly's friends, Esther and George, who solved the mystery of Madame Mallais.

Esther and George were talking about their books when Milly and she arrived for tea, chattering each on their own topic, not listening to each other. "George's *Resonant Poisons* has sold six hundred copies," Esther said without the slightest jealousy. "My novel sold ninety-four copies in three years." She sounded rather proud of it. "Would you like tea?" She had a husky tenor; it was strange to hear a man's voice offering tea.

"Would you like to make love with me?" George Vittal asked Perdita.

"No, thank you," Perdita said.

"Then I'll have to read you my poems." He held her hand; Perdita drew it away gently, he took it again. She smiled, drawing her hand away again and closing it decisively into a fist.

" 'The masks have nothing to say,' " George began.

"Art is like marriage and forgery is like friendship," Esther spoke over him. "In friendship, power always has its downward curve. One's strength to manage rises always higher until there comes a time one does not win, and though one may not really lose, still from the time that victory is not sure, one's power slowly ceases to be strong." Esther must have tremendous breath control, Perdita thought; once she started a sentence, she could go with it forever. "It is only in a close tie such as marriage, that influence can mount and grow always stronger with the years and never meet with a decline. It can only happen so when there is no way to escape."

" 'I want to love you,' " said George, " 'but to love you halfway. . . .' "

"I broke away from marriage well enough," Milly said. "Anyone can do it."

"You and Henry are not divorced, he is your art instead of art." Esther appealed to Perdita. "She must have art, for Milly to be without an art is to be without air. She thinks she does not want to breathe. Teach her to sing."

"I don't want to learn how to sing," Milly said.

"I can teach you some basic voice production," Perdita said without thinking. This was not forgetting music as she ought, but working up any excuse. "It doesn't matter," she said. "If you don't want to sing any better, then don't."

"It's nothing to be angry about, after all," Milly said.

"I'm not angry," Perdita said.

"You are angry," Milly said, "but you're a good woman and a good woman can't be angry."

" 'I know all sorts of people,' " said George Vittal teasingly. " 'Mostly/They're not up to their destiny/Their eyes move indecisively like dead leaves. . . .' "

"*You* must *write*, Milly, that is how you must apply yourself." Esther's young-man voice had a sort of arrogant innocence, Perdita thought; Esther never would have to consider husbands or children, or anyone but herself and her friends. "You must let your life lead you," Esther said. "You cannot live according to other people's ideas, they will certainly never make you happy."

Perdita thought of Madame Mallais, who had taken herself back in such a timid way, doing her laundry and dreaming of paintings while her husband did them. "Women cannot just *let* their lives lead them," she spoke up to Esther. "I know a woman who spent her life taking in laundry and waiting for her husband; but she wanted to paint."

"I know a woman with a story like that," Milly said.

"So do I, Milly," Esther said.

"Taking in laundry," George Vittal said, "that's Mallais's wife. She wanted to paint?" Ridiculous, his tone said. "Mallais must be destroyed," he said, "but Madame Mallais? One needn't bother."

"Why can't a woman paint?" Perdita asked.

"If she wanted to paint she would paint and especially after her husband died she would paint," Esther said. "Mallais has been dead for ten years and what is she doing now?"

"Oh, she's a good woman," Milly said, "she's taking care of her sick brother and her grandson, or of her husband's reputation—"

"No, she isn't," Perdita whispered suddenly. Under the table, her hands clenched together. She ought to have seen earlier.

"She's not a good woman?"

Madame had been taking herself back. "She has been painting," she said out loud. "She *has* been painting."

"No one cares," Milly said, "of course, she's a woman!"

"I care," said Perdita softly. Madame was in terrible trouble. She had not dared to sign her own name; she had signed—*oh dear Heaven, Dotty's painting.* Could she have done that? And could she have fooled all those experts who knew Mallais?

It wasn't likely, but it didn't matter. What it showed Perdita was how unreconciled she was to her own fate. *I know lots of people*, George had recited; *mostly/ They aren't up to their destiny—* She was not living up to her destiny of being a good mother and a good wife; she was not even trying.

Because, if Madame Mallais was painting, Perdita was glad.

Chapter 68

Reisden returned from tea at Dotty's to discouraging news. Again, Monsieur Delestre, who was to give the final approval to his loan, had not arrived from Switzerland. The Friday signing was to be put off to Saturday, when the banker would certainly have arrived.

The other five messages on his desk were from Barry Bullard. They met at Maison Choi.

"I got news," Bullard said. "In the Normandy provincial exposition, 1863, 'Ippolyte Duféray supposedly painted a *View of the Somme River, with Cows*. Got a gold medal. Duféray then turns around, says to the judges, 'This ain't mine, I signed it, but it was painted by my talented foster daughter, Suzanne.' " Bullard took a deep breath and burst out. "It was a bloody *shadder*," he said. "Armand-bleedin'-Inslay-flamin'-'Ochstein said it was a bloody colorful shadder, and I should 'ave seen the like before. I can forgive 'im lying but not saying I don't know me business."

"Madame Mallais? I don't think it can be true. She doesn't have the outlook. I think it's Mallais."

"She's got the stock."

Reisden told Bullard his theory. "She used to paint, Jean-Jacques paints copies, Gastedon . . . there's no lack of potential forgers. But Inslay-Hochstein supports the paintings. Cressous, who is really an expert, thinks his Mallais is a Mallais. And I think it is. It's Mallais doing the painting."

"I dunno," Bullard said. "Why? I wish I knew wot they were doing."

"How," said Reisden, "burgle the house?"

He drove to Courbevoie. The moon was high in the sky, more than half-full; he stopped his car on the Levallois bridge and looked upriver toward the clumps of lights marking the houses on the steep bank. He picked out the Mallais house, a dark block; a single oil lamp shone through the shutters.

He had called Daugherty from Jouvet, and Daugherty had gone shopping. The equipment was set out on the kitchen table: an electric torch wrapped in black tape, leaving a slit over the lens; Perdita's string-mesh marketing bag; a length of thin cord. Reisden laid the last items on the table: a stethoscope and a stick of African black, left over from André du Monde's amateur production of *Othello*.

"This is very stupid," Reisden said nervously.

"I'll go in," Daugherty said. "You don't have to."

Reisden shook his head.

They turned off the lights and watched the house below them, made indistinct by the fog and gaslights shining above the wall. Daugherty whistled under his breath. They waited until the last light went out behind Madame Mallais's shutters, and then waited an hour more. The St.-Denis bell struck eleven. Reisden buttoned his coat to his chin, hiding his white shirt and collar. Over his pale skin he spread *vaseline boriquée*, then the black makeup, and put on black leather gloves.

This was the plan. After Reisden was in the attic, Daugherty would come to the Mallais front door, pretending to be lost. He would wake up the household. Reisden would recognize Mallais's voice—or not. The household would go back to sleep, and Reisden would leave with any evidence he had found in the attic.

Utterly stupid. "Like something out of Arsène Lupin," he muttered. "Right. Ready."

They made their way down the clay path to the bottom of the garden, carrying the ladder from the shed, a double-ended wooden ladder such as is used for painting. They leaned it against the wall. Reisden hefted it to test the weight—far too heavy—climbed, and knelt on top of the wall. Madame Mallais's wall-building efforts had not extended to the usual broken glass on top; thanks for small favors. "Push the ladder up," he whispered. Daugherty grunted as he lifted it; Reisden hauled, cursed, balanced it, and let it seesaw over to the other side. The space between house and wall was so tight that the ladder almost stuck; Reisden jerked it back before it scraped, then let it slide down until one end rested against the ground. He climbed down, then tilted the ladder to rest against the house wall, just under the sill of the attic window.

Carefully, without hurry, he began climbing the ladder toward the window, as a burglar would in the ordinary course of business. Doing this while wearing theatrical makeup was comforting; its smell and the masklike sensation made everything slightly unreal. He braced himself against the window frame while he tested the shutter; locked, of course. He eased his penknife up between the shutters, felt the obstruction of the catch, and flipped it up with a jerk of the wrist. The heavy shutter swung open.

The attic was full of pictures.

Hard to tell how many, the attic was not a complete room but a low gabled storage area like a country granary. The paintings were all turned against the wall.

By now Daugherty was on top of the wall. From inside the attic, Reisden pushed the ladder away from the window. Daugherty caught it.

Now he was in the attic, with no way to get out until Daugherty returned.

The room was so low that he couldn't stand upright. He flashed his improvised dark lantern and saw paintings everywhere, small and large, in stacks, in rows, leaning against each other. He knelt down, counted roughly, and began to look at them. The first few looked like Mallaises: studies of the Grande Jatte, the Pont de Lavallois, Notre-Dame at dusk. If they were forgeries he couldn't tell.

The next looked like a Cézanne.

He pulled it out carefully, making no noise. Mallais was still the painter, but a Mallais who had seen the big Cézanne retrospective at Vuillard's: the retrospective of 1906, six years after Mallais had died. The painting showed one window of a Parisian building, creams and yellows in every shade from new wood to alabaster. It was a curious and wonderful painting, intensely color-conscious in little more than shades of white; but when had Mallais painted like this?

For minutes he almost forgot where he was, and simply looked at the paintings. More Cézanne, a touch of Gauguin. Studies for what must be *The Old Apple Tree,* an intensity of fading pink made from green, blush, a ripening brown; the bloom was blowing from the tree, filling the picture with a pink light. A study for *Spruce and Shadow,* which he set aside. The Renault and Citroën plants and the "Pont Noir" at twilight: frail, sensual plums and reds, rusty electric yellows, and under a streetlight a man in a bowler hat propositioning a woman, their faces and figures sketched dark indications, her dress a startling forest green. Colors, intense colors, beyond anything that the painter could have seen in field or garden, color passionately moving against color, the boats and barges and trees of Paris breaking apart from the pressure of pure color, drowning and dissolving in color, bursting with light.

The most recent paintings were hung on bits of wire against the chimney wall: they were still drying. One dark-toned canvas after another, studies of rain, of umbrellas, hunched shoulders of horses under gaslight and electric light. He moved his improvised dark-lantern torch over them, then stared at one and took it down.

It was his car, his dark green Mercedes parked at blue dusk on the high street. One side of the hood was up; a man in a black driving coat, holding an electric torch, was looking intently, with complete focus, down into the bright confused colors of the engine. There was an airlessness, an inward-drawingness, about the picture; the face, not very clear, was molded of shadows and the reflections of fire. Even the light was artificial, except for the dusk that hung like a blue reminder at the edges of the frame.

It had been a November evening, November two months ago, just after he had been shown the house for the first time; the car was misfiring, he had set a spark plug wrong and jammed it, and while he had worked at it, worrying it as he was worrying at the relationship with Perdita, an old Frenchwoman returning from her shopping had stopped to look at him. Try as he might, he could not recall her any better than that. But he did recall her.

From almost under his feet he heard the indistinct twang of her voice. He went absolutely silent, feeling like a voyeur.

"Mademoiselle Perdita's young man, talking about colored shadows at your opening, maybe he was just saying hello to me, but you know his cousin owns *Evening Light,* and he's sharp. I don't like it much."

Reisden closed his eyes. *Your opening.*

"Old woman," the man said affectionately. An educated voice, as Perdita had said; an old voice, trembling and in pain. It had been fourteen years since Reisden had heard Mallais speak; he was barely sure whom he heard now.

Behind him the open window shutter groaned suddenly.

"Do you hear something upstairs?" she said.

Shit, shit, *shit*, he hadn't closed it.

"Dainged shutter's blown open, likely. I'll go see."

Where was Daugherty? There was absolutely no hiding place in the garret. Reisden thrust the electric torch into his pocket and flattened himself on the floor, black in the dark. From below, she pulled down the stairs leading to the garret; a wavering fan of light illuminated stirred-up dust motes.

"I know you," Mallais said. "You'll be there half the night looking at them."

A sigh from her, half a laugh. "Was it worth it?" Madame Mallais asked. "Was it really worth it, for them paintings?"

"Don't you know it was?" the old man grumbled affectionately. "Good hands, you—what was that? Virgin Mary!"

The bell jangled again: Daugherty at last. Reisden heard frustrated discussion downstairs, one side speaking only English, the other only French. Worth what? What did you *do?* The Mallaises settled into bed; he heard whispered good nights, grumbles about a cat, and finally the small snores of the old people asleep together.

By feel, in the dark, he knotted one end of the cord around the handle of the shutter catch. He risked the light again to pick out the painting of himself and the *Spruce and Shadow* study. They just fit inside the string-mesh bag. Daugherty pushed the ladder toward him. He swung out the window and onto the ladder. He fed the cord through the half-closed shutter above the catch, eased the shutter closed, and with a quick jerk, as though he were starting an engine, pulled the knot loose and the cord free. Down the ladder with the paintings, switch the ladder from side of house to wall, up the ladder, hand the paintings down to Daugherty, pull up the ladder—the bastard must weigh a hundred pounds; a bit of Madame Mallais's mortar crumbled. Seesaw over, ease it down, climb down; and that was all.

"They are *both* painting." Reisden sat by the fire with a double brandy (in a teacup; they had no snifters). "He is alive. Some of the paintings are his; she said 'your opening, your paintings.' But this one's hers."

Daugherty was holding the painting in both fists, looking from it, to the study for *Spruce and Shadow,* to Reisden.

"Until the Romantics, painting was like plumbing or carpentry," Reisden said. "It operated on the apprentice system. In an atelier, there'd be a master, some journeymen, some apprentices or assistants." Van Dyck had painted only the faces and hands of his sitters; one of his assistants had done nothing but drapery. "Mallais's fingers were swollen when he sketched Dotty's portrait, four years before he supposedly died. I remember he dropped the pencil. Suppose he wished to paint, but was losing his hands, wasn't able to work as well or as quickly. What would you have done?"

Daugherty thought. "Wouldn't a said I was dead."

"Neither would I, and I don't understand that, but I think he trained her to assist him. But assistants become painters in their own right. Now, I would guess, she has the taste for it."

Daugherty looked from one painting to the other.

"That ain't legal, though?"

Reisden thought of the Inneses, the Blakelocks, even Corot blessing his students' Corots. One man's vision becoming a family's. "No. But understandable."

"They're painted the same way," Daugherty said. "He painted that one and she painted t'other?"

"I don't know what she's painted." Reisden shook his head. "You and I can't tell. I'll take both of these to Bullard. He can tell the difference." He pulled out his pocket watch: past two A.M. The tiny date hands had moved to Friday, January 21, Perdita's debut day. Bullard this morning, then the bank; Perdita's concert at Mrs. Bacon's this afternoon. He would tell Dotty about the marriage tonight. And in three days more he would marry Perdita.

They weren't ready. Tonight, in the Mallais house, he had felt something of the quality of the Mallais marriage, a durability one could touch, like stone. A quality, perhaps, of that shared work. He and Perdita didn't have that.

My dear Perdita— For the first time in a week he could write to her, if only mentally. *Madame Mallais is a forger.* But he could not write to her about the quality of that marriage, its warmth and durability, or on what it was based. After asking her to give up her own work, it was cruel.

Chapter 69

Apart from Pearl, Roy Daugherty's experiences of sex had been infrequent and commercial, like buying socks. On Saturday night he had escorted Milly and her little dog to her apartment, and all sorts of things had happened. He remembered incongruous things, the light still on, a pulled thread on the pillow sham, and Milly's pug watching them, panting and drooling.

All Sunday he had wandered around the city like a tourist. A lot of women in Paris had little dogs like Milly's. On the subway women carried poodles in baskets; bright eyes peered out from their muffs; in their arms, like babies, they held miniature schnauzers in little wool coats. On the quaiside, at one of those little bookstalls that perch on the parapets, Daugherty saw a postcard of a woman holding a dog. *Paris, Ville d'Amour*. He knew that much French. Paris, City of Love.

On a second look, he saw the woman was Milly.

Though he'd been favored by a Frenchwoman who was on postcards, he felt strangely diminished and disappointed. What he had got had been just a special sort of being a tourist, what a man should do when he was in Paris to prove he was a man. What he wanted was something more, not a postcard woman but a real one, not fairground glitter but gold.

What he wanted was what he hoped Reisden and Perdita were getting.

Reisden told him about the marriage while they were driving back to Paris. They had gone to the bank of the Seine, and they parked the car by a bridge and stood looking out over the water. It was just dawn and cold enough to bust rocks. On the other side of the river, outlined against the sky, was the Eiffel Tower in fading lights.

"You're going to be real happy," Daugherty said.

Reisden didn't say anything.

"Well, you are, ain't you?"

Nothing from him for a while. "Yes," finally, explosively, with a little uncertainty underneath.

Under the bridge stood a great statue of a man, maybe thirty feet high, a soldier with slop-britches, a flat cap, and a beard. Reisden said that Parisians measured high water on the Seine by how far it reached up "the Zouave." They talked about when the marriage would be, and where to rent the right kind of tailcoat and pants, and suchlike polite conversation.

"Well, ain't you?" Daugherty said again. "Happy?"

"Yes, certainly."

As soon as he'd got home and had breakfast, Daugherty went to see Perdita.

It was the morning of her debut, but she said she was just sitting around waiting, and she wanted to talk with him about Madame Mallais. Across the street from her building, a staircase led down to a cross street twenty feet below. They sat halfway down the stairs, looking down toward gray cobblestones and gray French buildings. Perdita was pale under her big hat. She offered him a peppermint stomach mint out of her handbag. He remembered, concerned, that she'd done that last week, and started to ask whether her stomach was upset; and then he was struck by a thought. Oh, land of mercy, what had the children got themselves in now? He'd better not ask, he didn't want to know more than he ought, he just congratulated her.

"Thank you," she said, holding her head high, the way she had when he'd caught her with Reisden.

She asked about Mrs. Mallais, and thinking he'd disturb her by what they knew, he whoffled around the subject until she came right out and asked him: had Mrs. Mallais painted any of those paintings?

"Well," he said, "yes. I guess she did."

Her and her husband painted them together, he explained, her husband mostly. She was a sort of—his assistant. She painted parts of his paintings. Bits. Once in a while.

"Never any of her own?"

Well, yes. Once. Once he knew of, for certain.

"She *did* it," Perdita said, and—well, there were no words for what she looked like; she hardly moved or changed, but she fisted her hands like she was rooting for the Red Sox, coming from behind in the last of the ninth, with three men on base and two outs: seven come eleven, Red Sox, go! "She *did* paint. She *is* painting." It moved him, some way he didn't want to be moved, because she looked so happy. He hadn't asked her yet whether she was going to be happy in her marriage, and he didn't dare to now.

"Her husband told her to do it," Daugherty said.

Perdita shook her head. "It was her idea."

"Honey," Daugherty said carefully, "it may not a been legal, what she done, so it's better if her husband told her to. They sold 'em as if the paintings was his."

"He must have let her. He thinks it's right. Mr. Daugherty," she said hopefully, "he must have authorized her to do whatever she did."

"It's forgery," Daugherty said miserably.

Her face went bleak. "You mean she will be punished for it?"

"She got to stop," Daugherty said, and added honestly, "at least. Reisden hopes he can work it so she only has to stop."

"You can't make her *stop*," said Perdita. "You cannot make her stop. She wanted so to paint. She must have thought about it for years, every day, Mr. Daugherty, while she was being a good wife and doing the laundry instead. Now she is doing it, and not because she wants to commit a crime, she is not painting for money, she is not trying to forge; she is painting for herself, she is doing her work because she has to; you cannot make her stop."

"Honey, you're being unreasonable," said Daugherty. "That would be the best she could hope for."

"When are you going to see her next?" she asked.

He and Reisden were going out tomorrow morning.

"I'm coming with you. You just can't do this and I'm going to say so."

That was that, she wasn't asking, she was telling him. Perdita asked to be taken back to her hotel; she'd see him and Reisden at the concert.

"Honey," he said before she went inside, "you going to be happy with Reisden, now?" He meant it a question but it sounded like instructions.

He found himself a café near the Madeleine and got a restorative cup of the little black café coffee. He doodled, idly, a lamplighter surrounded by rays of light, Perdita's hands passionately gesturing (he lost himself in lines, trying to get the grace and anger of them). *He authorized it! He thought it was all right!* Women were always saying their husbands'd told them to do it. He didn't get Perdita's hands quite right, and tried again on a fresh page, somewhat shamefully; it was only doodles.

On the plaza in front of the church was some sort of an excavation, a construction site, probably for the Métro. Some people had gathered round it. Daugherty put money on the coffee saucer and strolled over. They were all peering down the steps. At the bottom of the steps the floor had turned dark.

He looked more closely and saw that the darkness was water.

Chapter 70

Besides the sewers, other tunnels mined the ground below the streets of Paris. Ancient Roman lead mines, early Christian catacombs, and the remains of medieval wells shared the ground with railroad tunnels, the sewers, and, now, the Métro.

Digging for the Métro tunnels had several times broken into sewers. At St.-Michel a slow leak from a sewer had probably caused the short circuits a week ago. On Thursday, in the tunnels of the Gare d'Orsay, something more serious happened.

While digging for the North-South, the big new Métro line that would connect Orsay and St.-Lazare, engineers accidentally cut into one of the lateral sewers of the Left Bank General Collector, the largest sewer on the Left Bank. They immediately filled the opening with concrete and barricaded it. This repair should have been more than strong enough to withstand normal water pressure.

But when it rains above the Galeries Lafayette, it rains throughout northeastern France; and it had been raining without letup for days. The Yonne and the two Morvins had overflowed their banks days ago, and the soaked soil was as impermeable as stone; there was nowhere for the water to go but toward Paris.

In the most precipitous and dangerous floods, the Seine had

been known to rise by half an inch an hour. This morning, in Ivry, just upriver from Paris, a café owner by the river had started to whittle an hourly record on the pilings of his dock, because no one would believe him otherwise; the water was rising at more than an inch and a half an hour. In a day, if this kept up, it would be waist-high to a man.

Although it had not rained in two days, the Seine was so full that the sewers were not draining normally. By early Friday morning the Left Bank General Collector was backing up into its own side branches, one of which was the weakened lateral sewer under the corner of the boulevard St.-Germain and the rue de l'Université.

The sewer line broke. Infiltrating into the waterlogged soil, it weakened the honeycomb of small pipes and dirt between it and street level. It began to seep through cellar walls into basements along the rue de l'Université. But most of the water spread, explosively, into the unfinished North-South Métro line.

Chapter 71

Reisden had been working at Jouvet for about two hours Friday morning, and was on break to get coffee and rolls before phoning Barry Bullard. At the St.-Germain-des-Prés Métro stop, by the ruins of the old church, a crowd had gathered and was gazing down into the tiled entranceway. A heavy, frustrated woman was making her way up the stairs, leaning on a cane; she paused; her hat, decorated with a stuffed squirrel, nodded at knee level of the passersby as she looked up at them.

"*Tout est en panne,*" she announced bitterly.

"More short circuits?" a fussy-looking man in a bowler asked.

"No, it's water!" a younger woman said, waving frantically as she ran up the stairs behind the fat woman. "Water in the St.-Michel stop, Chambre des Députés, everywhere, everything's closed, excuse me, I'm late! Taxi? Taxi!"

Reisden thought of the mildewy stone basement of Jouvet and the records. He went down the Métro steps. The smell of the flooding was distinctive even by the *guichet,* a mix of rotten vegetables, feces, and clay, the smell of the sewers. In the worst rains, the Jouvet basement had that stink; it got into the file drawers, reminding him of the smell of autopsies.

Under the bright lights the station was as clean as a hospital, and the low, strong, white-tiled arches shone as if just sponged. From far down the tunnel Reisden could hear a faint roar as if a train were coming or a fire hose had been left open; that was all. A group of engineers were gathered round the tunnel opening. Reisden joined them.

"As for the river flooding," the portly, bearded Engineer Ducat said, "it will continue until Sunday, if the weather stays good, and the water will begin to fall on Monday or Tuesday. The sewer system should take care of it. But as for your cellar, monsieur, this is the problem."

He touched the tiled wall. The fingers of his glove came away wet, and at the place where he had touched the grout between the tiles, a bead of moisture gathered.

"Water pressure; the ground's full. This close to the river, monsieur, your basement will ooze water for the next few days, if not worse."

The engineers were looking down the tunnel, where water had pooled, deep enough at one point to cover the rails. Reisden looked too. Where the rails dipped below the surface, the water dimpled. Suddenly the surface trembled and slid, covering an inch of the rails at once.

Eight-thirty: Jouvet was gearing up for a full day of patient assessments and lab work, and they were shorthanded; several of the staff were late. Reisden went downstairs and felt the basement walls.

They were damp.

Nine o'clock. The usual patient assessments were under way on the ground floor, but the lab technicians were pressed into service to move the files. To minimize the weight, they would take only the drawers, not the cabinets.

Reisden called up the bank and said he could not make it this morning. That was all right; the proper official still wasn't back.

At nine-thirty the concierge's nephew arrived with extraordinary news: the low parts of Ivry suburb were under a foot of water. He had come into Paris by the Austerlitz-Orsay railway line, which ran in a cut along the river. "It's being kept open by pumps," he said excitedly. "The train wheels were splashing up water, whoosh! High enough to wash the windows."

"We'd better rush through that patient from Orléans," Madame Herschner said.

"I think we'd better rush through everyone east of Paris," Reisden said, thinking of the banker who inexplicably had not been able to return from the east.

The technicians began to pass file drawers one by one up the stairs, as well as bringing them up in the elevator. Rumors went up the stairwell with the files. The most spectacular one was that the North-South Métro stations were already closed all the way up to St.-Lazare.

At half past noon, at the corner of the boulevard St.-Germain and the rue de l'Université, part of the street collapsed.

In Jouvet they felt the shock first, as though someone had hit the building with an enormous rubber hammer; then they heard the rumble from the end of the street. By bad luck they had in the waiting room one Gimault, who had been in a mining cave-in and either had neural damage or was very, very scared. He screamed and rushed outside, breaking a pane in one of the glass doors. Reisden went after him and found him in the middle of the street, trembling, dripping blood from a cut hand, looking up at the sky: "*Tout va s'écrouler! Tout!* Everything's falling!"

At the end of the street, by the Boulevard St.-Germain, a section of the cobblestones had simply disappeared into the subsidence. From the hole could be heard the same rushing sound as in the Métro station. In spite of the cold and damp, an unmistakable foul smell rose from it. "Broken sewer main," someone said unnecessarily. Close to the hole, a small puddle was forming, perfectly square, the sign of some subsidence below.

"Back, everyone! *Y a rien à voir.*"

The section of the street was barricaded with pieces of planking and lengths of sewer pipe. Two policemen and a man in a bowler hat directed traffic away from the corner, but traffic immediately jammed on either side of the sinkhole. The boulevard St.-Germain is a main street of the Left Bank; fiacres, delivery wagons, taxis, and autos piled up like ants; a tail of traffic stretched down the avenue. The man in the bowler hat, a city engineer, began to mutter about overload on the pavement and further subsidence. In the confusion, drivers got off their boxes, expostulating with each other.

Even with the confusion, it was hard to believe anything was wrong. For the first time in days, it was entirely sunny. On the peaked roof of Jouvet, the slates gleamed as if waxed; the wood-and-iron wind flag swung back and forth in the breeze. Only the drawers being carried out of the basement and across the courtyard seemed sinister, like the baggage of refugees.

The attendant of Gimault, the miner, returned frustrated with his charge from the Orsay railroad station; the railway shuttle between Orsay and Austerlitz was closed, there was not a taxi to be had, there were no trams. Gimault must get to the Austerlitz railway station, the other side of Paris. Reisden volunteered his car. He should have ample time to take them there, check back at Jouvet, and get to the American Embassy and Perdita's debut before five.

But the traffic was almost as bad everywhere as on the boulevard St.-Germain. Everyone in Paris seemed to be on the street, fighting over taxis. People dashed in front of his bumper; horses danced nervously and chauffeurs leaned on their klaxons. The stolid bus horses in their blinders strained to tug their old square buses, which were so crowded that men were sitting on the window frames. He stopped and took two salesmen, also bound for the Gare d'Austerlitz.

"Why is the traffic so bad?"

"Part of the Métro's out." So it was true.

When he dropped them he took the route across the Austerlitz bridge, meaning to go back by the quais or the rue de Rivoli. Apart from the tangle of cars and horses, everything seemed normal, even cheerful. The Seine was ruffling white against the pilings; after the rain the normally hazy blue sky was pristine, the low sun picking out every detail of the freight depots, bridges, and factories upriver. The only sign of the flood was that a bench or barge mooring on the promenade, which would hardly have been wet yesterday, today was half-submerged, only a spray of water.

And then he looked upriver.

Upriver the sky was always hazy from the factories and the big smokestacks: the electrical generating plant at Ivry, the compressed-air plant on the quai de la Rapée. But this afternoon, above the tall stacks of the Ivry electrical plant, where he expected to see plumes of smoke, there was only clear sky. Something had shut down every factory in eastern Paris.

Reisden knew the connections between money and disaster. He had spent the past two months putting together the Jouvet bank loan. Money was not particularly tight in Paris; he had not had any more difficulty than one usually does, until this week, when the one bank official who was supposedly necessary to the approval had not arrived back from Switzerland.

He had barely read the papers this week, but he thought back over them now. Flooding in Switzerland, flooding to the east of Paris. Flooding upriver of Paris.

After a flood, money is very difficult to get; everyone needs to make repairs.

He went to the bank and persisted. There was no hurry, the bank said, and there was probably not. But at the beginning of a disaster, there is a conspiracy to believe that things will be fine. Say, "The loan rate will be two points higher next week, and I can't afford that," and you will cause a flurry of activity meant to prove you are wrong. For Jouvet's sake, Reisden was wrong, or overcautious, but he was ruthlessly persistent, and he got his loan; and after the papers were notarized, he stopped the car at a grocer's and bought canned goods, bottled water, and tins of the plain crackers that settled Perdita's stomach.

He wanted her to know he was thinking of her, protecting Jouvet for her, stockpiling for her; because the signing had taken until six-thirty, long after the bank had closed. Her concert was already over, and he had missed it.

Chapter 72

The Seine is rising toward the Mona Lisa.

The rain has stopped, the sun is out, the sky is a pale, clear blue; but the river stretches and extends itself, mottled and scaled with light like the skin of a great beast. The promenades show only as ripples; lampposts stick stiffly out of the current. The river has broken off the end of the Île de la Cité; the Vert-Galant has turned to water.

In the Salon Carré, under the electric light, yellow-green behind her glass, the Mona Lisa smiles, and the river winds itself around her shoulders like a snake. The tourists look at her, and then they look at the Seine. They are shocked and excited.

They say that all rivers are women, but a river in flood is a man. The water is angry, violent. The old lock at la Monnaie is being beaten apart, the wood streaming like matchsticks across the surface of the river, piling up against the arches of the bridges and making the water splash high. The Seine is wide, exalted, crude, powerful, a vision at the center of Paris, a field of water opening like a wound.

Leonard reads the papers. In the personals, "R" is asking "MONA LISA ARTIST" to meet him in front of Notre-Dame on Saturday night, ten o'clock. Confirm at poste restante, rue du Louvre. But in the Social Notes, among the pictures of pretty girls, there is a picture he recognizes: at the American

Embassy this afternoon, Miss Perdita Halley, student at the Conservatoire, will play—

No more letter writing. What the baron won't do for Leonard's woman, he will for his.

Leonard smokes his cigarette on the balcony. Inside, condensation makes the surface of the glass gray and hazy. He sees in the glass barely a hint of a man, a being of suggestion and mirrors, someone unknown, a monster.

Chapter 73

In the Embassy salon, Perdita tested the piano, crawled under it to fix a sticky pedal, and improved a few keys. Every time she heard someone coming, she scrambled up to be found sitting demurely at the keyboard, playing little girlish arpeggios. People in charge of pianos distrust people with felting files, which explains a great deal about some pianos. Four o'clock. An hour to go. The caterers were arriving.

Milly breezed in. "You're not an ideal woman," Milly said, "I can wait for you to admit it. Besides, we were in the neighborhood, weren't we, Nicky?"

"I'm not an ideal woman," Perdita said, "and thank you, Milly."

Perdita had not thought of asking Mrs. Bacon for the services of a maid. Milly helped her get into her concert dress: short concert corset that one can sit down in, lace underchemise, petticoat, lace-trimmed underskirt, then the Worth dress itself. Milly sewed the underarm hooks closed with a whipstitch and then carefully arranged the sash and sewed that on. Now the hair: loosed from its ordinary coiled braid, combed all out (it hung to her waist), brushed, smoothed back over "rats" to give it the fashionable puffs, coiled again in a Psyche knot at the back of her head, and packed solid with hairpins, including the two purely decorative gold ones that were all the audience saw. Paderewski's hair might flail in all directions but on a woman it would look sloppy. Small drop-pearl earrings, plain pearl necklace around her throat, and, courtesy of Milly, a little kohl and rouge.

Five o'clock minus fifteen minutes, and nothing to do but wait. Perdita walked up and down the *salle des dames*, took deep breaths, and ate a cracker and a peppermint. Her stomach was jumping, but this time with nerves.

"I'll go out and see how many are here."

They had done everything they could for publicity: cards to all the Americans living in Paris, announcements in the *American Register*, and even special cards at Madame Bacon's open house yesterday. Alexander's Madame Herschner had worked hours overtime. Nothing mattered, really, not even the critics mattered now; but it would be much better, coming out to play, to hear a lot of little murmurs and to feel that solidly packed anticipation that a good audience brings.

Milly came back munching. "It's a great spread and that usually brings them, but I don't see anybody except the vicomtesse. I told her you were still getting dressed."

Dotty opened the door. "Oh, Miss Halley, you're ready. But no one's here. Even Sacha isn't here. I don't suppose anyone is coming."

Perdita felt her knees giving way; she locked them. Alexander wasn't here. She thought of him before she did the critics. "I suppose," she said firmly, "that people are simply a little late."

"George isn't here," Milly said, "and I told him to come. He writes for three magazines."

They waited as long as they decently could, then started. Not a critic had come. Ten people sat scattered in acoustics meant for a hundred. Mrs. Bacon introduced her, talking about her various tours and honors, which sounded ridiculous in this empty room. Then she played. She played well; she knew she did.

She had had her Paris debut, and had been ignored as thoroughly as if she had never existed.

After the encore she excused herself and retreated to the ladies' room, where she leaned against the wall, not crying; she could have five minutes to herself but she couldn't cry. She reminded herself it didn't matter because she was giving up the piano. She drank a glass of water and returned, smiling, to thank her hostess and talk with her listeners. Everyone said the chocolate gâteau was excellent. Mr. Daugherty said she had done right good. The romantic-minded stranger who always shows up at a concert took Perdita's hand and held it very tightly, telling her how beautifully she'd played. The flustered old lady, who had sneezed during the largo, echoed him. "I'm so glad I walked down," the old lady twittered, "you mustn't *mind,* dear, usually there are *so* many more people, but it's this *dreadful* water in the Métro."

"What water?" Perdita asked.

"Why, it's practically a *flood,* and very sudden, too."

"I thought you knew," said Cousin Dotty. "The river has gone up two feet since this morning; the Orsay-Austerlitz tunnel is full of water; the North-South line isn't working. When I was coming past the Tuileries, *mobs* of people were waiting for the trams, they stared at my poor old coach so, I felt like Marie Antoinette. I thought you knew."

I *will* think she knew, Perdita thought. I'm marrying her cousin.

Finally, with everyone gone but Milly and Dotty, Perdita could retreat to the ladies' room. While she held her arms up, Milly snipped the seam stitches and she could breathe again.

"Sacha has completely deserted us," Cousin Dotty said from outside the door, "but I trust I may give you dinner?"

She sounded delighted that Alexander hadn't come. *That woman* had known before the concert that the trams and the Métro were out, and hadn't bothered to find out whether Perdita knew. Next week she would have to be nice to Cousin Dotty. Next week and for the rest of her life. "I'm afraid Madame Xico has asked me to come hear a pianist with her," she said.

Milly didn't say a word, thank Heaven.

Dotty left, taking the dress to her house. (She was good for something.) Perdita went into the *dames* to change her corset. Unhooking the tabs, she rubbed at the welts the corset bones had left, felt nausea crawling up the back of her throat.

She wouldn't think today about having no reviews.

It didn't matter, she reminded herself.

"Where shall we take Perdita, Nicky?" Milly asked. "To celebrate her not being an ideal woman?"

"Oh, Milly, you don't have to take me anywhere; that was to get rid of Dotty."

"Good little girls eat Friday dinner with their prospective sisters-in-law," Milly said. "Bad women go to Montmartre."

The Louvre closes at four. Leonard dresses in his best clothes, a black suit. The suit coat is long, reaching nearly to his knees. From above his cot, Jean-Jacques' copy of the Mona Lisa smiles. He gazes at her, in pain, resolute.

The Métro is not working. Leonard walks via the rue de Rivoli. He looks into the window of a knife store; and glitter, glitter, glitter, the blades throw electric light onto his face, as if the knives were the surface of a river.

He arrives late. There are many fewer people than he has expected. The girl is playing to an almost empty house. She doesn't look drugged today; Leonard likes her; she has pretty ankles, pretty feet.

The baron doesn't care about her; the baron isn't here. Following her will be easy.

Leonard is standing at the back of the room. He looks at himself in the mirror over Mrs. Bacon's Federal side table, above the crackers and cheese and desserts. A stranger is here, eating the cheese, with his hand to his mouth: a strong, dark man, ill-fitting his gentleman's clothes.

Leonard barely recognizes himself.

A knife, stuck into the pocket, has cut through the lining of his jacket. Leonard can see it, carelessly visible. He doesn't remember bringing it, and for one minute he feels disoriented. He threw that knife away, into the river. He thinks he did.

He moves toward the exit, where she will go. But from the front of the room, someone turns around, a woman with hennaed hair.

It's Milly.

Milly and Nicky and Perdita went to Montmartre. They took the funicular to the top of the hill, found the bar, and bought beer for the famous pianist, who played his own pieces, moody and sentimental, with trick titles like "Pieces That Look Like a Pear." Perdita wanted to learn one, but she would not be playing the piano anymore. They listened to a dark alto singing Gypsy songs, Hungarian sounding almost Spanish, lovely minor-key slides. At least she could listen, she thought. They ate sausages on the place du Tertre. ("I see somebody following us," Milly said mischievously.) They went to Aristide Bruant's bar, jammed elbow to elbow into a hot, noisy, narrow hovel, while the old *chansonnier* called them *cochons* and growled songs above their heads.

Milly drank a good deal of the beer and became quite high-spirited. They walked back to the Pension des Jeunes Filles, all the way from Montmartre, in streets full of other people walking, too. It still wasn't raining, and wasn't very cold; the atmosphere was almost like a festival. The Seine would stop rising Sunday, everyone thought, or Monday. The Métro and the trams would be working again tomorrow.

"It's a rotten thing," Milly said just before they reached the door of the pension. She was getting weepy. "You're really a good pianist, you know that?"

"At least you heard," Perdita said. Alexander hadn't, and had left no word. "Thank you, Milly."

"Oh, thank you, she says," Milly said. "But what does she do? I could have had something to say, but my husband took it all. Now your husband's taking yours. It's a filthy shame." She took Perdita's hand and fit a packet into it: a small round cardboard thing, the size of a box of rouge, sealed with string and wax. She closed Perdita's fingers around it. "Think. A teaspoonful of the powder in a cup of tea, that's all."

"Milly," Perdita said.

Milly kept her hands clasped around Perdita's. "You don't know what it's like to lose yourself. To have no words anymore, no way of saying who you are."

Perdita saw a chance. "You still can."

"Oh, no, no, I'm done for. . . . I could write more of La Midinette, I know the formula, she was a success, Henry wants more like that, but nobody's going to know about me—not even Nicky, will you, darling? They want what they want." Milly sniffled, deeply morose. "And you want to be loved, chérie; and your *husband* wants to love a good, solid, sweet, dependable girl-child-mama who sleeps next to him and has his baby, and you know it's a lie, he doesn't know what you are, but you'll become what he wants, because you like the lies best, you don't know what you are, you just know what you want to be," Milly said.

"It'll all seem much better in the morning," Perdita said.

"Yes, I ought to go home to bed," Milly said. "All alone with Nicky. . . . Do you know"—she leaned forward suddenly, and just as suddenly turned and shouted—"Leonard has been following us all this evening? He thought I didn't see him," she chanted, "but I di-id. Hello, Leonard."

Footsteps fled down the street. "Took care of *him*," Milly said. "He thinks it's his right to follow us. I hate men."

When Milly and Nicky were gone, Perdita stood with the box in her hand, ashamed to have it, ashamed even to throw such a thing away. Tomorrow she would burn her bridges and telegraph Mr. Ellis she was marrying. She knelt down, finding the sewer opening with her hand, and slid the box in. From the sewer came a deep-toned moan, like someone blowing across the mouth of a huge bottle.

She thought she heard footsteps returning. The mysterious Leonard? She pressed the buzzer hurriedly and was let in.

And Leonard, across the street, knows where she lives.

Chapter 74

"Ten people, my dear; such a disaster."

Reisden found Dotty in her salon, elegant in blue silk and diamonds, dressed for dinner but alone for once; Perdita had disappointed her, she said. She had been sitting at the piano, picking out Perdita's polonaise from the concert. "She was very good," Dotty said, breaking off in the middle, "rather fortissimo but quite in control. The encore was something aggressively modern, not a crowd pleaser, but then there wasn't a crowd. Too bad for her. . . . No critics either. Poor Miss Halley. Even you weren't there."

She closed the fallboard of the piano and sat, both hands on it, the fingers spread out, as if she would play, gazing at the piano she had brought from Austria. "Still I was quite jealous of her. Now," she said lightly. "What is going on?"

He sat on the window seat by her, leaning against the frame. He had arrived at Mrs. Bacon's long after everyone had gone, and had returned to Jouvet to help move files. Now the *premier étage,* the second floor of the building, was so full of file drawers as to be almost unusable, and water was leaking through the stones of the cellar. They were having to pump out the cellar, and he was exhausted, but the records were safe and he had his loan.

"You're going on," he said. "The twenty-seventh, whatever

happens, rain or hail or high water; you'll host her and bring in critics and your friends, won't you?"

"Oh, of course, darling," she said restlessly, looking at him.

Outside her window, crowds had gathered on the quai, lining the parapets. He opened the window nearest the Pont-Neuf and looked out. The Seine was enormously widened, a great black plain sparkling in the lights from the bridges. Across the river, the quaiside promenades were completely gone, and some of the lights on the quai had gone out as well. Men were leaning over the bridge with nets and sash-weights on ropes, snaring the wood and the bobbing barrels and bottles of wine the river was bringing.

"Eh, 'sieur!" a man called from the quai, holding up a dripping bottle. Laughing, he tossed it toward Dotty's two-hundred-year-old windows. Dotty shrieked. Reisden leaned out and caught it.

"Not bad," he said, looking at the half-soaked label. "Come outside, Dotty, we'll drink *vin ordinaire* out of the bottle and watch the river."

"Sacha, really." Dotty closed the shutters and snapped the catch. "You are procrastinating dreadfully. Never mind this nonsense, it'll be over soon. You promised to tell me what is going on with you, and I want it now."

She held out her hand for the bottle, which he gave her, and examined it as if it were the first installment of his secrets, and looked up at him; and then the smile faded from her face, and she stood holding the wine, and put it down on the carpet, and sat, still gazing at him, her face drawn.

She knows already, he thought. She always had.

"Yes," he said. "I am going to marry Perdita."

She said nothing at all for a minute.

"Dotty?" he asked.

"I *would* like a clarification or so," she said; "I do protest a little. All I've heard from you is that she didn't have any future here. You didn't want her. You wanted to give her up." She stood up and went over to her window with the fine view of the Seine. "Is it possible that Miss Halley is in an interesting state? She looked pale, and that dress did not quite fit her. Worth is not usually careless."

He didn't say anything; it would have been no use if he had.

"Sacha. Darling." She smoothed her skirt impatiently. "I really didn't think it of you. You know how to deal with that situation."

"I want the child."

She made an impatient gesture. "Have you had dinner, or anything like dinner?" she said. "I think really we should eat. I have had nothing."

A new Frérin, another girl from the one who had eavesdropped, brought in a tray. Soup and sandwiches, comfort food for the schoolroom; he felt like Tiggy. While he ate, he asked how Tiggy was taking the flood. She frowned. "He saw a drowned dog in the river, and he cried."

He wanted to wake Tiggy and hug him and talk the sorrow away, which, he suspected, would only make Tiggy remember it freshly. He drank coffee instead, while he told Dotty about the water coming through cellar walls. They were trying to make small talk, but couldn't go back to normality.

"So," she said, smiling a little tentatively. "You are to be a *père de famille.* You have decided you are in love. And she is going to be a mama, and one has a sentimental tendresse for a baby and the man involved; but what about her little career? With a baby to take care of, of course it's finished."

"I want her to go on here; I don't see how she can. Can you help her, beyond the twenty-seventh?"

She closed her mouth over that, thinking, her face suddenly older and quite pale.

"What?" he said.

"I simply—really, I think—oh, my dear, what are you doing? She, if you'll forgive me, is simply being loyal to her adventures, at the cost of what she can actually do rather well. You are playing a role, because you like to please women you like, and this girl is having a baby by you—which, apparently, you want. But what you are saying now is contrary to every moment of your intentions, lifelong, and I have known you for twenty years."

"You make it difficult to change intentions," he said.

"You are marrying this poor little girl because you have got her in trouble. That's all. She'll be terribly out of place. She *won't* get engagements, I can't have her at my salon forever. And you'll be twice as unhappy as she is; I know you, my dear; when you recover from being mad to marry her, you'll realize what you've done to her."

"Don't," he said.

"You know I'm right. Darling, you're hurting her."

"*Don't.* It's settled already, Dotty."

She stood and took his hand. The two of them were crowded together, awkwardly, between the leather chair and a little table.

"I want you to fall in love," she said, "of course I do, but delightfully, like an afternoon in summer in the country, and at the end of the afternoon one's simply been very very happy. You should have a sensual, pretty, obliging woman, and care about her not at all."

"Like Cécile de Valliès."

"She's perfectly the right thing."

"She's trivial."

"Don't confuse—" She hesitated on the word. "Don't confuse happiness with getting hurt, darling."

"This is not the same thing as Tasy."

"Why?" she said.

Yes. He looked at their two hands, enlaced, her long thin hand with the wedding ring and old diamonds, his with the Reisden signet ring. She is real, he thought, feeling a wariness so long-established that he had almost ceased to be conscious that he had it toward her. One always lies. One tells nothing that will lead anyone back to Richard.

"I'm not being fair to you," he said. "Sit down."

He took the signet ring from his finger and put it in her hand, closing her fingers around it. "Listen to me. Three years ago, in America, Perdita told me something I've never forgot. She said, there are moments when one can stop lying, but that if one dodges the moment, one loses the opportunity to stop. Dotty," he said, "there is a secret, a real one."

She gave a long, sharp sigh. "Is this what Miss Halley knows? And Mr. Daugherty?"

"Yes."

"And this is what happened in America?"

"Yes."

She leaned back, one arm against the silk armrest of her chair, her dress setting off her bright hair, her eyes bright, curious, and oddly amused, as if she were being given a long-expected gift. She held his ring in her left hand, running each finger of her right hand through it in turn.

"If you are angry at me, later, for not telling you until now," he said, "understand that I wanted to keep things simple between us. This is not simple. It is going to be difficult for both of us. This is the reason I thought I murdered Tasy."

She looked up, a flash of blue eyes.

"Twenty years ago in America," he said, "there was a boy named Richard Knight. He was the ward of his grandfather, William, who was richer than all our families combined and unfortunately not sane. In the name of discipline, William beat Richard: with his cane, with a chair, with a fireplace poker. Richard was going to die from it. But instead William was murdered."

"I know about this Richard," she murmured. "He was the one who disappeared, the one whose body you found."

"Richard supposedly saw the murder and was kidnapped and killed."

He watched her hands, not her face.

"That is not so," he said. "Richard murdered his grandfather and ran away."

Dotty's hand made a convulsive fist around the ring.

"I do not remember my parents. When I was a child, I lived in South Africa. My past was a series of lantern slides, without any sense or connection: a bug on a leaf; an elephant blowing water in a river; the top of a cigar box. None of them had anything to do with America. I want you to know," he said, "I remembered nothing about America. And for some reason, I don't know why, Leo von Loewenstein identified me as the son of Franz von Reisden."

"You had this," she said, opening her hand. "He told me so. He said when he found you, you had it in your pocket, tied with a piece of string. Your father had left it with you."

"I remember when Leo gave it to me," he said.

"You had it in your pocket," Dotty said, "tied with a piece of string because it was too large for your hand. You had poked a hole in your pants and knotted the string." She closed her hand around the ring again, opened it, stared at the ring on her palm.

"Leo brought me to Austria. I met you."

"We told each other everything," Dotty said. "Darling, it is far too late for you to have secrets from me."

"You and I had English lessons together. For an Austrian from South Africa, I knew English rather well. I've changed my accent since then, but, love, I gave bits of it to you. Say 'fire' or 'parlor,' and listen to Roy Daugherty." He could hear the faintest lengthening of the vowels in his own voice.

Dotty smiled, a twitch of the lips. "Darling, I assure you, I do not speak like Mr. Daugherty. And none of this is true. I know how this is going to end," she said, "because I know what happened in America."

"You *know*?" he said. "What do you know, Dotty?"

"Don't look like that, I wasn't going to tell you until you told me, though you will recognize I was hinting. At the time I talked to Elisabeth Harany whose cousin was consul in Boston, and she said that Gilbert Knight had been notoriously mad for years, he thought his nephew was still alive, and for some reason he decided Richard must be you. For weeks and weeks you didn't deny it—*there* is the mystery—and then you actually found Richard's body. It was terribly clever of you, but poor Friedrich Harany thought he'd have to get you out of gaol. I suppose that Gilbert Knight thinks you are Richard; but it is absolute folly for *you* to think so; how do you explain that you found Richard dead?"

"It was someone else's body."

"Oh, really, Sacha! Honestly! I suppose one has bodies to spare in America." Dotty stood and held the ring out to him with the very end of her thumb and first finger, as if it were something she had been forced to pick up from the street. "This is your ring. Put it on. It was your father's. You had it in your pocket. You had cut a hole in the edge of your pocket and tied it with a string. Leo told me. I remember it all. . . . Darling, you shouldn't ever tell people these things. You are my cousin.

I know everything about you. How could I possibly not know this?"

She was still holding the ring. He did not take it. She looked at him without blinking, as if he were her Mallais painting, a bibelot she thought of purchasing, a cabinet on which the gilt might have been replaced; her eyes searched his for incongruous details. She had seen something long ago, or she would never have asked him if Daugherty were black-mailing him; she saw something now; her face barely changed, but he saw in her eyes both disquiet and need.

"You are my cousin," she said very softly. "I know you, Sacha."

He said nothing. You are my cousin, he thought.

"If you were not my cousin," she said, "and were anyone I could in any way admire, you would not have cultivated my acquaintance under false pretenses. You would not have made me suffer for you. Nor would you tell me this now. I know you, Sacha." She held out the ring to him.

But as she did—he saw this clearly—her eyes dropped again to the ring, and as she held it out, she turned it between thumb and forefinger almost imperceptibly, uncomfortably.

And so, instead of putting it on, he brought it over to the candelabrum on the piano and looked at it himself: the worn, scratched setting, the carnelian with its tiny incised signet. He had never wondered where it came from. It had been Franz von Reisden's; he had never thought otherwise.

"What's wrong with it?" he said.

The corners of her lips tightened. "Darling—"

He held it out to her. She did not take it. She crossed the room and stood with her hand on the door handle, as if fleeing from him, ready to call Dumézy to fetch his coat and show him out.

"No, Dotty," he said. "We are not at all done."

She kept her back turned to him, saying nothing.

"Tell me what's wrong with the ring. I had better know that."

She turned to face him; a lady does not keep her back to someone with whom she is conversing. "Darling, how should I know? Am I an expert, like Mr. Bullard?" Her eyes slid away from his.

He turned and looked where she was looking: at the school-of-Watteau picture that had replaced her Mallais.

She was not an expert; she merely had a very, very good eye. She had asked him whether she ought to display her Mallais so prominently, whether she should send it to the retrospective. If she had done anything criminal, she would have simply refused to show it. No, she had sent it, distrusting herself, trusting "Armand."

"Dotty," he said. "How long have you known your Mallais wasn't right?"

She stared at him, wide-eyed, her blue eyes luminescent, almost innocent, as her ancestors would have stared at the enemy before a last-chance charge. "That is nonsense, Sacha," she said. "The painting came from the family directly; Armand Inslay-Hochstein sold it to me. My Mallais is quite as genuine as you."

Chapter 75

By the quai d'Orsay, outside the hotel, there was a party under the electric lights. From the Pont-Royal, men were snaring firewood, swinging sash weights on ropes. In the black water, barrels were oscillating and rolling, playing like seals, then dipping to disappear under the bridge. Someone snared one and set it up on the sidewalk on two chairs, then screwed a tap in. A waiter came out with glasses.

They had had a game between them, he and Dotty, when they had both been in Paris in 1896. They would ask each other vast questions, and have to tell the truth.

"What do you fear most?" he had asked.

Being laughed at, she'd said.

What do you want most?

"A Mallais!" She had just met Mallais. They had been walking in the Tuileries, he remembered, she eighteen, he seventeen.

Armand Inslay-Hochstein had offered Dotty a chance at a Mallais: a very handsome painting by an artist hard to collect. He had told her its provenance, which was flawless. He had also guaranteed it unconditionally. Dotty had taken it home— and hung it in her salon, as she would do; and Dotty had no electricity in her salon. No purple shadows visible at Dotty's; Reisden wondered if Inslay-Hochstein had thought of that.

And Dotty had known there was something wrong, or

sensed it; but had decided not to say so, until Barry Bullard had panicked her.

Under the lights of the Gare d'Orsay, a man in a bowler hat was leaning over the bridge, shining a light down at a vertical strip running up one of the pilings. It must be midnight; he was taking the height of the river. The height was passed through the crowd. Five meters forty, two meters above normal. A six-and-a-half-foot rise in two days.

Dotty had told him the debut had been a disaster, which meant she was Perdita's only chance, and what had he done? He counted them off on his fingers. He'd told her he was marrying. Was marrying Perdita, whom she distrusted. Because Perdita was pregnant. And incidentally he was not Dotty's cousin. What had he been trying to do? "Telling her the truth" didn't explain it.

He had been trying to lose Perdita her chances.

What do you want most? Love. Control. Not to be lonely, never to be left alone with the mess Richard created. Never to be unhappy alone.

What do you fear most?

Getting what I want, and to be unhappy with someone I have made unhappy.

What do you want that you shouldn't have?

Darling, Dotty had said, you are hurting Perdita.

What do you want that you shouldn't have? What is the one thing for which one cannot, can never wish?

Someone tapped him on the shoulder; he jumped and turned. "Daugherty."

"Been calling your name," Daugherty said.

"Sorry. I was thinking."

"Could see that," Daugherty muttered. Reisden made room for him. Daugherty had brought a couple of glasses of the *vin ordinaire*—after its passage down the river, very *ordinaire*, one should have drunk it through a mustache—and they stood, elbows on the parapets, watching the black water swirl in the river.

"Have you read *Crime and Punishment*?" Reisden asked.

"Don't recollect. I heard of the title. By some policeman?"

"A Russian novel," Reisden prompted. "Dostoëvskii."

"Don't read 'em."

Reisden nodded. "The hero commits a murder and is caught and sent to Siberia. He is humiliated, sullen, sick to death of himself; he denies everything; he doesn't want to live. Then he comes to a peace with himself. One sometimes wants that, the grand Dostoëvskian ending, prison and the Grand Inquisitor and repentance, and Sonia in the snow. A change of consciousness. . . . If I were sent to Siberia," he said, "Perdita would come with me. But in a month she would have made the acquaintance of someone in the Siberian Imperial Orchestra, and we'd be exactly where we are. She found a cellist once on a beach in New Jersey, and there were only four people but us on the beach."

What do you want that you absolutely cannot have?

Not Perdita. Not her alone.

What I have with you, Daugherty, and with her and Gilbert and no one else in the world: to have been caught. To tell the truth, to be believed, to take open responsibility for it and so to get beyond it somehow, to have it begin to be over.

He knew suddenly, devastatingly, why he had told Dotty. And it had failed.

Behind them, someone was trying to fish in the railway cut, flourishing his pole like a whip and laughing. "Esmé, my cousin's husband, used to fish," Reisden said. "Dotty told me that when Tiggy was small he once took the three of them to Courbevoie for the afternoon, and he and Tiggy fished on the bank while she walked round and saw the Mallais landscapes.

It can't have been much fun for him, he was a sport fisherman, trout and salmon, and from what she says she didn't spend much time with them that afternoon, but she told me, after she bought the painting, that it was the only time when they had all been really together." He wondered if she had seen the purple fishing shack that day. Below them, on the flooded quais, the still-lit street lamps made trembling streaks in the Seine. "So she bought her Mallais. We never see what we look at. We see what we see. Those lamps: light waves pass through the cornea, the lens, and the aqueous and vitreous humors, strike the retina; neurochemical impulses are transmitted through the optic nerve; and beyond that is consciousness, which distorts the lamp most of all. We never see the true street lamp, only light reflected in water."

"Still tell it's a street lamp."

"That depends; trouble the water enough and it's an Impressionist masterpiece. I find myself thinking of consciousness more and more unscientifically: a question of taking care, a question of what one"—he gestured for words—"earns the right to see?"

No one saw Richard. No one wanted to, not even himself. No one wanted to see whatever was happening with the Mallaises; they only wanted to admire the pictures. "Dotty wants her Mallais, I want to be Dotty's cousin," Reisden said. "All that is necessary, and healthy in its way. But I also want to see the real street lamp, and I want someone else to see it with me."

"Sounds like being a detective," Daugherty said.

"No. It's—" He looked for words. "It's having another pair of eyes to trust, when one doesn't trust one's own."

Chapter 76

Leonard knows where the baron's girl lives.

At dawn he goes to the rue de Rocher, where he has seen her yesterday. From the corner, he watches the door of the pension. It's early and dark; his breath steams in the cold air.

In the mirror of a puddle, in the reflection of a gas globe, the girl appears in her white dress, her skirt pulled a little up, pedaling as she plays the piano.

She is in danger. There is someone after her, a dark man.

Someone is threatening her, he tells her. He knows the name but will not say it. *Someone* cares for nothing but her body; *someone* has no heart.

He stares into the blackness.

Chapter 77

" 'Ruins and Deaths,' " the manageress read the *Figaro* aloud at six A.M. in the breakfast room of the Young Ladies' Pension. " 'Yesterday the Seine rose by sixty centimeters. The Service of Navigation believes that the flood will continue until Sunday. . . .' " According to the *Figaro*, all through the Île de France rivers had overrun their banks; flooded Lake Bourget now reached almost as far as Chambéry; the seafront was flooded at Marseilles. Upriver from Paris, Ivry and the other suburbs were flooding badly. Fortunately the weather had turned good; it was no longer raining, and the Seine would not rise for much longer. "Transportation is very unreliable," said Madame Audipat. "You young ladies will have to walk quickly to the Conservatoire, if you are to get the best pianos."

The day of a disastrous concert is bad enough; the next day is worse. Today, this very day, would have been Perdita's last at the Conservatoire; a lesson day, with one more dose of light-and-bright Chopin; the men in the class would know she had played yesterday, but today there would be nothing in the papers; and her stomach felt awful, and there was nothing she wanted less than walking quickly to the Conservatoire.

Today she was going to Courbevoie. She had left messages for both Mr. Daugherty and Alexander to call her here; and in the meantime she went back to bed.

She woke again, deliciously, at fully nine o'clock, and had a long deliberate breakfast in an empty dining room warm with sunlight. Nobody else's coffee was tasting gritty at the back of her throat. She had hot milk, and butter and honey on her bread. No one was at the pension piano, so she played on it, a piano-shaped object one step up from a window ledge; but she didn't have to play. She would not be number thirty-eight, but she would have a husband, a child, an easier life. How long had it been since she'd had breakfast in sunlight?

She had a visitor, Madame Audipat said with disapproving awe: the Vicomtesse de Gresnière.

From Alexander? About the marriage, the twenty-seventh, or Madame Suzanne, or what? They took Dotty's carriage to the Parc Monceau and walked on the paths, then sat on a bench and talked. Perdita wanted desperately to know whether Alexander had told Dotty about the marriage and Madame. Dotty wanted to talk only about yesterday's concert. She praised Perdita's performance and wanted to be sure that Perdita was prepared for her own salon. "You are taking my salon as seriously as Madame Bacon's, I hope."

"Yes, ma'am," Perdita said, keeping a bushelful of questions out of her voice.

"Good. I have been talking you up. Even with this annoyance of the weather, a few useful people will be there." Dotty reassured her that the Worth gown had already been pressed, set times on Tuesday and Wednesday for Perdita to try out the piano, and reminded her to arrive very early on Thursday so that Dotty's lady's maid could do her hair.

Dotty's own maid would do Perdita's hair? This was serious.

Dotty didn't offer Rosine's services for Monday, though, for the marriage; finally Perdita had to say something. "Did you see Alexander last night? I was worried when he wasn't at Mrs. Bacon's."

"He has—told me you intend to marry." Dotty paused, un-characteristically, and after a moment laid her narrow cold hand insincerely on Perdita's. "I am so sorry."

Perdita said nothing, indignantly.

Dotty lifted her hand away. "You know, my dear, Sacha's really not very—stable. He has had breakdowns; Jouvet is absolutely the worst thing for him. I'm very afraid he is heading into another difficult period. Whatever embarrassments might make you think of marriage can very easily be removed. I know what it is to be concerned for a husband's mind," Dotty said.

She did, and momentarily Perdita felt sorry for her.

"When I married I thought myself capable of everything. Self-deception, my dear, is the greatest of sins. I hope that you will at least defer any irrevocable decision about *him* until after Thursday. Thursday will be significant for you," Dotty said. "I do intend to have quite influential people there, dear."

Perdita went round the corner to the local brasserie, which had a telephone cabinet; she could not keep from calling him any longer. The connection to Jouvet was fuzzy and faint.

"Morning, darling." He sounded exhausted and was calling her *darling*, which was usually his word for Dotty. "I took a patient to the train and went to the bank. I got the loan but spent too long at it to hear you. I heard the crowd was very thin yesterday; I'm sorry."

"It happens."

"Did you play well?"

She smiled into the phone at him; dear Alexander, asking the right question. "Yes, I was terrific." She should have said the right answer, *Yes, now I'm ready to marry you.* "Alexander, Dotty was here this morning. What did you tell her?"

"I told her about Richard," he said. "She didn't take it

well." That would be an understatement. "Earlier she'd told
me I was involved in some scandal in America, that you
and Daugherty knew of it, and that he at least was using it
against me. If she's said anything of the sort to you, I heartily
apologize."

Someday she would turn Dotty to a grease spot. "No. She
didn't say anything like that. She wanted to make sure I was
taking her concert as seriously as I did Mrs. Bacon's, because
influential people will be there. I'm supposed to go there early
and be 'done' by her Rosine. She was friendly," Perdita said,
"more or less, though I don't know what she was thinking. But
she doesn't want me to marry you."

"That goes without saying," he said. "The rest surprises
me.—Just a moment, Madame Herschner wants something."
He covered the mouthpiece; she could hear him talking in
French.

"Do you know you're in the *Figaro*?" he said.

"A review?"

"Here you are, under 'Tea-time' in the late edition. Perdita,
this is very good. 'Can one still speak of female genius, that
overused word? We no longer know what to say when we find
the real thing. To us comes a great artist—a serious artist—a
beautiful, incomparable, unique artist!' This is very, very
good."

She sighed, half-amused by the hyperbole, half-pleased.
"Who could have written that? There weren't any reviewers."

"Not signed. Later in the column you have 'stunning' and
'worthy to be compared to Samaroff.' That'll do for Ellis."

But there was no question of Ellis, who wanted her to tour;
there was a little silence over the phone. "Congratulations,
love," he said quietly.

"Yes," she said.

"I'm afraid I see why Dotty visited you."

She did too. Dotty's friends had seen the papers. At the end of the review, "Tea-Time" mentioned that the young genius would appear Thursday at the at-home of the Vicomtesse de Gresnière. Dotty didn't want her salon star to desert her. "I'd better practice," she said. She had better, if she were to begin to make a good impression on Dotty.

But that wasn't the way she was supposed to make an impression on Dotty.

"When you're done," he asked, "will you come here? I want to talk with you. I may have gone to Courbevoie, but if so, I'll be back. Don't try to walk down, please don't; get a cab."

"I'm going to Courbevoie with you," she said. "I know what it's about. Mr. Daugherty talked with me yesterday. Alexander, you can't make her stop. I mean that. She's been talking with me," Perdita confessed. "Not saying that she painted, but near to. She wanted to paint all her life."

"Do you know," he said, "Perdita, do you know what she's done to her grandson? What, very likely, both she and 'Yvaud' have done because they want to paint?"

"Both of them?"

"I'll talk with you, but after I return; and you can't go, I'm taking the car."

"Alexander, I am going."

She wanted to be a dutiful wife to him, in every respect but that one, but they ended in almost a quarrel over whether he would take her to Courbevoie. "Stay there," he said as if she were a dog. "Do this for me. I'll send someone for you."

Do this for me. "All right," she said. "If you ask it. But don't go to Courbevoie without me."

Chapter 78

Milly Xico arrived at the panther's lair a little before ten. "I have something you want," she said, sitting down confidently in one of the two leather chairs in his office. He was pacing up and down the room, like his namesake, talking in English with Mr. Daugherty. She gave them both a brilliant smile. Her suit was coral orange, with a low-cut dull green silk blouse. She leaned forward, flashing branch coral, glass emeralds, and cleavage, and watched her effect on them. The American goggled and looked annoyed with himself. "Darling Sacha" merely raised one eyebrow.

"Monsieur de Reisden. Monsieur Dohairtee." She took from her purse several sheets of thin blue paper written over in purple ink, and a copy of this morning's *Figaro,* turned to "Tea-Time." She had circled the column in the same purple ink.

"You?" the baron said.

She fanned the sheets of blue paper like currency.

"My husband," she said, "my ex-husband writes for the *Musical Review, Musica, L'Illustration, Comædia,* the *Grande Revue,* he's a busy man, Henry, it's remarkable how many plays and concerts he attends. Your wife is an attractive girl, just Henry's type, he likes her. He will when he notices her. He'll think she plays tremendously well."

She handed the papers over, and he read through them as she spoke. They were good, she knew. It had been a long night.

"Henry is about to commit a horrible crime," said Milly.

Mr. Daugherty was watching them, as curious as Nicky, with the same bulging eyes behind his glasses.

"Henry's always in debt," Milly said. "A few months ago an American millionaire came to Paris and saw a painting he wanted. It's—" She licked her lips in the way that Henry had told her men couldn't resist. "I can't say. He asked Henry to help him steal it."

Mr. Daugherty leaned forward, squinting, as if it would help him understand French.

"Do you know George Vittal?" she asked.

"Ten Thousand New Perversions?"

"George thinks he's an anarchist. Henry's given him the idea of committing a crime for art's sake. George is going to throw a copy of—this painting—in the Seine. Six days from now, January twenty-eighth."

Her birthday. She picked up Nicky, burying her chin in the soft folds of fat at the back of his neck, looking at Perdita's baron with dark-circled feminine eyes, trying not to smile. "George is going to throw a copy in the Seine," Milly said. "But this American has confederates inside the museum. When he destroys the copy, they're going to replace the original with another copy. So it will appear that George stole and destroyed the original."

She opened her handbag and thrust a copy of George's *Resonant Poisons* at him. "I like George, but look at how George writes. How can I tell him not to throw the copy in the Seine? He'd throw the original if he had it." Milly considered this a stroke of genius, using George's own words. Men always believed other men.

"The American millionaire will pay Henry's debts, just for persuading George. George will get in terrible trouble. I still feel like Henry's wife, I can't let him do this, it's so *wrong*. If a *man* were to tell him—"

"What is the painting?" the panther said, right on cue, the book forgotten in his hand.

"The—" Milly brought out her handkerchief. "I can't say it." She dabbed at her mouth as if she were discreetly removing a piece of lettuce from her teeth. Behind it she was laughing. She turned the laughter into a tragic tremble. "The Mona Lisa."

This was his clue to gasp and say, "The *Mona Lisa*?" But he said, "The Mona Lisa? Are the copies being made by Jean-Jacques Mallais and Juan Gastedon?"

"Of course; you were there on Saturday."

"And what am I to do?" said the panther, laying down the book.

"Call Henry, or write him. Tell him you know what he's doing; he must stop or you'll contact the authorities. That would be enough. That," Milly said, dropping her eyes gracefully toward the sheets of blue paper, and then raising them to look adoringly at his face, "and you will have gained my eternal gratitude, monsieur, and that of your wife."

She rose; she fixed him with a look worthy of Sarah Bernhardt, tragic, queenly, self-sacrificing. She smiled at him bravely, once, and then plunged out the door before he could ask questions.

Nicky bicycled his little legs, growling, but she didn't let him go until she was around the corner. "Chou-*ette*, Nicky! Someone Henry doesn't even *know, calling* him, telling him not to steal the Mona Lisa—"

She could not possibly lose. Whatever the panther did, she was going to turn in the reviews; one got paid! If "darling Sacha" talked to Henry, good. If he didn't, Milly certainly hadn't counted only on him.

The Gare d'Orsay was crowded with travelers, grumpy and hungover; some had clearly spent the night there. Milly bought a telephone call and stood in line to use the apparatus. All around her, tales of woe: "But *I've* been stuck here since yesterday *noon!*" She closed the cabinet door and asked the operator for Julie de Charnaut.

"Milly?" Julie's pinched little voice barely made itself heard. "Do you know what Henry has *done* to me, I'm so ashamed, I'll commit suicide—"

"Oh, poor Julie." She listened. It was awful. "But you have to be brave. Julie, I've just found out, Henry's doing a terrible thing. We have to save him—"

"Really?" Julie said, sounding more cheerful.

"Yes, but you *can't tell a soul*—"

Milly never depended entirely on men.

The baron's girl does not come out with the other young women. Leonard waits for her, then has himself shaved at the barber's down the street. He is hypnotized by the fall of tap water, the glitter of the mirrors in the morning sun, the shriek of light against the razor's edge. He asks to be clean-shaven, like the baron. He buys a strop and a whetstone.

Across the street from the Young Ladies' Pension, by the stairs that lead down to the rue de Madrid, he swabs the knife with the whetstone until only looking at it would make a man bleed.

She has not come outside yet.

Today there was not a cab to be hired. Almost all trains from St.-Lazare to Courbevoie were badly delayed, Reisden discovered by phoning the station; although the flooding into the Métro was supposed to have been stopped, the electrical lines had been "compromised," that lovely French word that means one will need to string new wire, and the Métro toward Courbevoie wasn't running.

The cellar was leaking badly enough so that they had called a building engineer, and Reisden had to wait for him. He inspected the cellar with Levallet. The pump was not adequate; the floor was almost completely covered with water. Levallet smoked his pipe worriedly, poking at the footings of the huge beams, the *poutres*, under the tower. The air was thick with the smell of must and wet soil.

Daugherty arrived, ready to go to Courbevoie. Reisden put him and Levallet to work taking apart the vacuum apparatus; they could use the pump to keep the basement dry. The gas pipes and electric mains were at the bottom of the cellar stairs; those had to keep dry.

The extent of the flood could be mapped by the patients who didn't arrive. No one was coming from upriver, Ivry, Alfortville, or Charenton. Filling in for missing staff, Reisden took the patient histories of Leclerc, Fabien, possible schizophrenic, and Aubry, Germaine-Élisabeth, a minuscule toothless woman whose principal disease seemed to be passionate unorthodoxy. "Is it Christian to drown people? As for being God, a woman like me could do better!" He could do nothing; he paced restlessly, taking notes on a clipboard, thinking of the flooding cellar, thinking of Perdita waiting for him.

He put Eve Herschner in charge, leaving her the telephone number at Courbevoie. "If the engineer thinks we should brace the beams, do it." He collected Daugherty, who had been helping to move file cabinets into the courtyard, and they made their way toward the Young Ladies' Pension on the rue de Rocher.

It had begun to snow lightly. The electric tram service was out too. The horse omnibuses and gas omnibuses clopped and sputtered along the streets, swaying with the number of people on them; the horses leaned wearily into their collars, barely able to raise their hooves. It was faster to walk than to wait. Reisden set the pace on long legs and nerves; Daugherty trudged behind, head pulled down between his shoulders against the cold.

Today the Seine seemed not a plain but a barrier, immensely high and wide; the force of the water made the Pont des Arts tremble slightly. At the Vert-Galant, the willow branches made a dragging shadow in the current. Tiggy would mistrust him for having underestimated the flood; Tiggy would be frightened.

"Coulda taken your car," Daugherty muttered.

"We'll be all right once we get to the station. The trains are running to Courbevoie."

In front of the grand facade of St.-Lazare, pumps were jetting out water from the Métro; water hung in the air as it does downwind from the Versailles fountains, and rather than draining into the sewers, it was pooling several inches deep at the sewer openings. Inside the station, irritated people jammed the ticket counters; the trains were running, but the hall echoed with announcements of trains delayed, trains stopped. The suburban train had been delayed, they learned, but was expected at the most in half an hour.

"You get Perdita. I ain't going nowhere else I have to walk," Daugherty said. "Maybe I'll just take this next train, and you two can come out by yourselves."

"And leave me by myself with Perdita," Reisden said nervously.

"You two figure out who's painting what," Daugherty said. "I'll get the house warmed up for you."

Leonard sees Reisden arrive.

Reisden waited for Perdita in the Young Ladies' drawing room for male guests. It was tiny, spinsterly: flower pictures, small chairs covered in floral-patterned velvet, a piano decorated with mother-of-pearl. He felt loweringly masculine. He heard her coming down the stairs, step by careful step. My wife, he thought, and suddenly he could not look at her; his heart beat heavily, he sat down and looked at his feet. He heard Perdita explaining to the manageress, here was Monsieur de Reisden, who was taking her to stay for the weekend with Madame de Pouzy at Versailles. He took her small bag; he held her arm; he watched her signing herself out; instead of turning toward the Gare St.-Lazare, he marched her across the street and down the steps that lead to the rue de Madrid. Halfway down the steps there is a landing, and there he stood with her, the two of them sheltering in a shallow stone-framed doorway.

He could not look at her directly; down onto her hat with the orange feather, at her fingers against his sleeve, but he could not face her. He thought of William, and Tasy, of all the danger in which he was putting her, of all the things that had gone wrong, all of what she was losing. I can't do this, he thought, it is not right; she is not ready. I am not ready.

"Hello," she said brightly and breathlessly from under her hat. "Here I am. Yours."

Don't lie, he thought. "Oh, love, and I don't know what to do with you."

A man was looking down at them truculently, waiting for them to descend the stairs. Reisden waved him on; he and Perdita flattened themselves against the wall to let the man pass. But something was wrong. The man came down the stairs, but slowly, one by one; he glared at Reisden. There was something wrong about the look or set of the stranger's eyes, perhaps not even that, something indefinably wrong about his face, a suppressed violence and hesitation, something very wrong about that slow truculent descent. The two men stared at each other, the stranger above, glaring, offended; Reisden below; Reisden moved Perdita into the shallow protection of the door and stood in front of her. For a moment they were inches apart; then the man moved past, sidling away down the stairs, still watching them.

"What happened?" Perdita said.

"I don't know." He steered her quickly up the stairs. That is how Her Artist would behave, he thought, truculent and timid, and then decided, no, Her Artist would not have let him off so easily; it had been two men in a narrow place, and he had been thinking unconsciously of Her Artist; he had been making up a villain to simplify his feelings, because it is so easy to protect a woman against a man who is not oneself.

He took her to the St.-Lazare station hotel for lunch. He got them a corner table and sat looking out, her guardian dog, to keep her safe or merely to possess her. Apparently Daugherty had got a train; there was no sign of him. The next train to Courbevoie would be in an hour—or two, or three—and the restaurant and station were mobbed, not a seat to be had in the waiting room below, and the café almost out of coffee. He peeled back her glove and ran his fingers along the veins on her wrist. She was wilting against him. He remembered she was disturbed by the smell of coffee, because *she is having my child,* he thought, and was panicked.

"I'm nervous about the marriage." He would never last until Monday.

"So am I," she said, and smiled at him.

"Come outside; we'll see if we can find a taxi to Courbevoie."

The place de Rome was a mob of taxis, some of them available, but none of them was willing to go so far.

"Let's walk," she said.

"To Courbevoie?"

"No, just somewhere, to get some air." She wiped the mist from her face.

He didn't want to explain about Her Artist.

"Would you go to the hotel with me?" he asked her.

They were given a room under the eaves, something that with fewer stranded travelers would have been a servant's room. There was a narrow iron bedstead with a handkerchief-thin mattress, a deal dresser, a sputtering red-shaded gaslight vying with the gray light from the window. He locked the inadequate lock: a ceremony of possession, a ward against everything that threatened them, from the man on the stairs to their own differences. She stood in the middle of the room, feeling her way; she bumped up against the bed, sat down on it, felt the thinness and cheapness of the mattress. It was louche to take one's fiancée to a hotel. It implied one thing, as going with her to Courbevoie had. He sat down beside her and put his arms around her, but as if accidentally. He wanted simply to hold her, talk with her, be held. They had been talking too little to each other. He felt threatened, as if by the thief on the stairs, by himself, by her, by the fire between them that was so much of love, and was not quite love.

"I should take you to the mayor's office," he said, "and marry you this afternoon."

"I wish you would. Do you want to?"

"I think I want to have it over more than I want to do it this afternoon." He wanted the public ceremony they would have Monday, with Dotty there and Tiggy; he wanted it to be as much of a marriage as it could be.

She held his hands, pressing them to her cheeks. "I want to be yours."

"Love. Give me your ring." They unstrung her grandmother's thin gold keeping ring from its chain. " 'I, Alexander

Josef, take you, Perdita . . .' " He threaded the ring onto her finger, and gave her his signet, and prompted her from vague memories of the English ceremony of marriage; she said the words to him and fitted his forged ring back on his finger.

"Rehearsal," he said wryly.

"No, I want it to be real."

They made love, deferring to each other's fancies, as if carefully showing each other that they were delighted with each other and the marriage. Afterward they sponge-bathed each other with water from the pitcher and basin, the servants' substitute for a private bath. The sky had darkened to dusk, the room was lit by nothing but the red-tinged gaslight under its red shade; everything else was layers of shadow. He felt apprehensive, protective of her, a cave dweller at night.

She fastened the tags of her corset. She had to pull the bottom few together; they no longer slid easily in; and so he untied and loosened the laces. He cupped his hand gently over her stomach, protecting the child. The child steadied him. Life, he thought; life not death; a marriage, a child, a change. Please. She smiled uncertainly and closed her eyes for a moment.

"What?" he said.

"Oh," she said, "it surprised me. I'm not used to someone else changing how my corset fits. No one ever has. It's—intimate—" She quickly began pulling on the rest of her clothes. "It surprised me."

"You mean I'd better have let you do it. Or asked you before I did."

The back of her corset spread open an inch. The underskirt did not button properly to the corset cover. She unbuttoned the underskirt and arched her back, pulling and smoothing the laces. He wanted them to do this together, as they would do everything together; he did not want her to take back herself this way. He buttoned his own shirt collar; he would have been glad for her to do it. She could not quite get the corset back as it had been, and could not fasten one button of her skirt. She buttoned the suit coat over it, looking defensive, troubled.

"I'm sorry," he said. "I don't want you angry at me."

"I'm not angry. Everything's happening all at once," she said, smoothing the fabric down. "At least we're married. Almost married . . . I won't take this ring off again until it's the real one." She flourished her fist, a little graceful version of a cheer, and gave him a faint smile. "Monday."

"Monday."

She shook her hair out and began to brush it, quick anxious strokes, then gathered her hair up in both hands and twisted it into a knot. "Alexander. What will happen to Madame Mallais?"

"I don't know."

"She *must* be able to paint. She is good, Alexander; even that expert on the Impressionists thinks so."

He said nothing. He wanted to give her anything he could.

"She did what she *could*," Perdita said. "She didn't paint for money. She did it to paint. That's not forgery."

"I wish it weren't," he said.

"What will happen to her, then?"

"I don't know."

"Could Dotty do anything to make things easier for her?" she said.

Neither of them said anything.

"Would you ask her?" she said.

"Dotty and I are not asking each other favors at the moment."

"I'll ask her," she said. "I don't care anymore about getting reviews; but Madame Suzanne is important."

"Don't talk to Dotty about Madame Mallais."

"I don't want reviews."

"Not for reviews," he said. "There are already reviews. For Dotty; I want to know who did her painting before I disillusion her about it."

"There's the *Figaro* one," she said, half as a question.

"I have seen eight reviews," he said. "Enough Parisian quotes to fill a poster. Milly Xico wrote them all; 'Tea-Time' as well."

"Oh," she said flatly.

They had started with Madame Mallais; but after all it was not Madame they needed to discuss. "They're not real, but you can give them to—you can use them, if you like."

She went over to the bed and sat down, slowly, amid the tumble of bedlinen, their careful professions of love. He let her think of how she felt about those reviews—especially "Tea-Time," which she had thought genuine. She said nothing, making him do all the work.

"You wouldn't like to give forgeries to Ellis," he said finally, "but you ask everyone else not to be disappointed in Madame's forgeries."

She fisted her hands in her lap. "No, I'd use them," she said, "if there were a next concert."

"You're being perverse."

"Reviews are meant to get people to the next concert, Alexander. People don't start coming to concerts for music; they come because their friends are going, or there's going to be food, or a known person is playing. But sometimes they stay for the music. . . . So I would use the reviews, probably, if there were going to be a next concert."

"So," he said, "one endeavors to become known, for the sake of the music? That's rather close to Madame Suzanne."

"Alexander." She raised her head, defensive as one can only be of a bad argument, passionate about it. "She didn't paint in order to pretend to be her husband, and I don't play in order to get reviews. I'm glad when I get honest ones, good or bad; but for publicity, I don't mind if they review my dress or the refreshments or even my eyes; I don't *mind*. People come because of a puff piece in the papers; people come with their friends, or for the chocolate cake; and those all have value, because—" Her voice faltered. "Because I believe in what I'm doing. I believe in the music. If I did not believe in you and our marriage and our baby, I would take any reviews in a second, and I would appreciate them, and I would get all the use out of them I can. I'm sorry, Alexander, it isn't your kind of honesty, but that's what I would do."

"She signed his name to paintings she had assisted in or done," he said. "She drove her grandson out of the house because she was selling forgeries and he knew it. Don't let her get away with that. I would not respect you."

"She helped her *husband*. *He* approves of her," Perdita said. "He respects her. And whatever she did, her husband did it too."

She packed the last of her things and they left the room in a fragile silence. The elevators had stopped working; they took the stairs. He stood in the line snaking away from the desk, waiting to turn in the key. All the leather chairs in the lobby were full of people, most with luggage piled around them, clearly not hotel guests. The air was hot and vitiated, overbreathed by too many people for too long. By a potted palm, two children were sleeping, their coats covering them, their heads pillowed on parcels. Perdita sighed in the bad air.

He put his arm around her. She tensed.

"You're trying to protect her by mixing honest reviews with publicity."

"Alexander," she said, "most criticism of women isn't reviews; it's her clothes and her accent and her husband and never her work. Who would give an honest review to paintings by *Madame Suzanne*? Everyone would say she's her husband's wife and no wonder she paints like him, and she'd only be treated like a freak. But she *can* paint, she *should* paint, and of course she paints like her husband because she learned from him."

"Don't."

"You started," she muttered.

At the desk, a large family of Italians expostulated with the manager: but they had absolutely, absolutely had a suite for yesterday, they could not help it if their train had just arrived; they had nearly been wrecked. "We're from Bordeaux. . . ." A German officer, coming from Köln, said the Rhine was at 6m75, its highest level in twenty years; a trip usually lasting less than a day had taken him three.

Perdita took out her magnifying glass and her glasses and began to read her mail, holding it almost to the end of her nose. He was conscious of being snubbed. When they were together, she usually asked him to read her mail.

"I'll read," he said. "If you like."

"All right," she said. "Thank you," she added. She doled them out to him one at a time.

"Letter from Mrs. Bacon: you were marvelous, the audience was too small, hopes you will do it again." She frowned. "From a Miss King: she *did* so enjoy herself, she will *certainly* come to hear you again, and she will bring her *sister*. From Milly: you must not marry, you are too good. From—"

In one shudder of recognition, he knew the thin green paper.

Chapter 79

"Leonardo?" Perdita said. "Is it Leonard? Milly knows someone named Leonard; he was at the concert yesterday." She shivered. "Last night he followed us."

Yesterday, if he'd been at Mrs. Bacon's, he would have been in the same room with Her Artist. Today Her Artist had been waiting outside Perdita's door. Today they had passed him on the stairs.

Reisden bullied his way to the front of the telephone line. The Préfecture was unreachable, the operator informed him; phone service was failing all over the Île de la Cité. At the Sûreté, a harried police operator answered. "Anonymous *letters?* We're dealing with looting, monsieur."

Yuor a prety Girl. I am going to Take yu & yu will Unerdstan

B CARFEL OF THE MONSTUR

Her Artist was lonely, they had made him lonely; *don't answer his letters, don't talk to him....*

"I'm going to the Préfecture," he told Perdita. "They will look for Milly, who knows where this man may be found. You are going back upstairs and lock yourself in. He doesn't know where you are. I want to know you're safe."

"What about you?"

"For once," he said, "don't argue, don't have an opinion, *do* it."

Chapter 80

At the Préfecture, petrol lanterns and even candles were being unloaded. The basement had a foot of water in it; the police expected to lose their electricity.

Inspector Langelais had gone to Bercy to deal with looting.

"Give me paper and a candle." Reisden went into a deserted interrogation room and, warming his hands over the candle, wrote Langelais everything they knew about Her Artist. His name was probably Leonard. Reisden described the man on the stairs. He included the letter.

From the second-story room where he was writing, he could see the Boulevard du Palais and the Pont St.-Michel, black with people watching the river. Leonard might be insane but he was French, and tonight the Seine was providing the greatest free spectacle in France. Tonight he would go to the areas around the quais, the Latin Quarter, the Maubert, the Orsay.

There was nothing to suggest that Leonard knew about Courbevoie. Daugherty was there. Perdita would be safe with Daugherty until Leonard was found; he wasn't going to trust her in the central city until then.

He should have married her this afternoon.

Reisden crossed the river by the St.-Michel bridge, making his way through the crowds, conspicuously tall, alert for Leonard. Nothing. The students were crowding down as far as the lowest unflooded quai stairs, dipping branches or bits of wood into the Seine to test the current and seeing them snatched away. He stood under a haloed electric lamp. Nothing; no one moved toward him with intent. On the quai de Conti the lights had gone out; he unconsciously held his breath as he walked through the darkness. He did not run.

Tonight there was no party at the Gare d'Orsay, but no taxis either; the station was closed and dark. He loitered, his back to the station wall, scanning the people on the plaza.

No Leonard.

He turned south, through the street market at the rue Jacob, where the butcher shops and the bakers had closed early, back to the rue de l'Université and Jouvet.

"Monsieur le Baron! I tried to reach you at Courbevoie." Levallet shone the electric flash up at the tower. From under the window on the second floor spread a half-inch-wide crack like a lightning bolt, and at the corner another one spread to meet it.

"City engineer was here," said Levallet, puffing at his pipe. "We've got to brace it. The scaffolders are coming tomorrow."

The water might begin to go down Sunday, Levallet said, that was still the official word. "But we've had to turn off the pump. City engineer said, if we pump out the cellar, water pressure forces the walls inward. *Poum*, front wall scattered all over the street."

Snow was falling again, individual flakes turning delicately through the light. With the pump off, the water level in the basement seemed to be rising as fast as the Seine, at about an inch and a half an hour. The last few filing cabinets were still in the cellar, half submerged and beginning to float. Turning off the pumps meant water would reach the gas and electric lines tonight.

Reisden put Leonard out of his head. Without gas, electric light, or heat, Jouvet could not function. The mock funeral in the streets last Tuesday had been about times exactly like this; when a French company fell on lean times—and a great many were about to do so in Paris—management put the workers on *chô-mage*, without pay. For a smaller company like Jouvet, furloughing workers was not only an economic hardship but a betrayal. Even under the Commune Jouvet had never closed its doors.

Up in the lab, the technicians were in a group, talking, stunned. Two days ago the water had barely been running over the promenades, and now, look, close Jouvet? For how long? Dr. Jouvet had never had to deal with this.

"We'll have to close," Reisden said, "there's no way of keeping the lab functioning, and we aren't getting patients without the Métro or the trains." He knew what Dr. Jouvet would have done; it was financially risky, but they did have the money as long as the transportation breakdown didn't last long. The water was supposed to fall beginning Sunday. "We'll pay two-thirds salary—" There was a murmur of relief. He talked about where they would get salary and receive messages, and told them each to take equipment, supplies, and forms. They smiled, relieved for no reason; the water wasn't falling yet.

They filled the ambulance with more supplies, and Levallet drove it off toward Madame Herschner's apartment near St.-Placide. "And, Monsieur le Baron, you'll get married, and we'll be open again in a week!" Madame Herschner declared, and gathered up her umbrella. He smiled at her with what he hoped was the right expression for someone getting married.

For the first time in the three years he had owned it, Jouvet was absolutely deserted. He was a little at a loss. He was used to being too busy here, fielding questions. He turned off lights and checked the lab burners.

He went upstairs to the apartment, opening the tower window and looking for bulges at the corner of the building; nothing visible but the cracking. Down on the pavement, a shadow scurried across the street. A mouse, or one of the shadows that disturb tired eyes. Not a man.

Leonard has lost the baron and his girl at the railroad station; has stalked among the crowds at St.-Lazare, waiting for them. But it is only the baron he sees, finally, walking quickly around the mud puddles in front of the station. Leonard follows him as far as the Préfecture, and by that time he knows where the baron will eventually go.

He is there first.

He simply walks into Jouvet. The concierge is not in his office; the nurse is away from the reception desk, though there is someone there packing papers into an orange crate. He melts past the two waiting patients, into the warren of assessment rooms at the rear. Stairs wind around the open cage of the elevator, and Leonard climbs them to find himself in a cluttered laboratory. He ducks behind a pile of file drawers, stacked on the floor without their cabinets, as two men in white coats come past, one carrying a big microscope, one a box.

There is a door ajar into a dark office; Leonard ducks inside.

It smells like a museum, old fires and old wood, fragrant with age. Two leather chairs sit on either side of the fireplace near an elaborate carved desk. On the mantelpiece are two oil paintings; one is of the baron. Leonard takes out his knife and flourishes it at the leather, the polished surface of the desk, the paintings. He gouges a long scar across the surface of the desk, then rubs his ridged thumbnail across it, ashamed. He sits down in one of the fine leather chairs, staring into the fireplace, where a fire has been laid but not started. He gets up restlessly and spreads papers over the knife mark in the desk.

One of the "bookshelves" is canted back at an angle into the wall. It holds books but it is a door, and behind it is a stone-floored hall from which stairs lead upward.

Stone stairs, hollowed out with age. The plaster is grimy and scaling with damp. It's not the way Leonard thinks the baron lives, not the way the office is, not like *her* palace at the end of the Seine; this stair looks neglected, no one goes up it.

Leonard goes up.

Upstairs, the hall leads to a library. Leonard, who lives on a cot in the bachelor guards' quarters and has read only three books in his life, looks round in awe at the shelves of books, the white marble busts, the gilded Sphinxes, the piano through the portieres. By the library door is a coat tree, and on it hangs a long opera cape and a top hat. No one is here. Leonard moves into the next room, which has a piano. He lifts the velvet drape from the piano and touches the wood. In a row on the piano are little blue-and-tan Egyptian figurines. They look like moldy painted-marzipan mummies. Leonard picks up one and sniffs it, touches it to his tongue. It's cold, like the whole apartment, and dusty.

He goes back into the hall. He picks up the opera cloak, heavy red-lined black silk, and puts it around his shoulders, over his coat. In the mirror he sees himself, a gentleman.

The lights flicker and die, and the dark swoops in on Leonard. It has begun to rain again, or perhaps to snow; he hears a whispering against the windowpanes. The darkness is full of voices. He gropes his way toward the stone stairs, descending them with his hand patting the wall, feeling the curling bits of paint pick at his palm like fingernails.

Below him, on the staircase, is another man.

He has been caught by the dark too; he doesn't like to be left alone in the dark, he's swearing. He goes toward the lab; he lights a match and feels in a cupboard to find a candle end. The light shines in his face. It is the baron.

By the star of the candle, the baron finds his way down the dark stairs. Leonard comes behind him. The baron pauses once, looks up. Leonard flattens against the wall.

The baron crosses the vestibule by the waiting room. He opens the door, goes out, takes out keys, and begins locking the glass doors from the outside.

The waiting room benches are heavy wood, solid. Leonard turns one over with a thud onto the floor. The baron looks up sharply, but sees nothing. Leonard waits for him to go down the steps, then kicks at the bench leg. It gives with a crack. He scoops it up and stands by the glass doors.

Even in the cold, through the doors, the courtyard has taken on an unsanitary stink. It is snowing. The baron is by the car. With the candle, he is lighting each headlight. Now he has brought out the yard-long steel crank that starts the engine. He is fitting it into its grooves, trying not to kneel in the puddles where the candlelight glitters.

He cranks it to start the car, the ratcheting noise fills the courtyard, and Leonard's bench leg crashes through the glass-and-wooden door; he kicks his way through, scattering glass, and runs across the courtyard toward the baron, swinging the bench leg. The baron has been looking into the lights; he can-not see now. He tugs at the engine-crank, trying to free it for a weapon. At the last minute he gets it free and raises it over his head, a steel shaft a yard long; Leonard flinches back; but the baron hesitates one second, and Leonard rushes forward and hits him with the bench leg on the side of the head.

Leonard drags the baron onto the front seat of the car. He is bleeding from a scalp wound onto the leather upholstery. Leonard's knife is at his throat. Leonard could cut his throat, even by accident, or stab at the heart—he doesn't want to think about that—he can almost see blood spray, and he shiv-ers. Having power is right but frightening, and there is a part of Leonard, an ordinary part, that wants to wipe the blood off the upholstery, wants to make everything proper again.

Leonard pokes toward the baron's face with the knife, and the man blinks. Leonard moves the blade slightly away, obscurely reassured.

He upbraids the baron to give himself heart. Monsieur de Reisden, do you like ignoring me now? She's still in *that* place; I wrote you for weeks about her; do you care now?

The baron looks up at him now, conscious. He must want to fight but he doesn't move, because he knows about the knife. It is almost like a discussion they're having. Finally.

What Reisden saw first was his own candle, stuck with wax to the wooden dashboard of his own car. He stared up blankly into the light, and the blade of a knife moved across his vision.

"Take me to the M-Morgue," Leonard said from somewhere above him.

He turned painfully and saw Leonard. Leonard was holding the knife away from his body, pointed at Reisden, gesturing as if it were some new aid to conversation. I could get it from him, Reisden thought, and then tried to sit up. His head throbbed hugely; pain ran down his face. When he touched it, it was blood.

He must have shown pain. Leonard smiled, a strange mix of pride, scorn, and wistfulness, like an unsure novice in a fencing-academy who has scored a point off a more experienced man. Reisden reached up toward the steering wheel, trying to get up, and Leonard scuttled back and jabbed the knife toward him.

"D-don't m-m-move without telling me," Leonard said. "I'm the m-m-m-m-master here. Not you." He tried to snarl it. "I'll k-k-k-kill—"

Reisden could have killed him in the time it took to stammer out the sentence. He wanted to. As vividly as if it were happening, he saw himself bending to crank the machine; the motor catching; himself turning to whip the crank-handle up and knock the knife out of Leonard's hand. He felt the steel handle connecting solidly with bone. He could hear bones snap. How dare you threaten Perdita, you bastard, he thought.

He remembered his own voice pleading, *He doesn't know what he's doing; he's alone; catch him.* How pretty.

But Leonard was looking at him, trying to see what he was thinking, and for a moment, as Reisden looked up, their gazes met, and Reisden had to look away, as though he were the man with the knife.

"Don't kill me," he said, playing Leonard's game; Leonard smiled, reassured. "I'll take you where you want to go."

They start the car, Leonard holding his knife to the baron's throat, so that the baron is well behaved, and Leonard takes the crank into the backseat with him; it's another weapon. Reisden backs and turns the car in the courtyard. The wheels spin through water. The porte cochere doors are closed. They both get out again, without a word said, the baron opens the doors; they get in again, he drives out onto the street, they get out, close the doors, in again, simultaneous, both stepping on the mudguard at the same time, as if they are joined, mirrors.

Leonard leans back in the high rear seat, the knife pointed at the back of Reisden's neck.

Leonard has never been in a car before. He enjoys the sensation, the smooth speed. They negotiate the turn into the confusion of the Buci streetmarket. On the illuminated wall of a

patisserie-confiserie, she smiles at them: a garishly colored
poster advertising Mona Lisa *baci*.

Another car goes past them and its headlights shine into the
car. Leonard sees himself in the mirror of the glass windscreen,
a man in a top hat and opera cape being driven by a chauffeur.
A gentleman, her gentleman.

"What shall we do at the Morgue?" the baron said.

"*Rescue* her, of c-course."

The headlights shone momentarily into the car. Reisden saw
his own eyes staring out of a bloody mask, and behind him, in
the passengers' seat, Leonard leaning forward holding the knife
against his neck. Jules Jouvet's old top hat came down over
Leonard's ears; in his left hand Leonard held the yard-long
steel engine-crank upright, as a frightened petty king would
hold his scepter.

He recognized Leonard. He had seen him somewhere, before the steps this morning, somewhere on the edge of things.

Snow fell in sudden thickness like confetti through the
lights, making a confusion of the street beyond. Bright Mona
Lisa; a red-clay Etruscan mask; a mustached man in a brown
cap, carrying Jean-Jacques' parcel. A red-clay Etruscan mask
with what had looked like an accession number, but might
have been a museum acquisition number. The Louvre.

Behind them, lights glared again into the interior of the car.
The auto that had passed them had turned around at the cross-
street, the same car, a tall Panhard & Levassor; it was behind
them now. The light dimmed momentarily, then brightened
again; the chauffeur had slid the blue filters down over the
headlamps, as if to avoid blinding pedestrians. But whoever
was in the car did it a second time: dim, brighten.

"He's signaling you," Leonard said.

"I know."

"You c-called to them—"

Paranoid, too. "I didn't," Reisden said sharply. "And they are not from the police. It's some hero who saw my face bleeding." He wiped his face with his sleeve.

"K-keep driving."

"Yes," Reisden said. "Move the knife away. I may need to brake."

Leonard actually moved it away.

"Now hold on."

The snow was falling faster. Reisden turned into the warren of the Latin Quarter, with its ancient paving and near-alleys, down the rue de l'Ancienne Comédie. The P&L followed them. He made a quick turn by the dark courtyard of the École Pratique, where lights shone snow-haloed from the windows of Physio. Psych, and went the wrong way into the rue de l'École de Médicine, barely wide enough for his car. His lights flashed past Dr. Auzoux's; in the window, the two-headed kittens slept in their bottle. The car fishtailed down the street, slipping in the snow. He turned, cautiously because of Leonard; the P&L's lights had gone.

Reisden sighed, alone with Leonard again, and heard Leonard's sigh.

"The police don't know anything about you. They're far too busy with the flood." Reassure him; get him to talk. Reisden tried to remember what he knew about reassuring the mad. What would have reassured him?

"What do you plan to do?"

He listened patiently. Leonard wanted to give his victim to the river. This time it would work, Leonard said. Especially with help.

"The authorities will not release her body to just anyone. They're looking for a relative or friend."

Leonard thought over this. "They let g-gentlemen d-do anything."

Their run from the P&L had taken them by a side street into the Boul'Mich'. They turned left and passed the ruins of the Cluny; five minutes, less, to the Morgue. It was snowing heavily.

"They don't," Reisden said. "They will not release her body to me."

"D-don't joke with me."

Leonard jabbed the knife toward him, irritated with him.

Reisden saw the knife coming and put up his hand to stop it. The knife cut his hand, and suddenly there was an enormous amount of blood covering his palm. He looked at it stupidly. Defense wounds, he thought. He clenched the hand; blood dripped steadily through his fist. Leonard's jaw had dropped, his mouth was open; he looked terrified, and he raised the knife again.

"If you do that," Reisden forced himself to say calmly, "I can't drive."

"D-drive."

He got it somehow into gear without opening his fist; in first gear, they crawled up the Boul'Mich' and reached St.-Michel. The snow was building up on the windscreen; the only way to see was to reach around the windscreen and clear it by hand.

"You'll have to do that."

The two men looked at each other. Leonard climbed out stiffly and began scraping the windshield with Jouvet's cloak. He looked through the windscreen uneasily at Reisden. Reisden thought of accelerating, running him down. The windscreen immediately hazed and froze again; the wind was blowing water and diesel oil from the pumps trying to empty out the St.-Michel station.

"The policeman is watching us. D-drive."

They turned into the narrow rue de la Huchette; the car slithered on the paving, bumping once against the curb.

In five minutes they would reach the Morgue.

"What will you do when you get to the Morgue?" He was speaking consciously very slowly, rationally, trying to get Leonard to think rationally too.

"D-don't you think I have a plan? I'm not stupid."

"Tell me."

Leonard said nothing.

They reached the little square by Julien-le-Pauvre where the old locust tree grew, a heaped shroud under snow. The car turned onto the pont de l'Archévêché, and suddenly Reisden could see nothing beyond the whirl of snow and the cones of light from the bridge lamps.

The lights were out in the Cité. All of them were gone, even the lights of Notre-Dame. The green light was gone over the Morgue door.

Leonard, with a knife and three feet of steel to hit with, was going to approach the Morgue in the dark.

It is a plot. Leonard can see shadows moving by *that place*.

"It's a trap."

"It's the flood, Leonard. We'll stop here for a minute. We need to know what we are doing."

"Whatever I tell you, you're going to tell the police."

"How can I? The police aren't here."

"They are here." The car is crawling toward the darkness. Leonard shifts the knife to his left hand, leaning the engine-crank against the door frame. "I see them. They turned off the lights. They're coming."

"Leonard, no. It's all right."

"It's not all right," he almost screams. "You don't care, you don't care, nobody does but me—"

The baron turns around. "I don't bloody well care about her, but I do care about you—"

Nobody cares about Leonard but Leonard. She smiled at Leonard. She was the loveliest thing in his life. But she didn't care. *Help me,* she said. *I'm lonely, I don't love my life.*

What will I do without you? he said, but she didn't care. Pretending she loved him, then asking a dreadful thing, a thing that would make him worth nothing—

Leonard thinks of women's ankles, women's haughty eyes, women's faces turned away from gentlemen, the baron's girl winding herself around him like tentacles, two half monsters struggling to make a whole. Women love the false ones, the handsome faces, the heartless; what was he to the Mona Lisa? A friend to be used? Was that all he was? Where was love?

Oh, Leonard is so lonely! He brings the knife up and down, up and down, flailing against the unfairness of not being loved at all, never being understood. Help me! But no one helps. You cannot count on women, not on anyone, they care only for themselves, they're heartless, they don't love, they don't take trouble, they ask you for what you can't do and give nothing back. Until you get angry, a man gets angry, and he hits back—

And the knife connected; it grated across the radial bone of Reisden's arm; the pain was like being struck with an iron rod; and Reisden went mad. He did not even try to protect himself against the knife; it was too late; he simply went for the man, and while the knife sliced at him, he got the engine-crank. He tried to hit Leonard with it inside the car but his right hand was barely working, he could hold on to it but he couldn't grasp it or control it, it was slippery. He kicked the car door open and fell outside, leaning on the side of the car, and tried to raise his right arm and still couldn't; as Leonard followed him out the door, he managed to hit him; but Leonard still had the knife, and Leonard came at him again. They hit and slashed at each other—

"No one, no one," Leonard was crying.

All this time the car had been standing on the bridge, and though it was late and snowing, there was some traffic; a fiacre driver had stopped behind them, and now he got off his seat and came toward them, flourishing his whip officiously. "Eh, don't fight on the bridge, as if one needed that!"

Reisden pulled himself up, leaning on the car. "He has a knife," he shouted. There was blood all over the snow. The fiacre horse began dancing wildly, the driver stepped in front of the animal, his mouth an O, raised his horsewhip and brought it down across Leonard's face.

A policeman's whistle tooted. Leonard's head whipped around. He backed away, his hands held up in front of his face; blood was streaming from his nose, his cheek was cut open; he shook his head, terrified. The fiacre driver charged forward, past him, chasing Leonard toward the front of the car. "No," Leonard cried out, caught in the headlights, as if the car were about to hit him. The driver and the policeman closed in on him. He held out his hands hopelessly.

"Leonard," Reisden called out, "stop, give up—*please*—"

But Leonard saw the one direction from which no one was closing in on him. He turned and ran, and climbed onto the railing of the bridge. Only at the top did he look down, and he saw, under him, only the river.

"I'm a g-good man—*Help me*," Leonard screamed at Reisden, and jumped.

Chapter 81

The fiacre driver and the policeman took Reisden to the Hôtel-Dieu, the big hospital near Notre-Dame. He was passed to the front of the line at the emergency station, and lay in a half-stupor on a table, looking up at the ceiling, and was told that he was lucky. "Who was the man, a looter?" He was Leonard, Reisden said.

The corridors of the Hôtel-Dieu were full of stunned men and women. They carried American carpetbags or bundles tied in a tablecloth; they held crying children by the hand, fretful babies dozed against their shoulders; their overcoats were wet up to the knees, to the waists. "Alfortville," a Red Cross nurse said. "Ten thousand refugees." The policeman said Reisden would need to talk with someone at the Préfecture tomorrow. He lay in a cot in a darkened corridor, on his side, staring at the wall, shaking with adrenaline.

Over and over again, behind his closed eyelids, he fought with Leonard. Sometimes he could not raise his arm and Leonard grabbed back the engine-crank; it rose and fell and Reisden felt his hands being crushed, and then his skull. Sometimes he had it and beat Leonard to death. He looked down into the river and saw dark fragments of himself spiraling away. Dying and killing in that dark, he woke to find himself shouting in a tangled blanket. His right hand was half-numb; he pinched and rolled the blanket between his fingers to

convince himself he could move them, and stared into the in-
choate dark.

Leave the body at the Morgue. Don't answer his letters.
Leave him alone long enough and he will break.

At the end of the river, under a moonless sky, the bodies of
the drowned washed ashore. There was William, and Tasy,
and now Leonard. They were made of some thin pale sub-
stance, fragmented into shapes like ordinary objects, a handkerchief, a broken key, the handle of a cup, all needing to be
rescued. Reisden stood in yellow-brown muck, picking up fragment after fragment. *Help me.* Richard, a small boy, stood at
his elbow, pale but solid as Tiggy. "Why are you here?" Reisden asked him. "Go away. Die."

The gray light strengthened in the corridors and a nurse
turned off the oil lamps to save oil.

In the morning the hospital let him go. He got across the
square and leaned against the doorway of Notre-Dame, then
went in. He was not a believer, but he was Catholic; he lit a
candle for Leonard's soul, with one for William and one for
Tasy, and stood watching the flares of the candles, the small
fires twisting together.

The homily was being preached, on the Marriage at Cana.
We are water, the preacher said; make us wine.

He had himself shaved at a shop on the Île; the barber was
heating water outside, on the sort of wheeled cart used by
roast-chestnut sellers, and around its warmth gathered men in
bowler hats and tailored overcoats, holding their hands over
the coals. Reisden held his hands over it too; the others moved
away. In the barber's mirror Reisden saw a gray-faced man
with a slashed coat and stunned eyes, blood crusted in cuts
around his face and neck and soaking his coat collar, stitches
whiskering his jawline, a man who should be shunned, a man
half-mad.

Inspector Langelais had returned to the Préfecture. They visited the Louvre.

The palace was freezing and deserted; the basements were flooded. The guards at the entrance stamped their feet and held their gloved hands under their armpits. Langelais's request brought the director of personnel shivering from his quarters in the Mollien wing. "Leonard's dead? Strange duck," he said, looking at Reisden out of the corner of his eye, then looking away. Leonard was Leonard Legros, aged thirty, employed by the Ministry of Culture for the past eleven years. *Stutters badly; can read but not write,* ran the note attached to his file, and in a painfully traced signature, eleven years rounder and less mature than Her Artist's, Leonard had spelled his own name wrong.

In the guards' dormitory, they looked at his effects. Leonard had owned two uniforms, two suits, a suitcase full of badly spelled letters, and the Jean-Jacques Mallais copy of the Mona Lisa. He had lived and died alone; his only friend had been his victim. *Msieuer de Reisden, Why doant yo Listen to me,* Reisden read. The letter had never been sent. Reisden sat on Leonard's cot and read until he could not look at Leonard's handwriting without shaking. *I'm a good man*— Oh G-d, poor man, poor bastard.

The quai du Louvre was a sea of mud, and the parapets were being sandbagged against the rising river; in several places the quai was blocked with sliding hills of sand. At the Pont des Arts, debris had built up in great mats on the upstream side: long pale batons of wood for the bakery ovens, branches, entire trees, all covered in a slime of garbage. The bridge was almost damming the river, it was shaking, and water was splashing up and drenching the workers who were trying to break up the obstruction. Even today, on the quai de la Mégisserie, the birdsellers were displaying their parrots, their colored finches, their canaries; the birds shrieked and the little wings pounded, maddened, against their cages. *I am innocent, I never killed anyone—*

He went to the Morgue. The Morgue attendant peered at his battered face suspiciously. Because of the loss of electrical service and refrigeration, the attendant said, bodies were being removed as soon as identified. The Mona Lisa had been buried in a common grave on Saturday afternoon.

All through the gardens, on the quais, even from the roof of the Morgue, crowds watched the rising river.

Chapter 82

Milly met Jean-Jacques at the Café du Départ on Sunday morning. He grinned bashfully at her, his blue eyes shone, he had got at least one new hair in his mustache; to get up early for this, Milly thought, I must be pathological. He told her all about the Seine, pointing out the hydrographic scales and giving her the exact depth of the water. The flood was supposed to have stopped today, he said, but the snow ticked down on their umbrellas; he discoursed on floods and the structure of cities, oblivious to it all, his breath steaming and his bare knuckles red. Preserve me from engineers, Milly thought.

He'd brought her copy of the Mona Lisa, at least; she shifted Nicky's leash to her other hand and tucked it under her arm.

"By the way, Jean-Jacques, are you in trouble?"

Jean-Jacques' pretty upper lip got thin and his lower lip larger; his blue eyes darkened to the color of clouds before a summer thunderstorm.

"It's all right," Milly said. "You can tell *me*."

"I don't know anything about it!"

"About what?" Milly asked innocently.

"The woman who moved next door, and her boyfriend! I *told* Grandma she shouldn't ever sell—" He broke off.

"Listen," Milly said at her most soothing, "you tell me everything."

He glared at her with the black disenchantment of seventeen. "There's nothing going on!" he said, and took off, running down the snow-slick street.

Baffled, she stared at the parapets of St.-Michel. The pumps pounded; forced up from below, a great continual stream of water came shooting out of the hoses, jetting into the snow and cutting a path through it, making a confusion of sewer water and river.

By now there were no trams at all. It was foggy and snowing hard; she tramped along with the awkward painting under her arm, pulling her scarf up against the cold, dragging a reluctant Nick-Nack. She crossed the Pont de l'Archévêché in the wind, making her way among people leaning over the railing to see the river. Below her the river rushed, heavy, yellow, thick, and startlingly close, carrying pieces of wood, broken furniture, bits of paper, fruit peels.

By the bridge was parked a car she recognized, Sacha darling's big dark green Mercedes, which was being loaded onto a garage wagon pulled by two horses. Milly peered through the window. The leather upholstery hung in strips, and everything was crazed and splattered with blood.

Leaning against the parapet of the bridge, examining the river as carefully as if it were a madman, was Sacha darling himself.

He looked dreadful, his face bruised and scabbed with cuts, his right arm in a sling; he was shaking a little, with cold or nerves; and of course he was twice as controlled as ever, the gray eyes denying anything was unusual. "Madame de Xico." He could only whisper.

"Chouette, what happened to *you*?"

"Nothing."

Leonard was dead. He'd thrown himself in the river. What had he done? Killed a woman. Of course. Sacha stared over the mud-laden water, hatless, oblivious to the snow, shaking. Poor stiff-as-a-stick Sacha, he couldn't admit he hadn't been in charge the whole time, even of a raving lunatic.

"Leonard?" It was cruel of her, of course, but Milly could weave even this into her story for George. "Where's Perdita? Is she all right?"

Sacha darling turned pale, eyes wide.

Chapter 83

"I'll get her from the hotel," Milly said.

Easy to say. Milly got onto an overcrowded horsecar by offering to sing "Le Temps des cerises" for the passengers. "In Cherry-blossom Time" she warbled up the rue de l'Opéra, and "What Are Men Good For?" and "La Matchiche." Everyone hated to see her go.

At the Terminus, she found Perdita. All the girl wanted to talk about was the eternal Himself, of course. "I was sure Alexander was dead," she said. She put her hands in front of her face, but then banged her fists together, like a jockey's wife who has seen her husband fall at a fence, distraught and angry.

"What a state he'd have left you in if he'd got himself killed," Milly said soberly.

They made their way toward Jouvet, Perdita cautious on the slippery sidewalks. Milly carried her carpetbag, having left Jean-Jacques' Mona Lisa at the railroad station. In front of the station, all across the plaza, the water was at least an inch deep; the pumps were working so hard, and there were so many of them, that the air had taken on a smoky brown haze. They cut away from the traffic into the streets east of the Opéra, where, to Nick's delight, they found a butcher who had dog bones. "Buy extra," the butcher told them. Perdita, good housewife, bought steak and sausages for her irresponsible beloved, taking pains to make them the best. Dim dom boum, an interesting girl reduced to buying sausage. But you won't give up, Milly thought, not after you read my reviews; I can write when I want, me.

"What's in your bag? It's heavy."

"I'll carry it," Perdita said.

"I didn't say that."

"A tuning-kit," Perdita said. "Dotty's piano may go out of tune. If I play for her."

Milly opened the bag, looked at the tuning-handle and tuning-forks, and said nothing, briefly but eloquently and pointedly. Milly had heard about the Bösendorfer Concert Imperial. Perdita had run away to her beloved, with a tuning-kit.

"I'm not going to play the piano."

"Did you like your review? Wait till you see the one in *Harmonia*. People will be quoting it for years."

"I don't need reviews," Perdita said thornily, then: "Thank you, Milly."

"Why are you going right back to him, after he treated you that way?"

"I'm going to marry him."

"He doesn't need you, he needs sleep. If you go see him now, you'll spend the afternoon patting his hand and saying *poor dear* and wishing you could spit at him. And you're getting married tomorrow. What you need," said Milly cunningly, "is a little music."

Chapter 84

After waiting for Reisden and Perdita overnight at Courbevoie, Daugherty went back to Paris. Jouvet was deserted and dark, and the front door was smashed. Daugherty swore and heaved the door open. Inside, sitting in the waiting room with his head in his hands, was Reisden.

"You're in Courbevoie," he said.

"I walked back; son, what the h—l happened to you?"

The elevator wasn't working. Daugherty got Reisden up to the apartment and got him lying down on a sofa with a French comforter over him. "You want anything?"

"Look in Merck's for how much aspirin is a lethal dose," Reisden said. "A little less than that."

Somebody had beat him up, someone named Leonard, who had been crazier than a ginmill rat, and Leonard was dead, and all this had been happening while Daugherty was around and Reisden hadn't told him.

"I kind of take that hard. You coulda told me. Mighta done something."

The apartment was cold enough to freeze meat. The furnace was out. The apartment had no coal upstairs, no wood apart from the five or six logs piled in the fireplace. Daugherty wondered whether Reisden was going to try to do something about it himself or whether he'd ask for help.

He tried, getting up stiffly.

"Siddown," Daugherty said. "What you want to burn? Chair you don't like, or a bedstead?"

"Anything but the piano," Reisden said, and then awkwardly, "Thank you."

Daugherty burned a chair, and the velvet curtains and drapes, and the packing from all the books. And then, because Reisden still hadn't dropped asleep, he hefted one of the big solemn tomes. "How about that?"

Reisden took it and looked through it. "Old edition. All right."

It burned coppery green, slow as a log. The text was something about nervous diseases. The pages moved and Daugherty saw a dissected brain, white and black turning to black and gray.

"I couldn't help him," Reisden said. "Leonard. I hated him. I wanted to beat him to death; I knew what was happening to him and he asked me for help but I couldn't help him. Now he's dead."

Son, Daugherty thought, you got it all wrong; you got to learn how to take a lot of help if you're giving it. Especially if you go round hunting mad folks; this ain't the only time you're going to get beat up. Might do it once or twice myself. Daugherty looked round the apartment, which Perdita was going to come to as a bride the next day: little gimcrack tables with dead plants on them and those spindly chairs that fell over if you looked at them. Daugherty pointed at the tables, which Perdita would trip over.

"You ever thought of getting rid a these, doing a little clearing up, something?"

"There hasn't been time since last week."

"You been here three years."

Reisden smiled, a little shamefaced. "They'd burn," he suggested.

"What I was thinkin'." Daugherty went into the kitchen and came back with a hammer.

"I still have a sense she'll never live here," Reisden said. "She wants Madame Mallais to have forged paintings, and she wants Madame's husband to have supported her in it. She's vehement over it, I think, because she wants my support to tour. Tasy toured," he said. "Then it was just the way things were and it was difficult but it wasn't personal. Now there's a part of me that believes Perdita doesn't want music for itself but because it gets her away from me. And I give her every excuse."

"You know better, son."

"Not entirely; I'd get away from myself if I could, and I don't truly admire her for making another decision. My L—d, Daugherty, I can't protect her from me, I can't give her anything of value any more than I could Leonard, and we're getting married tomorrow."

"Well," Daugherty said, "leastways let's clear up."

Daugherty broke the legs off chairs and went downstairs and chopped up the broken bench too, and left the wood stacked by the fireplace. Reisden threw books into the fire, but left a pretty substantial pile to one side. Daugherty went down to the rue de Buci and came back with a scrawny chicken; he set it to boil in a pot in the ashes, with an onion and some potatoes, soup like he'd made for the boys. Reisden watched him like he'd never seen soup made before.

"Monsieur Mallais," he said. "Brother Yvaud. Whoever he is. He loves Madame; and if I'm right, he trained her to paint for him. Even if he is Mallais," Reisden said, "Perdita is right about this, Madame will be exposed as a forger, she'll be made to stop. For the second time. He didn't protect her."

"Nope," Daugherty conceded.

"What will he think," Reisden said. "What will he feel.—

Perdita's going out to Courbevoie for Madame's sake. I think I will be going to talk to brother Yvaud."

About then Perdita arrived, and the two children sat together in front of the fire while Daugherty went to find something to do elsewhere. He cleaned up the kitchen, throwing out newspapers left over from Dr. Jouvet's day.

He looked out once and saw them holding hands, the two of them grave and sad, sitting by the fire together, not speaking, as though they were protecting each other. It was a powerful picture, a sad one, and he went back in the kitchen and scrubbed at pots with years-old rust on them, but after a while he brought out his book and drew it out as best he could: Reisden and Perdita leaning against each other, but looking each in a different direction, ashamed.

Putting it on the page like that, he knew he would never forget it, though he'd have liked to.

He thought of Mallais: the sunset over the Seine, the girl standing in front of the rose hedge. That sad picture, *The Veil,* the dead woman. Daugherty understood now how it was different to be an artist. How much seeing Mallais had had to do; spring runoff and sunsets, sure, and naked women—but that wasn't all as easy as you'd think—and his own dead wife. Things he'd rather have forgot.

How could a man have stood to look at all of that? How could've Mallais borne it, seeing his wife dead and then having to look at her again, over and over, while he painted?

Daugherty wondered if Mallais hadn't taught his wife to paint just so he'd have someone to talk to who had seen as much.

Chapter 85

At a time when concert-going competed with the Folies Bergère and the vaudeville for popularity, no French concert manager would put only one item on his programme, even if it was Beethoven's Ninth Symphony. On Sunday the twenty-third, the special program of the Concert Colonne also featured the *Leonore* Overture, Ganaye's *Lieder of the Forest,* and Georges de Lausnay in Saint-Saëns' Fifth Piano Concerto. But whether it was Colonne's advanced age, the disruption caused by the flood, or the sheer size of the program, this was an off day. The pauses between movements and pieces were longer than usual, as players retuned their instruments because of the pervasive damp, and de Lausnay played Saint-Saëns' Fifth as if he had been adding two and a half to two and a half.

Perdita had studied the Saint-Saëns, and by the second movement, her right hand, against her skirt, was playing along with Lausnay, and with better expressivity, thank you; her right foot was tapping the carpet as if it were a pedal; but carefully, very carefully, so that Milly wouldn't notice. Her thoughts were the fantasies of students: What if de Lausnay broke his arm before the third movement, what if Colonne suddenly needed a pianist? And what would become then of her resolve to give up music? She was no longer a student; she was someone who had made her bargain, thinking shabbily of release.

Ganaye's *Lieder of the Forest* was gluey, awful. She let herself drift. Madame Mallais might agree not to sell her work, perhaps, but she must be allowed to paint. Paints and canvas cost money; Milly had told Perdita a big canvas could cost several hundred francs in materials. If Madame Mallais were bankrupt and needed paints, Perdita would buy them herself, she decided. (She wondered where her own money would come from, and whether she would need Alexander's permission to spend it.)

But if Madame Mallais painted, wouldn't she want an audience? Artists like audiences; people with enthusiasms and visions like to share them. Look what I can do with the piano! Hear this music! Hear what can happen!

"Milly," she said in the interval before the Ninth. "Let me tell you a story. But, mind"—Milly *was* a journalist—"only a story."

"M'hm," said Milly.

"There was a woman whose husband painted. He grew old and couldn't paint as well and he asked her to help him. She had painted too, when she was young. She learned his way of painting and she helped him; she painted in his style, with his ideas."

"Then she began to have ideas of her own," Milly said. "So her husband found a woman with no ideas, and the first woman has ended up in a ditch somewhere, or divorced, in a little apartment on the bad side of town. Making copies."

"No, her husband approves of her."

"I don't believe *that*."

"But someone else has found that she painted some pictures her husband is supposed to have done, and they want to stop her from painting. This while her husband is still alive, and approves of what she is doing."

" 'They' is your Sacha?"

"I didn't say that."

Milly patted her arm. "Everything is him with you," she said. "I'll be delighted when you fall out of love with him; you're like a woman who has just had her salon wallpapered and can't stop talking about it. Your Sacha will stop her, the way he's stopping you."

Perdita was not ready for the Ninth, because today it spoke to her on too many levels: the tremendous emotional quality of the music: fear, physical pleasure, solemn duty; its coloration, the horns like Milly Xico's brash nagging, like the taxi horns on the quai des Orfèvres; a flute like a child's voice; thoughtful, tender music, woodwinds and strings, her Alexander, finding his center in marriage, but treating marriage with so little care, so little of his intelligence; in the midst of joy, a bronze bugle call of longing; such complexity in the few notes of a theme. Around her, hundreds of people sat silent, men and women, magicked by these wordless truths. A wife's words are *I love you, I am devoted,* simple things, nothing else is expected of her, no subtleties, no variations or inversions of the theme, no development; a wife is as simple as a piece of string; but women understand the complex truths Beethoven wrote as well as men.

What made it wrong to silence Madame Suzanne was not just that she'd painted like Mallais; she was good enough to understand like Mallais, complex enough to paint like him. Even if she painted *very* like him—

Why must women stay silent, and do no more than understand, must they never speak? All the voices that women could have, paintbrushes, snare drums, violins, the piano. All the things that women could say. *I lost my words,* Milly had said. Madame Mallais had got hers, her brushes and canvases and tubes of color, not her name perhaps, but her voice. *I took myself back.*

What was wrong with the world, that a woman who saw pictures could not paint them? There were the clothes to fold, the children to take care of; the men who expected the women to fold clothes and take care; the daughters who did not have music, the sons who did; the necessity of everything that women did, and its second-classness; but why could there not be more, for someone, why could there not be more?

Madame Mallais had folded the clothes, but she had refused to be without a voice. She had no name; very well, she had signed her husband's. She had no training; she had learned from him. And she had painted forgeries, but with a voice, eyes, a mind; and with her husband's love behind her. *He* had heard her and believed in her.

"Joy, thou flash of light immortal," the chorus thundered, "Daughter of Elysium . . ."

And for once what Perdita heard in a piece of music was not the music but the words.

> "All men in the world are brothers
> In the shadow of thy wings.
> He who knows the pride and pleasure
> Of a friendship firm and strong,
> He who has a wife to treasure,
> Let him swell our mighty song! . . ."

Where were the women here? Only treasured wives, winged Joy, Nature's fruitful breast, footsteps strewn with roses; only the reward in the background.

Women were not Joy and Nature, no matter how many

men said it, no matter how long they said it, whether they were
Maître or Beethoven, it was not true. Take the music back, and
you hear sopranos and altos singing: they are not the voice of
heavenly choirs, they are women: they are not inspirations,
they are singers.

What would it mean, taking music back? It would mean,
not half measures and genteel music, but the real thing. It
would mean to squeeze out of that piano every note and more.
It would mean hurt too, and time, a heartless devotion, going
away for weeks and months; leaving a husband and a child
alone; loving some thing, some idea, as much as any person,
and knowing they sensed it, giving hurt for the sake of truth
and love. What terrible words those would be in a woman's
mouth, what disharmony; Perdita flinched from saying them;
but they would not go away; they would not let her go.

Real women really made art, and art for women was criminal, was heartless, it tore apart the world she wanted; and she
was one of them, she could not help it. She would marry
Alexander tomorrow, she could not help that either; but she
would be torn apart, moment by moment, day by day, until
she hurt Alexander and her child too badly and tore apart her
marriage, because her music would not let her go.

Chapter 86

With the breakdown of transportation and the flooding of the city incinerator, Milly wrote, *the Paris trash collectors fall back on the stratagems of ancient times. Carts and tumbrels roll through the streets to the Pont de Tolbiac, at the upriver end of Paris. Into the Seine fall wine bottles, fruitrinds, butcher paper, rotten vegetables, and the scrapings of plates. Some of this nauseating mixture is carried away by the water; some lodges against the bridges, mixing with the wood and debris already there and forming great mats, which must be broken up.*

Several of the bridges were now in danger. The lower-arched modern bridges, the recently restored Carrousel, the Pont Alexandre III, and especially the Pont de l'Alma, were underwater almost to the tops of their arches. *One has the impression of being able to reach out and touch the flood,* Milly wrote in her notebook, which was propped against the back of a shivering Nick-Nack on the parapet of the Alma. *The water is up to the Zouave's elbows. At ten in the evening, the Alma has been cleared of traffic, but I stand among five hundred people. We feel the bridge vibrate under our feet; we shiver under our umbrellas, awestruck at the gruesome and fatal spectacle of the Seine.* If the water rose further, there were plans to dynamite the central arch of the Alma in order to save the rest of the bridge.

And the water continued to rise. It had been supposed to stop; but it was not stopping. During the evening of Sunday, the Seine reached the ventilation windows of the Orsay-Invalides tunnel and began pouring through them into the tunnel and the station itself. The station floor was already partially flooded; now the water began to rise so rapidly that, by midnight, it was above the wheels of two locomotives trapped in the Gare d'Orsay.

Chapter 87

I n midmorning, Barry Bullard met Reisden and Daugherty at
Jouvet. Reisden was barely awake, but had dressed for the
wedding already, not being up to dressing twice; in Dr. Jouvet's gilded mirror he saw a grotesque Frankensteinian thing,
black-circled eyes, knife cuts sewn up with black thread, arm in
a sling, dressed in a custom-made gentleman's morning suit.
Bullard, a polite man, said nothing, asked nothing, only accepted tea courtesy of Daugherty's pot of boiling water, bub-
bling away over a fire of books. He had brought a wedding
present, a small oil sketch of the Seine in flood.

"I may 'ave bad news," he said, "or maybe very good."

Outside, it was snowing and numbingly cold. Even by the
fire it was chill.

"Let it be good," Reisden said. "We'd like some." He had
spent last night thinking about the cost of repairs to Jouvet. He
had a margin, but it didn't include the costs of being closed, or
of the flood.

"I looked at the brushwork of the two sketches you showed
me," Bullard said, clearing his throat, "comparing them with
other late Mallais work. Mallais starts with a 'ighly tinted
ground, then builds up 'is surface in layers. . . ." Reisden faded
out, leaning against the back of the couch. The light had a
headachy sharpness, and everything hurt.

"What?" he said, blinking awake.

"In my opinion," Bullard said, "the same person painted them all."

"Mallais painted them?" Reisden said, not understanding.

"*View of the Seine,* your picture, *Spruce and Shadow,* but also two paintings I looked at from the show, which they sold before 'e died, 1892 and '94."

"If Mallais painted the new ones, that's very good news."

"If it's Mallais," Bullard said. "If 'e did, flamin' good news and everyone's 'appy."

"But—" Reisden thought. "Perdita thinks Madame's painting too. Madame spoke as if she were painting."

"I 'ope not, I really do. Because if she painted the new ones, she's been painting for 'im for years." Bullard spread his hands in a helpless shrug. "It'll be a disaster, just like Inness or Blakelock; the dealers won't want even the right ones for fear they've got a forgery."

Going outside was disorienting. Jouvet was in the center of a shallow lake.

The rue de l'Université had the look of a trick photograph; the water had risen to the curbstones and all the buildings were reflecting in it. It was hardly an inch deep, but farther down the street, faded and flattened in the snow, the street had turned into a bizarre object, a tarnished yellow mirror, undulating against office buildings and iron-fenced courtyards.

A boat, rowed by two uniformed policemen, was moving slowly down the street as if on concealed rollers; a man in a bowler hat stood in the boat, calling something echoing and incomprehensible through a loud hailer. The boat was almost full of people Reisden vaguely recognized from the street. Roy Daugherty, who was wearing rubber boots reaching to his knees, waded out and waved at it, and they were treated to the sight of the rowboat gliding in through the porte cochere and drawing up to the steps.

"I'll close up here," Daugherty offered. "Got my gumboots, I can walk."

"We'll try to find a cab at the station; come to the hotel as soon as you can."

They were rowed as far as the rue du Bac, gliding along the street like Venetians, and walked up the slope toward the station. Today it was steeper. "Stay with you," Bullard offered diffidently, "until 'e gets 'ere?" Reisden nodded, conscious he was being ungracious. He slumped on a bench outside the station, blinkered with tiredness, watching the stairs where Leonard's Mona Lisa had sung. The clock in front of the station, like every outdoor clock they had seen, had stopped at 10:23; it was nearly noon.

"Not a cab to be 'ad," Bullard reported back.

"Have you seen Daugherty?"

"No, but come and see inside the station."

By the glass peristyle and the doors to the Orsay station, the crowd was elbow to elbow, craning forward. The main entrance to the Gare d'Orsay was on the second level, above the tracks. The water was almost up to the level of the doors. The vast green glass-and-studded-iron arches of the station, the café, the benches, the mahogany stands for postcards, books, and newspapers stood ready for crowds of travelers hurrying to catch their trains; the green-and-gilt railroad clock loomed over everything, though it had stopped; but the lower level of the station, where the tracks had been, was an enormous swimming pool, a dimly reflecting darkness whose surface was lit by the gray snowlight. In it floated pieces of wood, an engineer's cap, a newspaper. Sets of bronze-railed stairs led down into the water and on the surface a ring barely projected, not floating, but attached to something beneath. The surface kissed the top of it, rippled over it; it disappeared.

It had been the smokestack of a train.

It was intensely quiet, but from somewhere in the building came an echoing crack. A ripple spread over the surface from below the windows, then settled again.

"How did this *happen*," Reisden said. "Friday it was dry."

"Look outside!" someone shouted.

Outside the station, they looked over the terrace railing, down into the street. In the sidewalk all along the rue de Lille, glass-brick windows were set into the pavement, illuminating the tracks below. Usually one could see the train lights through them; now they were black, and one was leaking, squirting water up into the snow and onto the slippery pavement. Down the street, Reisden could see the pointed roof and wooden wind flag of Jouvet.

As they were watching, the windows began to give way. First one, and then in a rippling row, the glass-brick windows heaved up like the backs of animals, their iron frames buckling and the cement cracking around them; and as each gave way, water shot up from them, drenching the side of the building and the already flooding street. It was as if a row of fire hoses were spraying upward. A street tree swayed in its cage and jerked down, its roots sucked away; a garbage-tumbrel with a broken wheel scraped down the street, moved by the force of the water. For a moment there was so much water in the air that it stopped snowing; the flakes were melting as they fell. The water tumbled and was sucked down the slope of the rue de Bellechasse. Through the returning snow, they could see the progress of the flood down the street by the agitation of the trees.

Smoke and dust bulged out, surprisingly compact, then

suddenly swelled into a cloud that hid the end of the rue de Bellechasse. *Hein,* the crowd went, *eh,* as if at fireworks.

Reisden watched the dust slowly go more transparent and the outlines of the buildings darken to visibility against the snow. Above the mirror of the street, where he expected to see Jouvet's roof and ancient wooden flag, there was just the snow and the sky.

He stared for a long time at the blank place in the clouds. He thought of Daugherty last night, telling him he should take care of his house, building the fire out of furniture Perdita wouldn't have liked. *I might as well be useful because I ain't a going to leave.*

"Mr. de Reisden?" Bullard asked.

"How long has it been since we walked up here?" He sounded quite calm. "Do you suppose he was out of the building?"

" 'E'll 'ave got out, don't you worry."

"He would have needed to be out of the path of that wave." He saw Daugherty trundling through the water in his gumboots toward the avalanche of water tumbling and spraying down the street, carrying with it trees, a carriage, the garbage cart.

"You want to sit down? We'll wait for 'im."

"He'll come to the hotel," Reisden said, but he let himself be led inside the station. He leaned against the wall. Under the windows the water was agitated, moving in a perceptible current through the station, eddying around the banisters of the stairs. The water-level was no lower; the Seine was pouring into the station as fast as the water was invading the streets. Being on the street when the wave came would have been like being thrown into the Seine.

" 'Ave you got insurance?" Bullard asked.

"Not enough." *The archives,* he thought. "I've just lost all the company records." The archives. Perdita's piano. The d—n ushabtis.

"Daugherty liked art," he said. "Likes. He can draw a bit. I don't know him very well; he has two sons, I don't know how to reach them. I hope I don't need to."

He stood for a while, waiting, thinking about the archives, trying not to think about Daugherty. Five generations to build up that knowledge. He could think about it only as specific people. Five Dr. Jouvets. The Guérarts. *Demons in the streets; what concerns me, monsieur, is that they are always there.* He turned to the wall and stared at the glass panels until they blurred.

"What time is it?" It was still 10:23 by all the clocks.

"Twelve-forty."

"He'll go to the *mairie*." He could not think of anything else now. He did not want to ask Bullard to come, for what it might imply. Bullard came without their discussing it.

He had forgot to pick up the rings and favors; it was a task out of another universe, in a brightly lit shop on the rue de la Paix. Roy Daugherty's cigar cutter was among them.

Dotty, Perdita, and Tiggy were already at the *mairie*. Dotty stalked up and down, perfectly attired down to violet silk stockings and violet enameled buttons, furious that they had to wait for the other witnesses, doubly furious that Bullard was there and Daugherty was not. Bullard, embarrassed, made a pretense of looking at the paintings in the salle des mariages. Tiggy looked up at Reisden's face, frightened and trying to look brave. Perdita, in her white dress, stood silent in the center of the room, alone.

Daugherty did not arrive. Neither of the other two witnesses arrived either. They brought two passersby as witnesses. Dotty smiled icily, looking at the salle des mariages as if she were measuring it for new curtains. "Allons, allons," the registrar of marriages said and began; the breath steamed out of his mouth in clouds. The registrar asked if there were any objections to the marriage; there was a heavy-laden silence; Perdita cast down her eyes; Dotty narrowed her lips; Reisden said nothing. Tiggy, smiling with uncertain eyes, held out the two rings on the flat of his palm, like sugar for horses. Awkwardly, left-handed, Reisden fit the wedding ring onto Perdita's finger.

Outside it was still snowing, heavy sloppy granules. Perdita, looking lost, gathered her white silk skirts in one wool-gloved hand. As they picked their way through pools and rivulets, they saw through the snow shadows like sheds and low buildings, the superstructures of laundry barges, risen as high as the parapets. They looked *up* at the Bains de la Samaritaine. The river was everywhere, in the heavy snow and the yellow-brown mud that sucked at their shoes, and he and Perdita moved through it with infinite slowness, as though the tarnished gray light were coming through water.

The lights were out at Voisin's; the lunch table was set with candelabra. "This is very pleasant," Dotty said determinedly. Bullard had come with them, at Dotty's brittle insistence. Perdita said nothing. Bullard said nothing. Dotty carried on alone, chattering about the wedding and the flooding.

"Got here," Daugherty said. "Finally."

He was white, as if powdered; his clothes were torn; his face was covered with dirt and smeared with blood; but he was alive.

"Thought I was going to miss the whole thing, dintcha?"

Reisden stood up and pointed at Daugherty; his legs gave way and he half fell, half sat untidily on the floor.

Chapter 88

The arrival of Daugherty, and Reisden's bit of drama, utterly did for Voisin's. Dotty stood over his prone body and said, "And now shall we have the wedding toast, Mr. Daugherty?" and burst into tears. She nevertheless managed to get them all back to the place Dauphine and arrange for Daugherty's clothes to be mended. Reisden lay on Dotty's spare bed, still in the clothes he'd been married in; dealing with his shirt studs seemed as complex as climbing an Alp.

"How is the building?"

"Don't worry," Dotty said sharply.

So, Reisden thought. "How bad?"

"Lot of it's still standing," Daugherty said.

Details of Jouvet fell through his mind, like pieces of his life: the pattern of the parquet floor, the new microscope. He had forgot to wind the clock on his desk. The clock on his desk was now under tons of rubble. He thought of Tasy's recording, of the apartment where he and Daugherty had committed housecleaning yesterday, and of Dr. Jouvet, cross-indexing files for forty-two years.

"How much of the archives is gone?"

No one answered him.

"Me and Reisden got one or two things to say."

"Mr. Daugherty, there is no need—"

"Go on, Dotty," Reisden said. "It's all right. Help Perdita."

When she was gone, Daugherty sat down carefully on one of Dotty's chairs.

"How bad is it?"

"Most of the front of the building, and papers floating all over the courtyard. You got insurance and stuff?"

"I have enough cash to sell the company gracefully, but I don't think I'll own Jouvet anymore.—Daugherty?"

"Yeah?"

"Thank you for helping clean it up last night."

"Yeah."

There was a long silence. In the fire, a log snapped and sizzled, and then gave one of the short whistling exhalations one hears when a knot of sap wood gives up its liquid, or when a bit of trapped air is freed.

"I want you to know," Daugherty said, "you're wrong about a lot of stuff, but what you did with them records, that made sense, that was okay. It didn't work out, but that don't matter."

Reisden nodded. "I know that."

"You want to go to Courbevoie?" Daugherty cleared his throat. "Bullard's getting his shop cart, he can take everybody."

"Why not, there's disaster enough for everybody."

"I got to go find me my clothes, then."

Reisden heard voices from a distance. "Just a moment— Quiet. Stay here."

The head of the bed was by the grate of the heating system—which was doing nothing, since the furnace was out, but was open; and through it he could hear Dotty and Perdita in the salon. His first thought was that they had heard Daugherty and himself; then, shamelessly, he listened.

"——He should have married so as to weather such disasters. I blame you, *Madame* de Reisden, but now it is done; you carry his name and his hopes for a family. I cannot say I am pleased—"

Ach, Dotty.

"——but with my help you may be somewhat suitable," Dotty continued. "You will not become so by wearing orange feathers in your hat, or by walking the streets with a shining-new wedding ring, in a suit you cannot button. I shall teach you how to choose proper clothes, what servants you must have, whom you must know and not know. You shall honeymoon at La Gresnière, and I shall send down my old governess to coach you in etiquette and French. And I shall give you your career."

" 'Give' me a career—?" Perdita.

"By great good chance you have something the world may respect. My friends and I shall have you play for us," Dotty said. "In our salons. You will have your name in the papers."

I do not play to get reviews, Perdita had said. "I am really grateful," Reisden heard his wife say cautiously. "But I need to learn to run a household, madame, not to neglect it for the piano. I'm—slow."

Oh, he thought. Oh. That, at least, one could do something about.

"I shall require that you learn to run a household as well. Now," Dotty said, "the subject of Courbevoie."

Ah, yes, Dotty; now they were getting to it.

"You must dispose of that house without ever returning there. You cannot be considered reputable, living in your former house of assignation." Dotty paused. "There can be no other reason why you would wish to go to Courbevoie."

Perdita said nothing. Reisden listened. Daugherty said from the window, "Bullard's here."

"Go down and rescue Perdita," Reisden murmured.

The voices moved away. Reisden swung his legs over the side of the bed and stood up; the room darkened, and Dotty's gilded canopy bed and bedroom furniture rolled majestically, like carousel horses. Doggedly he began taking the studs out of his shirt. He was dropping them all.

"And where do you intend to go, madame, with Mr. Bullard, in a *van*? I will deal with this." Heels tapped decisively across the floor and down the stone stairs.

"Ain't she a dragon," Daugherty rumbled from downstairs.

"Find my hat, please, the one *with* the orange feathers," Perdita said crisply. "We must at least rescue Mr. Bullard from Cousin Dotty. Where is Alexander—?"

"Reisden's coming," Daugherty said in a loud voice.

"Well, ask him to come soon, please, he's the only one who can handle her—"

Reisden looked in frustration at the suit he should be wearing, dumped one of the pillows out of its sham, and rolled the suit in it. He buttoned his ordinary white shirt and put the dress jacket back on over it.

In the hallway, the mirrors confused him for a moment; he heard Dotty's voice below. "Mr. Bullard, I wish you to leave my house—"

"Dotty," he said.

"Darling," she said, half asking for his help and half warning him.

"Bullard," he said, "tell her."

"Mr. Bullard, I am not interested—"

"Mr. de Reisden brought me two paintings, oil sketches. 'E asked me to compare them with work sold by Mallais 'imself during the last two years of 'is lifetime, 'aving provenance from 'im. I did so. They appear to be by the same 'and—"

"Then my painting, Mr. Bullard, must also be by Mallais," Dotty said, brittle as glass. "I take it? After all these difficulties, have we not simply come to understand what everyone knows?"

There was a silence, a long silence. Reisden leaned against a mirrored wall. He was very, very tired. He wanted not to quarrel over who had painted the pictures; he wanted Perdita to have music in Paris. He wanted everyone to be happy, and he wondered which one of them would be the first to say *no*.

"Come with us to Courbevoie," Perdita said softly. "Dotty."

"Do you intend to cause a scandal? Do you feel you must say, Mr. Bullard, that a painter who is far, far better known, and deservedly, than you will ever be, has deliberately *encouraged* his ignorant wife to paint in his style while he was still alive?"

"He ain't dead yet," said Daugherty. "So you can ask him."

"You are all missing the point," Dotty said. "Sacha, you admire Miss—*Madame de Reisden*—for saying there are moments when one can stop lying, and that it will do one good, like a teaspoon of castor oil. That is not the point. You appear to think, all of you, that nothing counts but your own little glimmering fragment of truth. Mr. Bullard, you say the brushwork of those sketches matches paintings which have immaculate provenance, as does my painting. Should not one sometimes simply admit that what the rest of the world sees is right? Sacha darling, must one really *insist* one is unbalanced? *Madame* de Reisden, should one say one is a little piano student who cannot give up one iota of one's musical life? I know my painting is of the highest quality; it is a Mallais. I believe in it. One must decide what one believes, be responsible for what one believes. I think you must ask yourself, Madame de Reisden, if you believe *you* are of the highest quality, if *you* wish to be a success in Paris. If you wish something else—if you must be something else, something unvalued, peculiar, harmful—"

"Dotty," Reisden said.

"Dotty," Perdita said, "thank you for what you tried to do. But I have to go to Courbevoie. Alexander?" Her voice went breathy on his name.

"I'll join you. Leave us a moment."

He and Dotty were alone in the hall.

He went down the rest of the steps and stood beside her. He put his left hand lightly on her shoulder. She stepped back, shaking her head.

"Darling, I know how you will choose," she said. "It is your wedding day. Take her, take your package of little sketches, take your *wife,* go to your house at Courbevoie. But I live in Paris, Sacha. I go into society; I collect paintings. If you are going to make a scandal about Mallais, I must dissociate myself from—it."

They looked into each other's eyes. They had known each other for twenty years.

"Prove my Mallais is good," she said.

"I can't."

"Then," she said, "I will."

Chapter 89

It was amazing, Daugherty thought, how much stuff a woman could pack for overnight. Dotty brought sheets, blankets, clothes; Daugherty, waiting in the salon with Reisden, saw her come in and fit the collection of snuffboxes into a valise. "Aristocrat prepares for disaster," Reisden said in a low voice when she'd left, "by taking the portable goods and the heir." They went in two carriages: Daugherty, Perdita, Bullard in Bullard's van; Reisden, Dotty, and her boy in Dotty's carriage. Typical of her to take him, and him to go along.

It was snowing like a nor'easter. On the boulevard Haussmann, they jounced through mud while the cart wheels kicked up spray on either side. Snow and wind buffeted the sides of the cart. Bullard and Daugherty sat cocooned on a pile of snow-sodden draperies and quilting, with more quilts tucked around them. Perdita sat just inside, in more quilts, with her purple scarf around her hat to keep it on.

They were turned back from trying to cross the Seine at Neuilly and had to loop north toward the Pont de Levallois. Somewhere they stopped at a square where a German was selling hot sausages; they ate some with sauerkraut and warmed their hands over the brazier, while Bullard's horse Belle ate grain and tried to drink from an iced-over horse trough. Perdita stood shivering, shifting her feet as uneasily as the

414

horse, holding her gloves over the coals, then pressing them against her face.

"Some weddin' day," Daugherty said.

"I told her to come with us," Perdita said. "Well, here she is."

"Yup, no doubt about it. Snuffboxes and all."

He went to visit Reisden and Dotty in the other carriage. Reisden and the boy were playing Snakes and Ladders by lantern light and Dotty wasn't saying anything at all.

The snow turned to rain and the rain turned to ice. They reached Courbevoie close to midnight. The boulevard St.-Denis was an anthill of refugees heading toward the church, toward higher ground, toward anywhere. Bullard's horse struggled through a stream of wheelbarrows piled with blankets, chairs, pots and pans; by farm carts laden with iron bedsteads, chests of drawers, family pictures, and even a stove; past a moving cart where a family sat like Indians, staring straight ahead. A laundress went past, driving a goat cart laden with the sad-irons of an entire laundry.

It was too dark to see anything but the roof of the Mallais house and the line of gaslights beyond the garden wall. From the second story of the Mallais house Daugherty saw a light, a candle flickering through the hail.

Daugherty got the ladder, stood it up against the wall, and climbed it. The road by the river looked like the city was at war. Lit by the gaslights burning through the snow, soaked and dirty Arab-looking men in red trousers were hurriedly piling sandbags against the quai walls; behind them, men in blue shoveled sand into more bags, twisted the bags shut with a single motion like killing chickens, and passed them up to the Zouaves. Soldiers splashed calf-deep through river water, stumbling over hummocks of mud and piles of sand, shouting to each other.

Almost above the sandbags loomed the Seine.

"That wall is not going to last," Reisden said in a very quiet voice, as if shouting would bring it down.

Daugherty had brought a torch; he shone it down onto the Mallais house. He didn't like the look of it, just an ordinary French house, probably wood-framed underneath. Chunks of stucco had cracked away beneath the windows. If the flood got much worse, Madame Mallais was going to have holes right through the wall.

Didn't matter; if the flood got much worse, the sandbag wall was a goner.

"Still got the paintings in there, 'aven't they?" Bullard said.

The three of them dropped into the Mallais garden over the wall and splashed through water to the back door. The water was cold as the sea in January; even with his boots, Daugherty's feet went numb. Reisden pounded on the door, shouting in French; Daugherty kicked it. The whole thing gave way, splintering, and they were inside.

In the kitchen stood Madame Mallais.

She screamed and stared at them, wide-eyed. Daugherty's electric torch made colors blaze on the walls. More Mallaises than he'd seen, more than anybody'd seen; or more of something that looked a lot like Mallais. The old lady backed against the wall, blocking his view, screaming, holding her hands over them, trying not to let them see. Bullard went over and picked her up bodily and moved her aside.

"You said paintings in the attic?" Daugherty asked Reisden.

Reisden had said the attic was full; what he meant, it was *full.* Daugherty was first up the stairs; he held the lantern up, and flipped one painting out, and then another, and almost forgot where he was for a minute, they were so fine; he felt kind of calm, like looking at the ocean. He raised the lantern and looked at the paintings on the walls. Rain. Rain in Paris, rain on the Seine, rain in the dooryard, in the Mallais garden. Water rising. There was blue and purple in the gray, as if rain color had all the colors in it.

He looked outside. The soldiers were running around even more frantically.

Downstairs, everyone was talking in French. The Mallaises had two bedrooms, just like his house at home. Daugherty went into the empty bedroom and dumped the dresser drawers on the bed; that gave him three boxes, and he went upstairs and packed the first drawer full of paintings and eased it down the narrow stairway, out through the back, up the slope. The wall was in the way. He set the drawer down, found a shovel in back of the house, and pried under the wall, and about a three-foot section fell over in one piece. He climbed up the slope with the drawer full of paintings.

Perdita and Cousin Dotty were in the house with Tiggy. "Unpack this, or I'm gonna run out of drawers."

He'd been bumbling around, waiting to do something stupid, and now was his time to do it. So what if they were forgeries? So was that *View of the Seine,* and so was the spruce-tree picture, and if no one else cared for 'em, he did. Someone wanted to sell them, he'd buy them, take a trunkful home to Cambridgeport. They might be no Mallais, but they were Mallais enough for him.

Chapter 90

"Claude Mallais," Reisden said.

Time had shrunk the painter. He had lost all his hair and, in the cold, was wearing an American plaid cap, with earflaps, and a peasant's smock under a shawl. The skin of his face hung folded and creased from sharp cheekbones. Under a white, straggling mustache, his lips were purpled; the whites of his eyes were yellow with jaundice, his skin tanned with it. He squinted from pain, half smiled from it, showing false teeth. He lay propped on pillows in an ordinary bedroom: an iron bedstead, linoleum covered with cheap machine-made runner, wallpaper with a pattern of brown daisies. On the bed were seed catalogs open to advertisements for pears and flowering cherries, and momentarily the glorious paintings around the room seemed, not art, but simply apple trees.

"But it's not fair," Claude Mallais said. "The first new faces I've seen in ten years, and I know one of them. *You're* Mademoiselle Perdita's young man?"

"We are going to move you and the paintings," Reisden said.

"It's not fair at all. 'Zanne!" Mallais called.

"She's already gone up the hill." The Mallais house had begun to take on a silence, an air of ending, like that Reisden remembered from Jouvet. Bullard came in to take down the pictures. Daugherty was unhooking those in the hall.

Mallais looked up from his nest of pillows. He had bright blue eyes, which had been kind once and now were half-jocular, half-frightened, like those of a man prepared to bluff or plead. They were the color of Jean-Jacques' eyes.

"You came to the Nouvelle Athènes, once, more than once. A girl brought you; she didn't come back, you did. Sketched you while you weren't looking. A profile, and an air of suffering, as if a fox were eating your vitals under your cloak, like the Roman boy. You didn't want anyone to know about the fox. Thought I ought to tell you," Mallais sighed, "everyone has foxes; but you'd only have thought, 'The old man knows about mine.' "

That was exactly what Reisden was thinking now, in the panic that had dominated him for the last three years: *G-d, he knows about Richard.* "We don't have much time. I must ask you a question."

There was no time. Through the shutters of Mallais's window Reisden could see the soldiers fighting the Seine. Around the gaslights, glitters showed the height of the water, just at the top of the sandbags. Beyond the gaslight was blackness without distinction, no difference between water and sky, drowning Seine and drowned shore.

"Has your wife ever forged your paintings?"

"No."

Mallais was telling the truth; the eagle-beak nose and the chin jutted forward pugnaciously under his cap; but he was telling it a bit too self-consciously.

"In April 1907, Armand Inslay-Hochstein sold a painting, *View of the Seine.* Did you paint it?"

A hesitation. "It's real." It was the hesitation not of an outright liar, but of a person calculating whether the truth could fit within the words of the answer.

"What do you mean by 'real'?" Reisden asked. "Do you mean that you painted it with your own hands—"

He saw Mallais's eyes flicker at the word *hands*. Mallais's were under the covers.

Daugherty burst in. "Reisden," he said. "We gotta go," and pointed out the window.

Nothing to see except that the soldiers were not moving; they were staring up at the sandbags. But over the top of the sandbags, shining like fillets of mercury, water was trickling.

Daugherty scooped up Mallais with his bedclothes. Reisden, behind them, saw a lamp still on in the attic, took the stairs two at a time to blow it out, and took a final look at the Mallaises' bedroom. The bedside table was crowded with medicines: honey and vinegar, Bayer's aspirin, copper bracelets, the patent pharmacy of the arthritic. A pipe was clipped to a stand; a reading table stood on the floor, and on it lay a pair of glasses.

"Come on, Reisden!"

Outside Reisden heard the soldiers calling to each other, shouting, and the rumble of a motorized truck. No, not a truck: it was something being dragged along the quai, something huge; it was the shriek and rumble of a train.

He did a stupid thing: he pushed open the curtain and looked. The Seine came toward him like a wall.

The first rush of the water took the whole garden gate with it; the water poured through, momentarily, comically, rectangular as the doorway before it fanned and sprayed. The water was already foaming up the stairwell. He ran toward the back of the house, toward the window looking out over the backyard. Outside the window was an arbor, looking tumbledown under the weight of an ice-covered vine; below, already, a maelstrom of water tumbled where the doorway had been.

Halfway up the slope, Bullard was pushing a wheelbarrow; just behind him, Daugherty came stumbling, carrying Mallais over his shoulder, looking back toward the house. At the top of the slope stood Dotty, Tiggy, and Perdita.

He opened the window, judged the distance, and jumped. The water pushed him forward, sprawling, and knocked him over as if he had been hit from behind. He saw one of their lamps, or the lights from the house, below him; he ran toward it, tumbled, through a tornado, a sandstorm, quicksand, sleet. He was being battered against something, a wall; he thought for one panicked second that the water had sucked him inside the house, and then, for one long unforgettable moment, he was simply flying, pure smooth motion, as the flood took him, before he tumbled and slammed into shallow water, halfway up the clay slope of the garden.

He crawled farther up the slope, ice to the bone, dragged down by his overcoat, shuddering and cursing in gasps. He could see Daugherty's torch, still alight, violently waving; he was wading through the shallows, holding Mallais above his head. Bullard's wheelbarrow had overturned, spilling white rectangles into the water. Dotty was weaving back and forth at the edge of the water, and by her stood Perdita holding Tiggy's hand, looking out agonizedly into the dark.

He staggered across to them. Dotty shrieked; Perdita turned and hugged him silently, and Tiggy grabbed him around the knees, smearing himself with silt. Dotty hovered, murmuring in horror. Daugherty lurched past them, holding Mallais, whose mouth was open in agony, and behind them came Bullard and Madame Mallais, each holding a handle of the wheelbarrow.

And then, from the dark and cold, through the snow, boomed a vast explosion like a thunderbolt, a cannonading like the collapse of all of Paris. A red light rose in the eastern sky, a nighttime sun. It was far upriver—Ivry, perhaps, or Alfortville, all the way across Paris—but it was enormous. The sky bloomed red, like fireworks; the surface of the river turned to red brocade under red falling snow, and the explosion rumbled on and on.

On the quai de Seine, the municipal gaslights were still lit, the stubs of their lampposts outlining the disappeared quai. But the lower half of the garden was gone. The trees were all gone: the willow by the wall, the apple tree, the spruce. And there was no Mallais house, there was simply the blood-colored plain of water, with a tangle of current where the house had stood.

Chapter 91

"The soldiers—" Perdita said.

"They got away," Reisden said for Tiggy's sake.

Like mariners after a shipwreck, everyone staggered up to the house. They dragged mattresses into the salon for Mallais, and laid him by the fire, packing quilts under and over him. His thin arms made two lines under the covers, his hands were hidden again, but Reisden had seen them, and so had Dotty.

Mallais's hands were deformities. The knuckles were grossly knobbed, the fingers curved almost down to the palms.

Left-handed, painfully, Reisden stripped off his own soaked clothes; he was near to convulsive with cold. The water out of the taps was turbid raw Seine, smelling faintly of clay and rotting fruit. His wet bandages were packed with the same filthy water; he sat at the kitchen table, contemplating the work of rebandaging everything one-handed.

"Darling, I'll do that." It was Dotty, in the immaculate fawn-colored suit in which she had ridden to Courbevoie. She examined her pillow sham, seemed to conclude that it could be replaced, and began to tear it into strips.

Hands, he thought. He looked at the raw stitched slashes in his own palm. Laboratory work needs hands, a sensitivity of the fingers, just as art or music does, or painting. What would *he* have done if he had lost the use of his hands?

"He can still paint," Dotty said. "I told you that everything would be all right."

We see what we want to see. "He may be able to paint," Reisden said. "I wouldn't ask him to prove it."

"I don't need to, darling; the only question came when one thought he was dead. . . . Don't move. This will sting."

In the salon, in the hallways, all along the walls were paintings, piles of paintings, bureauless drawers full of paintings. Like a sleepwalker Madame Mallais moved from pile to pile, pulling out an apple tree, a bunch of flowers, the light across a kitchen table; she looked at them as though they were photographs. Her lost house, her lost garden.

Perdita came into the kitchen, looking at cans with her magnifying glass; she was making something for the Mallaises, who hadn't eaten. "Is this canned pears?" Perdita said.

"Of course it is," Dotty snapped.

Perdita said nothing. From hugging him outside, she had got dirt and silt on her best suit; she was wearing her red dressing gown for warmth. She moved around the kitchen, touching spoons and pans, opening the last of a bottle of red wine to sniff it, finding some cinnamon. Reisden noticed the amount of work she had to do only to find things in the kitchen. Dotty bandaged Reisden's arm a little more tightly than necessary.

"Do we have aspirin?" Reisden asked.

"Everyone has aspirin, darling," Dotty said.

"We don't," said Perdita. Reisden felt he had put her unfairly on the spot.

Daugherty put his head into the kitchen and withdrew.

"Dotty, what are you going to do to Madame Mallais?" Perdita asked.

"Darling, there is nothing *to* be done to her; she does not figure in anything; he is alive and painting."

"Where will they live?" Perdita asked. "They haven't anything now."

"They will sell a painting, I suppose," Dotty said, "since he is alive and can paint."

"Why did he say he was dead?" Reisden asked. Dotty looked at him as though he were on the wrong side.

"I'd like to know," he said.

"She *paints*," Perdita said.

"Miss Halley," Dotty said, "Madame de Reisden, your sentiment over artistic women knows no bounds, but you have made her a criminal and an artist when she is neither. Certainly not an artist," Dotty continued. "I believe I have actually found a specimen of Madame Mallais's work, and I shall be glad to *describe* it to you."

"You have?" Perdita said. "What did she paint?"

"Where is it, Dotty?"

"In the hall."

They dragged it into the kitchen. It was in the style of the 1860s, an almost photographically distinct painting bathed in a flat yellow light. In the middle of the canvas stood an awkward muscular young woman, a peasant, barefoot in a striped dress, holding a palette by one hooked thumb. On either side of her, two well-dressed people gestured at a picture outside the frame. On the left, Mallais, a young man, already bearded, held a finger up like a critic; on the right, his mistress leaned forward in a wicker chair. Between them the peasant girl stood in her striped cotton dress, painting the picture they were looking at: chewing at the wooden end of her brush, eyes wide and obsessed, staring at what only she could see.

How she strained to put something on the canvas; her lips

were drawn back from her crooked teeth, her head tossed back; her bare toes grasped the earth as if they helped her see.

"*Half*-clever," Dotty said, "*half*-good. The central figure has some interest, though she makes herself rather unnecessarily grand; but the other two are simply studio portraits, and the background is dreadful." It was, a haystack and a tree painstakingly made from muddy dots and splatters. "Old-fashioned and common, even for the time. Pre-Raphaelite. I suppose she could have illustrated books."

From the painting, Dotty had got a smutch of dust on her suit. "I must sponge this off," she said, and left them.

Perdita stirred the pears. For a minute he simply watched her; his wife, cooking in their kitchen. She turned the gas down to simmer and sat by him.

"Is it really not very good?" she asked finally.

"Provincial art museum," he said, "second floor, in the room devoted to local artists; donated by the artist's aunt. But the central figure's interesting. She could do faces."

She smiled heartbreakingly. "Young Married Women's Musical Society. . . . I'll bet they have their interesting days, too." She leaned her chin on her right fist. "Did you hear Dotty and me talk this afternoon?"

"Yes," he admitted.

"She was helpful," Perdita said.

"Ach," he said. " 'I shall teach you whom you must know and not know.' Our Dotty."

"I'll take her up on it," she offered.

I would like that. It was the easiest thing in the world to say to his wife.

"It just," she said softly, "it just never has seemed fair that even the ones who aren't much good don't get to *try* to be good. Someone always decides for women, chooses for them how much they have in them, and I'll bet someone decided for

her she only had this much talent"—she held her hands a narrow inch apart—"and so she only had this much space to put it
in. But you and I know, Alexander, when her husband trusted
her to do his painting, she could do it."

"Do you want us to make her a criminal, then?" he asked,
and heard *us* again.

"What would you do if it were me?" she asked.

Dotty is right, he was about to say to her. We should leave
things as they are. Let them lie about it. And he thought he
would say it, and then he thought of Leonard—and of himself,
who had wanted to be caught.

Be my wife, never leave me, play salon music in Paris.
Make me happy. Never get caught being who you are. He
moved his chair next to hers and put his arm around her.
Above all never leave me.

"How much talent do you have?" he asked.

"Oh—probably about that much." She held her hands the
same narrow inch apart.

He moved her hands a bit farther apart. "More than that."

She moved her hands apart, slowly, until they were as far
apart as they could be, her arms stretched out, open farther.
"*That* much, I *hope*." She put her arms around him and held
him, her face against his chest.

"If I asked you to use it," he said, "and it were not legal,
would you?"

"Yes," she said, muffled.

"Shouldn't I protect you?"

"From what," she said, raising her head, "from using it?
When you could teach me? I mean he could? And I wanted to
paint? What kind of a protection is that?"

Reisden looked up; Daugherty was at the door. He shook
his head.

She turned to him and took his left hand with both hers.

"Do you remember when I was trying to decide about marrying Harry, and you said, it's very simple, you can play music and be married too? I don't say anybody *can,* because it's so much, but no one had ever said that to me before about marriage. My aunt talked about trousseaus and pearls, and gratitude and being pure, but no one had ever said I could be a more complete person married than single. I think even if it isn't true, it—is true, somehow. That's what I hope he did," she said. "I hope he taught her everything, and trusted her to paint with him, and didn't protect her."

Oh my dear, he thought, salon music and the Young Married Women won't satisfy you.

"So," he said, "we can't let them get away with easy answers."

"No," she said.

"Not any more," he said, "than we can ourselves, love."

She put her arms around him, but "No," she said. "Not any more than us."

Chapter 92

In the salon, Bullard was examining the paintings. Perdita had brought in the stewed fruit and Madame Mallais was feeding it to her husband spoonful by spoonful. Daugherty, swathed in two blankets, massive as a South Sea chief, peered through his glasses at the paintings. Tiggy was looking sleepily at a painting of a horse. Somewhere Tiggy had acquired a black-and-white cat, which lurked under his jacket, blinking resentful green eyes.

Jean-Jacques had arrived, soaked. He had walked from Paris. He sat stricken by his grandmother and grandfather, guarding them, all nose and ears, his hair sticking straight up, in his damp underwear and his grandmother's shawl. He glared at Dotty, who, elegant in her suit, was sitting on the edge of the piled mattresses.

"You have never painted anything," Dotty was saying to Madame Mallais.

Madame Mallais nodded her head, frightened. "He painted them all."

"Mallais painted all these?" Reisden said.

Dotty gave him a sharp look. Monsieur and Madame Mallais nodded.

"When did you paint your most recent canvas?" he asked Mallais.

They looked at each other. Dotty stared at him as if he had begun singing drunken songs at a party: do be *quiet,* dear.

"Two years ago," Mallais said. "Maybe a year." Perdita was translating for Daugherty, who opened his mouth to protest. Reisden glanced at him sharply.

"And how do you paint, Monsieur Mallais?"

"With brushes strapped to my wrists," Mallais said. Madame Mallais nodded. Dotty nodded.

"Show me."

"No straps," said Mallais, "and I'm—" He smiled wearily.

"Of course he cannot paint *today,*" said Dotty.

"But ordinarily you could paint," Reisden said, "until two years ago, or a year. It will have to be less than two months ago, because we have a painting you must have done since November." He looked for it among the paintings. Bullard handed it to him.

"Really, darling, that is not you," Dotty said, "that is a mere impression."

"When I was in your bedroom, I saw a stand that would allow you to smoke your pipe without using your hands. Your wife feeds you," Reisden said. "But you can paint."

"Painting is important," Madame Mallais said.

"Why did you pretend to be dead?" Reisden asked. Daugherty nodded. The Mallaises looked at each other and said nothing.

"Everyone knows, darling, paintings go up in value after the painter is dead," Dotty said.

Both Mallaises looked at Dotty strangely.

"Why did you?" Reisden persisted.

"Thought they wouldn't believe me," Mallais said finally. "No one would believe I was a painter anymore."

"Because of your hands?"

"He has the arthuritis," Madame Mallais said.

"Were you painting from photographs?"

They looked at each other. "Yes," Mallais said with relief.

"There, darling, you see," Dotty said.

"I'd send 'Zanne out with a Kodak."

"I took the photographs," Madame Mallais explained carefully.

"Courbevoie wasn't far enough away from Paris," Mallais said. "All this area used to be fields. Then the suburban railway came in, and the trams; and all my friends decided to come out and visit the old man; and I was getting old, liverish, didn't even want to go to the Athènes. All those photographs around the house."

"He say photographs? I didn't see no photographs," Daugherty said.

Bullard repeated it in French.

"Threw them out," Mallais said.

"We threw them out," Madame Mallais said. "Then, the big Exhibition, the government asked a lot of the old men, the Impressionists, to come and paint in public. My old man couldn't do that."

Bullard nodded. Reisden remembered the pictures vaguely from ten years ago, one or another bearded man on a platform, as if at a sideshow, daubing away at a canvas.

"Couldn't," Mallais said. "That was the end. Couldn't do it. Couldn't think of an excuse not to. We thought of moving away from Paris, couldn't do that," Mallais said. "I needed the light on the Seine."

"The light in the garden," his wife said.

"So you went to Bergac," Reisden said.

Neither the wife nor the husband said anything for a few seconds.

"What happened after that?"

Jean-Jacques had known his grandfather was still alive, they said; otherwise the Mallaises had told only Armand

Inslay-Hochstein. Inslay-Hochstein had become their source of artists' supplies; when Mallais was ill, Inslay-Hochstein had brought the doctor. And: "I painted," said Mallais.

"He painted all the time," said Madame Mallais. "All by himself."

"Did he."

They had agreed not to sell anything, they said; but in 1907, two things had happened. The first had been the American stock-exchange panic. They had wanted to help Inslay-Hochstein, who had been Mallais's dealer ever since he had started selling.

The second had been the garden, *their* garden, which had been put on the market at the beginning of 1907.

They had given way to temptation. *View of the Seine* had been an old canvas that had never seemed quite right. They had pulled it out, squinted out the bedroom window, and seen a lovely purple gleam on the Grande Jatte.

"But they wouldn't sell the garden to us!" Madame Mallais said. She hadn't built the wall for spite, she said indignantly, Armand was still in trouble, and to help him, behind the wall they were painting *Spruce and Shadow*.

"You were going to say 'your husband,'" Dotty prompted her quickly.

But it was too late.

"Jean-Jacques," Reisden said. Jean-Jacques was sitting in the corner quietly, but the tears were running down his cheeks.

"They didn't do anything wrong," he said pugnaciously.

"I think they are doing something wrong now." He looked at Madame Mallais.

"No," she said uncertainly.

"You are making Jean-Jacques bear this," Reisden said. "That's wrong."

Jean-Jacques shook his head fiercely. "Stay out of this."

Perdita stood up. "It matters who paints a painting, madame."

"You don't know anything about painting," Jean-Jacques said. "You're blind."

"Do you remember, Madame Mallais, telling me how you felt when you saw Mary Cassatt's name? It would have mattered to me if it had been a married woman who painted them." Perdita's voice strengthened. "I wanted to find a married woman who loved her work and her family; who didn't hurt them or herself or her work, who was committed to all of them. If she exists, other women will know it's possible to paint and be a woman."

"How long have you been painting for your husband, madame?" Reisden asked.

"Sacha—" Dotty said sharply.

Madame pulled her apron up to hide her face.

"Ten years? Since you 'died,' Monsieur Mallais?"

"Oh, I really cannot stand this," Dotty said. "This is completely unnecessary."

"Longer than that," Bullard said. "'Ow many of these are yours, madame?"

"Any paintings that are *hers* must be instantly burned," Dotty said.

"No," said Perdita. "No, they shan't, Madame Suzanne—Dotty, you *shall* not, this is my house."

"Have you painted *things* that purported to be by your husband?" Dotty said. "Answer me." From behind the apron, Madame whispered something. Dotty paused for an icy moment.

"Mine?" she said. "My painting? Mine too?"

A long, frightened wail from behind the apron; it was answer enough.

Chapter 93

It took hours of negotiation to come to some agreement: Dotty paced the floor among the paintings, ready to throw them on the fire; the Mallaises, both frightened now, were willing to give her anything. What she accepted, eventually, was a trade: *View of the Seine* for a genuine Mallais of equal value. The sale of forgeries must stop. The painting of them must stop. This Dotty insisted on until long after Perdita had fallen asleep: Madame Mallais must never paint another picture. The negotiations jammed there, until Dotty put on her coat and threatened to go to the police; and then Reisden gave in.

He dropped asleep exhausted next to Perdita, haunted by Madame Mallais's desperate look when she had finally agreed to give up painting. *It wouldn't let me go. . . .*

Somewhere around midday, a lank-haired, unshaven specter stared at him from the bathroom mirror; he wandered into the central room, saw piles of paintings and Mallais asleep on the mattresses, found a chair, fell asleep again. In his sleep he heard voices—Tiggy, good; he dreamed, confusedly. He was standing in front of Madame Mallais's picture. Suzanne Mallais stood as she had, an awkward peasant girl in a striped cotton dress, chewing at the wooden end of her brush while she strained to make sense of an idea. *Art for a woman is difficult,* a woman's voice said. *Impossible* . . . He found himself awake, standing in front of the painting as it leaned on the back of a chair in the hallway: stunned, dunderheaded, every muscle stiff, feeling like Suzanne Mallais, in the middle, trying to grasp something only she could see.

Suzanne Mallais, by herself, caught forever between peasant and artist. He wondered what would have happened if she had painted herself differently. Would she have believed it? Probably not. We see of our reflections only the angles of light that reach our eyes. Everything else is secondhand.

Madame Mallais had begun to spread out the pictures, sorting hers from her husband's. Sitting on the piano bench, Reisden watched as she moved around the room with the slowness of old age, arranging canvases like squares on a quilt, shifting them from place to place. They took up the chairs; they were spread on the lid of the piano, next to the tuning hammer and forks; they leaned against the backs of the Mallais kitchen chairs and sofa; Madame Mallais even spread a few on the floor. Daugherty and her grandson helped her, hefting a particularly large canvas, piling others inconspicuously in a corner.

Dotty made sandwiches. Where had she found bread? But she had.

Perdita, waking, came into the room and found him. He took her into the kitchen, told her the results of the negotiation, and found her some plain crackers to eat. She leaned against him, the two of them in one kitchen chair; he felt the soft warm heaviness of her body against his and touched the contour of her stomach.

" 'Hem," Daugherty said. He had come in to fix Mallais oatmeal, he said, or whatever he could eat. They found something— bread in warmed red wine—and brought it into the salon. They took turns feeding Mallais.

"I got something to ask him," Daugherty said after they had finished.

"Why did he do it?" Reisden guessed, and asked Mallais the question.

"Had to," Mallais said. "Couldn't help it."

"Wa'n't what I was going to ask," Daugherty said. "Ask him what art's for. Why's it different from forgery."

Perdita translated the question. Mallais threw back his head and laughed, wincing from the pain in his neck; but for a moment he was the big handsome man again, the painter with the beard.

"Art's to fail at," Mallais said. "Art's not a whore for hire. She insults you, strips you bare, loses you your dignity, shows you you know nothing about loving her. She makes impossible demands—you know, mademoiselle."

"Art's not *she,*" Perdita said.

"It," said Mallais, "it, then, it changes you like an angel, it makes anything possible; and then you always try the impossible, because you know," the old man said, "you know it will work between you, for a while.—It doesn't matter who painted these, messieurs, they aren't forgeries. Without seeing them I would never have lived a part of my life," the old man said. "I would never have seen something important, and never have known it."

And he looked round at them, as if making sure they understood; and Reisden's wife nodded.

Chapter 94

Robbed of the garden, Madame had practiced Mallais's art on the streets. There was a magnificent canvas of the roofs of the Palais des Nations glittering in the sun of summer 1900, when Mallais had officially been underground for several months. A study of the Seine included the telltale wake of a motorboat; a cart horse stood in the shadow of the Métro excavations. Even though Madame piled forged canvases inconspicuously by the window, the extent of their crime was alarming.

Bullard drew him out into the hall. "I can't tell by brush-stroke which is Mallais and which Mallais-and-Madame. Not yet anyway."

"Is there any chance her paintings are not forgeries? He directed her."

Bullard shook his head. "They've got a sentimental value, is all. Mallais thought they were good enough to be Mallais."

Monsieur and Madame conferred. Madame Mallais looked over the relative size of the Mallais and non-Mallais piles, and surreptitiously shifted a painting from one pile to the other. "Madame—" Reisden shook his head. No more pictures migrated into the Mallais pile; she deliberated; two migrated out. The pile was small; they were not outstanding canvases; he was not happy.

He'd broken a cardinal rule of negotiation, to be certain that the parties can keep their agreements.

Tiggy had caught the nervous mood; he wandered from picture to picture, looking at them dubiously, stopping at the one of the cart horse drinking from the horse fountain at St.-Michel. Reisden beckoned Daugherty over. "Would you take Tiggy out somewhere? He doesn't need to be here."

"T'other boy as well." Daugherty nodded at Jean-Jacques in a corner.

"Have them play Snakes and Ladders together."

Jean-Jacques protested; Madame Mallais waved him away; he left reluctantly, giving her a rough little-boy hug.

Madame Mallais stood in the middle of the room, distracted; bent to adjust the position of one more painting; straightened up, an old woman, a servant, in widow's black, in the midst of color spread in circles around her like an audience. There were far too many of her forgeries and they were too good. Behind her stood her own young self between her husband and her sister, the real, dull Madame Mallais's work; but he had to remind himself that all the rest were fundamentally skills like those, a sensibility like those, because the rest seemed pure Mallais. The iris pond with the willow, the apple tree; men fishing in winter on the Grande Jatte; the garden by Notre-Dame, children at the zoo, the Vert-Galant in a summer sunset, shadows on Anne of Austria's window at the Louvre.

"We're ready, Madame Vicomtesse—" She glanced at her husband, twisting her hands in her apron.

Dotty gave her one dismissive glance (if you were a servant I should not consider you for *my* household) and moved among the paintings, a bright immaculate judge.

Perdita leaned back against Reisden; her hand found his. Against his ribs, she was holding her breath.

"Them in that section, Madame Vicomtesse, between the two chairs, those are Claude's."

Dotty knelt to judge an apple tree in springtime, a sketch of autumn leaves, a river scene. She stood; she frowned; Dotty bought for the name, but she also knew quality.

Had they taken the best and repainted them?

"I would like to see more," she said to Madame Mallais as if she were considering the pattern of a new sleeve. "Can this be all? Surely you have held some back for the family? Show me."

"Yes, madame, a few that are ours."

The family paintings were spread below the group portrait of Mallais, his mistress Camille, and Madame Suzanne. Most were portraits: Jean-Jacques about twelve in a Moorish vest; a bride drawing the gauze of her wedding veil through her ring; a young woman with a baby. Several of these were in the photographic style, Madame Mallais's work. There was a lush spring apple tree in pink with their daughter, young Claudie Mallais, reading under it. Reisden hoped this was the one Dotty would take, quite good, very decorative, clearly Mallais of the Mallais era. Dotty picked it up and considered it, then laid it aside.

"Perhaps—perhaps— No, what's this?"

In the shadows behind the triple portrait, she found and drew out a last painting. Dotty raised her eyebrows inquiringly, clearly pleased; for a moment Reisden could not see what it was, though, from her sudden indrawn breath, Madame Mallais knew.

"You kept *this*?" she said. "You didn't sell it?"

She turned it around, and, in a roomful of paintings that were very good indeed, it was so good it shocked. The painting *La Veille*, never exhibited since it had caused a sensation in 1870: Mallais's mistress Camille after death, white gauze veiling her body, one pale bare foot exposed. Orange daylilies, nearly red, were piled around her; an empty painter's easel was set up in front of her. Any other painter of the time would have made it an allegory: this was simple, the story of one afternoon before a woman was buried, when the flowers had been like this, the veil fallen wrong like this; it was a cry of grief.

She stood it against the back of a chair, and stood in front of it, considering the sensation it would make for her salon; and an odd, sad thing happened. It began to change Dotty. For a moment she was her blond, perfect self; and then, for another, and a much longer moment, she was a tired mortal, not so young as she had been. "No, it's far too morbid," she said, "one couldn't drink one's tea." She turned her back to it. Reisden took it from her, and faced it a moment himself. Terrible things happen, the painting said; you cannot stop them. Play the piano, study their traces in the nerves, do whatever you can; nothing will be enough to stop them; but it is better than doing nothing.

Dotty had not realized until now that she might find things she did not expect or want; but she had no intention of foregoing what she deserved. She walked among the paintings with the delicate starved condescension of a heron, searching for food in the shallows, finding nothing. From *La Veille* around the room, the paintings were Monsieur-and-Madame. Dotty paused at one after another, pouting her lips at a sketched detail of fashion, a car, a wide hat.

"This cannot be all," Dotty said.

Reisden and Madame Mallais were watching her. She became aware that she was the center of their attention, that she was in danger, in fact, of being judged. "Madame Mallais, come here. You know what picture I am trading. You shall tell me which of your *husband's* canvases is a fair exchange."

It was a splendid aristocratic move, to demand full value of the servants by giving trust. "Come, come, madame," Dotty urged and held out her hand.

Madame Mallais wrapped her hands in her skirts. "No, madame, I can't tell you."

"Surely you can."

Madame Mallais had taken on a frightened dignity. "No, I can't."

"Come here." A lady never insists, but a lady is not disobliged. "Let us look at them one by one."

Dotty paced across the room, back to the pie wedge of genuine Mallais paintings; Madame Mallais was drawn along with her. An apple tree, a river, autumn leaves. After the shock of the obvious masterpieces, they were, not second rate certainly, but oddly abstract.

"I don't know what I shall do, I really don't like any of these," Dotty said. She turned back to the part of the pie that was Madame Mallais's; hesitated for the second time; looked back at the genuine.

"Sacha, come here. Darling, do you notice something odd?"

She held out her hand to him.

"Perhaps you could explain to me—perhaps one of you could explain—why Monsieur Mallais's paintings seem to be so peculiarly timeless? An apple tree, autumn leaves, a river, very pretty; no people, no fashion, no motorboats! But yours, madame, the ones you have done for your husband:" She did not point, but she indicated, one after another. "That auto is a De Dion Populaire, isn't it? And that is a steam-bus. Those crowds, I think, are for Mademoiselle Fallières' wedding. Those are the *Matin* boat races. An unkind person might say that the difference between Monsieur's paintings and yours is only a matter of what can be seen in them."

No sound from anyone.

"Mr. Bullard," she turned on him, "with your famous brush strokes, what is the difference between 'his' paintings and those she did for him?" Bullard said nothing. "Sacha," Dotty said, "would you ask this woman *when* she began painting for her husband? Would you tell me which paintings are actually *his*?" She turned on Madame Mallais; she put her hand on the old woman's arm. It was the viscountess talking to the laundress suspected of pilfering handkerchiefs.

"I suspect, my dear, that you started painting for him some time ago."

Madame Mallais dropped onto the edge of her husband's mattress and put her face in her hands.

"Mr. Bullard, look at *La Veille*; that at least will show his style, if she has not repainted it!"

"'Zanne," Mallais said. With infinite slowness he pulled his ruined hand from the bedclothes and smoothed his wife's hair. She was sitting by her own young self, and both of them had momentarily the same look: panicked, caught with the palette in their hand. "Don't go after her," Mallais said to Dotty. "She never did anything wrong."

And Reisden understood.

"*Oh,*" Perdita said softly, questioningly, and he knew she had understood too.

"Keep your *View of the Seine*, Dotty," Reisden said. "It has provenance, everyone admires it, it is being written about. That is the one you want."

"How do you know what I want? You are the one who insists on awkward truths, Sacha," she said sharply.

"Dotty," Perdita said, "then you should have a forgery. But you won't get one."

"I think," Reisden said, "Madame Mallais should say it."

Madame Mallais looked up, biting her lips, and put her head back down on her hands, guilty and self-conscious; and nobody moved, nobody spoke, until he did.

"Once upon a time," Reisden said to Madame Mallais, "a woman I love told me that I had to tell the truth about something very serious to me, or I would lose the opportunity. I did," he said. "And for years I was intensely more unhappy than when I'd been lying.—Trying to tell the truth doesn't happen once. One becomes chained to it, one begins to see the consciousness and responsibilities and the connections it creates, one only half sees them; it starts out as a sentence, a momentary decision, and becomes a life. And one does fail," he said. "All the time. But I really do recommend it." He felt far too much in the center of attention, as she must feel; he leaned against Perdita. She held his hand.

"What matters," he said, "is not just the imperfections and the secrets, but being caught in them; how one's caught. That's what I mean." He had said more than enough.

"I'm *going* to play the piano," Perdita said quickly, like someone who needs to say something before she loses the courage, "any way I can, but I'm scared. That's my secret. I'm not good enough. I'll be a shallow person and a bad mother and a second-rate pianist.—Alexander thinks I have all the courage in the world, but I don't, I think about being publicly *bad* at things, especially in his eyes, and I mind."

"Oh, come on, old 'Zanne," Claude Mallais said.

"What?" said Dotty sharply. "What?"

Barry Bullard, examining *La Veille,* suddenly glanced over at the Mallaises, his eyes wide.

"It was a joke," Claude Mallais said. "Do you think any of us started out artists? No, this was forty years ago. I was a market gardener. She was a laundress. We weren't artists." He lifted his frail saurian head and out of his eyes gleamed the laughter of a lifetime. "It was a hot day. There was a boy fishing on the quai here. He came up to the house and asked for a cup of water."

"Can you imagine," Madame Mallais said timidly. "He was so cute, and sounded so grown up. And he saw the paintings."

" 'Promise me I can represent you,' " Mallais said. "He said that, with his fishing pole stuck up in the corner and his britches wet from fishing. 'You'll be my first artist.' He had a little card. Of course we thought he was crazy."

"*Armand Inslay-'Ochstein,*" Bullard said. "And 'e asked you if 'e could represent you."

"But he never asked," Perdita said softly, "he *never* asked who painted which pictures."

"Oh, Mademoiselle Perdita, it was both of us really who did—" Madame Mallais was wiping her eyes with her left sleeve; it was difficult to tell whether the tears were fright or laughter. "I knew it wasn't right," she said, talking to the edge of her sleeve. "But they just kept *being there* somehow— I would stand at my ironing board and see pictures on the shirts, and they wouldn't leave me, I would be all fidgeted till I did something about them. So Claude stood up for me," she said. "He let me do the painting, and he stood up and talked and pretended for me. Ma'am Vicomtesse, I'm sorry about your painting." She still called it *paingting*. "I painted it. I did that too—" Madame Mallais pointed timidly at one of the harmless "genuine Mallais" canvases—"and that," the apple tree, "and my poor Camille—" She pointed at *La Veille.* "Oh, ma'am." Madame Mallais looked around her; and suddenly, in the middle of the enormous riot of color, she stopped speaking, she simply looked. She turned round to see them all together. All that work; all those colors carefully mixed, every brush stroke separately felt and considered; all of the shadow part too, the late dinners, the unmended socks, the busyness, the weariness, the burdens and the lies; but look at the colors, her smile said, look what had happened, what a surprise, enough to make up for what she and all she loved had paid, enough, even to her, to make up for the unworthiness of the person who had been given so much to do and see.

"Oh, ma'am," said Madame Mallais, "I paingted them all, but look at them, aren't they beautiful!"

Chapter 95

On Wednesday morning, two days before her thirty-third birthday, Milly put her bare foot out of bed into water, and she became a refugee. Her flood emergency bag contained her silver toasting fork, three bars of chocolate, her own novels, two pairs of silk stockings, and Jean-Jacques' copy of the Mona Lisa, wrapped in a Chinese shawl. Let the necessities take care of themselves.

Across the mud and confusion of the fifth arrondissement, across the squelching gravel of the Luxembourg Gardens, Milly and Nick-Nack headed toward Esther's.

"Is Esther in? I've been 'flooded'. . . ."

The woman who answered the door was dark, short, a stranger, and in a dressing gown. From behind her floated a smell of omelette and onions. "I'm Alicia," she muttered. "Blatchford." Milly had never seen her before.

"Are you a writer?"

"Me? No."

"Are you an art collector?"

Esther came out of an inner room, in a robe, drying her hair. On the carpet-covered Renaissance table, a space had been cleared among the fans and the vases, and two spaces had been laid, intimately, with napkins and flowers, and on two of Esther's best Italian plates, someone had made ham-and-onion omelettes.

"This is Alice," Esther said. "She's American," as if that explained everything. Perhaps it did. "Do you want breakfast? She'll make another omelette, won't you, Alice?"

Alice glared out of dark jealous cow eyes, reminding Milly strangely of Henry's Julie. She could see Alice sometime in the future, weeping, walking up and down the paths of the Jardin du Luxembourg. *Milly, how Esther mistreats me. . . .*

Love, love, love! "No, thanks!"

The scope of the disaster could not be comprehended; it was either huge numbers or individual catastrophes. A sixth of Courbevoie was injured or homeless; water had reached the second floors and even the roofs of houses. (Milly thought briefly of Perdita.) At Ivry there was scarlet fever, threatening to become an epidemic. In Alfortville the water was up to four meters deep, thirteen feet. One could not see the disaster as a whole, only make vignettes. Milly and a man from *L'Illustration* photographed workers standing helplessly by a flooded carpentry shop, a pretty girl waving her umbrella as a soldier in boots rescued her, a dinghy carrying a coffin. On the Île de la Cité, they saw a diver rescuing records from the flooded basement of the Préfecture. *He comes up blowing air like a whale,* Milly scribbled. *His diving helmet off, he stands on the steps rubbing his forehead, stunned by the blackness.*

The flood was 7m89 on the Pont-Royal scales, and rising.

The Louvre was being closed.

Monsieur Homelli, administrator of the national museums, was holding a press conference in the courtyard. Though the Louvre was being closed down Homelli said emphatically, *nothing was wrong.* His mustache wagged, he talked, he pointed at the great bulk of the palace. What disaster could shake it? (Down in the basement, supposedly, one could hear the river roaring.)

"Will the Mona Lisa be moved?" Milly asked.

"Emphatically not, madame. The Mona Lisa is perfectly safe."

Around her, the other journalists scribbled; the onlookers nodded, reassured; they still had their Mona Lisa.

On the quai du Louvre, engineers hastily construct a cement wall two feet above the parapets and reinforce it with bags of dirt. Sappers barricade the gates of the palace with cement walls and sandbags; the last of the Louvre's twenty-two furnaces is shut down; in the basement, water has infiltrated three inches deep on the floors; terra-cotta heads and carved frames from Rubens paintings are left to drown if they must. . . .

Chapter 96

It is garbage that saves Leonard's life. He is sucked under, into roaring blackness; he bumps and scrapes against the bottom of a bridge; and then he is clinging to batons of wood from the bakery ovens, broken barrels of wine, branches, mats of garbage. With a rope under his arms, he is drawn kicking out of the water. Leonard is alive.

For what?

Even being rescued from death does not make Leonard impressive. He shows up at the Louvre on Tuesday morning. *"Tiens!"* says the guard captain. "We thought you were dead; we gave your cot to someone else." Leonard snatches his suitcase and his Mona Lisa back from the closet where they are waiting for someone to claim them. Several of the guards ask him about his scraped face and bandaged hands, but they grow tired of *c-c-c* and *g-g-g* and they don't listen.

Putting on his uniform, he goes upstairs to see *her.*

And there is something wrong with her. Her smile wavers. He stands in front of her, whispering his story to her, and she looks aside. She is not listening.

Leonard stands in the deepening gloom, his lantern held high, watching the Mona Lisa. The flicker of lantern light makes her frown, look away, stare; then she smiles at him luminously, but Leonard no longer believes it. Her eyes are swirls of brown paint.

Outside the windows of the Grande Galerie, the Seine batters at the top of the sandbagged parapets, steps from the walls of the Louvre.

George comes to see Jean-Jacques, but Jean-Jacques isn't there and Leonard is. George asks to buy Leonard's copy of the Mona Lisa. His eyes flick over Leonardo's painting in its white box.

"Nobody's stolen it yet," he says carelessly.

"D-do you want to throw her in the river?" Leonard asks suddenly. "You said you d-did. She's *not right*," he says urgently. "She *doesn't care*."

George laughs. "Happy birthday, Milly, if you're listening."

"I *don't like her anymore*."

Chapter 97

By Thursday afternoon, the twenty-seventh, no one was really expected to come to Dotty's open house. From Dotty's windows, one could look up and down the river and see nothing but disaster. All down the Left Bank, the sandbags at the top of the parapets had given way. On the quai de la Tournelle, the awnings of shopfronts fluttered like broken wings, then were ripped away. The *bouquinistes'* stalls perched on a hump of parapet, isolated, an island in the river. Outside the Vicomtesse de Gresnière's, the sandbags were still holding, but the river was above street height; it was hypnotic, desolate, and Reisden and Daugherty sat on two of Dotty's little gilded chairs, out of the way of caterers and servants, watching it.

Daugherty looked around to see they weren't overheard. "What happens with the Mallaises? What're they going to do?"

"According to Bullard, they should move to Italy and sell the paintings as Mallais forgeries."

"At least they ain't going to jail. But ain't anybody"—Daugherty lowered his voice—"anybody ever going to know she painted 'em?"

"Probably not."

That morning, Reisden and Bullard had gone to see Armand Inslay-Hochstein. In Inslay-Hochstein's impeccable office, they had all had coffee and freshly baked beignets—in the flood, the ultimate status symbol was now fresh bread. Inslay-

Hochstein had given them a tour of the gallery memorabilia, including souvenirs of Mallais. A Mallais vest, Mallais's sketchpad, one of Mallais's palettes. They all somehow had kept straight faces, as though these relics were important, the property of a great dead painter.

And perhaps they were important, Reisden thought. What an absurd painter Madame Mallais would have been, and she had known it. A peasant woman does not hold a palette, any more than a blind married woman becomes a touring pianist, or—G-d knows—an eight-year-old murderer matures into a husband and father. So she had found someone else—married him, or he had had the grace and luck to marry her. And between them they were Mallais.

Among Bullard, Reisden, and the dealer, there had been a very diplomatic conversation. They had all spoken in awe of Mallais's work. Everyone was delighted that the questions about it had been satisfactorily answered. So, as a kind of homage to Mallais, they had all done favors for each other. Inslay-Hochstein had expressed the greatest respect for the services of Cazenove-Bullard and anticipated using them frequently. He mentioned a certain eighteenth-century armoire that made Bullard's face break into a grin. And Dotty would soon have the chance to buy another good picture.

"And nothing for yourself, Monsieur de Reisden?" Inslay-Hochstein had said when Bullard had gone off to inspect the armoire.

"Two things," Reisden said. "First. I've been in business only three years, this is my first company, I've overextended myself because of the flood, and I don't intend to lose Jouvet. I want your advice, or if you know of someone better, I want his. Second."

"Second?" said Armand Inslay-Hochstein.

"Tell me when you knew about Mallais."

Milly was standing by the mirrored hallway, counting the arrivals. Pretty good; the salon was getting crowded; the *Figaro* review had brought them in. There was George, at least; he was going to do Miss Halley for next week's *Presse.*

Miss Halley—Madame de Reisden, bah.

Downstairs, a footman was taking coats and cloaks, furs and umbrellas.

In the doorway, a man with a package was waiting forlornly, as if he knew that he was not the caliber of personage to be invited to one of Dotty's parties.

It was Leonard.

"That day," Inslay-Hochstein said.

"The same day?"

"I was waiting at the train station to go back to Paris. It came to me. She had asked about advances for canvas and paint. He had just laughed at me."

"And what did you do?"

Leonard had moved out of sight. Milly craned her neck to see.

"What did I do . . ." said Inslay-Hochstein. "I was fourteen. One knows one is fourteen; it is one of the difficulties of that age. And I had found a painter, Monsieur de Reisden, a dream painter. But she had red hands, she had crooked teeth, she was shy. You remember, my father was a dealer, my uncle was a dealer, I knew what was necessary to succeed."

"And so?"

Milly rose and made her way inconspicuously out of the room, into the hall, where she could see Leonard downstairs in the mirrors.

"I could have gone back, like a good boy. I could have told them that Mallais was not a painter, with his beautiful beard and his painter's air; and she, just barely Madame, she would never be a painter. And there they would be still, a market gardener and a laundress, blameless bystanders of life; and you and I, Monsieur de Reisden, would sleep complacently at night instead of being in our uncomfortable quandary." Armand Inslay-Hochstein's young son had pushed open the door, a toddler still in curls and a long frock, swinging his silver Renaissance rattle in his hand. "I accept my difficulties," the dealer said, tousling his son's hair, "and he will have Mallais."

It isn't right, though, Perdita had said in bed last night. *Women look up to other women. Other women should know about her.*

You're asking her to do what she can't, he had told her. *She wasn't capable of it. You are.*

"Perdita's going to tour," he said to Daugherty, as casually as he could, looking across to the piano. "She'll be here until sometime next year; then she'll ask Ellis to represent her."

"Huh. You ain't—?"

"No. We aren't getting divorced. She goes, she comes back."

Marriages strain under distance and hard work. He had spent the last two days at Jouvet. The archives might be salvageable, with a lot of work and effort; most of the building was still sound, including, thank G-d, the lab. (The piano had not got a scratch.) But he would be working hard, at two jobs, and there would be a very small child, and a very odd father to look after him. William's grandson, with a child.

What would happen? He didn't know. There was every chance the marriage would fail, or worse.

"How does one raise a child?" he asked Daugherty. "If one's a man doing it alone but for the servants." The servants and a few demons.

"Don't know, son, didn't know I could do it until I had."

"I am looking for any expertise. Would you ever like to come here again, perhaps while she's away?" Reisden said. "On a visit, perhaps to give advice."

Watch me, he felt he was saying nakedly. Keep me from hurting my child. *Help help help,* like poor Leonard.

Daugherty cleared his throat. "Visit. Anytime. Sure. Only—"

There was a short, embarrassed silence.

"Well," Daugherty said. "I been thinking there's two things I could do. One, I could go back to Boston. I been to Boston, it won't languish without me. Two. I could do something else. Don't know what. Thinking about the Mallaises again. Maybe if they just need someone to help for a while"—Daugherty hesitated—"to fetch and haul and such, I—" He cleared his throat again. "Eventually I got to go back to Boston, I guess. But maybe they could use some help, is all, right now."

"You don't have to. Not for our sakes."

"Ain't nothing to do with either of you for once," Daugherty said. "Has to do with me."

"Oh?" Oh.

Milly glided down the stairs, Nick-Nack's claws clicking along behind her. Leonard was still hesitating, hovering. He held the package under his waterproof wool cape. It was large and flat and wrapped in brown paper. Milly recognized its measurements.

"Leonard—" She thought of the bloody upholstery in Sacha-darling's car and shivered. "Nicky! Wait here for Mama." It was barely raining, but raining; she needed something to wrap around her shoulders. "That Chinese shawl," Milly said to the footman, "the one around the painting."

"'Course I don't know French, but I can point to things out of the dictionary. . . ."

"You could learn."

"Learn?"

"French."

"Huh. Me?"

Me? Learn? No one does, Reisden thought; seldom; only artists. And art is something one fails at, a quixotic enterprise, like love or building a city on a flood plain. Still— There was a stir around the door; he saw a glimpse of a white dress, Perdita's. She and Dotty were behind the glass door, looking for someone. He moved and Dotty pointed; he realized they were looking for him, and found himself smiling.

"Lookit," Daugherty said, "here she comes."

And now Perdita followed Dotty through the rows of little gilded chairs, smelling candle-wax and the musky, aromatic smell of Dotty's house; and Dotty stepped aside and Perdita faced the piano. She heard bits of music talk and gossip, *Maurice Ravel, Julie Rivé-King, Madame de Fourché's salon on Tuesday night.* And then the silence spread around her, and she took her seat and placed her hands and waited.

In the moment before playing there is always that silence. It is exalting, but it is frightening. You are only who you are, you have only yourself to bring to it. She felt her child press a little against her corset; she felt the ring on her finger. She felt unworthy.

> *I know lots of people. Mostly*
> *They're not up to their destiny—*

Busy with nothing done, unworthy, inadequate; but married to Alexander, having his child, making a life with him, and being here, now, in this silence. How would she ever do it?

Even if you can't live up to your destiny, you can at least have one.

Caught, Alexander called it. Responsible. Connected.

The silence began to resonate around her; she heard in it the little vibration of the strings of the piano, a reflection of sound, a cage, a voice; she chose it; the silence changed to music; and she put her hands down on the keyboard and began to play.

Milly was back among the audience for most of the first half of the concert. At the interval she made her way to George, who was declaiming on sex to a horrified countess.

"What do you think?" she asked. "Pretty good?"

"We'll see when the reviews come out."

"Leonard's alive," she said casually.

"Was he dead?"

"Didn't you know he murdered someone and jumped into the Seine?"

"Good for him."

"I'm serious. He came here today with the Mona Lisa, he was going to give it to that man over there, the one by the vicomtesse, with his arm in a sling. See his face? Leonard nearly killed him." Leonard had given Milly a note with the painting, so wet the envelope had given way. *Pls Help*, they read in runny purple ink. *Wht shal I do Now I doant kno what to Do she Frtens me*

"Good, Milly," George said. "Good one. Very elaborate. And where is the Mona Lisa now, Milly?"

"You don't think I'd give it to darling Sacha, do you? It's downstairs in the cloakroom wrapped in brown paper, waiting for you."

"Happy birthday, Milly," George said.

"Ask darling Sacha about Leonard. My birthday is tomorrow," Milly said, handing him the cloakroom ticket. "And I'll be on the Pont-Neuf at noon."

Chapter 98

O*n this night we have become history*, Milly wrote. *At the Pont d'Alma, the Zouave is only a bust. At the Pont-Royal the top of the hydrographic scale is underwater; the water captures the date above it, "1740," the greatest Paris flood ever previously measured, and the Seine rises, and rises. There will be a new date there soon, above them all; this is the Great Flood, 1910.*

But good news, madame. In Alfortville and Ivry, in the drowned train yards of Bercy, the engineers see a high-water mark of silt and oil above the surface of the water. Tomorrow, January 28, a little after noon, it will crest in central Paris, and begin to recede.

Not so easy, Milly thought. For months "Madame" will be cleaning up. Pumps and mops and buckets, eau de Javel and disinfectants of all kinds will be twice their usual prices. Madame's electric lights will not work, the Métro will be dark, there will be layoffs, there will be sickness.

But tomorrow, a little after noon—

Chapter 99

On Friday morning, January 28, a bit before noon, in a dreadful freezing rain, Milly Xico and Nick-Nack took up their station on the Pont-Neuf, waiting for George.

On the upstream side of the Pont-Neuf stood everyone from the place Dauphine: Madame la Vicomtesse with her little boy, and Monsieur de Reisden, and—ugh—Madame de Reisden. Good G-d, how married they looked already. She leaned against him, turning her head to talk with him, soft and confident, a married woman. They were under one umbrella now, which he was holding in his left hand; his right hand was out of its sling, against her hip, almost onto her stomach, and her right hand held his as if she were delighted to have him feel her on the street; she was in a heavy coat, but what a gesture! Someday this dream of love would end like all dreams; she would be an old woman eating at a café with her dog; but now, no use at all, the girl was mired in marriage, stupefied by marriage, there was no use talking to her.

No sign of George.

Milly moved toward the parapet, shoving her way through the crowd of hats and elbows, holding Nick-Nack in front of her like a muff with teeth. On one of the pillars, someone from Bridges and Highways had improvised a hydrographic station. Lowered over the parapet on a window washer's chair, an engineer was making markings on the bridge pillar with a grease crayon. They were waiting for the crest, the highest point of the water, which would come through just after noon.

The water had taken on a different look, not so hurried, almost languorous, darker.

"The water's still going up, but barely, barely," an elegant young woman murmured. Milly gave her a second look, saw the engagement ring on her finger and the telltale soft happiness, and shifted Nick-Nack to her shoulder, sighing with boredom.

Why should she be bored? She and George had taken the package away from Madame Chinchilla's and opened it. George had said it wasn't the real one, but had taken it away. He'd taken it to Henry, who was in a panic, and Henry was peeling himself away from George like cheap veneer. And they had heard this morning that Leonard had given himself up, been arrested for murder, which was more than even Milly could have hoped for.

Milly had heard all this, and much more, this morning from Julie-les-Fesses, who had wept in fear, and packed her bags, and had left by the Gare du Nord for whatever destination a train would take her.

At the side of the bridge, men were shouting. A man flourished a net and hauled his trophy up onto the bridge, near the happy couple, the vicomtesse, and her son.

It was a dog.

It was large and hairy and filthy. Its eyes gleamed crimson and crazy, the eyes of a dog who has ridden a tree or a branch or a stick through who knows what water, under who knows what bridges. It retched horribly, shook a pound of mud off itself, and lurched against—the vicomtesse's little boy, who already had his arms around its neck.

"Oh, maman, can we *keep* him?"

The vicomtesse stared at the dog, paling. The little viscount looked up at her pleadingly. The dog stared at the vicomtesse. He moaned, showing teeth that would chew the legs off chairs, closed his eyes, and put his chin trustingly on the little boy's shoulder.

"Oh, Nicky, Nicky, Nicky," Milly said, "the vicomtesse has a *dog*."

How do you make a woman happy? Take a woman who is getting a little old for the life she leads, a woman whose husband has betrayed her, whose savings account is flat, whose apartment was on the rue de la Bièvre and is now half-filled with stinking sewage.

How do you make a woman happy? Give her power. Give her money. Give her chocolate from Pihan's, a box of chocolate, every day for the rest of her life, and to toast it, a silver toasting-rack with ebony handles. Give her anything she chooses, hats from a modiste, good boots, English boots, a different pair for every day of the week. An apartment on the boulevards, a house in the country, and that ultimate luxury, more than an attentive lover or a secret admirer will ever provide, a double bed where, except for her dog, she sleeps entirely alone.

Give her the Mona Lisa.

Leave the real Mona Lisa in George's hands? Or Henry's? Oh, no, thank you. It was in the concierge's office of the theater on the boulevard Poissonière, wrapped in a Chinese shawl.

It was Jean-Jacques' copy George had finally opened in the café they'd taken it to—and when he'd opened it, after reading Leonard's letter—after having heard what Sacha-the-panther had said about Leonard, and the rumors of Henry and a rich American that both he and Julie had heard—

George wouldn't show up; he wouldn't have the nerve. But George had escaped Henry; he'd turn respectable before he'd work for Henry again.

George was right, one should celebrate the flood, something should go in the river. "Let me get in my handbag, Nicky; there:" Milly had brought *La Midinette à Paris.* The first copy off the presses, the one—can you believe this—Henry had given her as if from himself, and written in it, too. *To my dear little Wifey, from her poor big old Hubby, who couldn't live without her.*

"Oh, do you like that book?" The elegant girl. "I like it too. It's my favorite book. Don't get it wet!" Milly was unconsciously holding it under the water streaming off her umbrella. "It's so precious. I wish I could meet her."

"Her?"

"Milly, the authoress. Of course she wrote it all herself," the elegant girl said. "She must have! Only a woman could know so much about love. Look, let me show you my favorite, favorite scene, look, he proposes to her, and she tells him—" The girl flipped through the pages, shoved the book back into Milly's astonished hand. "Here it is, I don't even have to look at it, I can recite every word, but *you absolutely must read this book,* it will change your life forever—"

Milly looked down at her own book as if it had turned into a snake in her hand.

" 'Let me drown in you,' " the elegant girl recited. " 'Let me be nothing but you. I want to live in your house, sleep in your bed, wear your clothes. I want to eat and drink you, I want to think you, to live you—' "

Terrible. Not the words, but the girl who had written them. Yes, absolutely yes, she had written them; but who else than the girl she had been could have been so horrifying in her single-mindedness? Who could have seen so much, the fall of a raindrop, the cats rolling in the corner of the garden, and so little about Henry?

"I want to be just like her," the elegant girl said, "I want never to think of anyone but *him*. But sometimes I do. I can't help it, I'm just not perfect."

You are just like her, Milly thought, poor girl. And when you're a few years older, what will you read? There's nothing. Girl grows up, girl falls in love, girl gets married; woman might as well be dead, stabbed and thrown in a ditch. Milly was standing just at the parapets, and she turned to her right and her left and saw women, ordinary women, thin women, fat women, a woman with a forehead as bulging as Juan's, a pretty woman getting a little old, a woman with a tender sensitive profile and big ears. What will you all read?

There was George!

"I have come to free you from the tyranny of Art!" He was standing on one of the benches built into the parapet. Above his head he held the Mona Lisa. "Today, representing the genius of the twentieth century, I spit on the rotted corpse of Art and cast her in the Seine—"

"He's some poor madman, don't pay attention."

Milly certainly wasn't paying attention. Her mind was full of stories, sly half-frivolous stories, subversive stories to be passed from hand to hand like the secret consciousness of women.

"That's the Mona Lisa, isn't it?"

Why hadn't she brought a pencil? "Do you have a pencil?" she asked the girl. She began scribbling on the blank back sheets of *La Midinette à Paris*. The elegant girl squeaked. "Shut up! I'm writing."

George had got to the climax of his speech. He held the panel up. He looked up at the rainy sky, the fog-rheumed buildings, the dull black crowd below him, and finally at the panel in his hands; and he smiled, as a man smiles plunging into something out of control, a man who has found the love of his life, his ideal, too precious to let go, a smile both distrustful and blessed; and with a grand gesture, he cast her into the Seine.

"Was that the Mona Lisa?"

Who cares whether George escaped Henry; leave that to George; and when it came to it, who cares about Henry. Milly didn't. But she, herself, Milly, ah, there was someone to care for, there was a girl to love: herself, poor talented and deluded and gloriously imperfect little writer, who had cared so much for her Roland. Never mind, Milly thought, he's gone, but you've got me.

She had been using the blank back sheets of *La Midinette* as a notebook; she ripped out her own new words, worth saving for now, and threw the rest overhand, and up the paperback flew, over the parapet, spreading its pages like a fluttering bird. It shed a saved token of love, a rose; and gone were the sighs of love, the delusions and devotion, the drowning in love; Roland had gone to his club, his job, another woman; what was left? Lovers and friends, dogs, singing, good steaks at a café: everything. Nicky barked at this stick he couldn't catch; a wind caught the book, a page tore out of it, and it fell into the Seine, one more piece of trash; but Milly looked out over the water and the limitless sky, and for a moment it seemed to her she saw, through the wind and the rain, a mysterious smile.

Afterword and Acknowledgments

"The history of 'Suzanne Mallais,' like that of Marian Blakelock, is among the most fascinating women's stories in the annals of Impressionist art. An uneducated woman, formerly a laundress, but with some small early canvases to her credit, Madame Mallais may have helped her husband with his painting during his lifetime; but after his death in 1900, she took him over. Starting with some canvases he had left half-finished, over the course of some six years she taught herself to paint in his style. Her principal motive seems to have been a need to deny her husband's death, for very few of these canvases were sold as by Mallais; instead, Madame Mallais took the far more unusual and interesting tack of painting as her husband would have done had he lived. For nearly two decades thereafter, her own canvases explored the interaction between Impressionism and the twentieth century. . . ."

No.

Madame Mallais never painted. Esther Cohen has no readers; George Vittal never threw any *Mona Lisa* off the Pont-Neuf; even Milly, whose books ought to be still available in Livre de Poche paperback editions, never wrote a word. The persons in this book are fictional, and any resemblance to actual persons, living or dead or yet to come, is a mere impression, or a forgery.

The flood is a forgery too, a collage of newspaper stories,

engineers' reports, eyewitnesses' accounts, and over three thousand photographs. In January 1910, after an autumn of rains,
every river in northeastern France crested almost at once, and
their floodwaters raged through Paris. It was the fastest flood in
recorded Parisian history, the highest flood since at least 1658,
and the most devastating. Its effect on Paris was far greater than
I have been able to show here; but what is here is fairly accurate.

The picture of early Cubism is less so; the knowledgeable
reader will spot details from several years of art history. The
Mona Lisa was actually stolen in 1911, in a bizarre and complicated plot involving Picasso, Apollinaire, Apollinaire's
friend-cum-secretary Géry Piéret, and some Iberian heads
Piéret had stolen from the Louvre. John Richardson has pub-
lished a delicious account of it, which will appear in the second
volume of his splendid *Life of Picasso*.

No forgery is done without help. My family was endlessly
supportive while the book was done . . . and done, and
done. . . . Thank you, Fred, Mariah, Justus, and Helen (and Vicious, and Gracie the Vampire Kitten). My agent, Jane Otte,
and my editor, Clare Ferraro, publisher of Ballantine Books,
lent unstinting support and enthusiasm to the project. Julie
Garriott provided brilliant line edits, and Nathaniel Penn,
Clare's indefatigable assistant, kept the Xerox machine hum-
ming and the lines of communication open.

The members of the Cambridge Speculative Fiction Work-
shop performed wonders on the manuscript; thank you, Sari
Boren, Steven Caine, Pete Chvany, Jr., Alexander Jablokov,
James Patrick Kelly, Steven Popkes, David A. Smith, and Paul
Tumey. Kathryn Cramer and Martha Ramsey gave me essen-
tial insights; Rachel Goodwin, Laurence Senelick, and Pam
Strickler saved me from idiocies too embarrassing to mention.
The ones left are all mine.

Thanks also to the staffs of the Widener and Houghton

libraries of Harvard University, the Boston Public Library, the Brookline, MA, Public Library, the New York Public Library, the Bibliothèque Nationale, the Musée Picasso, the Musée de la Ville de Paris, the Musée d'Orsay, and WHRB Radio, Harvard University.

For their help in Paris, thank you, Michelle Lapautre, Christine and Sacha Jordis, Dr. Michael Berger and his family, the staff of the Hotel St.-Jacques, and N. Lee Wood and Norman Spinrad. Postcard dealers, collectors, and flood fans shared their treasures. Elaine Sternberg rummaged round the deluge with me; Léon Lapautre provided *minous plaisirs*.

In Boston and New York, Betsy Wilkinson of Childs Gallery, and Abbot W. Vose and Elsie Oliver of Vose Galleries, gave me information about the operation of art galleries and let me tour; I am particularly indebted to Bill Vose for information about unconditional return and family forgeries. Robert B. Wyatt provided Paris postcards, advice, support, and recipes. (Bob, look at the ginger cakes.) Laurence Senelick and Julie Garriott (again!) introduced me to recordings of singers and the *caf'conc'* scene of the day. "Oh, what a joy it is when someone loves you so. . . ." Laurence Senelick translated "When Someone Loves You So"; the rest of the translations are mine. Laurie Mann ("Laure Cheneau," the radium painter) and Peter Lawrence appear courtesy of their generosity toward *Aboriginal* and the Brookline PTO; thank you both.

Every forgery needs borrowed feathers. To add verisimilitude to an otherwise bald and unconvincing narrative, quotes and misquotes from the works of Guillaume Apollinaire, Colette, Picasso, and Gertrude Stein are collaged throughout the book, in true forger's style without attribution. Milly plagiarizes George Bernard Shaw's review of Agathe Backer-Grøndahl. Reisden's discussion of the theory of consciousness is based on Alfred Binet's work. *Baedeker's Guide to Paris,*

1910 edition, and the eleventh edition of the *Encyclopedia Britannica* make unauthorized appearances. And every forgery must have one anachronistic detail: X. J. Kennedy is the author of the poem about rhinoceroses that (in somewhat altered form) Reisden recites to Tiggy.

In the midst of the flood, many men and women wrote down and photographed its details: the 1910 staff and special correspondents of *Le Figaro, L'Illustration,* and *Le Génie civil;* the staffs of the various governmental commissions on the flood; and the postcard photographers whose images preserve a unique moment in the life of Paris. They were the memory, source, and reality I worked from.

And finally, thanks to the city and people of Paris.

A wonderful thing happened the afternoon I arrived in Paris to research the flood. I'd gone up to Montmartre to look at the site of Picasso's studio and I decided to take a guided walking tour of Montmartre. One of the other people waiting for the tour was an old man, almost ninety, whose name I never got (I hope he sees this), and who had also arrived in Paris that day. It was cold and wet and our guide never arrived, but one of the women lived locally and said she'd take us round to the places she knew, so we all explored Montmartre together and then went out for coffee. We asked what each other did. I said I was a novelist from America and I was writing about the flood; and the old man said, "Oh. I remember it," and sang this song from 1910:

> *Ah, plaignez bis Paris,*
> *La ville sans pareille,*
> *Où tout est réuni,*
> *Les beautés, les merveilles,*
> *Depuis déjà huit jours voyez*
> *Que tout Paris est inondé. . . .*

Paris, where an old man will sing to a stranger, is still the city of the flood. The bathhouses and laundry boats are gone from between the bridges, but the *bateaux-mouches* still putter up and down the river, under some of the same bridges almost destroyed by the Seine. On the Pont-Royal you will see the hydrographic scales, and the mark above them, 1740, and above it the unbelievably high mark of 1910. On the rue de Bellechasse and the rue de l'Université, where the river struck, you will see small blue faience plaques on the walls. CRUE, they say, JANVIER *1910*, with a line; flood height, January 1910.

Paris floods; the city of art and love is the city of floods, it cannot last forever. But it is there now, much better than this pale forgery. Go there. See the Impressionists at the Musée d'Orsay. Stand on the Pont-Neuf; eat at the Café du Départ; ride the Métro to Courbevoie. Go to the Louvre and see the *Mona Lisa*. (Is it the *Mona Lisa*? Of course it is.) Throw something in the Seine. Throw this book, which is now over. And then try something new, something you cannot possibly do, something you are unworthy of.

It might work, in Paris.

It might work anywhere. Or it might not.

But at least you're in Paris.

Sarah Smith
September 1993–August 1995

About the Author

Sarah Smith has lived in Japan, London, and Paris. A Harvard Ph.D., she has taught film and eighteenth-century literature, and she now writes and designs documentation for advanced computer products. She is also the author of the *New York Times* Notable Book *The Vanished Child*. Ms. Smith lives near Boston, Massachusetts, with her husband and children and their twenty-two-pound Maine coon cat.